SHAKEDOWNERS

JUSTIN WOOLLEY

LONELY ROBOT BOOKS

For the misfits.

CHAPTER ONE_

Cᴀᴘᴛᴀɪɴ's ʟᴏɢ. *Galactic Central... 22... 16... point... shit. Hey, Quinn, what's the date?*

Sorry, sir?

The date.

September 12th, captain.

No, I mean Galactic Central.

Oh, I'm not sure. You'll have to do the conversion.

Quinn, Earth Greenwich to Galactic Central is an algorithm that's, like, a page long. I can't even remember how to convert between Celsius and Fahrenheit.

Captain, you know you're still recording, right?

Yes, Ensign Rangi, I know that. Just watch our heading, will you?

I'm not going to hit anything. It's space.

Look, everyone just be quiet for a minute. Captain's log. Galactic Central date... whatever, September 12th, 2233. Captain Iridius B. Franklin of the Galactic Federation freighter FSC Diesel Coast *recording. We're on approach to the Iota Persei system as part of a humanitarian mission bringing supplies to the mining colony on Iota Persei E.*

Humanitarian mission? We're carting a load of toy dogs.

Ensign.

Sorry, captain.

As I was saying, we're acting as part of a humanitarian mission to Victoria Station, the mining colony on Iota Persei E. This planet was recently attacked by Planetary Alliance forces and now, along with vital food supplies, we are delivering several hundred My PupPup artificially intelligent toy dogs for the children of the colony. We'll be dropping out of FTL momentarily and will enter orbit around Iota Persei E. End recording.

No one in the universe would consider the *FSC Diesel Coast* an attractive ship. It was a hauler, a starship built purely for function, with as much thought put into aesthetics as a sledgehammer puts into the meaning of life. It was constructed in the way of most ships: engines at the back, the bridge at the front, and, because this was a freighter, everything in between – other than some cursory living space – was the cargo bay.

Originally used as a mining freighter in the Frantle Belt, the ship's overall design was best described as agricultural. Clocking in at just over one hundred metres long, the *Diesel Coast* looked as sleek as a tissue box with two toilet paper rolls taped to the sides, and at nearly forty years old the ship's interior wasn't much better. Sure, the onboard systems had been upgraded over the years, but the upgrades had been ad-hoc at best. Everything was cluttered, additional computers having been tacked on awkwardly over the life of the ship. There were none of the smooth curves and stark whites of the fancy starships of the Federation fleet. The bridge, like the rest of the ship, was all squared edges and gunmetal grey showing through chipped and faded paint.

It was on this bridge that Captain Iridius B. Franklin spun a full three hundred and sixty degrees in his chair. He scanned the small crew around him, making sure they were all on task. There were only three others on the bridge, and they had nothing to do. Iridius knew they had nothing to do. They knew that he knew they had nothing to do. All this adjusting sliders and pressing buttons was just for show really. In truth, Iridius only wanted to test out his chair, happy it had been repaired and he could finally spin around without it making that irritating squeaking sound.

"Why do you bother with the log anyway, captain?" Ensign Benjamin Rangi asked from where he sat at the helm between the captain's chair and the view-screen. Rangi turned to look over his shoulder. The helmsman's chair didn't rotate, which was lucky, otherwise Iridius was sure Rangi would spend every mission with his back to the view-screen, cracking jokes and asking pointless questions.

"It's Federation Space Command protocol, ensign," Lieutenant Commander Kira Quinn answered from where she sat to Iridius's right. "Captain Franklin is required to record regular log entries in order to keep a record of ship activities in the event of an accident, emergency or investigation."

It was probably best that Quinn answered these sorts of questions because Iridius's answer would have been *because they make me.*

"Just seems like a waste of time on this ship," Rangi said. "Picked up a load of rocks. Delivered a load of rocks. Picked up green sludge in barrels. Dropped green sludge in barrels into the sun. Picked up toy dogs. Delivered toy dogs."

Iridius looked over at Quinn, his executive officer and second in command of the *Diesel Coast.* Before this mission, they'd made a delivery of fertiliser to 82 Eridani D. The inhabitants of that planet were a race of land-based sentient jellyfish that communicated solely through mind-to-mind telepathy. Staring at his XO,

Iridius wondered if he'd managed to pick that up. *Can I shoot him out the airlock?* he thought at her. She didn't react.

"How many of these My PupPup dogs are we carrying anyway?" Rangi asked.

"Chief?" Iridius prompted.

"Three hundred and six, sir," came a deep voice from behind him. Chief Petty Officer Gr'lak N'hlarkic Tre'laktor – Greg to his friends – was the load master of the *Diesel Coast* and the only non-human on the crew. A malignant, Greg came from a race of sentient tumours who grew on a large organism that enveloped their entire planet, splitting away once they reached full maturity. Basically, Greg was a living cancer. He was a nice guy though.

"Do they all have the same name?" Ensign Rangi asked.

"What?" Iridius said.

"The dogs. They're basically all the same dog, aren't they? Do they all come out of the box with the same name? Are they all called Rex or something?"

"Does it matter?"

"I just think it'll get confusing if suddenly hundreds of kids in the colony all have artificially intelligent dogs that look the same and answer to the same name."

Iridius shook his head. "Sometimes I think your intelligence is artificial, ensign. What's our ETA?"

"We'll be shutting down the BAMF in thirty-two minutes, captain."

"Excellent." Iridius slapped his palms down on the arms of the captain's chair and stood. "That gives me thirty-one minutes."

"For what, captain?" Quinn asked.

"For a nap." Iridius stepped down from his chair and walked to the back of the bridge. "XO, you have the conn."

Iridius descended the steel grate stairs to a corridor lined with grey pipes and orange electrical conduit. Directly ahead were more steps leading down to the cargo bay, which currently housed fifteen plastic crates containing three hundred and six toy dogs, and six crates of food and medical supplies which, on reflection, seemed like an odd ratio. Iridius turned left and walked to the door marked 'Captain's Cabin'.

He pressed the panel beside the door. The computer analysed his biometrics to verify his identity, then the door opened and Iridius stepped inside. He dropped onto his bed, but before the mattress had stopped its rhythmic bouncing the computer pinged at him.

Ping. "Good afternoon, Captain Franklin, you have one new notification. Your standing news search for Commander April Idowu has generated one new alert over the QEC-NET. Would you like to view the article, have me read it aloud, or cancel for now?"

It wouldn't be accurate to say that April Idowu was the one that got away – that would imply they had some intention of staying together. Iridius and April had spent three years in a relationship during their time at the Academy, almost ten years ago now, having both been fast-tracked into the command stream of training. Unfortunately, their relationship had ended with their opinions of each other unchanged from when they'd first met. April considered Iridius a lazy, often drunk, unambitious waste of talent, and Iridius considered April a pompous, perfectionist know-it-all. They had seen each other barely a handful of times in the years since. April had gone on to a distinguished career, and was now first officer aboard the Universe-class exploration ship the *FSC El Nino*, serving under the highly decorated Captain Roc Mayhem who, Iridius had to admit, was as awesome as his name made him sound. Iridius, on the other hand, had become a very young captain with a ship of his own – it just happened to haul artificially intelligent toy dogs, toxic waste and, one best-forgotten time, several hundred tonnes of Endorplorean landwhale dung.

So, if Iridius had such a low opinion of Commander April Idowu, why did he have a standing news alert set for whenever her name popped up in articles across the QEC-NET? Why indeed?

"Just summarise the article for me."

"*Yes, captain. Fleet Admiral Maria Ramirez congratulates April Idowu on her promotion to captain. Captain Idowu will be taking command of the newly constructed* FSC Gallaway, *the first of the next-generation Universe II-class starships. With advanced BAMF propulsion, the* Gallaway *is capable of reaching FTL speeds in excess of 6000c. It is armed with the latest threat detection and elimination systems, advanced shields, and the most comprehensive science and medical facilities ever embarked on a starship. Admiral Ramirez says, 'Captain Idowu and her crew will be leading Federation Space Command into a new era. She—*"

"Computer, stop."

It wasn't that Iridius doubted April deserved the opportunity – she deserved it more than anyone. But captaining a Universe-class starship and heading out on exploration missions into the great uncharted cosmos had been his dream, too. He hadn't joined Space Command to fly a hauler. But now, stuck as captain of this rust bucket, he would never get the chance to captain a ship like the *Gallaway*. April would go down in Federation history with a ship like that. The only thing holding Iridius back from the same type of career April was enjoying was the chance to prove himself on a decent starship. That, and the fact that he'd graduated at the absolute bottom of his Academy class because he was a lazy, often drunk, unambitious waste of talent. He also had a reputation for breaking every starship he captained.

Iridius sat up on his bed. The news that April was about to take command of the most advanced starship in the galaxy had given him a shot of envy right in the jugular. There was no way he'd be able to sleep now. Not only had his ex-girlfriend stolen his collection of Batman comics – including some from the twenty-first century – she'd stolen his dream ship, too. Well, if he wasn't going to get his nap he might as well have a coffee.

Iridius moved to the coffee press in the wall alcove. The ship's food synthesis system could make coffee – it could make nearly anything, given the plans for printing the correct chemical compounds atom by atom. However, fresh ground coffee from beans grown the old-fashioned way – well, grown hydroponically under synthesised UV light in synthesised soil with synthesised fertiliser – always tasted better. He tipped a spoonful of roasted coffee beans into his hand-grinder, closed the lid and clipped on the handle, then listened to the satisfying sound as he crushed the dried beans into powder. Even though hand-grinding beans took a couple of minutes, he liked the tactile, low-tech work. It gave him time to think about how his dreams had been crushed in a very similar way.

He stared out the porthole of his cabin. The glass was electro-tinted for FTL but the bright glow outside was still visible. When travelling faster-than-light there were no colourful lights or streaks of white as the stars whipped artfully past. Instead, the Doppler Effect turned the stars completely invisible, but brought cosmic radiation into the visible spectrum instead. So all that was visible was a diffuse white light, bright enough to burn the retinas out of your eyeballs.

When the beans were ground Iridius reached for a paper filter, remembering in that instant that he'd used the last one that morning.

"Dammit," he said, wondering if there was any way he could blame this on April too.

Not willing to give up on his much-needed caffeine, he reached into the garbage and pulled out that morning's used filter. Blowing on it, he put it in the coffee press, tipped in the ground coffee and filled it with water.

When his coffee was made he sat at the small table in his cabin, sipping the bitter black liquid that contained only trace amounts of bin fluff, and opened the latest issue of *Space Captain Monthly* on his holoscreen, flicking aimlessly through the articles for something of interest before changing to *Cosmic Playboy* – also for the articles, of course.

Some time later the intercom beeped.

"Captain, this is the bridge."

"Go ahead, ensign."

"Just letting you know we're five minutes from dropping out of FTL."

"Alright," Iridius said, closing his holoscreen. "On my way."

CHAPTER TWO_

IRIDIUS WAITED on the *Diesel Coast*'s bridge as they approached Iota Persei. A far-flung system, Iota Persei was best known for its mining operations and the small moon that orbited Iota Persei G, whose liquid water oceans contained mineral crystals that could turn the skin of most species a sparkling gold colour. Given the name Midas, the moon soon became a major tourist destination, and gold skin became a fashion statement among the wealthy – at least until the first cases of Midas's diarrhoea began occurring six months after the gold colour had faded. It was about as pleasant a way to die as it sounded.

"Why do they call it a bridge?" Ensign Rangi asked.

"What?" Iridius said, immediately regretting it. He knew better than to engage with the helmsman.

"The bridge. I was just thinking, no one's ever explained why it's called a bridge. I mean, it's not a bridge to anywhere. It's a room really – command room would be a better name than bridge. Why bridge?"

"Ensign," Iridius said, pinching the bridge of his nose, "stop saying the word 'bridge'."

As with most similar situations, Quinn provided the answer.

"Sailing ships were originally steered from the aft. When ships became steam powered the captain needed some way to see past the steam stacks. They built a raised platform that extended across the deck so officers could walk from port to starboard to check ahead of them. It was like a bridge. Ergo – the bridge."

"Well," Iridius said, "fascinating. Now, how far are we from dropping out of FTL? That's what you're meant to be focused on, ensign."

"Ten seconds, captain," Rangi said without turning back to the helm.

Iridius made a spinning gesture with his index finger and Rangi lazily spun to face the view-screen.

"Plenty of time, sir," Rangi said. "Popping the cherry in three, two, one... now."

Popping the cherry was a phrase pilots and starship helmsmen used in reference to the moment the Bedi-Alcubierre-Millis-Formelge, or BAMF, drive shut down – effectively popping the bubble universe that surrounded the ship. That bubble disconnected the ship from regular space-time and allowed faster-than-light travel. It also allowed them to avoid the troublesome effects of time-dilation.

The moment the bubble popped, the view-screen filled with lines of crackling orange as the ship's shields overloaded. During the first human test of faster-than-light travel a century and a half ago, a ship from Earth arrived at Alpha Centauri B and shut down its BAMF drive, releasing the enormous number of charged particles that had collected in front of the BAMF bubble. The resulting shockwave obliterated the entire planet of Mandor Trivani and caused the extinction of the primitive race of the Mandors – a species of intelligent, teddy-bear-like creatures. This incident led to the mandated use of shields to capture FTL particle dissipation. The downside of using shields to catch such an enormous amount of energy is that they usually overloaded, leaving the ship without a shield for some time – five to ten minutes in the case of a clunker like the *Diesel Coast*.

Once the orange light of the shields cleared, Iridius could see Iota Persei E floating ahead of them in the void of space. "Bring us into orbit, Ensign Rangi."

"Sure thing, captain."

The view of the planet shifted as the *Diesel Coast*'s thrusters reorientated the ship and Rangi used the fusion drive to bring it into an orbital insertion trajectory. As the *Diesel Coast* reached the planet, the curve of its aqua green surface filled the viewscreen, streaked with clouds of methane. Iridius heard the change in the hum of the engines as they powered down to provide just enough velocity to hold orbit. The planet turned on the screen before them like a rolling ball.

"Orbital insertion achieved, captain."

"Okay." Iridius turned to Quinn. "Call us in, I guess."

Quinn nodded, and tapped some buttons to establish a light beam comm-link with the colony below. "Mining Station Victoria, this is the *FSC Diesel Coast* requesting clearance for landing, over."

There was no response.

"Mining Station Victoria, this is the *FSC Diesel Coast* requesting clearance for landing, over."

Again, there was nothing.

"Maybe they don't want the dogs," Ensign Rangi said. "Can't say I'd want hundreds of toy dogs running around either."

Iridius didn't bother telling his helmsman to shut up. Instead, he focused on the sense of unease that was creeping up his spine. "Go wide band," he told Quinn. "See if we get anything."

"Mining Station Victoria, this is *FSC Diesel Coast*. Does anyone read? Over."

After several moments, Iridius spoke again. "Is there something wrong with our comms?"

Quinn shrugged. "There doesn't seem to be, captain, although it could be a, um..."

"A what?" Iridius asked, one eyebrow cocked.

"Maybe a Franklinism?"

Iridius's single eyebrow remained raised, the rest of his face neutral. "The *Diesel Coast* doesn't get Franklinisms. She doesn't do that to me."

Iridius's reputation for breaking starships was so widespread within Space Command it had even been given a name. If something odd happened to a ship while Iridius was onboard, it was dubbed a Franklinism. It would've been nice to have something more impressive named after him – a battle tactic, a diplomatic event, even an Academy drinking game would've been preferable, but Iridius couldn't deny the correlation between his presence and ship malfunctions. Every ship he'd been aboard during his time as a cadet had suffered some sort of impressive technical failure. From propulsion to computer systems to life support, he'd caused just about everything to go haywire. Even the FSC chief engineer, Commodore Nyquist, came to witness every door on a starship being fused closed and the simultaneous malfunction of the onboard water system, causing waste product to be ejected into the air. The incident affectionately became known as the porta-potty incident, named for its similarity to a twentieth-century prank. But the *Diesel Coast* had never given Iridius any trouble and, as ugly and plain as she was, he loved her for it – even if she was named for a coastline on Earth forever associated with a mid-twenty-first century ecological disaster.

"I'm sorry, captain," Quinn said. "There doesn't seem to be anything wrong with our comms system but it's well overdue for an upgrade. Refit of haulers isn't a high priority for the FSC."

"You seem to be telling me things I already know, lieutenant commander. Feel free to jump back in when you have some useful information."

Quinn recoiled slightly before gathering herself, a red bloom spreading over her neck. Most people might not have noticed, but Iridius knew his crew. "Yes, sir," she said.

Iridius felt a pang of guilt. He hadn't meant to chide her, but the *Diesel Coast* had never malfunctioned on him the way other ships did. Something else was up, and it was making him edgy. He hit the comms button to the engine room.

"Junker?"

There was a crashing sound, like a tray of metal objects being knocked onto the floor. A procession of inventive curse words followed, then a woman's voice came on the line. "Yes, captain. What's shiftin'?"

"Are you messing with my systems again?"

"No, sir."

Iridius waited a beat without saying anything.

"Well, yes, sir," Junker said, "but not right at the moment. Something wrong?"

"We can't establish communication with the colony."

"Comms should be fine, sir."

"Alright, well let me know if you notice anything odd. Franklin out." Iridius turned his attention back to the helm. "Ensign Rangi, bring us geosynchronous over the colony."

"Aye."

The helmsman worked the controls to bring the *Diesel Coast* into a location above the mining colony and hold them there.

"Junker," Iridius said into his comms again, "you ever fix that long-range scanner?"

"Uh, it's on the to-do list, sir."

"You know that means we're blind to incoming FTL signals," Iridius said. "There's a myriad of threats out here – Alliance warships, pirates... Greg's mother-in-law."

"That only occurred once, captain," Greg said. "She now

understands that my wife Tr'gork N'hlarkic Gren'trok does not travel on the ship with me."

"Alright, so we can't scan from orbit," Iridius said, ignoring him. "Quinn, if we buzz the station, can we use short-range scanners?"

Lieutenant Commander Quinn nodded. "Aye, captain. What are you wanting to scan for?"

"Any short-range signals, life signs, whatever's down there."

"Life signs?" Ensign Rangi asked. "You think something's happened? Another attack?"

"I don't know, but bring us into a fly-by of the colony."

"Roger."

"Captain," Quinn said, "if you're concerned there's been another Alliance attack, we should contact Space Command. We're not equipped to deal with anything like that. We're just a hauler. FSC regulations state that we should contact Earth to request assistance."

"Let's just see if there's anything going on down there first," Iridius said. "It might be nothing. Get ready to scan. Ensign, bring us down."

The *Diesel Coast's* engines hummed back to life. Ensign Rangi manoeuvred the ship and fired the engines in retrograde burn, slowing the ship to lower its orbit. Eventually, as the *Diesel Coast* entered the thin atmosphere and descended through the haze of methane clouds, the view-screen became obstructed by the flickering orange and blue of atmospheric entry.

Generally, starships don't need any sort of aerodynamic appearance because, as is widely known, there isn't any air in space. Any pointy ends and wing-things are purely the addition of enthusiastic designers. The problem for the *Diesel Coast* was, as a small freighter, it wasn't equipped with its own shuttle craft, and so was often required to enter atmosphere when visiting a planet. In other words, despite being one of the few ships that could use a pointy end and wing-things, it had neither, lending it all the aerodynamic capabilities of a brick.

Once they were well and truly into the gravity well of the planet, the *Diesel Coast* rotated the nozzles of its engines and burned hard as it bricked its way towards the surface. They flew low over Iota Persei E. Unlike the rough, craterous terrain of most rock planets, the methane cycle here meant methane rain, combined with harsh winds, left the surface smooth like rolling dunes. They passed over several large methane lakes that glistened a rich azure in the sunlight before the ship reached the three domes of Mining Station Victoria. The domes of the colony were built from hexagonal sheets of metal riveted to a frame beneath – not the expensive high-strength glass composite of some tourist resort. This was a working colony; the residents weren't here to admire the view.

Ensign Rangi may have been an incredibly annoying individual with the attention span of a three-year-old on red soda, but he was a hell of a pilot. The *Diesel Coast* skimmed no more than fifty metres over the ground, rolling in a steep turn around the domes of Victoria Station before pulling up and regaining altitude. No easy feat for a brick.

"Scan complete, captain," Quinn said. She looked at him. "No life signs detected."

"None at all?"

"No, sir."

"Our short-range sensors do actually work?"

Quinn nodded.

Iridius's mouth drew into a thin line. "Anything else strange show up?"

"No, sir, nothing," Quinn said. "Wait, there's a signal coming from inside."

"What kind of signal?"

"Oh, it's not important, just a low-charge signal from a remote mining plasma cutter."

"Sounds like a distress call," Iridius said. "Ensign Rangi, bring us in to land. We'd better investigate."

"Captain," Quinn said, "I don't think we should be doing that. Something has obviously happened. As a cargo ship, we are not equipped to deal with what might be another attack or even a biological event. Protocol says we should return to orbit and contact Federation Space Command so they can send an appropriate response."

"Quinn, I'm sure I don't need to remind you that Federation law also states that any vessel detecting a distress signal is required to respond and render assistance."

"Yes, sir," Quinn said, "but this is a low-battery warning."

"That's how you're choosing to interpret it," Iridius countered. "As captain of this vessel I am choosing to interpret it as a beacon of distress. Ensign Rangi, land us."

"You got it, captain."

The *Diesel Coast* turned and flew back to Victoria Station. The ship touched down on a landing pad near the largest of the three domes, and a roof extended up over the pad, enclosing the ship in a sealed landing bay that would be pressurised with breathable atmosphere before the airlock into the station would open.

"Alright," Iridius said, standing, "let's find out what's going on."

"Captain Franklin," Quinn said. Iridius looked at his second-in-command. "I don't think we should be doing this."

"Your concern has been duly noted," Iridius said. He pressed the comms on his chair. "Junker?"

"Yes, sir?"

"Get hard suits ready for me, you and Quinn, and get the rifles out of the cage."

"Yes, sir."

"You intend to enter the colony?" Quinn asked.

"We can't do much investigating sitting in here, can we?"

"Do you think a team of three will be enough?"

"Not enough for football, Quinn, but fine to have a quick poke around. Besides, we need Ensign Rangi ready for a quick escape if necessary, and Greg isn't qualified on the AR-80."

As a malignant, Greg was a member of a race vehemently opposed to violence of any kind. As such, his service in the FSC was conditional on him not being required to use weapons.

Iridius knew Quinn was nervous. "Look, Quinn, if there are no life signs then there are no enemies either. We'll be wearing hard suits, so biological threats aren't an issue. This isn't a big deal."

She nodded, though it was hardly enthusiastic.

"Alright," Iridius said. "Rangi, you have the conn. If I call it in, you better be ready to go." He walked towards the stairs at the back of the bridge, then turned back. "Also, if you see us running for our lives, take that as your cue to be ready to go."

"You got it, captain," Rangi said. "I'll keep her idling."

———

When Iridius and Quinn walked into the cargo bay, Technician First Class Samira 'Junker' Nejem was popping open plastic cases and removing the hard suits used for extra-vehicular activity. She was dressed in blue coveralls, her dark hair shaved on one side and the rest pulled up into a short ponytail. The straps of her coveralls just obscured the words FSC VALKYRIE, which were printed across the back of her white t-shirt.

The *FSC Valkyrie* was a battlecruiser – one of the few ships built purely for combat in the entire FSC fleet. The mandate for the FSC had long been exploration and scientific research.

However, the rise of the Planetary Alliance and the war that followed some thirty years ago had led to a greater need for warships. The *Valkyrie* was one of these, and had been Junker's posting before the *Diesel Coast*. She'd been busted off that ship for illegally selling used components and for conducting unauthorised upgrades. She still wore the shirt, not because she was clinging to the memory of serving on a better starship, but because crew on haulers like the *Diesel Coast* didn't get cool shirts.

"How's it going, Junker?" Iridius asked as he and Quinn crossed the mostly empty cargo bay.

Junker had laid out the suits on the ground. They were all matte white with chipped and faded FSC logos. The suits were segmented into boots, lower leg, upper leg, lower torso, upper torso (which also comprised the built-in air supply and life-support system), upper arm, lower arm, gloves and helmet. Black flexible seals would connect each segment, allowing movement for elbows, knees, and other bits that were supposed to bend. Hard suits like these were actuator assisted and provided a good range of motion and dexterity, which was only marginally impacted by the gloves. Compared with EVA suits from the original days of human spaceflight they might as well have been swimwear – albeit swimwear that featured eight hours of oxygen, radiation shielding, ballistic protection and urine recycling. The entire front of the snug-fitting helmet was electro-glass, allowing good vision, automatic tint control and a customisable heads-up display that could be controlled, as with most suit functions, via the touch screen on the left forearm.

"They haven't been used in a while," Junker said, "but I tech inspected them about a month ago and they were good then."

"Good enough," Iridius said. "Suit up and we'll perform checks."

No matter how far space suits had come, there was still

nothing elegant about suiting up in one. The three of them stripped down to their underwear then pulled on the thin, tight-fitting spandex that was worn underneath to regulate temperature. Quinn and Junker ducked behind a cargo crate to do this. Although gender segregation was largely non-existent in the twenty-third century, there was still an instinct to leave some things to the imagination of the opposite sex.

It was possible to suit up in an EVA hard suit alone, but it was significantly quicker and easier to do it with assistance. They helped each other with the torso sections, then Iridius and Quinn collected the arm and leg sections of Junker's suit, sliding them on and locking them in place. Junker keyed the control panel and powered up the suit, allowing her much freer movement so she could assist Iridius with Quinn's suit.

Iridius was the last to suit up, just as he always ensured he was the last to shower, the last to eat, and would be the last into the ship's escape pods if it ever came to that. There were a number of leadership tenets he held true, but none more so than to never put your own wellbeing before that of your people.

"Alright," Iridius said once his suit was powered up. "Helmets on."

They pulled on their helmets, listening for the click of the bolts sliding home, and checking that the control panel showed good seal around the neck joint. Iridius watched as the HUD projected up across his vision and then faded to transparent. It would remain that way until he manually activated it, or the helmet detected the movement of his eyes to the edges of his view, where information was displayed. He looked to the left and the suit status indicators became visible – green lights across the board.

"System check," he said.

"Green," Quinn answered, her voice coming in over the suit comms.

"Green," Junker echoed.

"Air on, pressure on," Iridius said.

They each switched from breathing external air to using the suit's life support. Iridius felt the slight pressure change and heard the sudden muffling of sounds that meant his suit was now sealed off from the outside environment. His suit status was still green. "I'm still green," he said. "You?"

"Still green," Quinn said.

"Likewise," Junker added.

"Alright, let's get some weapons."

They moved to the weapons locker on the wall of the cargo bay. Iridius keyed in a code and the door popped open. He pulled out two bulky black AR-80 pulse rifles and passed them to Quinn and Junker before taking one for himself. Each weapon was already fitted with an ammunition clip holding eighty rounds. Iridius considered handing out additional clips, but decided if they needed any more ammo than that they were already so far in over their heads that it wouldn't matter.

Despite common expectations of the future, laser pistols never became feasible weaponry – the energy requirements were just too extreme. Instead, electronic pulse projectile rifles became the weapon of choice. At the end of the day, even after thousands of years of weapon development, there was still nothing as reliable as filling your enemy with holes made by fast-moving metal. That said, the AR-80 did have an underslung non-lethal microwave-based incapacitation beam, which was pretty futuristic.

"Rangi, this is Franklin. We're heading out into the station now. Seal and purge the bay and shut down artificial gravity generation."

"Aye, captain. Take it easy out there."

Double doors slid closed, sealing the cargo bay off from the rest of the ship. With a long hiss, all the air was purged from the cargo bay and vents opened to fill it with air from the station atmosphere outside. Essentially, the cargo bay acted as one big airlock – standard procedure to ensure the rest of the ship wasn't exposed to anything in the station's air. With a small lurch, Iridius felt the ship's artificial gravity shut down, his stomach not appreciative of the sudden change from 0.8g of simulated gravity to the 0.3g of the planet's actual gravity.

Iridius walked to the wall and pulled down the red and yellow striped handle for the bay door release. Even muffled through the suit, Iridius could hear the thrum as the door mechanism worked. The cargo bay door began descending, opening up the entire back of the ship and forming a ramp to the ground.

Iridius didn't turn to look at his executive officer as she stepped up beside him, but in his peripheral vision he could see her fingers drumming against the body of her rifle. Lieutenant Commander Kira Quinn was a certified genius, with degrees in biology, physics and law, and an almost encyclopaedic knowledge of whatever she wanted to retain in her planet-sized brain. She was among the smartest officers in all of the FSC. Why, then, was she second-in-command on a piece-of-junk hauler? Because where FSC officers required nerves of steel, Quinn had nerves of chocolate – they had a tendency to melt in hot situations. Given time and space, she could solve just about any problem in the universe, but turn up the pressure and her composure went out the window.

They descended the ramp and entered the long corridor that ran from the landing pad to the main bubble of Victoria Station. The first thing they passed was a row of toilets. Six different types. These were species segregated rather than gender segregated – not because of humility or speciesism, but for purely functional reasons. Having these six toilet types was pretty standard. This was the minimum number that could cater for all species in the Federation – eighty-seven at last count.

There was a time when humanity stared out at the stars and thought they were alone. The universe seemed a vast place filled with nothing but existential dread. Once the people of Earth unlocked the secrets of FTL flight and became a truly space-faring race, it hadn't taken long for them to kick over the rock of the galaxy and discover just how many grubs and bugs were crawling around underneath. Life, perhaps even more than people suspected, was abundant out in the black of space and, in most cases, surprisingly similar. Most species were DNA-based, most were carbon-based with a smattering of silicon lifeforms. Most walked upright with arms and legs or something equivalent, and most used verbal language. The key repeated word in that sentence is 'most' – there were always some outliers that freaked out even the most well-adjusted xenobiologist – but on the whole, life seemed to have a bit of a pattern going. Still, Iridius had no idea how at least three of those six toilets worked.

Approaching the sealed door into the colony, Iridius saw that the control panel was dark, a single red word displayed: OFFLINE. Iridius turned to Junker. Other than being the only member of his crew who wouldn't lose their head in a firefight, this was why Iridius had brought her along. "Junker, can you get us in?"

Junker approached the panel, pulling a multi-tool from a pouch at her waist. She popped the front of the control panel off and started examining the wiring inside. After a moment she cut two wires and joined them together. She tapped the touch screen a few times and the door retracted into the wall.

They entered, and found themselves in the space dock of the station – three other corridors like the one they had exited ran off to other landing pads. There was space for the large six-wheeled cargo transporters to move around as they loaded or unloaded cargo from ships, and a sizable door for them to access the cargo processing area. Up a short staircase on a mezzanine level that overlooked the cargo area was the dock control room, security checkpoint and personnel entrance to the station. Iridius led Junker and Quinn up the stairs. Victoria Mining Station was not an enormous production facility, and didn't have the type of large spaceport associated with some of the planet-scale mining operations across the galaxy. However, Iridius still expected to see people around. They hadn't detected life signs, but if there'd been an attack there should be evidence of it: damage to the facilities, or bodies strewn around. There was none of that. The screens were all dark, the lights were the dim orange of backup power, but everything seemed in its right place. Other than the absent staff.

Iridius stepped forward and felt his foot slip out from under him. He stumbled, but managed to maintain his footing, thanks to the low gravity. He looked down. He'd trodden in something, a kind of pink slime. He lifted his boot and a thick glob dripped down from the tread on his sole. Iridius examined the goo. "What's—" But he stopped mid-question when he saw other puddles of the slime around the space. One was dripping down the side of a chair in front of the dock monitoring station. There were two spots of pink on the floor at the security checkpoint.

Oh.

"I suppose that explains why there weren't any life signs," Iridius said. "This isn't just goo, it's people goo."

"Oh shit," Quinn said. "I knew this was a bad idea."

"Get a grip, Quinn," Iridius said, "we're in completely sealed suits. Are there any airborne contaminants? Anything that might tell us whether this is something biological?"

"We shouldn't be here," Quinn said. "We shouldn't be here."

"Quinn!" Iridius snapped.

Quinn turned to look at him. "Right," she said. "Sorry." She pulled out her tablet and tapped at the screen, watching it for a moment. "Nothing recognisable as biological, captain – either

bacterial or viral. Air quality is perfect. Wait, there's something
—" Quinn stopped.

"What is it?" Iridius asked.

"My tablet just stopped working."

Junker pulled her tablet out. "Mine, too."

"There's some sort of electrical interference," Quinn said.

"Alright, let's do some digging the old-fashioned way," Iridius said. "Junker, take a look at dock control, see if you can get backup power to the computers. If you can, send any records of ships coming and going from the station back to the *Diesel Coast*. Quinn, see if you can find any sort of log that might tell us what the hell happened here. I'm going to push through to the main station and see if people met the same fate there."

"Are you sure we should split up?" Quinn said. "It was advised against in Academy training. They called it the horror movie rule."

"That must have been one of the classes I missed," Iridius said. "You've got your orders. We collect as much information as we can to send back to FSC Headquarters. Keep comms open and keep your suits sealed. No red-shirts today."

Red-shirts was the name given to members of the FSC killed during away missions. Originally, the uniforms of the FSC had consisted of white tunics and black trousers. The name red-shirt reflected the look of that uniform after injury. Although the Federation also had species with both green and blue blood, the term had stuck.

"Aye, sir," Quinn and Junker replied in unison, Quinn markedly less enthusiastically than Junker.

Iridius approached the door through to Victoria Station, a plain stainless-steel door. There was no separate entrance to the station because, let's face it, a mining station like Victoria didn't attract tourists who needed a dedicated entrance. The only people coming to Victoria Station were workers or haulers who didn't care whether there were nice white-walled entranceways with streamlined security screening and a 'Welcome to Victoria Mining Station' sign.

The control panel beside the door was dead. The space dock was comprised of the same atmosphere as the station, so the door shouldn't have a fail-safe seal. Iridius pushed the ends of his gloved fingers into the gap in the centre of the door and pulled outwards. When the doors parted enough, he slipped his hands in, pushing until the two halves of the door locked open.

Beyond was a space almost like a small lobby. The walls were industrial grey with yellow, blue and green lines painted on the walls, splitting down different corridors to indicate directions to station facilities. Iridius walked towards the corridors that branched off from the lobby. The power was offline to the doors here, too, but one of them was slightly open. Peering through, he saw several piles of pink goo lit by the orange glow of the backup lighting. There were three others arranged together in front of the nearby holographic information assistant, which was now offline, too.

"Looks like more of the same out here, unfortunately," Iridius said. "Nothing but pink goop."

"I managed to route backup power to the dock computer," Junker said over the comms. "There are no records of ship movements. They've been deleted."

"It's the same here, captain," Quinn said. "There are no logs. All of them have been erased. In fact, almost all the data in the station computer network seems to have been deleted or corrupted."

"I guess that rules out an accident," Iridius said. "So, we've got an attack, but for what? The Alliance might attack the station again, but they'd do it with some purpose – they'd either take control of the station or at least steal some equipment, but it doesn't look like that's happened. The only thing the attackers have done is goopify every resident of the station."

"Captain, don't you think that's trivialising it? These were people," Quinn said.

"You're right," Iridius responded. "I apologise. We'll just say they've been gooped. Is that better?"

"Not really."

"Look, in times like these, sometimes you've just got to try to see the... bugs!"

"See the what, captain?" Junker said.

Iridius didn't reply. Ahead, making its way up the corridor towards him, was a cloud of hundreds of black bugs. A swarm. They moved in a turbulent mass, growing out in one direction before shrinking in and then bulging somewhere else. Iridius stepped back and the swarm compressed to pass through the door then billowed out again, coming to a stop in front of Iridius. It hung in the air as if it was watching him, evaluating. Iridius could see now that what he had thought were insects were actually clusters of smaller things that clung together as amorphous blobs. There must have been hundreds or thousands, maybe even millions of tiny black specks. For a moment nothing happened, then Iridius felt a strange sensation run through his body, a subtle buzzing that seemed to fill him. His eyelid twitched, the muscles in his arms and hands jumped and the swarm flew upwards and swirled around the lobby space above Iridius.

"There's some kind of swarm here," Iridius said over his comms. "Looks like insects, but I think they're nanomachines of some sort."

The swarm whirled around the room in a chaotic mass, but eventually the radius of their orbit grew smaller until they were buzzing around directly above Iridius's head. He clutched his rifle and thumbed off the safety switch. Without warning, the swarm dived down, engulfing him. Iridius waved his rifle, trying to swat them away, but it was futile – the swarm just parted, leaving him swinging at nothing. Looking up, Iridius saw some of the swarm still above his head. He aimed his AR-80 and fired wildly into the mass. His bullets cracked into the roof above. If any of the swarm were hit, they didn't show it.

Iridius's comms crackled as if picking up some kind of interference from the turbulent cloud of micro machines. "*You.*" Static and high-pitched tones in his ears seemed to be resolving themselves into words. "*You.*" Then more words through the squealing, buzzing interference. "*You. Are. Us.*"

"Captain!" Quinn's voice came over the radio. "Captain, what's going on?"

"Get back to the ship!" Iridius said down the open comms line. "Now!"

"Captain, what's happening?" This was Junker.

"Just fucking go!" Iridius roared.

"Roger that," Junker replied without a second of hesitation. There was a brief silence, then he heard her speak again. "Come on, commander." A pause. "Quinn!"

"Huh? Oh right, running now."

Iridius began swinging his arms in front of him, moving forward as the swarm buzzed around him. Then, as quickly as it had appeared, the swarm peeled away and flew towards the door to the space dock.

Iridius lifted his rifle and fired again into the black cloud. The swarm simply opened voids around Iridius's bullets, seemingly able to predict the path of the projectiles. Realising that firing bullets was about as useful as throwing rocks at a Tartusian sandstorm, Iridius activated the AR-80's underslung microwave weapon, then fired. The weapon was completely soundless, apart from a rhythmic clicking to tell the user they were firing, but the swarm reacted. It stopped, and suddenly dispersed. Some of the black clumps broke apart into the smaller nanomachines they were made up of – so small that Iridius couldn't see them drop to the ground. Iridius continued to move his rifle, aiming it wherever the densest part of the swarm seemed to congregate.

A strand of buzzing black, almost like a tentacle, reached out from the main body of the swarm and snaked through the air towards Iridius, wrapping itself around his rifle. Even as he kept his finger planted on the trigger, the clicking of the microwave ray stopped. Having somehow disabled his weapon, the tentacle retreated into the main swarm. Iridius switched the weapon back to bullets, but when he pulled the trigger that firing mechanism was dead, too.

Iridius watched as the swarm headed out the door and into the space dock. He chased after it and saw Quinn and Junker disappearing down the corridor towards the *Diesel Coast*'s landing pad. Now that he wasn't surrounded by a swarm of machines, Iridius suddenly noticed the warnings flashing up on his helmet's HUD. Apparently, his suit had been damaged. An EVA suit was constructed of hardened glass, titanium-based alloy and carbon nanotube composite, and yet somehow, in the brief amount of time they'd surrounded him, those bugs had managed to inflict damage to the exterior of his suit. It was still environmentally sealed, but given enough time those things might have been able to burrow through. What the hell were they?

Iridius broke into a sprint. It didn't really matter what they were. They were going after his crew. Suddenly, another thought struck him. Maybe they weren't going after Quinn and Junker. They were obviously intelligent, and if they had any objectives beyond this mining station they would need a way off-world. Those little bastards were going after the *Diesel Coast*.

"Rangi," Iridius said over his comms, "do you read?"

"Aye, captain."

"Remember what I said about running for our lives?"

"She's ready to fly, captain."

"Captain," Junker cut in over the comms, "these insects you mentioned. I assume that's the black swarm about to overtake us?"

"Hit them with your microwave," Iridius said as he ran along the corridor. He watched as Junker and Quinn lifted their rifles. The swarm stopped suddenly, dispersing itself, just as it had when he'd fired at it, as if trying to limit the amount of the swarm being exposed to the radiation. Iridius knew it wouldn't stop them, but it would hold them up. He ran through the swarm – the EVA suit he wore shielded him from the microwave radiation. Mostly.

"Come on," he said as he ran past. "Just hold the microwave on them and keep moving."

More tentacle-like threads forced their way out against the microwave, reaching for Quinn and Junker as they turned and awkwardly tried to run while firing a steady stream of radiation behind them. As they ran out onto the landing pad, Iridius spoke over his comms again.

"Rangi, close the cargo bay door!"

"I'm sorry, Dave, I can't do that."

"What?!"

"It's that movie."

"Rangi!"

"Captain, I can't close the door with you outside."

"Dammit, ensign, that's an order!"

"Acknowledge that."

Iridius, Quinn and Junker jumped up onto the *Diesel Coast*'s closing cargo bay door, using the low gravity to aid their leap. They scrambled down into the bay, slipping and sliding as the angle of the door increased. Rangi had already reactivated artificial gravity. As they hit the floor of the bay Iridius spun back to see the door seal closed. It didn't look like any of the nanomachines had made it in, but Iridius wasn't taking any chances. "Get us out of atmo and away from this rock," he said over the comms. He felt the ship move beneath him as the *Diesel Coast* lifted off the pad. "Quinn, Junker, mag down."

"Aye, captain."

The three of them activated the magnetic seal beneath their boots – the same system that held people to the external hull during space EVAs.

"Rangi, tell me when we're out," Iridius said.

A tense minute passed before Rangi's voice came over the comms. "We're in the black, captain."

"Alright. Quinn, Junker, confirm you're mag locked?"

"Confirmed," they both replied.

"Open the door again, Rangi. Vent the cargo bay to vacuum."

"Aye, sir."

As soon as the cargo bay door unsealed, the air inside the bay exploded out into the vacuum of space. Iridius felt the pull as it rushed around him. His whole body angled towards the opening door but his boots held him pinned to the floor. Most objects in the cargo bay were mag-locked or bolted down, but those that weren't – a bunch of Junker's tools, the plastic crates the EVA suits had been stored in, and a tablet that had been left on a bench – were sucked out into space. But Iridius knew that any of those nanobugs that might have made it through the closing door were now being vented, too.

After thirty seconds of venting, Iridius spoke over his comms again. "Alright Rangi, that should do it. Shut the door and give us atmo."

The cargo bay door began closing soundlessly, now they were in the vacuum of space. Once it was sealed Iridius saw air blast in through the vents around the roof – white sprays at first, as the water used to humidify the air condensed in vacuum. Eventually, as the cargo bay pressurised, this stopped, and after another minute or so a large green light above the cargo bay door blinked on. Ensign Rangi came over the comms to confirm.

"Cargo bay at atmosphere."

"Acknowledged," Iridius said. "Let's unsuit."

"You want me to contact Earth, captain?"

"Negative, ensign," Iridius said. "This wasn't a Planetary Alliance attack, it was something new. Some sort of intelligent swarm of nanomachines. We'll go to Earth and deliver a report ourselves. Plot a course."

"You got it."

Iridius disconnected his gloves and dumped them on the floor before removing his helmet. As soon as the seal cracked, the reassuring hum of the ship returned. They helped each other out of their suits and put them on the floor.

"I'd clean up the suits and put them away, sir," Junker said, "but the crates have gone the way of the *FSC Dodo*."

"It's fine," Iridius said. "Just leave them and come up to the bridge."

The three of them hurried up the stairs from the cargo bay to the bridge, Iridius already speaking as he reached the top. "Ensign Rangi, you ready to engage the BAMF?"

"Affirmative, captain."

"Punch it then."

As the crew of the *FSC Diesel Coast* gathered on the bridge and Ensign Rangi prepared to engage the ship's BAMF drive, none of them were there to see the almost imperceptible movement in the cargo bay. From the pockmarks that had been eaten into Iridius's EVA suit, tiny nanomachines that had buried themselves there and clung to the suit even during the depressurisation of the cargo bay floated up into the air. They coalesced together in a loose form, and after a second of what may have been contemplation, they found a suitable host for the vast intelligence they were linked to, and locked on. They'd found a form with its own artificial intelligence system, along with a body that had suitable appendages for movement. This was a system they could use to rebuild and continue their mission. The nanobugs entered one of the cargo crates aboard the *Diesel Coast*, and in the short time before Rangi engaged BAMF, the tiny machines altered the onboard systems, created a suitable neural-net simulation and uploaded as much of the ancient intelligence that controlled them as they could. And in that moment a My PupPup toy dog became the most advanced synthetic intelligence in the galaxy. Oh, and Captain Iridius B. Franklin, bottom of the Academy class of 2221, was giving it a ride straight to Earth.

CHAPTER THREE_

"Approaching Earth," Ensign Rangi said. "Passing lunar orbit and slowing to the new approach speed of fifteen hundred kilometres per second." Rangi groaned. "Jupiter's nuts, these new regulations suck. We might as well be walking."

Iridius leaned forward in his most captainly pose, his elbow on the arm of his chair and his chin perched between his thumb and forefinger. "On screen," he ordered.

Materialising in front of them, the image magnified so that the planet filled their entire view-screen, was the slowly rotating globe of Earth. Homeworld of humanity. The white of shifting, churning clouds covered the surface of the blue marble as it hung stark against the black forever of space.

Whenever they flew to Earth, Iridius always had this image displayed so he could announce their arrival to the bridge. "Here we are. Welcome to Sol C. Welcome to the cradle from which homo-sapiens crawled out to meet the vast galaxy. Earth," he said. "What a shithole."

How humanity had managed to slip into the Galactic Federation and in just one hundred and fifty years gain such a crucial and widespread role, no one was really sure. Earth had gone from an outer spiral arm backwater to the home of Federation Space Command Headquarters and a hub of shipbuilding and diplomacy. Iridius couldn't help but think some bribery or corruption had been involved, but of course this was the twenty-third century. That sort of thing didn't happen in the twenty-third century. Humanity was honest and peaceful, and would never have agreed to any underhanded deals, such as selling off large tracts of land in Africa for use as alien weapons test facilities, or having Australia completely removed from the planet so it could be used as an exhibit in the Garlax Zoo. You know, for example.

"Sir," Quinn said, aghast. "You can't say that about Earth."

"Why? What's Earth ever given to the galaxy?" Iridius said. "Denim jeans and herpes?"

"Us," Quinn said. "Humanity."

"Exactly. That's what I said, herpes."

"It's our homeworld."

Iridius waved a hand dismissively. "Yes, look, I understand how important Earth is from a historical perspective, but it's still a half-destroyed ball of pollution. And sure, atmospheric carbon removal and planet-wide re-vegetation has been underway for a couple of hundred years, but my family originally hails from Liverpool, and my grandfather moved to Procyon C, a planet with an arsenic atmosphere, because he wanted to live somewhere with fresher air."

As the *Diesel Coast* drew within two hundred thousand kilometres of Earth, Quinn opened a channel. "Earth Approach, this is Lieutenant Commander Quinn of the FSC *Diesel Coast* requesting transfer to Freighter Control."

"*FSC Diesel Coast*, this is Earth Approach, confirm. Transferring you to... belay that, *Diesel Coast*, I'm receiving a notification that you should proceed directly to FSC Headquarters."

"Earth Approach, this is Iridius Franklin, captain of the *Diesel Coast*. On whose authority are we being transferred?"

"Orders are from the Admiralty, captain. Bring your vessel into geosynchronous orbit above marker point six and an automated pilot will land you at FSC HQ. Earth Approach out."

Iridius drummed his fingers on the arm of his chair. It was odd they were being sent to FSC HQ. Usually they'd be relegated to a freight depot, like all haulers. He could understand it if the Admiralty already knew what they'd found on Iota Persei E, but they hadn't reported in yet. This wasn't the early days of FTL space flight, when communication still couldn't exceed the speed of light and all interstellar communication had to be conducted via faster-than-light probes. Quantum Entanglement Communication had been in use for almost a hundred years, providing near-instantaneous communication throughout the galaxy. The *Diesel Coast* had been sent to Iota Persei E only after the colony had been confirmed as secure following the earlier Alliance attack. There'd been no mention that everyone had been pink-gooped, and there'd have been no point sending the *Diesel Coast* with supplies if they had. Obviously Victoria Station never had a chance to communicate, and the *Diesel Coast* was the first ship to land after whatever had happened. Iridius would be willing to bet in a Diluvian Kill-Casino that these nanomachines had nothing to do with the Alliance.

"Alright," Iridius said. "Do as instructed and bring us into orbital insertion above marker point six. Where is that? Puerto Rico?"

"Aye, captain," Rangi said. "Looks like we're third in the queue."

In just over four minutes the *Diesel Coast* was entering orbit above the Indian Ocean, in a location close to where the continent of Australia had once been. Ensign Rangi initiated a burn to put the *Diesel Coast* into a transfer orbit that would end with it maintaining an altitude of thirty-six thousand kilometres above marker point six.

During their manoeuvring orbit, the *Diesel Coast* passed within several hundred kilometres of the FSC's major orbital shipbuilding facility, *Rutan Station*. The station was constructed from eight circular sections, like thin donuts lined up, each a hundred metres apart, the inner diameter slightly over three hundred metres. Massive tubular sections connected the donuts, making the whole station look like the frame of an enormous cylinder. Visible within this cylinder was a starship nearing the end of construction, the *FSC Beagle*. However, docked to one end of *Rutan Station*, shining fresh white in the starlight, was a ship that drew Iridius's attention. It was the sleek form of the recently completed *FSC Gallaway* – the new flagship of the fleet, and the ship that April Idowu would soon be commanding.

"Rangi," Iridius said, "magnify our view of Rutan."

Ensign Rangi pressed some buttons and the construction station filled the view-screen. The *FSC Gallaway* looked even more spectacular than he'd imagined.

"Look at that," Iridius said. "Now that's a ship. It's got everything – advanced propulsion, weapons, laboratories, everything a starship captain could want. Imagine what I could do with a ship like that."

"You don't need a ship like that, sir," Junker said. "You've got the *Coast*."

"Yes, Junker, I'm aware of that. That's my point. That's why I'll never achieve anything. A captain needs a ship like the *Gallaway* to do anything of value. You know who tells stories about the captains of haulers? Nobody."

The *Diesel Coast* had been waiting in geosynchronous orbit for almost half an hour when a voice came over the loud speaker. "*FSC Diesel Coast*, this is ALEO."

ALEO – Automated Landing from Earth Orbit – was a weak AI system used for piloting spacecraft down to landing pads at particularly busy spaceports. Human helmsmen were perfectly capable of executing the landing manoeuvres themselves, but the majority of them were more than happy to let ALEO take over, not only because regulations required it, but because no one wanted to be that pilot who collided with one of the quagmire of satellites orbiting the planet, or somehow managed to spear an enormous starship into a building.

"Helmsman, please accept my handshake request with your vessel's control system." The voice of ALEO was synthetic, and incredibly realistic. It was supposed to be gender-neutral, but always reminded Iridius of his Aunt Wallace, which brought back terrible memories of holiday lunches with the extended family and ruby-red lipstick kisses planted on his cheek. Ensign Rangi turned to look at Iridius. After a moment of hesitation, Iridius nodded and Rangi hit the button to accept the request.

"Thank you. Your vessel, the *FSC Diesel Coast*, is seventeen versions behind on flight system firmware. A note has been placed on your maintenance schedule. This version of ALEO is compatible with your flight system, but some newer safety features may be unavailable." *Same old passive aggressive message*, Iridius thought. *Tell someone who'll actually authorise us to get any decent maintenance, you stupid computer.* "Your descent time will be approximately sixteen minutes. Sit back, enjoy your landing, and thank you for using ALEO."

Iridius sat back in his chair, but he didn't relax, and he wouldn't enjoy the landing just because some computer told him to. He'd never been a fan of handing over control of his ship to anyone, especially not an AI. Even if it was a very limited AI, it was still a synthetic intelligence, and that made him nervous. The Federation had regulations in place to prevent the development of any AI that might become self-aware and go rogue, but Iridius still didn't like them. That was one benefit to captaining a ship like the *Diesel Coast* – it was so old that it didn't have an onboard

AI and could never support one, because its systems were too limited.

Unlike their landing on Iota Persei E, re-entry and landing on Earth was not a simple glide-slope descent. ALEO regularly fired thrusters and even initiated in-atmosphere pulses from the ship's fusion drive to alter their course, changing their descent vector multiple times to avoid satellites, space debris, and other ships.

Fifteen minutes and fifty-eight seconds later, the *Diesel Coast* was landing at Federation HQ in Brasilia, Brazil. Being on Earth, the landing pad did not require a dome or other pressurised structure. Instead, they landed on one of many exterior pads. It was still separated from the main building by a walkway that was currently barred by a thick automated gate for security purposes, but at least they'd be breathing real air for a change. That's what Ensign Rangi called it, "real air". Iridius preferred "polluted garbage gas".

Once the landing legs of the *Diesel Coast* had settled on the pad and the ship systems had powered down, Federation HQ contacted the ship, advising Iridius that he could stand down his crew for shore leave as long as they remained within the recreation spaces of HQ. Iridius, on the other hand, had an appointment with Rear Admiral Emilia Merritt of Fleet Command in one hour. Before her posting to Fleet Command, Merritt had been commandant of the Academy and had held that post during Iridius's time there. Iridius had a less than perfect record at the Academy, and so had spent more time with her than most cadets. *Another meeting with Metal Merritt.* Iridius supposed he'd better take a shower and drag out that rarely-used dress uniform.

————

Iridius smoothed his tunic, trying to buy a few more seconds before knocking on the door, even though Rear Admiral Merritt could probably see his silhouette through the frosted glass. Iridius had to push down the feeling that he was about to enter the commandant's office for yet another lecture after a night of drunken frivolity or having forgotten to show up for an exam. He might only be in command of a hauler, but he was still a captain in the Federation Space Command. He would enter the room like one. He lifted his fist and rapped on the door.

"Come."

Iridius entered the office and snapped his body to attention. "You asked for me to come directly, admiral."

"Ah, Captain Franklin," Merritt said. "You're actually slightly early."

"Yes, ma'am," Iridius said. "Would you like me to come back?"

"No, no, come on in and sit." Merritt gestured towards one of two empty chairs in front of her desk. "It's just a nice change from our previous interactions."

Iridius sat. The window of Merritt's office looked out on the lush gardens in the centre of the square-shaped Federation HQ building. Hopefully his crew were down there getting the rest they deserved, especially Quinn and Junker. What they'd seen on Iota Persei E would have rattled them, even if they wouldn't admit it. In truth, it had rattled him, too. The understanding was starting to hit home – all those piles of pink goop had been the residents of Mining Station Victoria: men, women, children.

"Would you like some water?" Merritt asked, lifting a glass jug from the desk.

"Yes, thank you, ma'am."

"You seem to have lost the tardiness you carried through your years at the Academy," Rear Admiral Merritt said as she poured sparkling clear water into a glass and handed it to Iridius. "It's nice to see."

"I like to think I've come a long way since then, ma'am."

"Good," Merritt said. "I should hope so. You've always been an intelligent and talented leader, Iridius. Your Academy career was one hell of a wasted opportunity."

Iridius took a sip of water. "Yes, ma'am."

"You drank away your chance to graduate near the top of your class."

"Yes, ma'am."

"Squandered your potential and finished dead last, lucky to make it through at all."

"Yes, ma'am."

"You could have been—" Merritt stopped herself. "I'm sorry, captain, you'll have to excuse me, it's easy to fall into old dynamics. Fact is, I haven't seen you for a few years and I'm glad to see you've got command of your own ship quite quickly. You were unaware of this, but you were almost expelled from the Academy."

"I am aware of that, ma'am," Iridius said. "I think you threatened me with expulsion on at least six different occasions."

"No, what I mean is your discharge was already prepared. I just refused to authorise it. I saw your potential, even if others didn't."

For a moment Iridius was speechless. He couldn't picture Metal Merritt fighting for him behind the scenes. "Thank you, ma'am. I don't know what to say."

"You don't have to say anything. My job was to get the best officers into the FSC. I thought you would be one of them. You can thank me by doing well in your command."

"Yes, ma'am, but it's just a hauler."

"No," Rear Admiral Merritt said, "it's not *just* a hauler. It's your chance to repair your reputation and build your career back up to where it should be. Plenty of captains prove themselves post-Academy. Some even work their way up from haulers to exploration or combat vessels. A true starship captain makes the best of the situation, whatever it is."

"Well, thank you ma'am, I'm just trying not to break it."

"Ah, yes," Rear Admiral Merritt said, "your famous ability to cause malfunctions in starships. That's actually why I've called you here."

"It is?"

"Yes," Merritt said. "I know you've undertaken shakedowns before. Your ability to take a ship through its test voyage and find every fault that can possibly occur is invaluable to FSC engineering staff."

As an unexpected perk of his reputation as a captain who breaks starships, Iridius also enjoyed a steady stream of work as a shakedowner. Before every starship's maiden voyage, before the majority of the new crew even stepped aboard, the starship would be taken on a shakedown cruise. This first flight out of space dock was designed to test the integrity of the vessel and ensure its systems were fully functional. Any defects or faults discovered during shakedown could then be rectified before the crew took over. Usually, a shakedown was undertaken by some of the crew who would eventually be part of the ship's complement, plus testing engineers and mechanics, but given his ability to bring the most extreme issues to light, Iridius was often called upon to captain a shakedown cruise. It wasn't exactly a high-profile job, but at least he got to do something different every once in a while.

"I guess everybody's got a talent, ma'am," Iridius said, unable to keep the sarcasm from his tone. "I suppose I should resign myself to my fate as a shakedowner."

"It's not all that bad, is it?"

"Ma'am," Iridius said, "with respect, taking new ships on a solar system lap because I'm exceptional at breaking things isn't the career I'd imagined, even for an Academy fuck-up." He caught himself. "Excuse my language, ma'am."

"Please," Merritt waved it off. "Fuck-up you might be, but having a side job as a shakedowner while maintaining your own command is actually something of an achievement."

"Hooray," Iridius said, with the same enthusiasm one might have for unflavoured porridge. He took another sip of water.

"What if I told you I've got a special shakedown assignment for you?" Merritt said. "Someone has to take the FSC *Gallaway* out for a spin."

Iridius choked on his water, spraying droplets over Rear Admiral Merritt's desk. He hastily wiped the drops of spittle away as he recovered his composure. "Sorry, you want me to command the *Gallaway*?"

"Shakedown command," Merritt clarified, "but yes. You'll be the first captain to take her out of the dock."

"Fuck a duck," Iridius said. "The gronking *Gallaway*."

"Yes."

"Uh, sorry again ma'am, but of course," Iridius said. "I'd be honoured."

"It's got a skeleton crew prepped and will be ready for its shakedown cruise in two or three days."

"I'll need my crew, too," Iridius said.

"Your crew?" Rear Admiral Merritt asked. "From your hauler?"

"Yes, ma'am," Iridius said, "from the *Diesel Coast*."

"I'm sure the *Gallaway*'s skeleton crew will be more than enough. They'll be serving on the ship, after all."

"I'd like my crew, too, ma'am," Iridius said. "They've always come on shakedowns with me. They're just as important as I am."

Rear Admiral Merritt looked at him for a moment and then turned away. She touched the surface of her desk and a holo-screen shot up in front of her. She flicked through some screens, and Iridius watched her type the words '*Diesel Coast*' into a search field. Merritt brought up the ship register and navigated to the crew files. Obviously, as a fleet commander, Merritt had access to the crew files of every ship in the FSC fleet.

"First Officer: Lieutenant Commander Kira Quinn," Rear Admiral Merritt said. "Exceptional record, exceptional scientific mind, exceptionally bad under pressure."

"She's getting better," Iridius said.

"Helmsman: Ensign Benjamin Rangi. One of the top flight school graduates in his year, a natural at flying everything from atmospheric aircraft to the Universe-class simulator. Unfortunately, his record is littered with minor breaches for insubordination, and a myriad of complaints about him 'not being able to shut up'."

"Yes," Iridius said. "Rangi's annoying, but I've never seen anyone fly like him."

"Load Master: Ah, he's a malignant, and of the N'hlarkic strain, too. That's enough said really, and you don't need a load master for a shakedown cruise."

"He's a nice guy," Iridius said, "and he does more than load master. He's got substantial engineering knowledge."

"Lastly, you've got a technician, Samira Nejem. Oh yes," Merritt said, "I know her. She's the technician that got busted off the *Valkyrie* for selling refurbished fusion and BAMF components to ship crackers and parts dealers. She was court-martialled for stealing Federation materiel and busted down from chief petty officer to first tech."

"Yes," Iridius said, "but the key part of that is that she's a technician who *could* refurbish fusion drive and BAMF components."

"Captain Franklin," Merritt said, and Iridius didn't miss the sudden switch to using his rank. "I understand your loyalty to your crew, but the *Gallaway* has a designated crew already.

Those who are here on Earth and whose conversion training is complete will act as the skeleton crew for your shakedown cruise. As *interesting* as the crew of your hauler are, they won't be needed for this assignment."

"Ma'am," Iridius said, readying himself to give this everything he had, "I may have been a disappointment to you during my time at the Academy, but I hope you know that I greatly admire and respect you. And with all that due respect, I think you're wrong. They're all fuck-ups in their own way, like me – we're the losers of Federation Space Command – but I want my crew with me because I see in them what you saw in me. I see their potential, even if others don't. If nothing else, they deserve their shot at being aboard a ship like the *Gallaway*."

Rear Admiral Merritt stared at Iridius. "They won't be doing anything while they're aboard."

"Yes, ma'am. I understand."

"Fine," Merritt said, "you can bring your crew along for a glorified pleasure cruise."

"Thank you, ma'am. I know they'll appreciate it. I'll be sure to tell them it was you who gave permission."

"I don't care whether you do that or not. That's something you still need to learn about command, captain. It's not about making friends."

"Understood, ma'am," Iridius said.

"The shakedown will be a one-week, fusion drive around the solar system, BAMF to Alpha Centauri B, standard tests including weapons, and then home."

"The usual run."

Merritt nodded. "You'll get more details when you get aboard and meet the crew. You're expected aboard the *Gallaway* at 15:00 hours. You can leave on a shuttle up to *Rutan Station* momentarily. We've already cleared the *Diesel Coast* to stay berthed where it is for the duration."

"Of course, ma'am."

"Good." Rear Admiral Merritt nodded. "That will be all." She reached for her own glass and took a sip, indicating that the conversation was over.

"Uh, ma'am," Iridius said.

The rear admiral looked at Iridius as if wondering why he was still there.

"I assume this means we're not here to discuss what happened on Iota Persei E?"

The confusion on Merritt's face was answer enough, but she still said, "What happened on Iota Persei E?"

"We were tasked to deliver supplies, ma'am."

"Yes, for the colony to recover from the Alliance attack, and toys for the children. I am a fleet command admiral, captain, I tend to know things. Why exactly do we need to discuss it?"

"Um, because when we arrived there wasn't anybody to deliver supplies to. Everyone on Iota Persei E is dead."

This time Rear Admiral Merritt was the one to spray water over the desk. "What?! Another Alliance attack?"

"No, ma'am, I don't believe so. Everyone was, well, they'd been turned to goop."

"Turned to goop?"

"Yes, ma'am."

"You don't think that perhaps this was the information you should have led with?"

"I didn't want to interrupt, ma'am," Iridius said. "You were saying such nice things about me."

Merritt gave Iridius a zero-Kelvin glare. "I assume you're trying to be humorous. This is not the time, Captain Franklin."

"No, ma'am."

"What exactly happened?"

Iridius ran the rear admiral through everything that had happened, from the time they attempted to communicate with

Iota Persei E and received no response, to landing (he may have glossed over the fact that the distress signal was a low battery signal), to finding the pink goop, and then finally escaping the nanomachines.

Rear Admiral Merritt took in his report with a passive stare. "Thank you, Iridius," she said. "I understand responding to a distress signal, but at the first sign of trouble you should have contacted Earth. A vessel more equipped to deal with the situation would have been dispatched."

"Yes, ma'am," Iridius said. "I just thought people might have needed assistance."

"Very well. We'll send a ship to investigate whether or not these nanomachines you've described are responsible for the deaths of the colony inhabitants, and whether they pose a further threat. Is there anything else you need to mention?"

"Uh, what should we do with the supplies that were meant for Victoria Station?"

"I'll organise to have them unloaded now."

"And, just to be clear..."

"Yes, Captain Franklin?"

"Am I still taking the *Gallaway* for a shakedown cruise?"

"Yes, Iridius," Rear Admiral Merritt said. "Despite my better judgement, I'll leave you slated for shakedown command of the *Gallaway*."

Iridius fought the urge to fist pump in celebration. "Yes, ma'am. Thank you, ma'am." He stood and drained his glass. "You know," Iridius said, "back at the Academy I always used to think the jug on your desk was full of vodka."

Merritt stared at him. "If I was meeting with you, Iridius, it probably was."

CHAPTER FOUR_

While Iridius Franklin was en route to *Rutan Station*, mentally preparing himself to take shakedown command of the *FSC Gallaway*, some important developments were taking place back at the landing pad where the *Diesel Coast* was parked.

Stevedore First Class George Reed strongly believed sixteen-hour double shifts could get in the sea, preferably right in the soupy centre of the Great Pacific Garbage Patch where they could be eaten by the mutated mega-sharks that probably lived there. He was sure the rest of his dock worker crew shared this sentiment, having been dragged – just thirty minutes before the end of their double shift – from the Brasilia Space Port to Federation Space Command Headquarters, where they'd been tasked with unloading unused supplies from a hauler.

"What's it even doing here, Reedy?" George's crewmate Lennox Melendez asked as the cargo bay door of the *Diesel Coast* was opened. "Sure, it's FSC, but it isn't exactly the gem of the fleet, is it?"

George shrugged. "I don't know, Melendez. I was told the same as you. Unload the cargo crates and return them to the port."

The cargo bay door stopped with a gentle clunk against the concrete surface of the pad. After being with this crew for sixteen straight hours, the last thing George wanted to do was talk to them. Still, he'd been thinking the same thing. A hauler like this always landed at the port – it was usually only FSC shuttles and diplomatic spacecraft that landed directly at headquarters. What did he care, though? Once they got this hunk of junk unloaded, he could get home, have a cold beer, and finally get off his damn feet.

"Could be a top-secret ship," said Alfie Hall, the third member of the crew assigned to this task. "I've heard some of the FSC's most advanced ships get disguised as haulers or mining ships so they don't get targeted by the Planetary Alliance."

Alfie Hall was the FNG of the group – the Fucking New Guy. George looked at him. He felt sorry for the kid. He was young, enthusiastic, and wanted nothing more than to join Space Command. Unfortunately, he had neither the background nor the grey matter to get into the Academy, or even join as enlisted crew. Instead, he worked as a stevedore, a docker, a cargo lumper. That wasn't the reason George pitied him, though – he was a docker too, after all. No, George pitied Hall because Hall actually believed he was part of the FSC and that this job was just the first step on his journey to becoming captain of a starship. The sooner young Alfie realised he was just a dock rat, and would likely remain a dock rat forever, the better.

"I don't think so," George said. "I've unloaded the *Diesel Coast* before. The only thing secret about this old bucket is how it manages to get in and out of atmo without falling to pieces. Come on."

George walked up the cargo ramp with Melendez and Hall following, guiding the hovering cargo lift between them.

"What's in the crates though?" Hall asked.

"Nothing top-secret," George answered without looking

back. As they approached the twenty-one cargo crates loaded in one corner of the cargo bay, George noticed a scattering of tools and a pile of EVA suits on the floor that hadn't even been put away. He didn't think the crew of a secret FSC mission would leave the cargo bay in this state, even if they were flying a fake hauler.

"What's the manifest say?" Hall asked.

"Nothing classified, if that's what you're thinking," George replied.

"Come on, Reedy," Melendez said, "humour the kid. It's got me curious, too."

George sighed. "Fine," he said, pulling the small hardened tablet off his belt. "It's not going to…" George trailed off as he looked at the screen. "My god, it says here there's twenty-one crates of highly classified plans of Alliance ships stolen during a black-ops raid."

"What?!" Hall said, his excitement palpable – at least until he saw the way George was looking at him, eyebrows raised to betray his sarcasm. "Oh."

"It says," George continued, "there's six crates of food and medical supplies and fifteen crates of something called My PupPups."

"The toy dogs?" Melendez asked. "I bought my niece one of those things. Drove her parents nuts. Why is a hauler carting those around?"

"Aha! Exactly!" Hall exclaimed, finger raised as if he'd just solved a murder. "Sounds like a cover."

"It's not a cover," George said.

"Let's look then," Hall said.

"We're not looking in the cargo crates."

"Why not?"

"Um, because that's illegal," George said, wondering why he needed to say this.

"We're not going to take anything," Hall said. "I just want to have a look."

"Those crates do have a habit of popping open if they get knocked off the top of a stack, Reedy," Melendez said.

"No."

Hall looked at George. "I bet you fifty bits there's something other than toy dogs in those crates."

George stared back. "Fifty bits? Do you even have fifty bits?"

"I've got it. You want to make the bet?"

George shook his head at Alfie's audacity. "Fucking new guy," he muttered. He had to admit, it hadn't taken Hall long to figure him out. He did like a bet. It wasn't that he was a problem gambler – the only problem was that he tended to lose more than he won. He knew he was being manipulated, but he didn't mind relieving an idiot of his money. If Hall really wanted to see inside one of these crates and have his conspiracy theories squashed, and was willing to give up fifty bits to do it, who was George to stop him?

"Alright," George said, "if one of the crates happens to fall off the stack and it's got My PupPup dogs in it – which it will – you owe me fifty bits."

Hall nodded. Melendez grinned – whether it was because of excitement or because Hall had managed to convince him, George wasn't sure. It was probably the latter.

"Bring up the lift," George said as he stepped up onto one of the crates and then clambered up the next to reach the top of the stack. Melendez and Hall brought over the hovering lift, a small platform that used reversal of artificial gravity to make moving cargo crates and pallets easier. They positioned the lift next to the stack and used the controls to raise it up. George began shifting the top green crate and, with a slightly off-angle shove, it slipped off the stack, bounced off the edge of the lift and fell, landing on its side on the deck with a thud. As expected, the lid of the crate popped open a crack. It didn't come all the way off, but it was open enough that someone could take a quick look at what was inside.

"Oh no," George said. He glanced around and then inclined his head towards the crate. "Go on then, Hall."

Hall quickly looked around before stepping forward. He wrung his fingers together nervously, as if he actually expected to find something other than toys, then leaned forward and looked into the gap. As he did, there was a crunch and the lid popped off completely, as if it had been shoved with some force from inside. Hall stumbled back, landing heavily on his arse.

From inside the box came quiet whirring and clicking sounds, and then marching out in rank and file came row after row of small white dogs. Obviously modelled on some sort of small terrier, they were covered with synthetic white fur, had realistic black noses that shone with a damp sheen, and their tongues even hung out in a simulation of panting. But there was something odd about them. The way they moved, the way their fur was identical, right down to the streaks of grey, and especially the cold, lifeless look in their eyes put them right on the edge of the uncanny valley.

"What the hell?" Melendez exclaimed as she jumped down off the cargo lift to take a closer look.

"There," George said, "you owe me fifty bits, Hall."

"Yeah," Hall said. "I guess I do."

"Okay," Melendez said, "how do we get them back in the box?"

Hall watched as the thirty or so dogs from the cargo crate came towards him. "Stop," he said. "Go back in the box." None of the My PupPups responded. They continued towards him. He hastily stood. "Halt. Switch off." The little dogs continued with their small, clicking steps, ignoring Hall's words completely.

"They're dogs," Melendez said as she moved up beside him.

She looked down at them and pointed a finger in a stern show of authority. "Sit."

Simultaneously, the rows of dogs stopped and sat down on their haunches, looking up at Melendez and Hall.

"There," Melendez said, "I told you. Now let's pick them up and put them back in the crate." The dogs all cocked their heads to the side and watched Melendez. "Yes," she said, "you're all very cute but don't give me that look. We have to put you back."

The My PupPups straightened their heads and then, bursting off their rear legs like they were spring-loaded, they leaped into the air. Half of them landed on Melendez, the other half on Hall. Both cried out in surprise and then screamed as the My PupPups began biting and clawing at their faces. They swatted desperately at the small dogs that clung to them, tearing at their eyes and faces, biting and gripping with mechanically powered jaws.

"The fuck?!" George said from where he remained perched on the stack of crates. Melendez spun, tearing one of the toy dogs from her face, revealing torn and bleeding skin as she threw it across the cargo bay. Hall fell back, flailing, and screaming about his eyes.

George finally moved. He jumped from the stack of cargo crates and hurried over to the terrified Hall, grabbing furry white shapes and pulling them off him. Behind him he heard crates shifting and dropping to the ground. He turned to see lids flying off and more My PupPups emerging from the crates. Before George could call out for help some of them launched at him. He managed to swat away the first couple, but he soon became overwhelmed as twenty or more attacked. They focused on his face, just as they had with Hall and Melendez, disorientating him, covering his mouth and muffling his shouts for help.

He realised some of the dogs were heading for the cargo bay door. At first he thought they were trying to escape, but then in his peripheral vision he saw one of the My PupPups jump up and bite the cargo bay door handle. Another leapt up and did the same, and then a third, until their weight was enough to flip the handle down. George heard the sound of the cargo bay door closing.

George struggled against the possessed children's toys, but was on his back before he even realised he'd fallen. He tried to put his hands up, to pull the dogs off and protect his face, but they clawed at his eyes. He found himself wondering, oddly, why anyone would give toy dogs teeth and claws. As his vision turned from the sight of white synthetic fur to blurring red and eventually black, he felt something clamp around his throat. The mechanically actuated jaws of a My PupPup squeezed, crushing his windpipe and leaving him, despite the desperate pulsing of his diaphragm, unable to draw breath. Before he died, Stevedore First Class George Reed's last thought was not about the unfairness of his fate, nor regrets about the way he had lived his life or how much he'd left undone. No, George Reed's last thoughts were how goddamn typical it was that this happened on a sixteen-hour double shift.

CHAPTER FIVE_

STEPPING onto the bridge of the *FSC Gallaway* Iridius felt an unexpected surge of emotion. At the forefront was a nervousness he was careful to keep hidden. He'd never been responsible for a ship anywhere near this important before and didn't want to make a complete arse of himself. Something going wrong wasn't what worried him. His job was to help iron out any bugs in the ship. What worried him was ensuring that the malfunction wasn't his fault. For example, not crashing the galaxy's most advanced starship into the sun.

Iridius felt awe, too – awe at even being on this bridge, but especially in knowing he was captain of this vessel, if only for the shakedown cruise. Iridius had to admit there was also a slight smugness. According to all official records, the first captain of the *FSC Gallaway* would be Captain April Idowu, but he'd have been in command of the *Gallaway* before his ex-girlfriend and, officially or not, they'd both know it.

The bridge of the *Gallaway* couldn't have been more different from that of the *Diesel Coast*. *This* was what a starship bridge was supposed to look like. Where the bridge aboard the *Diesel Coast* looked like a prison laundromat, the *Gallaway*'s bridge looked like an artist's impression of the future. Everything was sleek and curved, the white walls lit from below, giving the circular room an almost ethereal quality. The floor was navy blue, and a glowing pattern of blue concentric circles was set into the roof. From the elevator door where Iridius stood, the bridge descended two more levels. Down the first flight of steps, in the centre of the bridge, was the captain's chair. To its right was a chair with a console curving around it – the executive officer's station. To its left was another station with a console comprised primarily of a large holoscreen. This was a station the *Diesel Coast* didn't have – the tactical officer's station. The tactical officer was responsible for weapons and strategic shield control.

In front of these three chairs, another flight of steps descended to the lowest level of the bridge. Here, two prominent chairs faced forward with low consoles in front of them. These were for the helmsmen. Arcing away to the left and right of the helm was a semi-circle of other stations, engineering, scientific, communications, something else, that one, and some other things Iridius should probably know about but didn't. At the front of the bridge, following the curve of the white wall, was the view-screen, at least four times larger than the one on the *Diesel Coast*.

"Captain Iridius Franklin, I presume."

Iridius turned. It was a Zeta Reticulan – known more commonly as the Greys. One of *those* aliens, the original bug-eyed butt-probers. There weren't many of them in the FSC, mostly because there were a lot of humans in the FSC and ever since an incident where a small Zeta Reticulan scout ship had crashed near Roswell, New Mexico some three hundred years ago, relations between humans and Zeta Reticulans had been strained. It didn't help that the Zeta Reticulans still looked down on humanity as a lower species, a primitive bunch of apes that could be easily disorientated with some fancy lighting effects and abducted for useful experimentation. It had been a bonus for the

Zeta Reticulans that no other humans ever seemed to believe the stories of those who'd been abducted. Eventually the truth came out about Zeta Reticulan experimentation on humans, and there'd been tension between the two species ever since.

"Yes," Iridius said, "I'm Captain Franklin."

"Sir," the Grey said, "I'm Commander Mul. I'll be executive officer of the FSC *Gallaway* when Captain Idowu takes command."

"A Grey XO," said a voice from behind Iridius. "Watch your butts, everyone."

Iridius turned and shot Ensign Rangi a fierce look of disapproval and immediately regretted having him aboard.

"Please excuse Ensign Rangi," Iridius said, turning back. "He lacks the filter between the stupid gland in his brain and his vocal cords."

Commander Mul looked from Iridius to Rangi and then back again. His expression was hard to read, as Greys' always were. Their enormous oval black eyes never seemed to change, they had no noses, and their mouths were small slits at the bottom of their faces. "And these are the passengers you've brought along with you?"

"They're my crew, yes," Iridius said, his regret at having brought Rangi along instantly replaced by fierce loyalty. They were like a family – he was allowed to berate them and regret them and regard them as a bunch of losers, but if anyone else said anything degrading, his hackles would rise in instant defence. "You'll be acting as XO under my command then, Commander Mul?"

The Grey looked at Iridius with the same disapproving look he had given Rangi. At least, Iridius thought it was the same. The Greys needed little cards they could hold up: "I'm angry" or "I'm disappointed" or "I'm a little grey twat".

"Your command, sir?" Mul said.

"That's right," Iridius said. "Will you be my XO?"

"Oh," Mul said, "for the test flight, you mean. I thought you were implying you'd be taking actual command of the *Gallaway*."

"Well," Iridius said, "I will be taking command for the duration of the *Gallaway*'s shakedown."

"Captain Idowu is the commanding officer of this ship. You'll just be acting captain for this short voyage."

Iridius decided it was best to step away from this. It wasn't worth having a spat with the XO three minutes after he set foot on the bridge. "Let's not get too caught up in semantics, shall we, Commander Mul? I'm just asking whether you'll be acting as my XO during shakedown or if you'll be remaining behind."

"I will be acting as your XO, yes sir," Mul said.

"Great," Iridius said. "I'm looking forward to working with you then." *You little grey twat.*

"We're just going through final checks, sir," Mul said.

"Good." A long pause followed – not so much a pregnant pause; more like a pause that had eaten too many burritos. Iridius wondered if Commander Mul was going to offer any more information or, after a while, if he was ever going to speak again. It seemed Iridius was going to have to drag everything out of him. "Okay, so, are you going to introduce me to my crew?"

"I'll certainly introduce you to Captain Idowu's crew, sir."

Iridius clenched his teeth to keep from saying any of the things he wanted to say. He noted how much Commander Mul's head looked like a balloon, and wondered if it would burst if he pricked it with a pin. *Little grey balloon-headed twat.* Iridius forced a smile. "Great. Let's get started then."

Commander Mul gave Iridius the briefest of rundowns of the bridge crew. The two helmsmen, Ensign Wesley and Ensign Smith, were cardboard cut-out fly-boys. Clean-cut, handsome and with borderline narcissistic smirks, they were the type of pilots who wouldn't have looked out of place with oversized goggles, leather caps, and long beige scarves flowing out behind them in the wind as they leaned casually on a fencepost explaining to the nearest woman that they were, in fact, pilots. They turned in their seats to nod when they were introduced. Iridius never actually figured out which one was which – not that it mattered. He was sure their personalities were no more distinct than their looks.

Lieutenant Latroz, the tactical officer, was next to be introduced. She was a Siruan, a race from Sirius B that were humanoid-ish in appearance and extremely tall, at least seven feet. All Siruans were a purple-brown colour, differing only in the distribution of shades and pigments. Their skin was a flexible carapace of bony ridges and points – a little like the shell of a spiny turtle, but thin enough to bend and twist. The Siruans were famous for two things. Firstly, all of them were female – at least all the ones anyone would ever meet. The male of the species was a small, spherical creature that, without going into explicit detail, was inserted completely inside the female during the reproductive process. Once the female Siruan had been impregnated, she absorbed the male completely as nutrients for her baby which, after seven months, would be born as either a single female or a litter of male sphere-things. Whether the male Siruans had actual intelligence was unknown. Female Siruans were thought to be able to communicate with the males in some way, but discussing this was a serious taboo among Siruans, so no one really knew.

Secondly, Siruans were known for their skill in combat and warfare, which was why they often took tactical or security roles. Latroz nodded at Iridius. Iridius returned the gesture, thinking to himself that Lieutenant Latroz was goddamn terrifying.

The communications officer, Ensign Herd, turned and waved to Iridius when he was introduced. He was human but one of the Babels, an odd cult-like group who were committed to pursuing the goal of transhumanism through mechanical or computational augments to their bodies – a belief that had been coming in and out of fashion since the early twenty-first century. This was useful in a comms officer, as Ensign Herd had embedded a translation chip in his brain, allowing him to communicate with an extraordinary number of species without requiring computer translation.

Rounding out the bridge crew was Lieutenant Commander Ish Kaku, an engineering officer Iridius had met before. It was hard to forget their first meeting, as Kaku had been covered in expelled ship sewage at the time.

"Good to see you again, Captain Iridius," Kaku said.

"You too, lieutenant commander," Iridius said. "Here's hoping we get through this relatively unscathed."

"I brought a rain jacket, sir," Kaku said. "Just in case."

Iridius smiled. At least there was someone onboard he might be able to have a tolerable conversation with.

"We also have several technicians onboard to tend to major systems, primarily working for Lieutenant Commander Kaku in engineering, but not all scientific and support staff will be embarked for the shakedown cruise," Mul said.

"Medical?" Iridius asked.

"Yes. I believe Doctor Paine is down in sick bay performing an inventory stock check."

"That's an unfortunate name for a doctor," Iridius said.

"She is very talented."

"No, I'm sure she is. It's just funny because doctors treat pain and her name is Paine."

Commander Mul stared at him. "Indeed, sir."

Little grey balloon-headed humourless twat.

"Alright," Iridius said to the entire bridge, "continue your checks. We'll be pushing back from the station in two hours."

"Why don't you and your crew go and settle into your quarters, sir? I'll call you when we are ready to leave."

"Thank you, commander. Carry on then," Iridius said, his tone implying that leaving was completely his idea.

As they entered the lift, Ensign Rangi spoke. "Well, he's a bit of a dick, isn't he?"

"Consider yourself reprimanded for speaking that way about a superior officer, ensign. However, for once, I actually agree with you."

―――――

Iridius killed the next forty-five minutes by unpacking his clothes and browsing articles on the QECNet. As he was reviewing the systems on board the *Gallaway*, there was a knock on his door. He opened it and saw Quinn standing in the doorway.

"XO," Iridius said, "what can I do for you?"

"Sir," Quinn said. Iridius could tell she was nervous; she was clearly about to ask him something she considered outside regulations. "I know it must have been you who ensured we were included on this shakedown cruise and I appreciate that, as I'm sure the rest of the crew does. It's just, on the other shakedown cruises we've been on, we've actually been doing our jobs, but it doesn't seem like the *Gallaway* crew are going to involve us at all. What exactly are we supposed to be doing over the next week?"

"Look, I know this is different to our normal shakedowns, but this ship is different. This isn't a hauler or a mining ship. Hell, do you remember the last shakedown we did?"

"Yes, sir. It was frozen food transport."

"That's right – basically the *FSC Mister Whippy*. But this is the *FSC Gallaway*, Quinn. It's not just another space-faring ice-cream truck. We have to understand that the crew might be a little hesitant in including us. Besides, if you don't have to do anything why don't you just consider it a week off and enjoy cruising through space in the most advanced starship in the galaxy?"

"Sir, FSC regulations state that all crew should be actively engaged in a mission when not on shore leave. During periods of shore leave FSC personnel are not eligible to receive ship-board pay allowances. There isn't a category allowing for personnel to be inactive while aboard an FSC starship."

"Yes Quinn, relax, I know that." He didn't. "No one is going to dock your pay or penalise you for slacking off. Your presence aboard this ship has been approved by Fleet Command. Aren't you excited about being aboard the *Gallaway*?"

"Yes, sir. Of course."

"Well then," Iridius said, putting his hand on Quinn's shoulder and looking her in the eyes. "Enjoy yourself, alright? We're not doing shakedown on some hauler they rushed through construction. We're on the fleet's flagship. I doubt anything's even going to go wrong."

"*Red Alert. Red Alert.*" The announcement blared throughout the ship. "*Red Alert. Red Alert.*"

"Well," Iridius said, "except maybe whatever that is. Come on, let's head to the bridge."

Iridius and Quinn made their way to the elevator. When they reached the bridge Iridius saw the lights illuminating the space had turned red, casting everything and everyone in a scarlet tint.

"*Red Alert. Red Alert.*"

"What's going on?" Iridius asked.

Commander Mul was in the captain's chair. He spun to look at Iridius. "Captain Franklin," Mul said. "I hadn't called you back to the bridge yet."

Iridius strode onto the bridge. "Commander Mul," he said, "I returned to the bridge because there seems to be a red alert occurring. As captain of the ship, I don't need to be called back to the bridge for that."

"Ah, yes, sir," Mul said.

"Testing of the alert system is not part of the pre-flight checks for this mission," Iridius said. He wasn't going to admit he'd only finished reading the mission plan and so only knew what was and wasn't included in pre-flight checks as of about twenty minutes ago.

"No, sir," Commander Mul said. "There seems to be a problem. We're not sure what caused it."

"Ahem," Iridius spoke the word, rather than actually clearing his throat. Commander Mul looked at him expectantly. "You're in my seat," Iridius added.

"Sir, I—"

"Commander Mul," Iridius said, "the captain is on the bridge."

"Yes, sir," Mul said and, after a beat that bordered on insubordination, relinquished the chair.

"*Red Alert. Red Alert.*"

Iridius lowered himself into the captain's chair of the FSC *Gallaway*. Externally, it looked like he was simply sitting down. Internally, he squealed like a little girl who'd just been given a pony. "Alright," he said, turning to look at Lieutenant Latroz. "I'm going to assume you've made several attempts at shutting this racket off?"

Latroz nodded. "Aye, sir."

"Okay." Iridius looked at the arm of the captain's chair. There were a lot more buttons and dials and slider-things on the touchscreen than he was used to. He flicked through until he found comms controls and hit the button for a line to engineering. "Lieutenant Commander Kaku," he said.

"Here, sir," came the reply.

"At least one of those technicians you've got down there is an electrical technician, right?"

"Yes, sir," Kaku said. "We're trying to isolate the problem but even if we disconnect the circuit, the speakers aren't shutting off."

"Wait one minute," Iridius said. He flicked the comms to Junker's quarters. "Junker," he said. "Get down to engineering and see if you can help turn off this goddamn noise."

"A Franklinism already, sir?"

"I wish you wouldn't call it that, Junker," Iridius said, "but probably."

"Red Alert. Red Alert."

Iridius used the comms again. "Greg, can you head to engineering to assist Junker in dealing with this noise?"

"Aye, sir."

He switched back to engineering. "Kaku, two of my people are coming to assist."

"Aye."

"Quinn," Iridius said, turning to look at his XO, "go to the XO's station and pull up full electrical schematics of any systems that might interfere with the speakers. We've dealt with an issue like this before, so you should be able to help Junker isolate the fault."

"Yes, sir," Quinn said, "on the *Pixie Blue*. I remember." Quinn moved to the XO station and hovered, a little lost, when Mul didn't move.

"Captain Franklin," Mul said. "I believe we agreed earlier that the crew from your hauler would not be involved in the operation of this ship."

Iridius, his patience thinning, the repeated blaring of the red alert announcement certainly not helping, spun in his chair to face Mul. "Commander Mul, I do not recall agreeing with you about anything. FSC regulations state that all crew aboard a ship should be actively engaged in a mission. There is no pay category allowing personnel to be inactive while aboard an FSC starship. The crew of the *Diesel*

Coast have been temporarily transferred to the *Gallaway* and are receiving full shipboard pay and allowances. I'm simply following FSC regulations by having them use their skills." Iridius caught Quinn's eye and resisted the urge to give her the 'thank you for your help, we are now victorious' thumbs up. "As we have just discussed, Lieutenant Commander Quinn has dealt with an issue similar to this in the past. Please allow her to undertake the order I've given her."

"Sir," Mul said, "I am XO of this vessel. I would prefer if—"

"Oh, for fuck's sake," Iridius said.

The bridge was quiet. Well, apart from the electronic voice declaring there was a red alert, as if they hadn't figured that out yet.

"Sir," Commander Mul said, "I do not appreciate such language being directed at me."

Iridius took it all back, everything he'd ever thought about Ensign Benjamin Rangi. If there was one person in all of Federation Space Command who should be shot out of an airlock and left to be excruciatingly elongated by the gravitational forces of a black hole, it was Commander Mul.

"Stand up," Iridius said. He was stern, but he didn't yell. That was another of his key leadership tenets: a captain should never yell at their subordinates.

"Red Alert. Red Alert."

Perhaps he should revise that tenet to say that a captain should never yell at their subordinates unless they are trying to be heard over an excessively loud red alert signal.

"Commander Mul, I have given you a direct order. Relinquish your station."

Finally, on the brink of reportable insubordination yet again, Mul stood and stepped to the side. Quinn looked at him apologetically, which Iridius wished she hadn't, before sitting in front of the station. "Junker," she said into her comms. "Are you there?"

"Roger. I'm in engineering with Lieutenant Commander

Kaku and Greg. I'm pretty sure the fault is the same as the one we had on the *Pixie Blue*, but the systems on the *Gallaway* are obviously *way* more complicated. Could you pull up schematics for any systems running parallel to either the alert system or the speaker system? Greg will talk me through it here."

"Already done that, Junker, patching it through to you now. Got it, Greg?"

"Aye, ma'am," Greg's distinct voice came over the comms.

Iridius let them work. There was a reason he wanted them to work on faults like this – they'd seen them before and knew how to work through them. Individually, despite their faults, his crew were good at their jobs. Together, like some synergistic force, they were outstanding. Within minutes, the blaring red alert siren ceased and the lighting around the bridge returned to normal.

"Sorted, cap," Junker said over the comms.

"Thank you, Junker," Iridius said, looking sideways at Commander Mul, who stared back defiantly. "Ensure you give Lieutenant Commander Kaku a full account of what happened for his engineering fault report."

"You got it."

"Thanks for your help, Quinn," Iridius said. "You can give Commander Mul his station back now."

"Aye, sir," Quinn said, immediately vacating the seat, just as, Iridius had to bite back saying out loud, Commander Mul should have. Mul sat down without comment. Iridius had no idea whether it was even possible, but he thought he saw a tinge of pink, anger or maybe embarrassment, flush across the commander's elephant grey cheeks.

"How far did you get through pre-flight checks, commander?" Iridius said.

"Almost complete, captain," Mul replied.

"All primary ship systems checked?"

"Yes, sir."

"Life support?"

"Yes, sir."

"Good stuff. Well, what's say we push back?"

Commander Mul looked over at him. "We've still got some systems to check through."

"I don't mean you push back against me, Commander Mul. I mean we push the ship back from the station. There are no checks we can't do under sub-light drive until we get out past lunar orbit, right?"

"No, sir. That should be suitable."

"Excellent. Ensign Wesley, prime the thrusters and power up the fusion drive."

"Sorry, sir, but actually I'm primary pilot at the moment," said the helmsman Iridius had thought was Ensign Wesley but was apparently Ensign Smith.

Iridius would not give Commander Mul the pleasure of even glancing at him. "I guess you'd better prime the thrusters and power up the fusion drive, then."

"Aye, sir."

"I'll call it in, Herd," Iridius said. Normally the comms officer would communicate with other ships or stations, but the FSC flagship setting off for its shakedown cruise seemed like the kind of occasion when the captain should do it. "*Rutan Station*, this is Captain Iridius B. Franklin of the *FSC Gallaway*, requesting undocking and push back for departure on the shakedown cruise of Space Command's newest vessel and future flagship. We look forward to seeing her through this last step before she sets out to explore the galaxy, bringing peace and diplomacy wherever she goes."

"Ah, cap, you're still talking to me," Junker said.

"I know," Iridius replied, a little too quickly. "I was just going to ask what you guys thought of that as a, you know, official sort of start to the mission announcement thing."

"Yeah," Junker said. "Right. No, sounds great, cap."

"Alright then," Iridius said. He adjusted the comms channel so that he was broadcasting to *Rutan Station* this time. "Rutan Station, this is Captain Franklin, requesting undocking and push back for departure on the shakedown cruise of the *FSC Gallaway*. We look forward to seeing Space Command's newest flagship through her final step before she sets out to explore the galaxy."

"Yep," Junker said. "Still me."

"Oh, Jupiter's balls," Iridius said. He looked at his touch-screen again and very carefully changed his comms to contact *Rutan Station*. "*Rutan Station*, this is the *FSC Gallaway*. We're ready to go."

"Captain Franklin, this is Rear Admiral Merritt. I'm gathered here with Admiral Retlax and Admiral Stewart. We expected a little more ceremony on your departure, being that you're taking Space Command's future flagship out of dock for the first time. You could have at least attempted to make a stirring announcement."

Iridius took a deep breath and let his cheeks balloon out as he exhaled. "Yes, ma'am. Ah, we're all looking forward to taking the *Gallaway* through her paces and making sure she's ready to explore the galaxy. A one small flight for us, one giant leap for the FSC type of thing."

"Right," Merritt replied in a tone that clearly suggested otherwise. "Godspeed then, *Gallaway*. We'll see you in a week."

A controller at *Rutan Station* cut in. "Docking clamps are clear, *Gallaway*. You're go to push back."

"Roger that, *Rutan Station*," Iridius said. "Helm?"

"Aye, sir," Wesley or Smith replied.

"Push us back."

With a hum little louder than an old-fashioned refrigerator, the *FSC Gallaway*, pride of the Federation Space Command fleet, began floating back from space dock.

"We are clear of *Rutan Station*, captain."

"Bring us around to bearing zero nine zero attitude zero," Iridius said.

"Aye, sir."

The *FSC Gallaway* turned away from *Rutan Station* and Earth. The moon was currently on the other side of the planet, so the only thing on the view-screen ahead of them was space, the big black – and Iridius B. Franklin got to take the most advanced starship ever constructed out there.

"Punch it."

The *Gallaway* accelerated away from Earth. Once they'd passed lunar orbital distance, Iridius gave the order to activate the BAMF drive. The helm did so, and the *Gallaway* slowed to a stop before encasing itself in another universe and vanishing with a middle finger to the laws of physics, leaving the universe utterly confused about what had just happened.

CHAPTER SIX_

"FULL STOP."

"Full stop, aye captain."

The *FSC Gallaway* had spent three days performing manoeuvres around Alpha Centauri. It was the perfect place for ship testing – humanity had already wiped out all sentient life in the system, so there was no need to worry about doing it again. Iridius and the crew had run through all the standard manoeuvres they had to test: the BAMF drive flight from Sol to Alpha Centauri, orbital entry and exit, and every preprogrammed evasive manoeuvre, plus they'd cycled most of the onboard systems. There'd been only a few minor faults. Intra-ship communication cut in and out a little; the fusion drive had failed to prime once, but that had been a control system issue rather than an issue with the engine itself; and there was a funky smell in the kitchen, which Iridius was convinced was the food Lieutenant Latroz had been eating. All in all, it had been a fairly uneventful trip, which Iridius supposed was a positive for his first command of a *real* starship. Plus, now they were onto the fun stuff.

"Alright," Iridius said rubbing his hands together, "weapons tests."

"Sir, before we get started on weapons testing I have a small concern," Commander Mul said.

"Of course you do," Iridius muttered.

"Sorry, sir?"

"Nothing," Iridius said, "please continue."

"We are yet to receive any communication from Earth," Mul said. "We have sent our report each day, but have not received anything in reply. I would have expected Earth to respond at least once."

Mul's concern had been tickling the back of Iridius's mind, too. He wasn't surprised Earth hadn't confirmed receipt of their reports; what surprised him was that they hadn't been asking for more frequent updates. They'd handed Iridius Franklin their most advanced starship – he'd thought Rear Admiral Merritt would be up him like Ferran Gut Leeches to make sure he wasn't screwing this up. Maybe she really did have faith in him.

"I'd thought that too, commander," Iridius said. "Maybe they aren't too worried, as long as we're sending in our reports. Could also be a glitch though, I suppose. Herd, does everything seem alright on comms?"

"Aye, captain," the communications officer said. "All seems fine."

"Quinn," Iridius turned to his XO, "do you want to check the quantum entanglement field?"

"Aye, sir," Quinn said. "I'll look into it."

"Captain," Mul said, "perhaps I should—"

"Nope," Iridius said, cutting him off. "I need you focused on weapons testing."

"Certainly, sir."

Iridius wouldn't say the crew of the *Gallaway* were any happier about having Iridius and his crew onboard after three days, but at least Iridius had figured out how to keep them occupied. The trick was to give them jobs they considered more important than what the crew of the *Diesel Coast* were doing. The only *Diesel Coast* crew member Iridius hadn't yet managed to get involved was Ensign Rangi. It wouldn't surprise Iridius to learn that Wesley and Smith had their arses superglued to their chairs at the helm. To their credit, they had managed to split helm time perfectly, so he couldn't pull them up for being active at a station for longer than regulations allowed. Luckily, of all Iridius's crew, Ensign Rangi was the one most content to be kicking back with his feet up. He was on the bridge now though, not wanting to miss the weapons testing.

Iridius had been looking forward to this, too. He'd always been successful in war games at the Academy, both in space and in simulation. Weapons testing wasn't quite the same, because they'd just be targeting drones, but still, at least he got to blow things up. "Latroz," he said, "are the drones prepped?"

"Aye, sir."

"Alright, let's begin with railgun fire at ten kilometres. Launch a target drone."

"Aye, sir."

Latroz hit some buttons on her console, and moments later a drone, high-luminosity lights flashing from green to red, was shooting away from the *Gallaway*. It travelled out to the nominated range and then stopped.

"Helm," Iridius said, "bring us broadside to the target but hold view on the drone."

"Aye."

The *Gallaway*'s thrusters fired soundlessly into the vacuum of space, old reliable Newton's third law giving the ship the push it needed to turn broadside.

"We're in position," Wesley confirmed from his seat at the helm.

"Latroz, engage railgun defence matrix."

The hull of the ship reverberated with a pulsing *thwack-a-thwack-a-thwack-a* as the ship's defensive railguns fired. They used the principles of quantum electrodynamics to accelerate solid tungsten kinetic rounds towards the drone – a fancy name for what was essentially the equivalent of space cannonballs. Just over half a second later the drone erupted in a glowing blue cloud, a phosphorous flash designed to provide visual confirmation of the drone's destruction.

"Bring us to bearing one eight zero attitude zero and we'll fire the other battery."

Several more tests followed, including altering the range of the drone, setting it on an approach vector to simulate a missile, and operating the railgun matrix while manoeuvring. Once Commander Mul had concluded satisfactory operation of the ship's defensive weapons, it was time to move on to offensive weapons testing.

"Ready to have some fun then?" Iridius said, not receiving anywhere near the enthusiastic reply he'd hoped for. Surely the *Gallaway*'s crew had enough personality to find at least some enjoyment in chasing a drone through the black and blasting it into a puff of molecules. Maybe not old humourless-football-head, but the others seemed like they at least knew the theory behind fun. "I'll take your sudden shift from silence to near silence as a yes, then. Latroz, prepare a drone with an Alliance cruiser sensor signal, give it a full suite of evasive manoeuvres and prime some ship-buster missiles."

"Aye, sir."

"Launch the drone."

Another of the target drones flew off into space. This time it was lit up red, with a tracking marker on the view-screen. A simulated enemy.

"Drone has engaged evasive behaviour. It's trying to outrun us," Latroz said.

"This is exciting, isn't it?" Iridius said to her. "Don't you think this is exciting?"

"I find little enjoyment when there is no real enemy, captain."

"Right," Iridius said. "Well, I think it's exciting. Ensign Wesley, bring us into pursuit and hold our distance at one thousand kilometres. Latroz, prepare to engage target with missiles."

Wesley did as ordered, and the *Gallaway* began pursuit of the target drone, now too small to see with the naked eye, but still wrapped in a bright red target reticle as the ship's sensors kept close tabs on it. Out here, in the dark of space, there was no way to hide. The large energy requirements of a starship – even one as small as the target drone – meant the heat and mass signatures were impossible to conceal. With the element of surprise completely removed, space warfare was essentially the equivalent of two people standing in the back of brightly coloured pickup trucks throwing rocks at each other as they drove past at several kilometres per second.

Once they'd held a stand-off distance of one thousand kilometres for a short while, Iridius leaned forward in his captain's chair and, with a completely unnecessary finger-gun gesture, said, "Fire."

The missile exited one of the *Gallaway*'s tubes with eye-popping, nose-bleeding, brain-squashing acceleration. Once it was away, the target drone immediately sensed the incoming missile and began evasive manoeuvres, limiting itself to the delta-v appropriate to an Alliance cruiser. The computer on board the missile immediately began plotting a targeting solution based on known evasive patterns, and without any of the countermeasures available to an actual Alliance ship the drone only lasted about half a minute before the missile caught it on an intercept course and careened into it at just under fifty kilometres per second.

Just as Iridius opened his mouth to issue orders for the next test, another of the *Gallaway*'s missiles fired. He turned to look at Latroz. "I think it's dead, lieutenant."

She turned to him, and her expression wasn't one you wanted to see on the person in charge of all the missiles. "That wasn't me, sir."

"I'm sorry," Iridius said, "are you saying you didn't fire that live, extraordinarily dangerous, highly advanced nuclear warhead anti-ship missile?"

"No," Latroz said.

"What about that one?" Iridius said as another missile left the *Gallaway*'s weapons bay, followed by another, and then another. "And those?"

"I'm afraid not, captain," Latroz said.

"I didn't think so." Another six missiles launched in quick succession. Iridius watched the missile tracking on the viewscreen. The first missiles were already slowing and turning. "Commander Mul, can you confirm those missiles we've fired are targeting us?"

Commander Mul looked up from his station. "Confirmed. We're under missile lock. I don't understand how this is happening."

Iridius tapped at the console on the arm of his chair as more missiles let loose from the *Gallaway*. "Engineering, shut down all power to the weapons bay."

"Aye, sir."

"Latroz," Iridius said without missing a beat, "shields to full and take us to red alert please."

"*Red Alert. Red Alert. Red Alert.*"

Despite how irritating that announcement had been a few days ago, there was something oddly reassuring about it now.

"Give me a count," Iridius said. "How many missiles did we fire?"

"Twenty-two missiles away, captain," Commander Mul said. "No more firing now that power's been cut to the missile battery."

"Turn us around, Ensign Wesley. One seven zero attitude ten, full fusion. Start preparing a BAMF trajectory back to Earth and get the drive spooling," Iridius said. "Lieutenant Latroz, status on railgun point defences?"

"We didn't have a full ammunition load when we left Earth. After testing we're down to thirty per cent."

Down to thirty per cent point defence ammunition, not yet ready to BAMF, and left to evade twenty odd missiles. This was a lot like a test they'd undertaken in the simulator back at the Academy. If Iridius recalled correctly he'd done alright then – or maybe his ship had been destroyed. That had been almost a decade ago and it was fairly safe to assume he'd been hungover. He had the *Gallaway* now though, that had to mean something.

"First missile incoming in ten seconds," Commander Mul said.

"Evasive manoeuvres please, Ensign Smith," Iridius said. "Keep our cross-section down, stern to the missiles."

Smith began inputting commands into the helm. "Executing evasive patterns."

The thumping of railgun fire started soon after – a spray of tungsten rounds blasted into the path of the missiles. "Missile one destroyed," Latroz commentated from her station at Tactical. "Missile two and three destroyed. There's a salvo of six approaching now. They're splitting."

"Put a tactical window on screen," Iridius said. A small picture-in-picture window appeared in the top left of the bridge's massive view-screen. It showed the *Gallaway* as a blue triangle in the centre and the nineteen remaining missiles as bright angry red dots swarming towards the ship. Six of them were close, splitting into two groups, just as Latroz had said. Three continued to approach from the stern while the other three arced away, seemingly going to miss until the *Gallaway* turned towards them. Iridius watched the screen as the ship manoeuvred. "Is there a reason we're turning back into the path of those three missiles? That seems like the opposite of evasive manoeuvres."

"Ah," Smith said from the helm as he punched some buttons. "Changing evasive pattern."

The *Gallaway* changed its course, attempting to turn back away from the three missiles, but it took a lot longer to turn the ship than it did for the missiles to correct. They wouldn't hit broadside, but they were still going to hit. The railguns roared again, and the three red dots approaching the rear of the ship blinked out of existence. Two of those approaching from the other side vanished too, but one got through, and hit the ship's shield with a flash. The hull shuddered.

"Port shield down to forty per cent but holding," Latroz called.

"Spread the shield power back around the ship," Iridius said. "Looks like we can't keep them on our stern." Iridius watched the remaining missiles on screen. Three of them continued in and vanished as the rail guns thumped. Half the others seemed to be on a collision course but then spiralled back out, away from the ship. The others accelerated ahead and turned in sharply, just as the *Gallaway* changed direction, too.

"The missiles are anticipating our evasive pattern," Commander Mul said.

"More than that," Iridius said. "It's like they know exactly what we're going to do."

"They do," Mul said. "These ship buster Mk III missiles are programmed with FSC standard evasive manoeuvres as the basis of a machine learning algorithm in order to predict the movements of enemy ships."

"Bet someone thought that was a genius idea at the time," Iridius said.

"Yes, sir," Mul said. "I simply never anticipated we would be attempting to evade our own missiles."

Iridius looked at the Grey. "You programmed them?"

"I spent some time with FSC weapons development before this posting, captain."

"Tell me, commander, do Zeta Reticulans understand the concept of irony?" Iridius said as the railguns roared again, shearing through another salvo of missiles.

"Railgun ammunition at fifteen per cent," Latroz said. "Ten missiles remaining."

"Shields are at sixty per cent," Mul said.

"The missiles are splitting up again," Latroz said. "They appear to be separating into groups to target the most likely evasive patterns based on our trajectory changes. One of them is coming up from stern." The railgun turrets fired again. "It's destroyed, but railguns down to ten per cent."

"How many direct missile hits can we take at sixty per cent shields, Commander Mul?" Iridius asked.

"It depends on location and separation period, captain," Mul answered, "but worst case would be shield failure after a salvo of three or four."

"And we don't have enough railgun ammunition to rely on point defence?" Iridius already knew the answer, but thinking out loud always helped him with a tense situation.

"Most likely not, sir."

"Smith," Iridius said.

"Aye, sir." The helmsman turned to look at him.

"Get up."

"Sorry, sir."

"Get out of that chair," Iridius said in the clearest don't-argue tone he could manage. "Rangi, get your arse to the helm."

"Huh?" Rangi said from where he was sitting at one of the unused consoles.

"Get on the helm," Iridius repeated. "We're not going to get out of this with preprogrammed evasive manoeuvres."

"Sir, I can manually fly the evasive patterns," Smith said.

"You see what you just said," Iridius replied, "*the* evasive patterns. I don't want you flying the same shit you got taught at the Academy – that's what's programmed into those missiles anyway. Get up." Smith relented and Rangi took his place at the helm. "Ensign Wesley, how long until we can BAMF out of here?"

"Two minutes, captain."

"Ensign Rangi," Iridius said, "do something to keep us alive for two minutes, would you?"

"Aye, sir."

Rangi took manual control of the ship just as a salvo of five missiles came in from the starboard side. The railguns peppered shots at them before the sound dramatically stopped, followed by the flash and shudder of the ship being struck by a nuclear detonation.

"Railguns are empty," Latroz said. "Five missiles remaining."

Under Rangi's manual control, the *Gallaway* rolled and dropped in attitude, suddenly departing from any known evasive pattern. The remaining missiles streaked past where the ship would have been and Rangi altered course again. He slid the throttle on the fusion drive to full, increasing the ship's acceleration but at the cost of manoeuvrability.

"You can't evade at full speed," Smith said from where he stood, still hovering close to the helm he'd been forced to give up. When Rangi ignored him, Smith looked to Commander Mul. "He can't evade at full speed, the thrusters won't overcome the ship's forward momentum."

"I'm not going to evade them," Rangi said. "At least not yet."

"You can't outrun them!" Smith said, growing more agitated. "Their acceleration is too high."

On the tactical screen the red dots had turned and begun chasing the blue triangle. They were some way behind, but they were gaining faster than Iridius would like. It always gave him pause that here, on the bridge of a twenty-third century starship, hurtling through the black of space surrounded by energy deflector shields and armed with nuclear warhead fusion engine missiles, the tactics of space combat still compressed down to what looked like a 1979 Atari game.

"He's heading for the debris field," Commander Mul said.

Iridius turned his attention to the main view-screen and saw that the little grey football was right. Rangi was flying towards the Mandor Trivani Cloud – the collection of rocks and dust left over after humanity accidentally obliterated that planet.

"Rangi?" Iridius said. "I see your plan here and firstly, let me commend you on your wonderful initiative, but, just so I'm crystal clear on this, we're not going to beat these missiles there unless we hit the debris field at full speed, right?"

"Pretty close to it, captain."

"Right, good, good, and you're also aware that some of those rocks are pretty big?"

"Yes, sir."

"Good." Iridius drummed his fingers on the arm of his chair. "Carry on then."

"One minute until BAMF," Wesley said.

"Fifteen seconds until missile impact," Latroz said.

"At this speed we should reach the debris cloud in twelve seconds," Commander Mul said.

"Well," Iridius said, "I told you this was going to be exciting."

The Mandor Trivani Cloud grew exponentially bigger on the view-screen. Iridius considered what he was looking at. The planet was pretty well vaporised, so what was left of it was quite small and spread out, but still, he didn't know how Rangi was going to react in time to avoid colliding with at least some of those bigger bits. As they reached the cloud and flew into the scattered remnants of Mandor Trivani a few flashes popped up on the view-screen as large rocks hit the shields. Ensign Rangi immediately slid the throttle down, past full stop and into full reverse, and at the same time fired all port-side thrusters. Iridius felt the vibrations ripple through the floor as the ship's control systems tried to do the impossible task that Rangi had just asked of them. Rangi immediately fired thrusters to nose up the *Gallaway* and carry it over a small asteroid-sized chunk of planet. One of the missiles slammed into the rock, detonating and sending rock fragments into another missile.

"Three missiles left," Latroz called.

"BAMF in thirty seconds," Wesley added, "but captain, we can't safely BAMF out of the middle of all this debris."

"Rangi?"

"I know that, sir."

Iridius left him alone. Rangi flew the *Gallaway* like it was a dart racer ripping through an asteroid course. Of course, it didn't behave like a dart racer – it was too big and heavy, and collected its fair share of rocks along the way. Still, to his credit Rangi's piloting skills would have made him competitive in a dart race even if he was flying a dishwasher.

"Ten seconds to BAMF."

The remaining missiles still gave chase, but eventually their onboard systems made them turn less aggressively and take a more conservative flight path. Rangi took a turn around an asteroid and one of the missiles speared into it. Rangi pulled the *Gallaway* up travelling perpendicular to the disk of the cloud.

"You've used up their delta-v," Smith said in disbelief. "The missiles are dropping off."

When the *Gallaway* emerged back out of the Mandor

Trivani Cloud, Rangi punched it up to full fusion drive again, putting some distance between the ship and the missiles, which had slowed to dodge the last of the debris, and come out of the cloud.

"BAMF ready!" Wesley almost screamed the confirmation.

"Full stop," Iridius said.

Rangi brought the ship to full reverse to lose all speed.

"Incoming!" Latroz called as the missiles bore down on the suddenly slowing *Gallaway*.

"As soon as we stop, fire the BAMF," Iridius said.

A second later, as soon as the *Gallaway* came to a complete stop – necessary for the BAMF to work – Wesley engaged the FTL drive. There was a shimmer on the view-screen as the ship was enveloped by the pocket universe. The last two nuclear missiles detonated on the *Gallaway* – or rather, where the *Gallaway* would have been had it not just popped into another universe, safely accelerating away at well past the speed of light.

CHAPTER SEVEN_

When the BAMF bubble surrounding the *Gallaway* burst, and the shimmering of the fragmenting shield cleared, the sight out the view-screen was not what the crew had expected.

"I know we were in a rush, Ensign Wesley," Iridius said, "but you were supposed to take us to Earth."

"That is Earth, sir."

"No," Iridius said, "you see, Earth is a sort of blue-green sphere with some swirly clouds on it. That is a ball of fire."

No one spoke. The crew of the *Gallaway* stared out the view-screen at exactly what Iridius had described. The planet Earth, cradle of humanity, home of Federation Space Command headquarters, was consumed with a yellow-orange glow.

"Zoom the view-screen please, Commander Mul," Iridius said. There was no response. Even the Zeta Reticulan stared in shock at the sight before him. Human and Zeta Reticulan relations may have been strained, but they were technically on the same team now, and despite what people might say neither wanted to see humanity's homeworld reduced to a lifeless rock. Iridius spun to him. "Mul, I said zoom in."

"Right," Mul said, snapping free of the sight of a burning Earth. "Zooming in, captain."

Iridius wasn't sure what he'd expected, but zooming in didn't make things seem better, it just provided a higher-definition view of a planet-wide nightmare. The surface of the globe, once home to billions and billions of sentient beings – human, animal and extra-terrestrial alike – was now completely covered in molten lava.

"Alright," Iridius said, "who left the oven on?"

The bridge crew all turned to look at him.

"Sorry, I honestly can't help myself. It's like my pressure relief valve. Seriously though, we've only been gone four days. How does that happen to Earth in four days?"

Some of the crew opened their mouths, some even made shapes with their lips, but none of them spoke.

"Somebody say something!"

"Sir," Commander Mul said, "I don't think we should approach."

"Oh, we're going to approach," Iridius said. "Bring us into orbit, Ensign Wesley. Commander Mul, do a long-range sweep. Tell me there's something left down there. If not, there has to be something left in orbit."

Iridius touched some controls on the arm of his chair. "Earth Approach, Earth Approach, this is Captain Iridius B. Franklin of the *FSC Gallaway*, do you copy?" There was no response. Iridius looked down at his controls, swiping through and changing the comms settings. "Lunar Base Armstrong, this is Captain Iridius B. Franklin of the *FSC Gallaway*, do you copy?" Nothing. "Armstrong Base, is anyone there?" Again, silence. He adjusted to a wide comms blast. "This is an all-frequency broadcast from Captain Franklin of the *FSC Gallaway*, is anyone receiving? Lunar bases? *Rutan Station*? FSC Space Command?" After waiting a long moment Iridius shut off his comms link. "Goddamn it," he said, his anger, fear and frustration all surfacing. "Herd, keep trying to raise someone, anyone. Mul, what have you got?"

"Nothing from the surface of the planet on the long-range scanners, captain. All FSC space stations appear to be in orbit still, but none are transmitting. Lunar bases are still there too, but all non-responsive."

"This is impossible," Iridius said.

"My parents were down there," Quinn said.

Iridius looked at her. She hadn't taken her gaze from the view-screen, and her eyes were shining with brimming tears. Iridius almost made a crack about how he wished his no-good parents had been down there, but didn't. Instead he said, "I'm sorry, Quinn." He looked around at the bridge crew. "I'm sorry to anyone who had people down there. I know it doesn't look good, but there's always a chance people evacuated off-world. There's not much I can say right now, other than that we're going to find out what's happened here. Someone must be responsible for this, and the Federation Government must have responded."

The crew of the *Gallaway* still seemed distant, like they weren't really there. Iridius knew, as captain, it was his job to pull them back. He'd start by keeping them busy. "Ensign Wesley," he said, "keep us on an orbital entry trajectory. Don't bother with the new approach speed restrictions – I don't think anyone is going to book you. Ensign Herd, prepare a quantum entanglement communication for Tau Ceti. Encrypt the communication for Federation Government Eyes Only and load it with all the images and sensor information we've gathered since dropping out of FTL. Tell me when I can transmit an accompanying message. Quinn, get on that sciencey-looking station down there and see if you can figure anything out from the long-range scans. Latroz, have we got shields back?"

"Partially, captain. Shields are at fifty-seven per cent recharge since BAMF."

"Bring them up with as much power as you can for our approach – just to be safe."

"Aye, sir."

The *FSC Gallaway* slowed to a planetary approach speed as it passed lunar orbit range, but just as Iridius had instructed him, Ensign Wesley didn't slow the ship to the regulated fifteen hundred kilometres per second.

"Captain Franklin," Ensign Herd said, "you can transmit whenever you're ready."

Iridius hit the button. "This message is for the Federation Senate and is an urgent request for assistance. This is Captain Iridius B. Franklin, currently in command of the *FSC Gallaway*. We have been undertaking shakedown operations in Alpha Centauri and have returned to the Sol System. On our arrival we found Earth," he paused, "well, kind of on fire. There's been some sort of planet-wide catastrophe. We can't establish contact with anyone on Earth, in orbital stations, or at any of the lunar bases. There are no distress signals. No nothing. Please tell me there's been some sort of response – that rescue ships were already launched and are on their way to some safe planet of tropical islands and cocktails? We are standing by for instructions." Iridius switched off the comms.

"Coming up on orbital entry," Ensign Wesley said. Iridius felt the acceleration change, albeit dampened by the artificial gravity, as the *Gallaway* reversed its fusion drive and slowed for tangential orbital insertion around Earth. This close, the image of Earth on the view-screen showed the recognisable shapes of the continents. At least some areas of landmass seemed to have survived complete obliteration, though they still looked dark against the yellow-orange glow of magma and flares of plasma that seemed to boil and burst up from the surface.

"Life signs?" Iridius asked, looking over at Mul. The Zeta Reticulan commander was watching his console and when he glanced up, even though his face had the emotional range of an eggplant, Iridius knew the answer.

"Incoming QEC transmission from the Federation Senate," said Ensign Herd.

"You can play it for the bridge, ensign," Iridius said.

Ensign Herd pressed some buttons on his communication console to broadcast the transmission to the entire bridge.

"Captain Franklin of the FSC Gallaway, this is Senate Secretary Baloo Baluuk on behalf of the Federation Senate. Your orders are to remain in orbit of Earth and await the arrival of the FSC El Nino. First Officer of the El Nino, Commander April Idowu, has been field promoted to captain and will be assuming her command of the FSC Gallaway on her arrival. She and Captain Mayhem have been on government business and have been given new orders to investigate the Earth situation. Federation Senate out."

"Investigate the Earth situation," Iridius repeated. "They don't know what's happened here."

"I do."

Everyone turned to look at Lieutenant Latroz.

"Have you found something on the scanners?" Iridius asked.

"No, captain," Latroz said, "but I've seen this before."

"You've seen Earth looking like a toasted marshmallow?"

"Not Earth, obviously, but I've seen this done to a planet before."

"What are you talking about, lieutenant?"

As if suddenly realising she'd said something she shouldn't have, Latroz turned to look at Commander Mul. He shook his head just the slightest amount, but it was easy to catch even the smallest movements of that giant grey balloon.

"What?" Iridius asked, his tone betraying his annoyance. "What do you know about this?"

"I'm afraid that's classified, captain," Commander Mul said, and Iridius was sure he savoured every word of that godawful sentence.

"I'm a Federation Space Command captain, Commander Mul," Iridius said. "That automatically gives me Security Status Five. Now tell me what the hell is going on."

"You're the captain of a hauler, sir," Mul said. "You might have the highest ordinary clearance, but you don't have Alpha Security Status."

"We're not going to compare the sizes of our appendages again, are we, commander? As captain of this ship, I'm ordering you to tell me what you know about this."

"I cannot be ordered to release Alpha Security Status information."

"What the hell is Alpha Security Status and why haven't I heard of it before?"

"It's a level of clearance above the standard, sir."

"And you have it, do you?"

"Yes, sir."

"And I don't?"

"No, sir."

"Okay, and does this Alpha Security Status still work on a need-to-know basis?"

"Yes, sir."

"Well, given the circumstances out that view-screen, I'm pretty confident this is a situation where I need to know what in the gronking black shit of space is going on, don't you?"

"Sir, I—"

"Earth has been destroyed, you big grey turnip! Your clearance doesn't matter right now. Tell me what happened!"

Mul looked from Iridius to Latroz. "Alright, lieutenant, go ahead."

"As I said, sir, I've seen this happen to a planet before. It's the result of a Quantum Fission Catalytic Exothermic Reaction Device," Latroz said. "They call it a planet-slagger, or an overkill bomb. When launched at a planet it causes a catalytic reaction in which matter splits on the quantum level and releases extreme heat, turning the surface of the planet into molten slag and causing the atmosphere to combust."

"So Earth's been attacked," Iridius said. "By who? Planetary Alliance?"

Latroz shook her head. "No sir, see, that's the thing. The Alliance doesn't have weapons like this. The only government with planet-slaggers is the Federation. That's why it's classified Alpha."

"The Federation doesn't have weapons like that," Quinn said. "The Federation Charter forbids the use of weapons of planetary destruction."

"That may be what is in the Charter," Mul said. "But we do have them. Again, that's why it's classified Alpha."

"Why do you think the Planetary Alliance have never been more than an annoyance to the Federation, captain?" Latroz said. "The planet I saw slagged like this was Cygni C – first home of the Planetary Alliance. I was an ensign on the FSC *Valhalla* when they did it."

"That goes against everything the Federation stands for," Iridius said.

"For the Federation to stand for anything, captain," Commander Mul said, "it must first and foremost stand. There are always groups that would seek to tear it down."

"Let's say I believe you, hypothetically at least, and the Federation does have weapons capable of toasting a planet," Iridius said. "Why would they use one on Earth?"

"*Gargarin Station* was armed with one," Commander Mul said. "It was permanently aimed at Earth."

"The main FSC station orbiting Earth had a bomb capable of destroying Earth that was permanently aimed at Earth?" Iridius said. Where *Rutan Station* was the FSC's orbital shipbuilding space dock, *Space Station Gargarin* was its administrative and security facility in orbit. Iridius looked to the view-screen. Even though it was small from their current orbital location, he could see the glint of *Gargarin* as it rounded the Earth, the sun reflecting off the shining surface of one of its outer rings. It was a small station compared to something like the Rutan shipbuilding facility, but highly advanced. Its structure was a series of concentric rings of decreasing diameter affixed to a central spire, giving it an appearance reminiscent of a child's ring-toss toy. It was still lit up as if all systems were operational, rotating slowly about its central axis.

"Yes, sir. *Gargarin* held an overkill bomb as a safeguard."

"A safeguard?"

"Yes, sir. A lot of Federation member homeworlds are targeted with them, in the event of a rebellion or loss of the planet to an enemy. Control is held by the Federation Government."

Iridius looked around the bridge. "Have I stepped into some sort of evil mirror universe here? Do I need to grow a goatee?"

"I'm afraid not," Mul said.

"Right, so are we actually suggesting the Federation bombed Earth?" Iridius asked.

"No," Commander Mul said. "I don't believe that is the case. There's no reason for Earth to be eliminated in that way. Humanity has a major position in the Galactic Federation. It must have been an accident."

"An accident?" Iridius said. "Like a 'whoopsie I leaned on the wrong button' accident? That's not an accident, Commander

Mul. An accident is knocking a cup of coffee over on some paper-work, not flash-frying a planet."

"Humans accidentally turned Mandor Trivani into rubble," Rangi said.

Iridius shot him a look. "Whose side are you on, ensign?"

Rangi shrugged. "Just saying."

"Captain, I've found something," Quinn said. "There's a ship docked at *Gargarin Station*."

"Excellent work, Quinn," Iridius said. "Also, please note there are waves in the ocean and clouds in the sky."

"Not anymore," Rangi said.

Iridius gave Rangi a look that he hoped expressed just how unhelpful that comment was. He knew his comment hadn't exactly been useful either, but he was the captain so he could get away with it.

"What I mean, captain," Quinn said, "is there's a ship docked at the station that shouldn't be."

"Which ship?"

Quinn hesitated.

"Which ship, Quinn?" Iridius asked again.

"It's the *Diesel Coast*, sir."

"I knew you were going to say that," Ensign Rangi said.

The *Diesel Coast* should have been down on the landing pad at FSC HQ, turned to molten slag like everything else on the planet. Instead it was in space, docked at the orbital space station from which the planet-slagger had apparently been launched. Iridius's first instinct was to communicate with Earth and find out who'd stolen his ship, but of course that was a dead end – to the tune of ten billion people dead.

"Life signs on the station?" Iridius asked.

"Still none," Mul replied.

Iridius ran his fingers over the rough stubble on his cheek. "If the planet was hit by one of these planet-slaggers, why are the stations empty and the lunar bases non-responsive, too? Could the residual effects from one of these bombs cause that? Radiation or something?"

Latroz shook her head. "No sir. Aboard the *Valhalla* we launched it from orbit and were quite safe."

If the stations were empty, something else was happening here, something deliberately planned. What in all the black vacuum did Iridius's rust bucket hauler have to do with it? What should have been a dream assignment was turning out to be a nightmare couple of days – even worse than the time they'd had to deliver replacement equipment to Proxima Centauri C after their facility for production of synthetic fertiliser had gone haywire, creating what was unimaginatively being called Poo Planet. Come to think of it, during his time in Space Command, he'd had a lot more encounters with excrement, synthetic or otherwise, than he'd ever expected. But at least Earth hadn't been destroyed on any of those occasions – and if it turned out the *Diesel Coast* had something to do with it he was sure he'd wind up in more shit than ever.

"Commander, can we dock with *Gargarin Station*?"

"We have access codes to deactivate the automated defences," Mul said, "but we have our orders from the Federation Senate. We are to await the arrival of the *El Nino*."

"And we will," Iridius said. "But if the *El Nino* was in the Tau Ceti system on government business they won't be here for almost twenty-four hours. They didn't say we couldn't attempt to gather more information while we're waiting.

"Ensign Wesley, prepare to dock with *Gargarin*."

"*Do not attempt to approach this orbital construction. We are present. We will destroy your ship.*"

Iridius looked around with his eyebrows raised. The booming electronic voice had come through every speaker on the bridge. "Okaaaaay," Iridius said, dragging the word out in a way that made it very clear that things were not, in fact, okay. "Where did that communication come from, Ensign Herd?" Iridius asked. "Did you authorise it?"

"No, sir. I did—"

But Ensign Herd was cut off as the voice echoed through the bridge once again. *"We do not need to be authorised."*

"I am Captain Iridius Franklin of the FSC *Gallaway*. You will identify yourself and announce your intent."

"We are the Aegix. We have intent only to do as we are programmed. We are preparing for the coming of the Synth-Hastur, the Devourers of the Stars, the Great Living Storm of Steel, the Lords of Interstellar Space and the Harbingers of Forever War."

"Well," Iridius said, "that doesn't sound great."

There was a lengthy pause.

"It is not."

"There are no life signs aboard that station. What are you? An AI?"

"We are the Aegix. We are hive intelligence. We are swarm."

"Right," Iridius said. "See, I always knew it was only a matter of time before some AI went full cooky-dooky. I'm also going to make the flying leap and assume you're the ones responsible for the ball of molten rock that used to be Earth."

"We have done only as programmed. We were preparing your species for the coming of the Synth-Hastur, but the sentient occupants of this planet tried to destroy us. We were forced to retaliate, shutting down life support for all orbital facilities and the settlements on this world's moon before eliminating the population of the planet with your convenient weaponry. We must prepare all life for the coming of the Synth-Hastur. No attempts to interfere with our function can be tolerated. We have accessed your wide data network and now understand there are many more species in the galaxy that require preparation. Do not attempt to approach

or you will be eliminated. There will be no further communication."

"You listen to me, you crazy AI. You don't get to make demands of an FSC vessel after you've seized control of an FSC space station and murdered billions of people. You will relinquish control of all facilities or it's you that will be eliminated. Does that sink into your programming?"

The booming synthetic voice didn't respond.

"Do you understand?"

There was still no response.

"Hello?"

"They said *there will be no further communication,*" Ensign Rangi declared in his best impersonation of an autocratic robot voice.

"Yes, thank you, ensign. I know what they said." Iridius turned to Commander Mul. "Will that approach code still deactivate the station's defences with this hive mind thing in control?"

"I can't be certain, captain," Commander Mul said, "but if I had to speculate, given they appear to have been able to remotely control the life support systems of all orbital stations and the lunar bases, I think we have to assume they have already taken control of station defences."

"Lieutenant Latroz, how are our shields looking?" Iridius asked.

"Back to full charge, sir."

"Helm, bring us on an approach to *Gargarin*, but do it slowly."

"Aye."

"Captain Franklin," Commander Mul said, "I wish to raise numerous points of opposition to what I believe you are considering. One, we have been ordered by the Federation Senate to wait for Captain Idowu. Two, you have no idea what the capabilities of this Aegix entity or entities are. Three, you are the shakedown captain of this vessel. Ordinarily you are captain of a hauler and I do not believe you have the authority to take us into such a hazardous endeavour."

"I understand your concerns, commander, and I acknowledge them, but right now we are the only ship here. The *El Nino* will not arrive for an entire day. Look at what this hive intelligence did to Earth in four days. Do you think it's still going to be here in twenty-four hours or do you think it'll be off to destroy more inhabited worlds? I might ordinarily be the captain of a hauler, but I went through the same academy as every captain. I wouldn't be able to do anything about this situation with the *Diesel Coast*, but we're on the *Gallaway*, the most advanced ship in the galaxy – let's use it. If we don't stop this runaway computer right here and now there's a chance no one ever will."

As Iridius spoke, the bridge dropped into the now-familiar scarlet hue as red alert was declared.

"The *Gargarin* has deployed an external railgun battery," Latroz said, and then half a heartbeat later, "it's fired a short burst."

Out the view-screen there was a flash from the station, and then a second or two later there was a flicker of movement as glowing projectiles tore through the vacuum of space ahead of them.

"They fired across our bow," Latroz continued. "A warning shot."

"Full stop," Commander Mul called to the helm.

"Belay that!" Iridius demanded. "Continue on. Prepare to evade."

Ensign Smith and Ensign Wesley turned to look at the captain and first officer.

"Stop us now, Wesley," Mul said. "As executive officer I am relieving Captain Franklin of command of this vessel. I believe he is acting unlawfully, against the orders of the Federation, and putting the vessel and her crew in danger."

Ensign Wesley, with no small amount of hesitation, tapped at the helm and slid his hand down the touch screen throttle control to bring the FSC *Gallaway* to a full stop.

"Is that how it's going to be? You're going to attempt to take this ship off me?"

"It's not your ship. It's Captain Idowu's ship."

"April isn't here!" Iridius burst out before calming himself. "We need to do something about this situation now."

"I have no doubt I speak on behalf of the rest of the *Gallaway*'s crew when I say we'd prefer to await the arrival of Captain Idowu before we attempt any sort of attack. You are leading us against an unknown enemy powerful enough to destroy the Earth."

"You're speaking on behalf of the crew, are you?" Iridius asked, incredulous.

"Yes," Mul said, "I believe I am."

"Well," Iridius said, "Lieutenant Commander Quinn is usually the one who lets me know exactly which FSC regulations I'm breaking at any given time. But you see, there are a few FSC regs that all captains know, even me, the captain, as you seem to enjoy pointing out, of a lowly hauler. One of the regulations I know is a real doozy. I'm sure you've heard of it before – Federation Space Command Regulation 166. In case you don't remember I'll do my best to paraphrase it for you. It says that only the executive officer of a starship (that's you) may relieve the commanding officer (that's me) of command either under medical advice of the ship's doctor or by placing the commanding officer under arrest. In order to place the commanding officer under arrest the situation must be an obvious breach of lawful behaviour, and on investigation the subordinate officer must demonstrate that retention of command by the commanding officer would seriously and irrevocably damage the interests of the Federation. There's also the bit that says the subordinate officer must act alone. If crew consensus or action is involved in the relief of command, this constitutes mutiny.

"So to be clear, Commander Mul, you must place me under arrest. You must be confident that relieving me of command and not attempting to destroy the entity that has admitted to the annihilation of Earth and the intent to continue finding every sentient species in the galaxy is in the best interests of the Federation. And you must not involve crew consensus in your decision to relieve me, lest you be guilty of mutiny – which, oops, you just admitted is exactly what you're doing, because you believe you are speaking with the crew's consensus."

"Oh snap," Ensign Rangi said. "That's an antimatter-level burn."

Iridius should have immediately berated Ensign Rangi for this comment, but he didn't, because he had to admit it was indeed an antimatter-level burn.

Commander Mul stared at Iridius without responding.

"Admittedly I don't know much about Zeta Reticulan anatomy, but what's it going to be, commander? Do you have the balls?"

Commander Mul lowered his head until his enormous black eyes were looking at the ground. Zeta Reticulans may not express emotion on their faces the way humans do, but some body language, it appeared, was universal.

"Given the circumstances I won't press charges, but you are relieved of your post for the moment, Commander Mul. Quinn, you'll take over as my XO."

"I'll excuse myself from the bridge until required again for duty," Commander Mul said. He walked away from his console and moved to the rear of the bridge, where the elevator doors opened with a science-fiction swoosh. Commander Mul entered the lift without saying another word, and the doors closed in front of him.

"Right," Iridius said, "Quinn, take your station." He turned to the rest of the crew. "Whatever is on that station destroyed Earth and now wants to head off and target the rest of the galaxy. Does anyone else have any objections to raise about us blowing the thing out of the black?"

No one did.

"Sir?" Latroz spoke hesitantly, as if she – the enormous muscled warrior who could crush his skull like an overripe pear – was afraid of him.

"Yes, Latroz?"

"I have to agree with Commander Mul's assessment that our codes will not disable the station's defences. A direct attack on the station is a tactical error."

"Thank you, Latroz," Iridius said. "I suppose it's lucky I never intended to directly attack the station then, isn't it?"

"You didn't?" Latroz asked.

Iridius looked at her. "Despite what some people might believe, I'm not a moron, lieutenant."

"No, sir, sorry, sir."

"You were going to feint, hey cap?" Ensign Rangi said. "Like when those pirates had a go at us in Rigel?"

"That's right, ensign," Iridius said. "Lieutenant Latroz, the *Gallaway*'s shuttle is the new-generation stealth variant, correct?"

"Yes, sir."

"Good. Perhaps I should have outlined this first to avoid that confrontation with the commander, but I'm used to working with my crew. For the rest of you, the plan is simple. We feint the station, making the Aegix think we are attacking but are over-whelmed by their defences, at which point we retreat. During this manoeuvre I take a small away team and leave aboard the shuttle in stealth mode. We breach the station, shut down the station defences from the inside and then make our escape on the shuttle again. Once the shuttle is clear, the *Gallaway* reengages the station and blows it out of the black."

Lieutenant Latroz stared at the captain. "As tactical officer aboard this ship I would not consider that plan simple. But I like it. I haven't breached a space station for combat in several months. Permission to go to the armoury and prepare the shuttle."

"Very good, gather enough weapons for four of us," Iridius said. "Ensign Rangi, go with Lieutenant Latroz. You'll be joining the away team. Myself and Junker will be the other members." Iridius tapped at the comms on the arm of his chair. "Junker, head to the shuttle bay."

"You got it."

"Quinn," Iridius said, "you'll run tactical."

She nodded.

"Wesley, continue on towards the *Gargarin*. Prepare to turn hard starboard and bring us broadside to the station to absorb their railgun fire."

Under the control of Ensign Wesley, the FSC *Gallaway* hummed and began moving through the vacuum of space once again, headed for *Space Station Gargarin*. From here – if you ignored the orange glow of molten lava that covered the once-blue marble of Earth below – everything seemed just as it should, the station rotating slowly about its axis as it hung silently in Earth orbit. There was nothing to indicate that all life aboard had been exterminated and the station was now home to a synthetic intelligence of unknown origin.

"The station's defence turrets are all coming online now," Quinn said.

"Arm missiles," Iridius said. "Make it look like an attack run."

Red Alert. Red Alert.

"We're targeted," Quinn said, and then after a beat, "they're firing."

On the view-screen *Gargarin Station* lit up with flashes of white all over its surface, pulses as the station's defensive railguns erupted to life, silent in the vacuum of space.

"Hold course," Iridius said.

The view-screen flashed with impacts on the ship's forward shields as the railgun fire struck them. The ship shuddered. The barrage of small railgun shots carried enough momentum that even the motion of the three-hundred-metre-long starship was affected.

"Shields down to sixty per cent," Quinn reported after the volley of railgun fire ended.

"Fire a six-missile salvo."

Quinn did so. Iridius watched as the missiles streaked forward, acutely aware of what had happened the last time they'd used the *Gallaway*'s missile system. This time though, he hoped the fact that there was something else to target meant the missiles wouldn't turn back and have a go at them. This time, the six missiles did what they were intended to do and streaked off towards the station. Just as Iridius had anticipated, the missiles were met by another volley of railgun fire, tearing through them and causing them to detonate before they struck the station. When the missiles were little more than tennis ball-sized chunks of debris floating away into space, *Gargarin* opened up with another railgun bombardment aimed at the *Gallaway*, this one even more intense than the first. A veritable hailstorm of heated tungsten railgun rounds flew towards the ship.

"Quinn, full power to the port side shields. Wesley, hard to starboard," Iridius called. This was their cue to retreat, giving the appearance that they'd attempted an attack run but the station's defences had overwhelmed them. They turned away, increasing their speed, still feeling intense shuddering as the railgun fire peppered along their port side.

"Shields at fifty... forty... thirty per cent," Quinn said as the impacts continued to pound into the thin layer of energy that protected the ship's hull. If that shield failed, the railgun rounds would tear through the hull of the *Gallaway* like ball bearings through wet paper or, as in Iridius's experience, like parental criticism through self-esteem.

As Ensign Wesley guided the ship away from the station the railgun rounds decreased in frequency until they drew out of range and the *Gargarin*'s turrets stopped completely. Iridius stood. "Take us out of range and drop anchor, Ensign Wesley. Once shields are back up, run in for another simulated attack and retreat. I'm heading to the shuttle bay to launch with the away team. Lieutenant Commander Quinn, you have the conn."

CHAPTER EIGHT_

THE ANCHORING SYSTEM of the *Gallaway* automatically fired small bursts of gas from the thrusters to keep the vessel from drifting too far as they waited for shields to recharge. In the shuttle bay Iridius, Latroz, Rangi and Junker were suiting up for EVA – full suits, as it was likely the life support on board *Gargarin Station* would not be functional. Unlike the awkward hopping, shimmying, jerking dance required to slip into the EVA suits on the *Diesel Coast*, the *Gallaway* had an auto-suit system. Iridius stood against the EVA station on the wall, arms and legs wide, and the fully armoured powered exoskeleton combat spec suit, complete with black and grey digital camouflage paint job, was fitted piece by piece by robotic arms and secured in place. It was an efficient system that only made Iridius flinch once, when a robotic claw came forward to clamp his codpiece down.

Once in their heavy combat suits Iridius powered up, watched the HUD swipe across his vision and had the sudden sensation that the suit had disappeared. He was free to move, unburdened by the weight of the armour, as the exoskeleton amplified his strength and supported the shell of the suit. Latroz walked between them and passed out AR-85 pulse rifles – the next model up from those on the *Diesel Coast*.

"Systems check," Iridius said.

"Green," Latroz replied.

"Green," Rangi replied.

"Green," Junker replied as she moved her arms and legs in place, jumped up and down on the spot, and did all the things that Iridius desperately wanted to do in the advanced combat suit but wouldn't, for fear of looking, well, exactly like Junker did. "Fucking green, these things are awesome."

"Alright," Iridius said, "let's load up."

The four of them boarded the sleek, arrowhead-shaped shuttle. This small craft, despite only being a transport shuttle, was just as advanced as the ship it called home. Capable of FTL in its own right, with full stealth capability and manoeuvrability to rival a dart racer, it was ten metres long and still more ship than the *Diesel Coast*. It wasn't capable of full cloaking – no one had managed to perfect that technology yet – but it could sneak up on just about anything that didn't hit it with a direct scanner beam. Once aboard, Ensign Rangi naturally took position in the pilot's chair. Iridius hadn't needed to tell him he'd be flying. The shuttle could be flown completely by the onboard autopilot, but that required the use of sensor arrays that would greatly affect the stealth capability. Manual piloting was more difficult, particularly as they drew near the station and would attempt a leech manoeuvre – clasping themselves to the station's outer hull – but stealth was the priority, so they'd have to fly without sensors. Wesley and Smith were capable helmsmen, but Iridius didn't think they could pilot by feel the way Rangi could. The four occupants strapped themselves tightly into their seats, Rangi in one of the two forward-facing pilot positions and the others in the wall mounted seats in the rear. The shuttle was not large enough to have an artificial gravity system, so once they cleared the *Gallaway* they'd be in zero-g.

"Beginning feint run," Quinn's voice came over the comms. The crew in the shuttle waited. Iridius counted out seconds until they felt the reverberation of railgun fire hitting the shields. As the railgun fire ceased, Iridius knew the *Gallaway* would be turning away.

"Clear to launch, shuttle one," Quinn said. "Good luck. No red shirts."

"No red shirts, you got it," Rangi said. "Shuttle one launching."

The shuttle lifted off the deck of the shuttle bay and hovered. It turned slowly on the spot, rotating through one hundred and eighty degrees until the bow of the shuttle pointed out the shuttle bay door. The fusion engines at the back of the shuttle glowed as Rangi increased the throttle and they accelerated away from the *Gallaway*, the raw acceleration pinning them back into their seats far more than they'd experience on a starship with more efficient inertia control. With the sudden removal of an artificial gravity field and the burst of forward acceleration, Iridius had the stomach-turning sensation that down had suddenly become towards the rear of the shuttle. He breathed deeply and exhaled slowly, taking a moment to override his inner ear and tell his body that no, he hadn't lost his balance.

The shuttle moved forward, emerging out from the relative safety of the *Gallaway* and into space, a tiny object drawing away from its mothership in the vastness of the black. Hopefully the move was timed so they were hidden as the ship turned away after its fake attack run. Iridius never really enjoyed the idea of a shuttle craft in open space. It made him feel like one of humanity's early astronauts – a maniac in a tin can – the equivalent of a paper boat being set adrift on the Pacific Ocean. He knew it was an irrational thought really – given the scale of the black, being in a larger starship wasn't actually all that much better. Space, with apologies to Douglas Adams, is big, and no matter what ship you're in, you are not.

"Engaging stealth," Rangi said, the pilot seemingly unaffected by the acceleration shift. Pilots always seemed less affected by the tumbling of acceleration vectors. "I've always wanted to press one of these buttons. Would have come in handy for us on the *Diesel Coast* a few times, wouldn't it, cap? A button that makes the ship go completely quiet and disappear. Pretty cool."

"Yes," Iridius said, "I wish I had a button like that I could use on people."

As Rangi engaged stealth mode there was little change inside the shuttle. The windows – apart from a small section in front of the pilot – turned completely black and the hum of the engines decreased somewhat, but outside, the shuttle shimmered, active camouflage making it almost completely invisible to the naked eye as the light was bent around the hull. Shrouds dropped down around the engine exhausts, leaving just enough exposed to allow thrust to escape, but even this was temperature inverted, with extremely powerful endothermic heatsinks dropping the temperature of the exhaust closer to the two-point-seven Kelvin of surrounding space. Communication was blocked. Radiation emission was blocked. Everything that could be detected to show the shuttle as an object distinct from the vacuum around it was tempered to be almost non-existent. What was left should avoid detection by broad sensor sweeps; only someone directly targeting their location with high-gain sensor pings would find them. All this meant the inside of the shuttle began to grow increasingly hot. Studies were yet to determine whether the radiation being hoarded by the shuttle was enough to cause lasting damage to the occupants. Iridius pushed that thought aside. They wouldn't need to stay in full stealth for all that long, and he'd never really wanted kids anyway.

Ensign Rangi flew the shuttle completely visually, arcing around from the cover of the *Gallaway* and emerging all but invisible to station sensors. He flew a wide, curving path to ensure the shuttle didn't approach from the same bearing that the *Gallaway* departed on. There was little more they could do but hope that the shuttle's advanced stealth mode meant they remained unseen and undetected by the Aegix.

Iridius's hands grew clammy with nervous sweat as the spire of *Gargarin Station* grew increasingly large in the small amount of window still clear at the front of the shuttle. Rangi, usually a fan of pushing a craft as fast as possible, took the shuttle in at a painfully slow speed. Every instinct Iridius had was screaming that the longer they took creeping up on their prey, the greater the likelihood they'd be spotted, but he forced his primitive monkey instincts down. They weren't slinking across some savannah towards a buffalo – this was space, and they were invisible but for the faint emissions they were radiating out into the black. The slower they went, the less obvious those emissions would be.

Rangi kept the shuttle to a speed of only one hundred kilometres per second, so it took twenty minutes to reach the station. For this period of the flight, the shuttle coasted along at constant velocity, leaving the occupants floating up against their restraints in zero-g. During their transit, Iridius filled them in on the plan, such as it was. They would leech the shuttle onto the hull of the station and cut their way in. Once inside, Latroz would take point and they would proceed rapidly to electrical engineering in the main spire, where Junker would lead them through disabling all station power to shut down the defence turrets. Then they would backtrack to the shuttle and return to the *Gallaway*. Apart from these discussions, they mostly sat in silence. Iridius left them to their thoughts, sure they were preparing themselves for the dangers of the mission ahead, or reflecting on those who had been exterminated on Earth and its orbital and lunar bases. At least, that's what he thought they were dwelling on until Ensign Rangi spoke.

"It looks a lot like a ribbed dildo, doesn't it?"

"What?!"

"The *Gargarin*," Ensign Rangi said. "It looks a lot more phallic than most space stations. Why do you think that is?"

"Focus on the mission, Rangi," Iridius said.

Sitting in the pilot's seat, Ensign Rangi shrugged his broad shoulders. "I'm focused on the mission, captain, don't worry. I'm going to stick us on the side of that shaft like a genital wart."

Junker chuckled. Even Latroz let a smile crack through her rippled and bony face. Iridius just shook his head. He didn't berate Ensign Rangi – there was no point, and he trusted him to do exactly what he said. That's what mattered about the helmsman's performance, even if from now on, every time he looked through the window Iridius couldn't help but see the FSC's advanced space station as a giant floating sex toy.

"Decelerating now, manoeuvring for a leech on the spire as close to electrical engineering as I can," Ensign Rangi eventually said in a half-whisper.

"You don't have to whisper, Rangi," Junker said.

"I know," he said, still in that same stage-whisper. "It just feels more stealthy, doesn't it?"

Iridius felt his weight shift towards the front of the shuttle as deceleration kicked in. In front of them, *Gargarin Station* was rapidly approaching, or rather, they were rapidly approaching it – it was always hard to tell in space. Rangi worked the controls, using tiny thruster pops to pitch the shuttle upwards at a high angle of attack to their flight vector. Now came the difficult part. Assuming the stealth systems of the shuttle had kept them hidden from *Gargarin's* sensors, Ensign Rangi faced the task of landing the shuttle belly-first onto the station with an impact gentle enough that it didn't trip any foreign object impact alarms. As they drew closer, closing in on the station with a relative speed of only a few kilometres per second, Rangi pitched the shuttle more. Iridius knew Rangi would have lost sight of the landing location but the station loomed above them – or in front of them, or beneath them, depending on which frame of reference you wanted to use. Rangi, like all starship pilots, had incredible spatial awareness, and Iridius knew he'd be holding the relationship between the shuttle, the reference points he could see on the station and their landing location in his mind as much as on the computer. They decelerated more, pitched more, and Rangi made subtle adjustments to their orientation and heading. Soon, they were moving in under one of the station's enormous rings and the gunmetal grey surface filled the view out the window. They coasted in completely belly-first towards the main spire, Rangi flying by feel and memory, taking prompts from the proximity numbers flashing over his screen. He fired thrusters, once, twice, a moment's wait, then again. They seemed to be barely moving relative to the station now.

"We're on," Ensign Rangi said.

Iridius looked at him. "We're on?"

"Yes, sir."

"Huh," Iridius said. He hadn't felt a thing. "Nice work."

"Very good flying, ensign," Latroz said. "I am impressed by your skill in delivering us to our enemy."

Iridius looked from Latroz to Rangi. The two of them looked at each other with an obvious intensity. Oh god. Was the organic armoured warrior alien woman flirting with his pilot? And was Rangi ready to reciprocate? It was hard to imagine that anything could make Iridius more uncomfortable than flying in a shuttle towards a space station controlled by rogue hive intelligence – but there it was.

"Prepare to cut through," Iridius said, undoing his seat

harness and letting himself float upwards. He pushed himself out over the floor of the shuttle and engaged the mag on his boots, which were suddenly pulled down and locked to the floor with a clunk. The others, apart from Rangi, who stayed in the pilot's chair, did the same.

"We've got a good seal," Rangi said from the front. "I'm ready to engage cold cutters."

"Engage," Iridius said.

"Roger."

Iridius felt jolts and vibrations through the floor as the cold cutters on the bottom of the shuttle extended to touch the hull of the station and began tracking around in a circle, super-abrasive particles embedded in a gas blasted out to slowly cut into the surface of the hull. It was slow going, but faster cutting methods like plasma couldn't be used because the heat involved would be detected by the station's sensors. Iridius, Latroz and Junker, the three who would be going aboard, geared up with their rifles, grenades and explosive charges and double and triple checked their gear while they waited for the cutters to breach the hull of *Gargarin Station*.

"Cutters are indicating they're through," Rangi eventually reported.

"Alright, let's open the hatch."

"Wait," Junker said. Iridius looked at the first technician. "If this thing is a machine intelligence, it probably killed everyone aboard by venting the station to vacuum. If we open the hatch with a pressured cabin it's pretty likely the pressure differential will get detected. We need to pressure match the inside of the station."

"And if we vent the shuttle to vacuum and the inside of the station isn't?" Iridius asked, though he suspected he knew the answer.

"That'll be detected, too," Junker confirmed.

Everyone looked at him. Decision time. So far his limited contact with the Aegix had given him the distinct impression that if humans couldn't be prepared, whatever it was that actually meant, then the Aegix wouldn't have an issue venting a station full of them. "Seal your suits, go to onboard air supply. Rangi, vent the shuttle."

"You got it, cap."

Rangi closed the doors between the cockpit and the rear of the shuttle, sealing himself in an area that would maintain air and pressure. The shuttle outside Iridius's suit dampened into silence as the air in the rear section was flushed into space. They waited for the venting process to finish before Iridius said over suit comms, "Open the hatch."

In the floor of the shuttle was a manual hatch. Latroz bent down and turned the handle. Soundlessly, with only the vibrations through his feet alerting Iridius to the grinding of the lock, Latroz pulled the hatch inward. Stuck to the bottom of the hatch was a circular piece of thick steel, its edge ragged and sharp from where the abrasive had blasted through. The piece that had been cut from the hull remained joined to the hatch by mag claws so that it wouldn't fall inwards into the station. Once it was out of the way, a one metre diameter hole was revealed in the hull of *Gargarin Station*.

"Go," said Iridius.

Latroz nodded. She disengaged her mag, floated up to the roof of the shuttle and pushed off, clutching her rifle to her chest to float down through the hole. As she cleared the shuttle she twisted in the air and landed on the floor of the station, standing sideways to what Iridius currently considered down. It was indeed vacuum inside the station, but the artificial gravity was apparently still on. Iridius went next, following Latroz's lead and deactivating his boots, pushing up and then down through the hole in the hull. He wasn't quite as practiced at leech entry as

Latroz, though, and once he passed through into the station he wasn't quick enough to register the shift in gravity and contort his body to get his feet under him. He hit the floor face first with a crunch. Junker followed and was somewhere between the two, flailing a little and stumbling but ultimately ending up on her feet. Iridius stood and brought his rifle up in a ready stance as quickly and as unashamedly as he could, avoiding his subordinates' eyes.

The inside of the space station was dark. The main lights running along the roof had been deactivated and the corridor was lit with an eerie mix of faint orange emergency lighting and the green, red and blue light emanating from their suits. Iridius's suit auto-enhanced the limited light to give him a brighter view out of his helmet. But the enhancement began to flicker, dropping in and out before settling on an unenhanced vision of the dark corridor. Iridius switched on his helmet-mounted torch – a circle of white light illuminating the wall ahead of him. Latroz and Junker followed his lead, their own enhanced vision giving out, too, which concerned Iridius. They'd been blessedly clear of Franklinisms aboard the *Gallaway* – at least since they'd returned to Earth and discovered the Aegix – but now their all-important EVA combat suits were glitching. He tried to tell himself he'd never had a Franklinism on anything but a ship system before, but this suit malfunction felt an awful lot like one.

"Latroz, you've got a station map highlighted with the fastest route to electrical," Iridius said. "Bring it up and let's move. The sooner we cut power and get back to the shuttle the better."

"Aye, sir," Latroz said as she adjusted something on her forearm suit controls and then headed off down the corridor. The spotlight from her head torch swung from side to side as she scanned ahead, bobbing up and down as she walked.

It didn't take long for Latroz to come to a halt, her head torch illuminating a shape slumped against the wall. As Iridius approached, he saw the shape was actually two people. They were sitting against the wall, dead, their skin already showing the taut, crinkled texture of vacuum drying. The bodies of all those the Aegix had killed in the lunar bases or on the orbiting space stations would stay like this forever, mummified, never decomposing. When Iridius looked closely he saw the two figures were holding hands. They had faced death together and now their fingers would remain intertwined for all eternity.

"Still a better love story than *Twilight*," he said.

"What?" Latroz asked.

"Nothing, don't worry about it. Push on," Iridius said. "It might sound harsh, but we know everyone's dead. No point dwelling on it."

They moved on, proceeding quickly but carefully under Latroz's well-trained lead. They passed more bodies – human, mostly, but also Haptids, Zeta Reticulans and Venusians, different species from across the Federation that had all fallen victim to inevitable death once life support had been cut off and the station vented to vacuum. The elevators were non-responsive, so they descended the steel grate steps between decks until they reached the level where the main electrical systems should be located. As they emerged from the stairwell, Iridius saw the array of large electrical relays, power converters, transformers and control systems that indicated they were in the right place. Iridius really had no idea what he was looking for, but Junker was already making her way towards a control station.

As Junker tried to reactivate the dormant controls, Iridius caught sight of movement in his peripheral vision. He spun, bringing his rifle to bear and saw a familiar sight illuminated by his head lamp. He couldn't hear them in the vacuum of the station and they moved differently without air, skittering along the floor, walls and ceiling of the corridor, moving more like spiders than flying bugs, but it was definitely the same black nanomachine creatures they had encountered on Iota Persei E. A swarm. A probably intelligent swarm. A probably hive mind intelligent swarm that now had a name. The Aegix. The puzzle pieces Iridius had already suspected clunked uncomfortably into place.

"Sir," Junker said over comms. "I think those are the same bugs from Iota Persei E."

The *Diesel Coast* was parked here, and the same swarm they'd been exposed to before was here. Oh boy. "But we couldn't have brought them back with us," Iridius said, finishing his thoughts out loud. "We purged the cargo bay, and we would have known if we'd dragged that many with us."

The tiny black machines crept down from the roof and walls to join those on the floor. They stopped moving a short distance away, covering several metres of the floor, twitching and rippling like a living rug.

"Something else is coming," Latroz said.

Standing in the darkness of an abandoned space station surrounded by desiccated corpses and hearing the words *something else is coming* was never going to be a pleasant moment. Iridius expected to see some horrific creature appear, something grabbing hold of the wall with a clawed hand, crushing the metal slightly and rounding the corner with a huge gaping maw dripping slime venom. To Iridius's relief this was not what happened. Instead, what appeared was a small, white, fluffy dog. The black swarm parted like a miniature Red Sea as the dog walked somewhat stiffly through them.

"Ah, what is that?" Iridius asked.

"That," Junker said, "is a My PupPup artificially intelligent toy dog. Those are the things we *did* bring back with us."

"Oh," Iridius said, looking at the dog and feeling that final puzzle piece slam into place. "Fuck."

"They must have flown the *Diesel Coast* up here."

The My PupPup dog stopped around two metres from Iridius. It tilted its head to one side and stared. Then Iridius heard a voice through his helmet's comms channel. *"You were warned not to approach this station."*

Iridius looked at the dog. "Um, hello little dog." He bent down on one knee. "I am Captain Iridius B. Franklin of the Federation Space Command vessel *Gallaway*. Is that you speaking to me?" Iridius had always hoped to be among the pioneers who made first contact with a new species. He just never thought it would involve speaking to a toy.

"We are the Aegix. You may address this unit. It is currently housing our interactive consciousness, though we are in the hive, we are swarm."

"As an FSC captain I am authorised to make first contact and establish diplomatic talks in order to avoid any further hostilities between our species." The plan of sneaking aboard, disabling the power supply and then escaping completely unnoticed had gone to the dogs, no pun intended, so this seemed as good an approach as any. "If we are to avoid conflict, we need to understand each other. Why have you attacked this planet?" Iridius asked. "You've killed billions of people."

"This information has been provided already. We must prepare for the coming of the Synth-Hastur. The inhabitants of this planet attempted to interfere. There can be no interference."

"Look, if it's anything like Iota Persei E, you just started turning everyone into pink goop. You are the aggressors. I'm sure the people of Earth were just trying to defend themselves."

"We were preparing them for the Synth-Hastur. This is our function."

"What do you mean, 'preparing them for the Synth-Hastur'? Preparing how? Turning them into food? Are the Synth-Hastur your creators?" Iridius asked, not sure if he was trying to buy time or whether he really expected to make progress.

"*We are the Aegix. We were not created by the Synth-Hastur. We were created before the last coming of the Synth-Hastur, half a million of your Earth years ago. We are the Aegix.*"

"Oh, I see, you're the Aegix, are you? I must have missed the first six thousand times you said that. What do these Synth-Hastur want?"

"*The Synth-Hastur come to destroy. As they always come. They come to cleanse this galaxy. The Synth-Hastur are the Devourers of the Stars, the Great Living Storm of Steel, the Lords of Interstellar Space and the Harbingers of Forever War. The galaxy must be prepared. The galaxy must be prepared. The galaxy must be prepared.*"

"Okay," Iridius said, realising that he might have been more right than he'd like about this AI being completely bonkers. "And so what happens to me and my people now?"

"*You have already been prepared.*"

"What do you mean? How have we been prepared?"

"*Not the others, just you.*"

"What are you talking about?" Iridius asked, incredulous.

"*Your colleagues will be prepared now.*" These words were somewhat more menacing than one might expect coming from a small white puppy.

"Wait," Iridius said, but the My PupPup, or at least the Aegix that had taken possession of it, didn't wait. The swarm moved forward, skittering along the floor towards Iridius, Latroz and Junker with an irregular arachnoid motion that triggered fear and disgust in the evolutionary recesses of their brains. Iridius lifted his rifle, remembering the response of the robotic creatures on Iota Persei E.

"Hit them with microwave," he said as he fired into them. Just as had happened in Mining Station Victoria, the bugs hit by the radiation were immediately stopped. Most of them spread apart to avoid the strongest of the microwave blasts. "Back up and keep firing."

The three of them fired as they retreated, heading for the stairs back to where the shuttle remained leeched to the side of the hull. Unlike the mining station, the bugs here stayed on the floor and walls, making them easier to target with the microwave blasts. They managed to hold the bugs back – until they couldn't anymore. Without warning, the three of them stopped moving, stopped firing and the swarm kept coming. It took Iridius a moment to realise it wasn't his rifle that had malfunctioned, or at least it wasn't only that. He couldn't move his finger to squeeze the trigger, and he couldn't lift his feet, no matter how hard he tried. Not only that, his suit's HUD had vanished.

"I can't move," he said. "Give me a status on your suits."

There was no reply. It appeared comms were down, too.

"*Your extra-vehicular suits are under our control. Further aggression will not be tolerated.*"

He could hear that though – not that he wanted to.

"*The galaxy must be prepared. The galaxy must be prepared.*"

The swarm came forward, covering the floor, parting around Iridius's feet and splitting off to make its way towards Junker and Latroz. Iridius couldn't turn to look; his body was frozen, his helmet locked in place on the torso of his suit. He forced his head to turn to the side as much as he could, and in his peripheral vision he saw the black bugs of the swarm crawling up Junker and Latroz. Iridius tried to move. He forced his arms out as hard as he could but it was as if the suit was actively resisting him. The Aegix had control of them. Their advanced EVA suits were suddenly nothing more than tombs, sarcophagi they were trapped in.

"Mother Earth fucking damn it!" Iridius howled with frustration inside the echoing box of his helmet. "Stupid fucking suit, move!"

With a flicker of text and diagnostic graphics, Iridius's HUD flared to life across his vision, his suit rebooted, and suddenly he *could* move. He immediately spun to Junker and Latroz. They were both all but completely covered with the crawling black of the swarm; the mechanical creatures looked as though they were already burrowing into the composite armour. He pulled the trigger to blast both of them with radiation, knowing their suits would protect them. The effect of the radiation was immediate. The bugs on Latroz and Junker either dropped to the floor and broke apart into their tiny nano-sized components or they scattered, moving in fits and starts like flies sprayed with a burst of insect repellent. Replacement swarm-bugs immediately began moving towards his crewmates like reckless cannon-fodder. Iridius prepared to fire again, but another group of the bugs who'd scurried along the floor behind him leaped up into the air, forming an arm that wrapped itself around Iridius's rifle. As soon as they had latched themselves on, the ammunition display on the rifle went dark, and when Iridius pulled the trigger it was completely unresponsive.

Iridius swore and tossed the useless rifle aside, then spun to face the My PupPup dog. "Leave my crew alone," he demanded as he stormed towards it, not knowing whether the dog or the synthetic being inside it could even hear him. There was no response. As he drew close to the dog, a large swarm of the machines came together in front of it in a churning, protective black mass. The bugs clambered over each other, stacking atop one another to form a pillar stretching seven or eight feet tall. The pillar sprouted two arm-like appendages at the top, and two more of the churning limbs at the bottom. The pillar rocked forward and then dropped onto its front legs, Iridius darting backwards as it fell. As the bugs rearranged themselves and the shape twisted and contorted, Iridius realised what they had made. They'd formed themselves into a large dog, or at least the best approximation the tiny machines could manage. It stalked towards Iridius, its jaws snapping. As the creature lunged, Iridius did the only thing he could think of. He screamed and swung his arm, fist clenched, in a wild defensive punch. The gesture should have been futile, but as his hand hit the side of the bug-dog's head the thing exploded. Iridius's hand passed into the amalgamated creature without much resistance, and his combat suit-enhanced strength almost threw him off balance. Somehow, as if blown by a gust of wind, the bugs disassembled and burst apart. They dropped to the floor, bursting into tiny, almost imperceptible spots.

Iridius, deciding to figure out how he'd managed that a little later, turned his attention to the My PupPup. The small fluffy dog looked at him and tilted its head to the side as if evaluating him.

"You have interrupted the swarm. You have interrupted prepa-ration. All life in the galaxy must be prepared. Further aggression will not be tolerated," the voice of the Aegix came through his comms channel yet again.

Iridius stormed forward towards the dog, lifted his armoured boot and slammed it down right on top of the fluffy little monster. The toy dog crunched satisfactorily beneath the metal and magnetic-powered stomp.

Iridius lifted his boot and stared down at the mangled robot corpse. "Bad dog," he declared.

There was a groan through the comms. "Really, cap?" Junker's voice said. "One-liners?"

Iridius turned to see Junker and Latroz moving towards him, Junker looking down at the shattered robot dog.

"You can move again," Iridius said, "and communicate. How are your suits?"

"All green," Junker said, looking to Latroz, who nodded to indicate that hers was as well. "The bugs tried to eat through them though. If we were in standard EVA suits they probably would have managed it already."

"You have any idea what happened?" Iridius asked Junker.

"You punched the nanomachine dog thing and it exploded. Seems like that put the whole swarm offline. Thought maybe you might know what you did, cap," Junker said.

"I have no idea," Iridius said. He knew that as captain of a starship he should probably try to sound more confident, but in that moment he was so lost he couldn't even feign confidence. "How did they get control of our suits in the first place?"

"It seems the swarm can hijack our equipment, somehow hack their way into our systems. If I had to guess I'd say they operate as a network of nodal points, and are basically hacking us in the same way they must have done to the station itself. Radio waves, wireless networking – our systems send and receive signals all the time. Everything's encrypted and secure, of course, but I'm guessing if this Aegix can control a swarm of nanomachines and get inside everything from My PupPup toy dogs to *Gargarin Station*, our suits aren't going to stop it."

"I believe that is an indication that we should undertake an immediate tactical withdrawal," Latroz said. "They will be sending reinforcements. Captain Franklin, if you are unaware of how you managed to regain control of your suit and eliminate the nanomachines, we need to head for the shuttle."

"We have to take down the station's defences if we're to give the *Gallaway* any chance of destroying it."

"Yes, sir," Latroz agreed, pulling a square brick of explosive from the belt she'd slipped around her combat suit. "We have lost any illusion of a stealth approach. I suggest we tactically withdraw while completing our mission with a secondary approach. We, as your people are fond of saying, do this loudly. Technician Nejem, I expect you can advise where to put this to ensure we disable the power?"

Iridius watched a broad grin spread across Junker's face. "Oh yeah, lieutenant."

"Alright," Iridius said, "plant the explosive and let's go."

Latroz and Junker hurried to the bank of electrical equipment, Junker guiding the alien warrior to a large electrical transformer that she insisted would see the whole place light up – something about coolant processes and heat transfer and unstable isotopes. Latroz planted the explosive against the side of the transformer, pressed in the detonator and armed it. Junker and Latroz returned to Iridius and the three of them retreated back up the stairs towards the shuttle. Even in the mid twenty-third century, when faster-than-light travel was possible and reality television had finally run its course, the concept of explosives had not changed considerably. You take a tightly packed block of material that is mostly inert unless triggered by a sudden input of energy, you put the block of explosive on the thing you want to make go away, you insert a smaller explosive charge, you get as far away as you can, and when you trigger the small charge the shock causes the larger explosive to release combustion gases at something close to eight kilometres per second – basically, it goes bang.

And bang it went.

It would be poetic to say the whole world shook, but it didn't really. Iridius certainly felt the explosion as they moved at suit-amplified speed back towards the shuttle, but the mass of *Gargarin Station* was enough to quickly damp out the vibrations shuddering through the structure. The plastic explosive they planted was enough, just as Junker had said, to cause follow-on blasts that tore through all the electrical systems in the vicinity, but the space station wasn't going to pop like an over-inflated balloon full of cheap special effects. This was a complex mega-structure with failsafe design, including isolated ring segments with reinforced double-bulkhead construction, auto-air venting, instant fire suppression and multiple redundancy in electronic, mechanical and structural components. There was no way a single explosion, like, say, a missile hitting a thermal exhaust port, would cause the entire space station to erupt – that would just be terrible engineering. But what did happen was, as their explosion ripped through the electrical systems, the station was plunged into darkness and the artificial gravity gave out. Somewhere below them there was another explosion and the floor shuddered again. The entire station might not be about to explode, but there was no guarantee the ring section they were in wasn't going to come apart and send them floating off through the black of space.

Iridius, Junker and Latroz switched on the magnetic attraction of their boots and their running changed into the long, loping steps of micro-gravity. It was an adjustment, but as people who'd spent the majority of their adult lives in space, it was one they made easily. As they ran around the final corner and headed for the shuttle, Ensign Rangi came over the radio.

"Captain," he said, "I know I'm supposed to be radio silent but we've got a problem."

"Tell me in a minute, Rangi," Iridius said. "We're on our way back. Prime us to break the seal and get out of here. Things are exploding."

"That's the thing, cap. There are some sort of tiny black machines crawling over the outside of the shuttle. The propulsion system has gone dead. We're not going anywhere."

Hearing this mid-bound, Iridius landed and then stopped. The hole through the hull was just up ahead. "Shit," he said. "Have you tried again?"

"Six times, cap."

Iridius let out a groan of frustration. "How come no one ever radios through with good news? When is someone going to radio through and say, 'Captain, I've got a report for you – you've won a year's supply of Gartoshin Whisky.' Are you still in suit, Rangi?"

"Just need my helmet and gloves."

"Alright," Iridius said, "come through the breach hole and meet us." He turned to Latroz. "Have you still got the station schematics up, lieutenant?"

"Aye, sir."

"Figure out the quickest route to the docking bays."

Latroz began tapping at the control panel on the forearm of her suit. A moment later Ensign Rangi was emerging from the shuttle and coming down the corridor to join them. "Back to the central shaft and down to the lowest ring," Latroz said. "But we cannot know the integrity of the passages, or even whether this ring is going to hold together."

"It's likely to be automatically sealed after the explosion anyway," Junker said. "We'll be cut off from any of the other station rings."

"Well, we need to get out of this ring in case it does break apart, and we need to get off this station before we get attacked by robot dogs or pink-goopified by their pet bugs, so we're going to have to risk it. If the shuttle isn't an option, we've got an old friend down at the docking bay. She'll get us out of here."

"The *Coast*," Junker said, part-realisation, part-question.

Rangi smiled. "Good thinking, cap. The old girl won't let us down."

The dull sensation of something exploding below them reverberated up through the floor again. Iridius spun to Latroz. "Can you get us there?"

The seven-foot-tall Siruan nodded and turned, leading them back down the stairs. They moved quickly through the level below. The explosion they'd triggered had been only one level further down and the floor here was buckled, bent, and in some places completely ruptured. The space was filling with a black-grey smoke, and frayed wires sparked and flared in the gouges in the floor. The four of them moved as quickly as they could through the dangerous surrounds, but even with the sensors in their suits displaying light, and infra-red enhanced vision showing through their face plates it was slower going than Iridius would have liked.

"Another set of stairs should be ju—"

Latroz's voice was cut off by a sudden explosion ahead of them. The chain reaction Junker had promised was apparently still chain-reacting. An enormous ball of fire erupted through the floor then was gone just as quickly as it had appeared, sucked away into the oxygen-less vacuum of space as the hull of the station was breached. Iridius watched as the floor and, more disturbingly, the walls ahead of them tore into shreds of metal and floated away. The gaping hole left an unobscured view of the burning surface of Earth and the rest of *Gargarin Station* stretching away from them – a sight that was both terrifying and beautiful. Iridius, Junker and Rangi's mag-boots kept them locked securely to the floor but Latroz, who'd been ahead of them, was too close to the damage. A section of internal wall slammed into her at high velocity and sent her spiralling out through the hole in the wall. The only thing Latroz's mag-boots remained secured to was a chunk of steel floor that had been torn away with her.

"Latroz!" Iridius yelled down his comms. "Latroz, do you read?"

When she didn't respond, Iridius, without a second thought, bent his knees, switched off his mag-boots and pushed himself off the floor as hard as he could. He tucked his arms in by his sides and torpedoed out the hole in the space station, his eyes firmly locked on Latroz's spinning shape, which was rapidly moving away. The combat EVA suits had very little fuel for untethered manoeuvring – they weren't meant to be used for space walking – but Iridius kept his legs pointed straight out behind him and fired the small thrusters on the outsides of his calves. He accelerated towards Latroz.

"Latroz," he tried her over the comms again but she still

didn't respond. She must have been knocked unconscious – he just hoped it wasn't worse than that.

"Captain," Junker said. "Watch your fuel."

"I've got it."

Iridius closed the distance between them, knowing he'd only get one chance at this. If he hit too fast and failed to get a solid grip on her, Latroz would go spinning off into space and they'd never be able to recover her. He still didn't know how he was going to recover himself yet, but one thing at a time. He kept his arms angled diagonally behind him, holding them as stiff as he could, and fired the small thrusters on the outside of his forearm to adjust his course. He hadn't done an untethered EVA since the Academy, and even then that had been in a purpose-designed spacewalk suit, not a combat suit designed for minor zero-g manoeuvring. Plus, unsurprisingly, he'd been hungover and not really paying attention. As he rapidly approached Latroz, Iridius swung his arms and legs forward, forming his body into a u-shape. He fired as much of the dry thruster fuel as he dared, having to blast the white spray for a lot longer than he'd expected to lower the relative velocity between himself and Latroz. He opened his arms and legs, ready to wrap them around Latroz, and hoped she'd forgive him for what was bound to be a very awkward and possibly suggestive embrace. When he collided – groin first, but luckily no one really noticed – he grabbed Latroz as tightly as he could, willing the actuators in the powered suit to clamp his grip down hard. He managed to hold tight and stay pinned to Latroz, but the impact had sent them tumbling. Iridius fought to keep his bearings as he saw the Earth pass below them, then the black of deep space, and then *Gargarin Station*. Earth, black, station. Earth, black, station. He turned his attention to his HUD, watching the display and ignoring the changing orientation beyond. Every time the station passed he fired his leg thrusters counter to the spin, and with each burst the spinning slowed until he had stopped turning and could keep his eyes fixed on the looming structure.

"Captain?" Junker said. "You alright?"

"Yeah," Iridius said, "I'm good." He said it even as he saw his HUD blinking a warning that he was low on thruster fuel. He was floating away, watching the shapes of Junker and Rangi grow smaller. "I mean, I probably don't have enough fuel to reverse the momentum of both of us, so I suppose that's not great."

"Is she alive?" Junker's voice this time. "If she's not you could... well... Newton's third law and all."

"No," Rangi said, a little too insistently. "I mean, you can't do that."

Iridius looked in through Latroz's face plate. Her eyes were closed but he could see her breathing. "She's alive," Iridius said. "And don't worry, ensign, I didn't jump after her to throw her off into space. Thanks for the suggestion though, Junker."

Even from there Iridius could see Junker's casual shrug.

Iridius loosened his grip on Latroz; now that their velocities were matched she wouldn't go anywhere. They were floating away from the station slightly, but the largest component of their motion was downward, or what Iridius currently considered to be downward, which was in the direction of his feet. In that direction lay some good news. He and Latroz were, with a little adjustment, headed towards the *Diesel Coast*. She may not have been the *Gallaway*, but in that moment her grey shoebox shape was glorious to behold.

"Okay," he said, "listen, I might not have enough fuel to come back but if I give a little nudge I can head us in the direction of the *Coast*. You should do the same. You're going to have to jump."

"I'm a pilot," Ensign Rangi said. "I sit in ships. I don't jump out of them."

Iridius was already holding his arm out to the side and firing his thruster to stop their slow drift away from the station and head back in towards it. "Junker," he said, "give him a push, would you?"

"Ha," Rangi said, "very fun – hey!"

Iridius looked back and saw Junker jumping out of the jagged hole, holding onto Rangi's arm as she did. As she pulled him out with her, his feet stayed attached to the floor inside. "Release your boots, Rangi!" Junker yelled. He did, and Iridius watched them float out of the station, adjust their body positions and fire thrusters to head in his direction, Rangi bumping into the hull of the station as he tried to adjust his trajectory.

"I thought you were a pilot," Iridius said.

"Of ships, cap," Rangi said, his voice borderline hysterical, "not death-trap EVA suits."

Junker grabbed hold of Rangi to help steady him. "Come on, fly boy," she said. "I've got you."

Confident Junker could get Rangi back on the straight and level, or the straight and falling, as the case may be, Iridius turned his attention to his destination. Combat suits contained none of the advanced trajectory or flight controls of spacewalk suits, so he had nothing to judge his approach with, other than by eye. He didn't want to fire his thrusters for too long and slow too much because he didn't want to accidentally reverse his vector. He didn't want to come in too fast, either – because bouncing off the *Diesel Coast* and floating away into the forever of space was inadvisable. He pulled himself back in close to Latroz to keep their centre of mass from being too eccentric to his thrust vector, then fired his leg thrusters.

They lasted only a second before they began spluttering and then stopped. His HUD display had changed from low thruster fuel to empty. They were still headed for the *Diesel Coast* with way, way too much speed. Iridius's mind raced. He wished Latroz was awake – her thrusters could slow them – but there was no point wishing for unavailable options. If he spread himself parallel to the top of the *Diesel Coast* it was likely he'd bounce straight back, instead of skewing off at an angle that would send him spinning away into the wild black yonder. There was the risk he'd shatter his faceplate, though, and then he'd have the unpleasant experience of having his eyes snap-frozen. As he was weighing up between the quicker vacuum death or the long, slow death of suffocation, someone grabbed him.

"We got you, cap," Junker said.

Iridius saw Junker next to him, and Rangi on the other side, grabbing hold of Latroz. With all four of them linked together, Junker and Rangi twisted themselves around as best they could and fired their thrusters towards the *Diesel Coast*. They expelled all their fuel, cutting their velocity enough that when they struck the top of the hauler with a sudden metallic thud, they managed to get their mag-boots to stick as their knees buckled under them. Iridius and Rangi held tight to Latroz, whose boots were still carrying some fractured floor from *Gargarin*, and managed to keep her from bouncing off. Junker moved to the maintenance hatch in the roof of the *Diesel Coast* which, thankfully, responded to her access code. Condensing air sprayed out from around the hatch as it opened into the small airlock below, which meant the ship's life support was probably still functional.

The airlock for the maintenance hatch was small, only meant for one person at a time, so Junker went in first. Iridius and Rangi lowered Latroz through next, sealing the hatch behind her and letting Junker drag her out. Then Rangi entered the ship, and finally Iridius. He sealed the airlock, his suit confirming on the HUD that he'd entered an artificial gravity zone. He waited for the air to cycle and pressurise, and when he walked out of the airlock onto the mezzanine platform that ran around the perimeter of the cargo bay he saw that Junker had already removed her helmet and Latroz's. Iridius grabbed at his helmet's release, and when his suit confirmed the atmosphere of the ship was safe it unlocked.

"She seems alright," Junker said, "but I'm no expert, not even on humans and definitely not on Siruans."

Iridius nodded. "Help me carry her down."

The three of them moved her down to the floor of the cargo bay and lay her on her side. The crates that had housed the My PupPups were scattered around the space, broken open and empty. That confirmed his fear. He'd brought the Aegix back from Iota Persei and they – or it – had somehow managed to take up residence in those stupid dogs. He pushed his worries about that aside for now – they had a more pressing concern.

"Junker, you stay here with her. Rangi, let's get to the bridge."

Rangi hesitated for just a moment, looking at Latroz, then followed Iridius up the steps to the bridge. The lights automatically came on as they entered the space. Everything looked as it should. Systems seemed to be comfortably at idle and there were no nanomachines or robot dogs to be seen. Iridius sat in the captain's chair. It wasn't as comfortable as the one on the *Gallaway*, but it felt very much like home. Rangi sat at the helm and Iridius saw him running his hand along the edge of the console. Ben Rangi felt just as much at home here as he did.

"Start her up, Rangi," Iridius said, "and get us out of here."

"You got it."

Iridius watched as Rangi quickly ran the ship's start-up procedures. All systems seemed to respond as they should. The fusion drive hummed, but they weren't going anywhere. "Rangi?"

"Docking clamps won't let go," he said from the helm. "They're holding onto us."

"Full power," Iridius said.

"Captain, that will—"

"Fuck some shit up," Iridius finished for him. "I know. Just do it. Tear the clamps off."

Rangi smiled. "Aye aye, cap." He throttled the ship up to full power without completing the undocking and the sound of groaning metal filled the ship as it pulled against the docking clamps. The hum of the ship's fusion drive grew louder, and the metallic groan was punctuated by the crack of overstressed metal suddenly failing. The ship lurched, jolting to a stop again as the remaining docking clamps held strong. Iridius almost fell out of his chair, and Rangi splayed forward across the helm console. The engines fought to accelerate the ship away. There was another pop and lurch and then, with some grinding, tearing sounds, the final clamps gave up their defiant hold and the *Diesel Coast* flew away from *Gargarin Station.*

CHAPTER NINE_

"*Gallaway*, this is Captain Franklin, do you read?"

"Captain, it's Quinn, go ahead."

"We've disabled power to the station defences and are escaping right now. Bring the *Gallaway* around and unload some missiles into that thing."

"I assume that's you in the *Diesel Coast*?"

"Yeah, that's us, long story."

"Not really that long," Rangi said. "We got attacked by My PupPups and nanobugs and the shuttle's fucked."

"Yeah, actually, that's about it," Iridius said. "Start your attack run, *Gallaway*."

Through the *Diesel Coast*'s magnified view-screen Iridius watched the unnecessarily streamlined shape of the *FSC Gallaway* come blasting back, heading into a banked turn in another unnecessarily but admittedly impressive way, the fusion drive at full burn. A long stream of blue-white trailed out behind it.

"Captain," Quinn's voice came over the comms, "the *Diesel Coast*'s sensors might not be registering this, but an external bay door on *Gargarin Station* just opened and there are multiple small objects emerging."

"Weapons?" Iridius asked.

"I don't think so," Quinn replied. "They're sticking together, moving in a swarm, but they're bigger than the nanomachines. We're scanning and isolating a magnified view of them. Huh."

"Huh?" Iridius said. "Quinn, what do you mean, 'huh'? You don't say huh. You say 'interesting' or 'this is a bad idea'."

"They're dogs, captain," Quinn replied.

"My PupPups?"

"Yes, but it looks like they've been modified. They're moving under their own thrust."

"Oh good," Iridius said. "They've made space dogs, have they?"

"They're in pursuit of you," Quinn said, "accelerating fast."

"Roger," Iridius said. "We're being attacked by space-faring dogs. How much threat can they possibly be?"

"I'd advise a risk-averse approach, captain," Quinn said. "We really don't know anything about this enemy."

"I've got them on sensors now, cap," Rangi said from the helm. "We're accelerating as fast as we can but they're pushing some serious g's. Be on us in thirty seconds."

"Keep going," Iridius said. "Take us straight for the *Gallaway*. Quinn, we're coming right at you. We're going to try to keep ahead of them. We'll pass above you and once we do, you open up the defensive matrix railguns on the dogs. That should shred them."

Rangi turned the *Diesel Coast* directly into the path of the *Gallaway* and headed straight for it, playing a thousands-of-kilometres-per-second game of chicken.

"We're closing on the *Gallaway*. Twenty seconds out, but the dogs will catch us in ten. I can't outrun them, sorry cap."

"It's alright, Rangi," Iridius said, "it's not your fault. Our old faithful just isn't fast enough."

"The swarm is closing on us," Rangi reported. "Half a kilometre out... a hundred metres... impact."

Iridius waited, gripping the arms of his chair in readiness. He sat with his eyebrows raised and waited some more. "Impact, was it?"

"I think – yeah, they're going around us," Rangi said. Out the view-screen Iridius saw the swarm of dogs splitting around the *Diesel Coast* and reforming ahead of them, continuing on a vector straight at the *Gallaway*. They were close enough that Iridius could make out individual dogs. They were the same fluffy white robot dogs he'd seen on the space station, but they had definitely been modified. Their forelegs had been extended into appendages that ended in large metallic clawed feet. Their rear legs had been tucked back and were secured to a small propulsion device, something that must be immensely powerful for its size. Their heads had been modified too, the white fur peeled back to reveal a metallic skull, that much larger eyes had been wired into. So the Aegix had altered the robotic bodies it had taken up residence in, Iridius thought, but they were still just toy dogs. What could they possibly do against a ship like the *FSC Gallaway*?

In answer, Quinn came over the comms again. "We've got no shields!" The swarm of dogs was moments away from reaching the *Gallaway*.

"What?" Iridius asked.

"We're losing systems one by one. Shields are down. Railguns are down. Propulsion has ceased."

Iridius enhanced the image on the view-screen. The *Gallaway* was drifting in space, unable to manoeuvre or defend itself. The swarm of dogs hit the front of the ship, spreading themselves out and landing over the nose, right up past the bridge to the observation deck on top of the ship. They used their extended front legs to stop themselves from rebounding or sliding off.

"They're on the hull," Quinn said.

"I see them," Iridius replied, "but I'll go back to my previous point – even if they've interrupted your systems, what are those toy dogs going to do to the hull of a Universe-class ship?"

The toy dogs were happy to oblige him with an answer. They pointed their heads down to the hull, and after a moment the red of cutting lasers burst from their newly upgraded eyes. Two beams from each of the hundred or more dogs now attached to the hull of the *Gallaway*. All over the hull Iridius could see the white-yellow flare of laser burning through metal, insanely bright against the dark of space.

"We're picking up breach attempts all over the hull," Quinn said. "Can you see what they're doing, captain?"

"Fucking laser eyes," Iridius replied, partly in answer to Quinn's question and partly in disgusted surprise.

"Laser eyes?"

"Yes, they've got lasers coming out of their eyes," Iridius said. "Hold tight, *Gallaway*, we're coming to assist."

As the *Diesel Coast* continued towards the now-drifting *Gallaway* Iridius set his mind to tactical evaluation.

"They just ignored us," Iridius said, more to himself than anyone else. "Rangi, are our systems all online?"

"They seem to be, cap," Rangi answered.

"Either they don't think we're a threat or they're unable to access our systems like they have with the *Gallaway*."

"Maybe they know there's not much we can do."

"I don't know, if they could shut us down why wouldn't they have done so?"

Iridius glanced up at the view-screen and saw the My PupPups continuing to gouge into the hull of the *Gallaway*. The *Diesel Coast* had been their lifeboat in escaping *Gargarin Station*, but Iridius still felt that familiar tug of inferiority, knowing there was nothing the *Diesel Coast* could do to assist. The *Diesel Coast*'s defences, just the cursory railguns and chaff it was fitted with to help escape from pirates, would be no help. Even if they brought those guns to bear, they couldn't target the individual dogs, and their railgun ammunition would tear right into the *Gallaway*'s hull.

"Cap," Rangi said, interrupting Iridius's concentration – not that it mattered, because his brain was coming up empty – "we've picked up an incoming ship."

"Good or bad?"

"It's FSC," Rangi said, "a couple of minutes out. Signature confirmed. It's the *FSC El Nino*."

April. She was here to take command of his ship – er, her ship. The one that was currently being crawled all over by four-legged laser-eyed robots possessed by a synthetic demon. Iridius tapped at the controls on the arm of his chair, but before he could hail the *El Nino* they received a transmission.

"*Diesel Coast*, this is Captain Roc Mayhem of the *FSC El Nino*. The *FSC Gallaway* is not responding to communication, what's the situation?"

Such a cool name.

"Captain Mayhem, this is Captain Franklin."

"Who?"

Great. Just great.

"I'm currently in command of the *Gallaway*."

"You're on the wrong ship then, son."

Iridius resisted the urge to reply with 'yes, sir', reminding himself that he was a starship captain, too. "It's a long story," he eventually said. "The *Gallaway* is adrift, all systems down, and currently being attacked by a synthetic intelligence calling itself the Aegix that's taken control of toy dogs. You—"

"Toy dogs?" Mayhem interrupted.

"That's right. My PupPups."

"I bought my daughter one of those. I hate it."

"Well, you're going to hate these ones even more. You need to destroy *Gargarin Station* – that's where the Aegix seems to have based itself. Destroying *Gargarin* may destroy the Aegix."

There was no reply for a moment.

"My first officer has asked permission to speak to you."

Oh great. Iridius had been looking forward to this moment about as much as a barbed-wire wedgie.

"Iridius." April's voice came across the comms, carrying an impressive array of connotations: greeting, annoyance, blame, maybe even a hint of nervousness – or maybe Iridius was just hoping for that one.

"April," Iridius replied in a forced jovial tone, "it's good to hear from you. How are you? How's your mother?"

"She still hates you."

"Good, good to hear, great."

"What's the situation, Iridius?" April asked.

"And what have you done to Earth, son?" Captain Mayhem asked, jumping back into the conversation.

"Look, not my fault, that one," Iridius said, "and neither is the current situation with the *Gallaway* – not directly, anyway. You need to fire on *Gargarin Station* now, before you get within range of whatever jamming technology they've used on the *Gallaway*."

"That's an FSC station, Iridius."

"Not anymore, it's not."

"Given your current situation, I'm not sure you should be dispensing tactical advice, son."

"You're not my dad!" Iridius burst out in frustration. There was a moment of silence.

"What?" Captain Roc Mayhem answered.

"No," Iridius said, flustered, "I mean, stop calling me son!" He sighed. Roc Mayhem was something of an idol of his, and this wasn't how he'd wanted their first meeting to go. "April, can you still hear me?"

"Yes."

"Look, this situation is completely fucked but trust me, you need to take out the station. We managed to get aboard and cut the power to the defence matrix, and this is probably the only chance we'll have before this Aegix thing and its nanobots turn the whole galaxy into puddles of pink goo. Remember when we were at the Academy and we undertook the Sector Four simulation?"

"I remember."

"Well, this is like that, except Earth's been destroyed and the whole galaxy is next. Trust me, I'm right about this. Tell Captain Mayhem to unload everything you've got on that station and do it now. I'd say you're almost in range of their control, and once you are you'll be as adrift as the *Gallaway*."

There was another moment of silence. Iridius imagined April and Captain Mayhem conferring. He just hoped he'd convinced April, and that she, in turn, could convince her captain.

"Alright, son," Captain Mayhem said. "We're firing."

The *Diesel Coast*'s view-screen erupted with coloured blue boxes as the ship's sensors picked up the flurry of missiles leaving the *El Nino* and identified them as friendly fire. They streaked towards *Gargarin Station*. Ordinarily, the station's railgun defence network would have come online and shredded the incoming missiles with a rain of fire of its own, but because Iridius, Junker and Latroz had succeeded in cutting the power, the station's defences were offline.

"*Your hostile actions are foolish. The galaxy must be prepared for the coming of the Synth-Hastur. Our alteration is the only defence for sentient life.*" The Aegix came uninvited across the comms network again. "*The galaxy must be prepared.*"

"Wait," Iridius said, suddenly realising he may have made an incorrect assumption about the relationship between the Aegix and the Synth-Hastur they kept speaking about, "what do you mean, your alteration is the only defence for life?"

"*The galaxy must be prep—*" The strange voice ceased as the *El Nino*'s missiles made impact. The space station took successive hits and then, after a slight delay, it erupted. The circular segments exploded, breaking up in what looked almost like slow motion, until the smaller explosions eventually combined into a massive spreading fireball that quickly dissipated as it consumed what fuel it could in the vacuum of space. All that remained were several large chunks of the station spinning lazily away and a large cloud of tiny debris expanding much more rapidly – a massive twenty-third century engineering marvel torn to shreds in seconds. As Iridius sat watching the destruction on the view-screen, Quinn came back over comms.

"Systems are coming back online," she said. "Hull breach attempts appear to have ceased."

"Bring us to a stop, Rangi," Iridius said, then looking at the view-screen he switched back to comms. "The laser eyes have stopped," he told Quinn, "and the dogs have lost their grip on the hull. They're floating away. I think it worked."

"The Aegix don't appear to be a complete swarm intelligence. The nanobots and the My PupPups they were controlling act as a cohesive whole, but they must need some sort of central brain, like a hive needs a queen. That must have been on the station," Quinn said.

"Good," Captain Mayhem said. "Now, hold your position, *Gallaway*, your captain's coming over." Iridius nearly confirmed that he was indeed before he realised what Mayhem meant. April would be taking over command of his ship, and Iridius would be back in command of the forty-year-old *Diesel Coast*. "Captain Franklin," Captain Mayhem continued, "you'd better come dock your hauler with the *Gallaway* too. We'll need a debrief and a handover for Captain Idowu."

"On my way," Iridius said before switching off his comms and then adding, "You big jerk."

"Sorry?" Captain Mayhem said.

Well, Iridius thought he'd switched off his comms.

CHAPTER TEN

BEING TOO large to land in the shuttle bay, the *Diesel Coast* manoeuvred to dock externally at the *Gallaway*'s freight loading station. Iridius helped move Latroz to sick bay and then made his way to the bridge. He hoped April had arrived before him so he could make something of an entrance as he walked onto the bridge. As it turned out, his nonchalant swagger while waving off the inevitable praise was only witnessed by Quinn, Greg, Smith, Wesley, Herd and, unfortunately, football-headed Commander Mul. There was noticeably less praise than he'd expected, too.

"Damage report?" Iridius asked, trying not to sulk.

"Captain Franklin," Mul said, turning to address Iridius, "Lieutenant-Commander Quinn was just filling me in on exactly that. All systems are functional, including shields, and the hull sustained damage but no breach. I need a thorough understanding of the *Gallaway*'s current state of functionality in readiness to provide a full report to Captain Idowu when she assumes her rightful command."

"Oh, we're doing this again, are we, commander?" Iridius said. "Never mind that I just led a team to infiltrate an FSC space station controlled by synthetic enemy intelligence and managed to disable the station's defence so we could destroy it, stopping a threat to the galaxy that had already eradicated all life on Earth and left it a ball of molten lava."

Mul stared at him. "If the *El Nino* hadn't arrived when it did, this ship – your supposed command – would likely have been destroyed."

"Do you think the fact that I'm only acting captain means you're immune to insubordination? I never ordered you back to the bridge."

"We are way past the jurisdiction of a *shakedown*," Mul said, "and stating fact is not grounds for insubordination. The real captain is about to arrive, so I've taken liberties to ensure my ship is ready for my captain."

Iridius clenched his teeth. In all the deep dark vacuum there was nobody who could grind his gears like this grey bastard. He was ready to jam his fingers into the Zeta Reticulan's nostrils and tiny mouth and fling him into the sun like a big grey bowling ball, but before he could, the elevator door opened.

April Idowu strode out onto the bridge of the *FSC Gallaway* and Iridius found himself with two completely opposing thoughts in his mind at once: *wow*, she looks so good, and *urgh*, she looks so good.

April walked onto the bridge with the same grace she'd always possessed. She was, and always had been, a force that took over a room. It wasn't just because she was tall, dark and had the kind of figure that looked good in an FSC uniform, it was also because she had an air of confidence about her. She was born to lead – she had the starship captain x-factor. In truth, this was very likely what had drawn Iridius to her when they'd first met; the same unshakeable confidence that had eventually irritated him so much. Her hair, as black as the space she'd made it her life's goal to explore, was shorter than Iridius remembered, and held back in a neat ponytail, pinned tightly at the sides.

She'd always had the potential, but now she looked command-ready.

"Captain Idowu, welcome aboard the *Gallaway*." Commander Mul addressed April with an air of creepy reverence. He even added a small bow. If he hadn't known any better, Iridius would have thought Commander Mul was just a little bit smitten.

"Thank you, you must be Commander Mul. I'm proud to have such an accomplished officer as my second-in-command."

"You're too kind," Commander Mul said. "I'm very much looking forward to serving under you."

Iridius had to force himself not to repeat the commander's words in a snide, mock impersonation like a six-year-old.

April looked around the bridge, greeting the crew by name and even throwing in some personal anecdotes, like asking after their children, because of course she'd done her research about each and every member of her crew. This casual, personalised entrance suddenly seemed much more impressive than Iridius's swaggering action-hero attempt. April nodded a greeting to the crew of the *Diesel Coast,* too. She knew Lieutenant-Commander Quinn but had never met the others, so gave them a much more cursory greeting. *See,* Iridius thought, *not so easy to seem like the perfect captain when you're just dropped in it.* April saved her final greeting for Iridius. Of course she left him until last. She'd wanted him to stew in the drawn-out moments prior to the dressing down she was sure to give him. Why did it constantly seem that Iridius was outranked by the other captains of Federation Space Command? Hell, even commanders like Mul thought they were higher up the food chain. April turned to him.

"Iridius," she said, with much more joy than Iridius had expected, "it's really good to see you. You look great." She opened her arms wide and embraced him. He instinctively hugged her back, trying not to think about the bumps and curves of her body as they pressed into him. He was confused, caught off-guard by the unexpected affection.

"You look great, too," he said. "Congratulations on your promotion."

"Thank you," she said as she pulled away. She looked at Commander Mul. "Captain Franklin is one of my dearest friends from the Academy, Commander Mul. I'm sure you've enjoyed your brief time aboard with him. It certainly seems to have been dramatic."

"Yes, captain," Mul said, "very dramatic."

"Where's Lieutenant Latroz?" April asked, looking around the bridge.

"Sick bay," Iridius said. "She's recovering from an injury sustained during our infiltration of *Gargarin Station*. Doctor Paine assures me she'll be fine – apparently Siruans enter a kind of self-imposed coma when injured, a trance state that aids healing. She should be back on her feet in a couple of hours."

"I hope so," April said. "I asked for her as my tactical officer specifically."

"She's tough," Iridius said, trying to ignore the feeling that April was berating him for breaking one of her toys. "She'll be fine."

The bridge door opened again and Captain Roc Mayhem strode onto the deck of the *Gallaway,* his chest puffed forward in a bulging display of power that would make the largest silverback gorilla proud. Silverbacks were now extinct, Iridius realised – after all the conservation work that had been done, they'd been blasted into non-existence because of a single bomb designed by the very species who'd been working to save them.

Mayhem looked around, taking in the sight of the sleek new bridge but giving away nothing. He was a large man, broad across... well, everything you'd expect to be broad on a hero of the

Federation. "You there," he said, pointing to Quinn, "you've been acting XO?"

"Aye, sir," Quinn replied.

"How'd the *Gallaway* fare during the attack? Have you prepared a full damage report?" He turned to look out the viewscreen, his eyes going distant. "Whatever happened to Earth, I have a feeling we're going to need every ship we've got."

"It's fine, we're fine," Iridius cut in before Quinn could respond. "Everything's fine." How many goddamn people wanted to act like captain of this ship? And why was everyone staring at Captain Mayhem like his testosterone-fuelled bridge entrance was so much more impressive than the one Iridius had tried just minutes ago? "All systems are fully functional, including shields, and the hull sustained minor damage but no breaches. Most importantly, which no one seems to have acknowledged, the existential threat to the galaxy has been neutralised."

"Captain Frantling, is it?" Mayhem asked. "Captain Idowu has told me a lot about you."

"Obviously not my actual name," Iridius said.

Captain Mayhem stared at him.

"It's Franklin," Iridius clarified. "Iridius Franklin."

"Sure," Captain Mayhem said. "Well, Franklin, as I was saying, Captain Idowu informed me that you were classmates at the Academy."

"We were lovers, actually," Iridius said, stupidly resorting to a display of sexual prowess that might have worked for Neanderthal Man. Iridius's far more civilised and supposedly advanced twenty-third century brain immediately looked at itself in disgust. *Lovers? What the actual fuck?*

"Yes," Mayhem said, "she mentioned you were in a relationship." The implied *no idea why* was plenty obvious to everyone. "I was referring to the fact that, despite your current command,"

Iridius guessed he wasn't referring to the Universe II-class exploration vessel but rather the rust-bucket currently docked to the side of it, "you seem like agood captain, and you made the right decision in a high-pressure situation. I respect that. That's why I agreed to follow your lead in destroying the station. Thing is, your orders were to wait for our arrival before you did anything."

"We didn't expect you so quickly. We thought you were in Tau Ceti. I considered it within the best interests of the galaxy to take action."

"I can see you like to take action, but you put the *Gallaway* and its crew in danger," Captain Mayhem said.

"Like you've never done that, Mayhem," Iridius shot back. "I've read up on some of your exploits. You flew your ship into an inverted black hole. You took on three Necroblaise death ships with the *El Nino*. You've led a team into the mouth of a planet-sized Scargalarg pus-dragon."

"The key word in each of those cases, son, is that it was *my* ship and *my* crew. The *Gallaway* wasn't yours to do that with. You and your crew were just the shakedowners."

"Roc," April said, "I know Iridius was just trying to do what he thought was right. Everything worked out."

"Apart from Earth being gone," Ensign Rangi interjected, as he was often prone to do.

"Well, yes, apart from that, ensign." April turned to Iridius. "Why don't you show me to the captain's cabin, Iridius? You can fill me in on how the ship has performed, and anything else I need to know on the way."

Iridius nodded and gestured for April to lead the way back to the elevator.

Iridius waited for the door to close. He let the moment of awkwardness at them being alone pass before he turned to her and said, "Look, April, thanks for sticking up for me back there. I do appreciate it but—"

April took that same moment to press the elevator stop button and turn to him. "What the hell have you been doing with my ship, Iridius?"

Iridius was a little taken aback by the sudden change in demeanour, but not for long. "Oh, here we go, I should have known better than to think judgemental old April Idowu wouldn't come out in force. As usual I'm still not up to your high standards of excellence, I see."

"No, as usual you were being reckless."

"Recklessly saving the galaxy."

"Oh, please. First of all, you don't even know the entire galaxy was at risk. Second, I meant everything I said to Captain Mayhem about believing you and trusting your instincts, but you should never have put the *Gallaway* or the *El Nino* in that position. You should have done what you were ordered to do and waited."

"I've already told you, I needed to act."

"No!" April's powerful voice almost rattled the elevator around them. "You *wanted* to act! You wanted it to be the only option so you could play the hero. Want and need are two different things, Iridius. This isn't some simulation at the Academy – this is real. Earth has been attacked, FSC headquarters destroyed and you decided to single-handedly attack an unknown enemy even though reinforcements were on their way. That is not being an FSC captain. That's being a reckless fool."

"It's alright for you," Iridius said, "you've got the command you always wanted. No one is going to give me that opportunity. I'm stuck flying a hauler. How am I supposed to save the galaxy in that? It's lucky I had the *Gallaway* and its stealth shuttle."

"You know what? I was happy when I heard you'd been given the *Gallaway* for shakedown. I thought Admiral Merritt had selected you because you'd changed."

"No," Iridius said, "she selected me because I haven't

changed. I've still got whatever curse causes ships to go stupid around me."

April shook her head and rolled her eyes at Iridius. "You see, that's exactly what I'm talking about. I thought you must have been taking responsibility, doing what you had to do to show you're not the same as you were at the Academy. But you are the same, aren't you? Still blaming everything and everyone but yourself."

"Oh, gronking black of space, don't bang on with that again," Iridius moaned.

"It's true, Iridius. I bang on about it because you can't get it through your thick skull. You blame not having the right ship, or not having the right opportunity – you always blame everything but yourself for your failures. The truth is, you had an opportunity most people would kill for and you wasted it because you were a lazy, often drunk, unambitious waste of talent. Nobody will give you your dream command on a platter – you have to earn it. You're not cursed. Curses aren't real. And most importantly, the starship doesn't make the captain – it's the other way around. Blaming everything else doesn't go any way towards fixing the problem."

"I suppose Roc Mayhem Space Boy Scout told you that, did he?"

"No, actually he didn't, but what he tried to tell you *was* true. Being a captain is about putting your ship and crew first, knowing when to take risks and when not to run your crew or ship into danger for the hell of it because you think it's your only chance at making a name for yourself."

Iridius stared at April. He felt that same sudden rush of attraction he'd always felt when she got angry. His mind ran off down the back streets of his memory towards all those nights of make-up sex after fights just like this one. Damn, they'd been good together. But they'd also been terrible together. Iridius pulled himself back to the present and shut down April's argument with the absolute genius of, "Yeah, well, whatever."

April shook her head and rolled her eyes again. She reached out and hit the button to send the elevator continuing on its way. "My god, I can't believe I was looking forward to seeing you. I really hoped you'd be a little more mature, but you're still just a child."

"You were looking forward to seeing me?" Iridius asked.

The elevator door slid open and April walked out. "I *was* looking forward to seeing you," she said without looking back. "Past tense."

"But still," Iridius said, "you were looking forward to seeing me. That's what you said. It wasn't that far in the past. Have you *missed* me, April?" He knew he was pushing it but, well, he was Iridius Franklin. Pushing it was what he did.

April ignored him, leading the way to the captain's cabin, obviously thoroughly familiar with the layout of the ship despite the fact that she'd never been aboard. Iridius was sure she would have explored every inch of the ship in virtual reality when she found out it would be her first command. When they reached the captain's cabin April stepped up to the door and pressed the door panel. Nothing happened.

"It'll still be coded for me," Iridius said. "You haven't officially taken command yet."

"Yeah," April said, "I suppose that's true. We can do it on the console in the cabin. Can you let us in?"

"Sure."

Iridius touched the door panel. The computer instantly scanned a large amount of biometric data – more than was comfortable, really – and the door slid open. The cabin was neat, which was lucky considering how he usually left his cabin.

The computer pinged.

Oh shit.

"Hello captain, your standing news search for—"

"Computer, stop! Cancel!"

"—Commander April Idowu has generated... okay, cancelling."

Iridius smiled, a broad, forced smile, which covered the situation about as well as painting a smiley face on a bomb. He laughed. "I have no idea what that was all about. What a crazy coincidence."

April slowly turned to look at him. Very slowly. Painfully slowly. "Maybe it's you who's been missing me, Iridius."

"No," he scoffed. "I was just... you know... I had it searching for you because... because I needed to know when you were coming to take over command. Yeah, that's it."

"Right," April said. "Well, I'm here now so I guess we'd better make the changeover official."

"Yeah, I guess we'd better. So, how do we set it up for co-captaincy?"

April looked at him. "I don't think there is a co-captaincy setting on a starship, Iridius."

"What? Wait a second, you don't want to be a co-captain?"

"Iridius, don't make this into a thing."

"Fine. I was just kidding."

"No," April said, "you weren't. Not really. It'll be easier if you just transfer command."

Iridius knew she was right. If he hesitated he'd find it even harder. He used secure biometric authorisation to navigate to the captain-only menu, where a number of high-level ship command options were available. He hit the buttons for transfer of command.

"Captain Iridius B. Franklin, service number 8537718, do you wish to transfer official command and all associated rights and responsibilities to Captain April H. Idowu, service number

8537678? This includes crew restructure as previously authorised."

"Yes," Iridius said. "Transfer the command."

"Transfer confirmed. Congratulations, Captain Idowu."

April smiled at him. Despite everything, it was a friendly smile of consolation. She knew this was hard on him. "So, now that's done," April said, looking at him with an intensity that both thrilled and terrified him, "why *did* you have a standing news search for me?"

Damn. He supposed it was too good to be true to think she'd just let that go.

Red Alert. Red Alert.

"Captain," Quinn said over the comms, "or captains, I suppose, we need you on the bridge immediately."

"Oh, thank the black," Iridius said as he took off out of the cabin, away from any discussion of feelings.

CHAPTER ELEVEN

"Captain," Commander Mul said as Iridius and April stepped onto the bridge.

Both Iridius and April simultaneously said, "What's going on?"

Iridius turned to look at her. "Sorry," he said, gesturing for her to continue. "Old habits."

She smiled the same consolatory smile, which now seemed a little too pitying for Iridius's liking, and made her way to the captain's chair, which Commander Mul vacated without any hesitation. "Status?"

"There's been a launch from Lunar Base Armstrong," Commander Mul said. "Unmanned probe, no known design or signature."

"Is it coming for us?"

"No, captain."

Red Alert. Red Alert.

"Switch that off," April said, and Commander Mul obliged, silencing the alarm and returning the lights around the bridge to their normal soothing hue. "What's its trajectory?"

"It's on a heading away from Earth, captain. Bearing two seven three attitude seventeen relative."

"You said everyone on the lunar bases was dead," April said, turning to where Iridius stood at the back of the bridge.

"They are."

"Who launched that then?"

"Captain, if I may?" Quinn asked.

Iridius said, "Go ahead" at precisely the same moment April said, "Yes?" April shot him a quick look.

"Well, to be fair, that was my XO this time," Iridius said.

"What are you thinking, Quinn?" April said.

"I'm thinking it's the Aegix," Quinn said. "It managed to shut off all the life support systems on the lunar base remotely, and it managed to access the *Gallaway*'s system remotely. It can likely activate a launch, too."

"Except the Aegix has been blown into teeny tiny pieces," Iridius said. "Besides, where did the probe come from if they're unrecognised?"

"Printers," Commander Mul interjected. "Armstrong has a large manufacturing facility. They probably built a probe."

"Ah shit," Iridius said. "It's an escape pod, isn't it?"

Quinn nodded. "That would be my hypothesis too. The Aegix doesn't seem to be a true swarm intelligence. It refers to its location and seems to need a central node that contains the equivalent of its consciousness. But it does seem able to transfer that central consciousness, just as it transferred itself onto the My PupPups the *Diesel Coast* brought back from Iota Persei and then to the systems of *Gargarin Station* and now, presumably, into that probe."

"I'm sorry," April said, "did you say the *Diesel Coast* brought this thing back? Just so I'm clear here, the artificial intelligence that destroyed Earth hitched a ride on your ship, Iridius?"

Iridius grimaced. "I was going to bring that up." He looked at Quinn. "I just thought we'd deal with the situation at hand first."

"This is your fault?" April stared at him, incredulous.

"Not really. It just happened to be my ship that was delivering artificially intelligent toy dogs to Iota Persei E – toy dogs the Aegix used to piggyback a ride to Earth."

"And they must have used the *Diesel Coast* to get up to *Gargarin*, too," Ensign Rangi said. "That's why it was docked there."

"Yes, thank you, ensign," Iridius said. "As quick on the uptake as ever."

"Another probe launched from Armstrong base," Commander Mul said. "And another, and another."

"I thought you said it needs a central consciousness," Iridius said.

"I believe it does," Quinn said, "but it's still an AI so it's possibly copying itself."

"Mul," April said, "get on tactical. Destroy those probes."

"Yes, captain."

Commander Mul began giving orders to Wesley to bring them into a better position for a targeting solution on the probes.

As the *Gallaway* began to give chase and fire missiles after the probes, Captain Mayhem spoke into his personal communicator. "*El Nino*," he said, "this is Mayhem. Lee, I want you to destroy the moon."

"Sir?" the surprised reply came from Lieutenant Commander Lee, Mayhem's new XO now that April had taken command of the *Gallaway*.

"I'm providing captain's authority for you to use the planet-slagger. Target Armstrong Base for the initial impact," Mayhem said. "And Lee, don't worry, there's no one left to look up at the night sky and miss it."

"Aye, sir."

Roc Mayhem turned to the bridge. "No point taking out these probes if they just keep making more."

April nodded.

"The *El Nino* has a planet-slagger?" Iridius said.

"All Universe-class ships do, son," Mayhem replied.

"Wait, so the *Gallaway* has one and I didn't even know?"

"Alpha Security—" Mul started.

"Yeah, yeah," Iridius cut him off. "Alpha Security Status, I know."

What bothered Iridius most about this wasn't that this ship was carrying a weapon of mass destruction he hadn't known about, but rather the fact that if a Franklinism like what had occurred with the missiles had happened to that bomb, they could have done some serious damage.

"The remaining probes are slowing," Quinn said. "Spooling up for FTL."

"Hit them now!" April called to Mul.

The *Gallaway*'s missiles streamed out after those probes that hadn't already been destroyed. As the probes slowed to engage their BAMF drives – a major disadvantage of the BAMF system was having to be stationary to activate it – the missiles caught up, hitting the probes and bursting them into fragments in a short-lived explosion of yellow-white. The final probe, the one that had first launched from Armstrong Base, came to a stop. Just as it activated its BAMF drive the *Gallaway*'s missile struck. The probe vanished. Whether it had jumped away into another universe or had been vaporised was not clear.

At the same time there was a flash of light as the planet-slagger launched from the *FSC El Nino* hit the surface of the moon, directly in the centre of Armstrong Base. Once the historic site of man's first moon landing where the Apollo 11 lander was still kept on display in a glass dome, it was now the impact site of a quantum fission reaction. Humanity had once stared up at the moon and strived to reach it. Now, it had annihilated it. Because the moon had virtually no atmosphere, the impact of the planet-slagger wasn't quite as impressive as it would have been on Earth, but still, it did the job. Armstrong Base was gone in less than a second, and the surface of the moon turned from the familiar white-grey rock into something that looked like bubbling red jelly, with the reaction moving out at incredible speed. The entire lunar surface was molten within seconds.

"Fuuuuuck," Ensign Rangi said, running the vowel out for several seconds, "that's a serious weapon."

Iridius couldn't help but agree.

"That last probe," April said to Commander Mul, "did we get it?"

"Sensors registered both a missile hit and a BAMF activation," Mul said. "I can't confirm, but it was likely hit."

"It better have been hit," Iridius said, "otherwise it's off to turn more people into pink goop, and we have no idea where."

"All we can do is warn all systems to watch for an incoming probe and destroy it immediately," April said. She turned to Captain Mayhem. "Roc, you'd better head back to the *El Nino*. I think we should make for Tau Ceti."

"No," Iridius said. All eyes on the bridge turned to look at him. He would have felt embarrassed if he wasn't so used to people looking at him with suspicion or exasperation. "Look, if I was a synthetic intelligence that could replicate itself I'd always leave a backup behind. It's likely the Aegix left a copy of itself on Iota Persei E when it hitched a ride on the *Coast*. If the *Gallaway* has a planet-slagger, you should go to Iota Persei and use it. If that's the last location housing an Aegix intelligence, it needs to be slagged."

April looked from Iridius to Roc Mayhem. The captain of the *El Nino* nodded. "You're probably right, son. I'll take a shuttle back to the *El Nino*. Plot a BAMF course for Iota Persei. We'll pay it a visit on the way back."

"There's a risk we'll experience the same interference from the Aegix as we already have," Quinn said. "The ship was completely vulnerable."

Iridius was about to comment on her tendency to raise the worst-case scenario but he stopped himself. "There's a chance," he said. "But we had no issues until we landed there." He looked at April. "If you BAMF in and immediately fire the planet-slagger it should be fine."

"Alright," April said. "Ensign Wesley, plot a course for Iota Persei." She turned and nodded to Roc Mayhem, who nodded in return and then exited the bridge.

"Okay then," Iridius said, "good luck, April."

"Where do you think you're going?" she asked.

"Uh, back to the *Diesel Coast*. This isn't my ship anymore."

"We'll piggyback the *Diesel Coast* with us. You stay here. You're the only one who's actually got any experience with the Aegix. I might need you." Then, as if to ensure those last words weren't left hanging in the air, she quickly added, "Plus, FSC scientists will want to examine the *Diesel Coast* so we'd better keep it quarantined."

"Right," Iridius said. He looked at Greg, Rangi and Quinn. "Looks like we're on loan to the *Gallaway* for a little longer. I guess that means I'm co-captain of the *Gallaway* after all."

"No," April said. "You're really not."

The elevator door hissed open and Latroz and Junker stepped out. "Reporting for return to duty, captain," Latroz said to Iridius.

"Good to see you back on your feet, Latroz," Iridius said, "but I'm not the captain of the *Gallaway* anymore. Captain Idowu has taken over."

"Ah," Lieutenant Latroz said, "that's a shame, I enjoyed your desire to take the fight to the enemy."

"Ha, see?" Iridius said. "I knew someone would be happy with that."

"Welcome back to the bridge, lieutenant," April said. "You're fully recovered?"

"Yes, captain," Latroz said.

"Good. Take your station, we're heading for Iota Persei to hopefully put an end to this."

––––––––

The *FSC Gallaway* dropped out of FTL with a lot more dignity than the *Diesel Coast*. Iridius still couldn't work out why that was, but the whole thing just seemed smoother. He didn't even feel the usual pang of post-lightspeed nausea. Even as the ship's shields caught the BAMF wave and were sparkling and fading away, April jumped straight into action.

"Latroz, get our shields recharging and prepare to launch the planet-slagger. Wesley, high fusion speed towards Iota Persei E. We want a fly-by, not an orbital insertion. Mul, I want to know everything happening on that planet. Tell me if so much as a bug moves near the mining colony."

As much as Iridius had hated it when she'd directed that type of authoritative tone towards him, he had to admit that seeing her take charge as captain of a starship was pretty damn sexy. Iridius saw on the view-screen that the *El Nino* had taken up position behind them off their starboard side – standard FSC two-ship formation.

"Approaching planet-slagger range on Iota Persei E in fifteen seconds, captain," Lieutenant Latroz said. "The weapon requires captain authority to fire."

April tapped at the arm of the captain's chair. "Captain's authorisation provided. Prepare to fire."

"Captain," Commander Mul called from the XO's station, "there's something on the far side of the planet. It's a ship."

"We've got the most advanced ship in the fleet. Why didn't we see it?"

"It was using a methane electrical storm to mask itself. It's moving now though, burning out of an orbital trajectory to close with us. Should be coming into view now."

"On screen then," April said.

The view-screen focused and magnified. Coming around the magnified curvature of the planet was a spaceship. At least, it was a spaceship in the sense that it was in space.

"What *is* that?" April asked, leaning forward in her captain's chair.

"That," Ensign Rangi said, "is a fucking giant My PupPup toy dog."

"Don't know if I'd call that a toy," Ensign Wesley said.

"Well, no," Quinn said, "but it seems like they've used the image of the My PupPup dog as the basis for a starship. It's like the form of the toy dogs has been imprinted on them."

The ship that broke orbit around Iota Persei E to engage the *Gallaway* was the same shape as the West Highland White Terrier used as a model by the My PupPup manufacturers. Its small legs were tucked up under its body. Its head, complete with pointed ears standing up to house sensor arrays and a mouth hanging open with a lolling tongue, stayed fixed on the position of the *Gallaway* as if it was staring at it. The ship was finished with a matte white over metal – at least they hadn't decided to cover it in fluffy white fur. Then again, maybe that would have been better, because this looked like one of those hairless sphinx cats Iridius's Aunt Wallace had kept that always freaked him out as a child.

"Within range for planet-slagger launch," Latroz reported, tearing everyone's attention away from the frankly ridiculous sight of the three hundred-metre-long metal dog flying towards them.

"Fire," April ordered.

The planet-slagger launched from one of the *Gallaway*'s missile tubes and hurtled towards Iota Persei E. The dog-ship reacted immediately, clearly expecting the attack. Its mouth opened and released a torrent of high-velocity metal, a railgun barrage that Iridius initially thought was targeted at the planet-slagger, until Latroz barked, "Incoming!"

"Shield status?" April queried.

"Online but at twenty per cent. They'll hold for one volley."

"Turn us away," April called to the helm.

The shields lit up the view-screen as railgun rounds began impacting.

"Ten per cent," Latroz called as the *Gallaway* turned away from Iota Persei E. The barrage continued. "Five per cent." The light show of high-velocity metal hitting a gravomagnetically acti-vated quantum chromodynamics shield was as impressive as always. The rings of colour, mostly blue but other colours too, depending on the velocity of the rounds and the wavelength of light released, would be easy to consider beautiful if it wasn't a sign of imminent death. "Shields down," Latroz called. The last of the railgun rounds struck the hull of the ship and the bridge rocked. "Damage to decks six, seven, twelve and eighteen. Hull breaches on six and twelve. Damage to secondary med-bay, lower galley and crew quarters. There's no one down there. I'm sealing and venting. The Aegix ship is manoeuvring for another barrage."

"Planet-slagger?" April asked.

"Impact in five."

The planet-slagger cruised through the methane atmosphere

of Iota Persei E. The barrage of railgun fire exited the mouth of the dog-ship on target to impact the now-shieldless *Gallaway*.

"The *El Nino* is breaking formation," Commander Mul said. "They're moving into the railgun fire."

On the view-screen Iridius saw that Mul was right. The *El Nino*, its own sensors able to monitor the *Gallaway*'s systems and recognise how vulnerable she was, had broken formation and was flying across the bow of the *Gallaway*, banking to display the underside of its hull to the railgun fire coming from the dog-ship.

"Planet-slagger impact," Latroz said.

On the other side of the *El Nino* Iridius saw Iota Persei E burst into flames. Unlike the moon, Iota Persei E did have an atmosphere, and being an atmosphere comprised primarily of methane, it was even more flammable than that of Earth. The bubbling of the molten remains of the planet's rocky surface was only just visible through the eruption of a planet-wide orange-blue methane flame – basically, an unimaginably large lit fart.

Flashes of impact could be seen all over its shields as the *El Nino* took the railgun fire intended for the *Gallaway*.

"*El Nino*'s shields are down," Commander Mul called out as he monitored Roc Mayhem's ship. "They're taking damage and the Aegix ship is preparing another barrage." The *El Nino* wasn't moving. It held its position, shielding the *Gallaway* from incoming fire.

"Ensign Herd," April said, "give me a channel to the *El Nino*."

"Go ahead, captain."

"Roc," April said, "get out of there. Don't do this."

"April, as much as I appreciate the assumption that we're sacrificing ourselves to save you," Roc Mayhem said across the comms channel, "we were just trying to buy time for your shields to recharge so we could both fall back. Problem is, we can't actually do that. Our systems are shutting down. Propulsion is offline."

"The Aegix," Quinn said, "same as what happened to us."

"Bring us around in front of the *Nino*, Wesley," April ordered. "Do it now!"

Ensign Wesley worked the controls. For a starship that weighed almost two and a half million metric tonnes, the *FSC Gallaway* was quite agile. Unfortunately, it was not agile enough to stop its momentum and turn back to cover the *El Nino* in time. Though Ensign Wesley tried his utmost to bring the ship to bear, it was impossible – even Ensign Rangi wouldn't have been able to bend the laws of physics, no matter his skill as a pilot.

The next barrage from the Aegix dog-ship hit the *El Nino* and, with no shields to protect it, the railgun rounds tore through the ship. Iridius watched as rounds of hyper-velocity metal pierced from the bottom and punched out the top of the *FSC El Nino*. The hundreds of railgun rounds broke the back of the Universe-class ship, and flares of yellow-orange burst out as the ship's internal atmosphere exploded through ever-widening holes in the hull. Like a destructive join-the-dots puzzle, the holes in the *El Nino* quickly linked together, and any hope that the ship or its crew could survive was lost. Until the construction of the *Gallaway*, the *El Nino* had been the pride of the FSC fleet. Now they watched in silence as it broke apart. April closed her eyes. The ship she had served on until only hours before, the crew she had served with, the captain she had served under, all lost. It happened slowly in the zero-g of space – small fragments spun off quickly, but the larger chunks of the ship separated and spread out like wood drifting apart on still water.

Iridius turned his attention to April. She'd opened her eyes again, but seemed transfixed by the sight on the view-screen, as if by staring at the vision of the disintegrating ship she might be able to uncover the trick, find the glitch that would reveal what she saw to be a lie. Iridius was far more concerned with the enemy ship, which had turned its attention back to them. He resisted the urge to say anything – he wasn't the captain anymore, and despite his attempts, his captaining of the *Gallaway* hadn't been as well received as he'd hoped. Still, April should be doing something. He cast his eye over the rest of the bridge crew. They were watching the destroyed *El Nino* and the approaching Aegix ship, and were glancing at April, waiting for her orders. Iridius knew it wasn't his place to command the crew, but the destruction of the *El Nino* seemed to have shaken April – not the best reaction for the captain of a starship facing a giant spacefaring dog controlled by a synthetic intelligence.

"April," Iridius prodded, as gently as he could.

She looked at him. The screens on the consoles around the bridge flickered ever so slightly. The Aegix was attempting to get into their systems. Iridius didn't know how he knew, but he could sense it. They were about to be immobilised the same as before, the same as the *El Nino*.

"April," Iridius nudged her again, "we need to act now."

She nodded, then turned back to continue watching the view-screen.

"Captain Idowu," Commander Mul said, "Captain Franklin is correct. The Aegix vessel is moving to engage us now."

Iridius watched April but she still didn't react. "April!" Iridius dropped the gentle approach and shouted at her. "Focus or I'm taking command. Don't make it like that exercise with the *Tolstoy*."

"Right," April said, finally shaken free from the shock of seeing the *El Nino* destroyed. "Ensign Wesley, bring us around, bearing zero nine zero and begin evasive action at full speed."

As the *Gallaway* turned and began evasive manoeuvres as ordered, April finally came to life. "Latroz, give me some intelligence on this ship. Have they got shields? Any weapons other than those railguns?"

"They've got some sort of energy shield that our systems can't classify. Can't get a lock on the frequency. They only seem to be carrying those railguns. Tactically, it's unlikely they need missiles if they're able to incapacitate enemy ships like we've seen them do. Propulsion seems low capacity; we've got a far superior acceleration profile. Normally I'd suggest that means we have an advantage, but after seeing what they just did to the *El Nino* my tactical advice is, unfortunately, to disengage and retreat."

"We can't do that," Iridius said. "Every sentient being in the galaxy is at risk. If we retreat, this ship could BAMF anywhere in the galaxy – maybe even straight to Tau Ceti." He looked at Mul. "Or Zeta Reticula." He turned to Latroz. "Or Sirius." Then back to April. "We can't let any other planets turn out like Earth."

"Keep on our course, Wesley," April said, "and plot a BAMF to Alpha Centauri B. I'm sorry, Iridius. I know you blame yourself for bringing the Aegix to Earth but I won't put my ship in a battle we can't win."

"It's not about blaming myself." It kind of was. "It's about saving the galaxy." Mostly because it was his fault the galaxy needed saving in the first place. "We've got the *Gallaway,* the most advanced ship in the FSC fleet. If we don't stop them, who will?"

April stared at him. "We need the whole FSC fleet. We can't do this on our own."

"They could go anywhere."

"I'm sorry, Iridius," April said again, and he knew that her decision had been made. Those were the same words she'd said when she'd broken off their relationship for the last time.

April, please, I know we can work it out.

I'm sorry, Iridius.

Iridius would have broken off their relationship anyway. He would have. It's not like she broke his heart or anything.

"April, if we BAMF out of here we won't know where they've gone. People are—"

"Our shields are down." Latroz spoke over the top of Iridius, which would have annoyed him had she not essentially been saying they were about to die.

"Get us out of here, Wesley!" April said.

"We're pulling away," Latroz said, "but if we stop to BAMF they'll be within range to fire on us."

Once the FSC *Gallaway* had shot away from Iota Persei E and put some distance between themselves and the giant space-dog, Latroz called out, "Shields coming back online."

"Good, full power to aft shields. Keep going, Wesley," April said. "When it looks like they've reached max acceleration I want you to drop our acceleration very slowly – don't go lower than ninety per cent of theirs. Draw them in closer. Keep just far enough out that railgun fire won't be effective."

"Yes, captain," Wesley said. He had the tone of someone obeying an order that seemed likely to get him killed.

"The exercise with the *Tolstoy*," Iridius said, more statement than question.

April nodded. "Thanks."

Iridius shrugged. "One of my finer moments. Happy for you to run with it, and it does seem like you're running."

April ignored the barb. "Latroz, can you estimate the lethal range of their railgun?"

"Taking into account round spread and time to evade is complex, but I'd suggest instant kill range for us is less than thirty kilometres, and significant chance of ship loss below seventy-five kilometres."

"Alright, Wesley," April said, "draw them in but keep us at around one hundred kilometres out, minimum. Quinn, from your experience at what distance can the Aegix affect a ship's systems?"

"Based on the limited sample set of encounters we've had, we've been closer to some element of the Aegix swarm than that each time."

"Alright," April said. "We'll just have to hope that one hundred kilometres is enough range that they can't get into our systems and we can surprise them quick enough."

The bridge fell quiet as the crew executed their orders. Other than Latroz, Wesley or Mul providing situational updates there was little conversation, but there was a buzz in the air. The crew all knew the situation they faced and the bridge was filled with that nervous energy all sentient beings seemed to give off in a flight or fight predicament. The air was a soup of high-strung emotion.

"I'm matching their velocity to hold our distance at one hundred kilometres," Wesley said.

"The galaxy must be prepared. Aggression against the Aegix shall not be tolerated. The galaxy must be prepared."

"It might just be my imagination," Iridius said, "but it sounds pissed."

"We're probably holding the right range then," April said. "It knows its weapons are ineffective from there and it can't catch us."

"Running is futile. We do not tire. We will chase you and eventually you will succumb. The galaxy must be prepared."

"Listen, Fido," Iridius said, "dogs used to chase stuff on Earth too, and you know what? Most of the time it ended with the dog getting flattened by a car." Iridius bent down and whispered into April's ear, ignoring the smell of flowers and coconut and admonishing his hormones to choose a better time and place. "It can hear us. Don't give the order out loud. I'll take the helm."

She turned to look at him, their faces close, their eyes meeting. She nodded. "Okay," she said to the bridge, "we could be running for a while. I need you to stay fresh. Wesley, you're relieved from the helm. Captain Franklin will take a shift as helmsman."

"Captain?" Wesley said.

"You have your orders, ensign," April said. "Get up."

Ensign Wesley did so with a look of confusion. Iridius sat down. He was only partly familiar with the helm of the *Gallaway* but, in all honesty, it wasn't that hard. Among the sliders, buttons and displays glowing across the blue touchscreen he immediately recognised the controls he'd need to do what April wanted. Sure, he couldn't fly a ship like Ensign Rangi – that required talent and skill – but the basics of flying a spaceship actually weren't much different than operating a microwave, not that he'd let a pilot hear him say that. They tended to get touchy about people implying they weren't as skilled as the pilots of old. Iridius got the attention of Ensign Smith beside him. Wordlessly he pointed at the BAMF controls on the helm in front of him. Smith nodded and readied himself to initiate the BAMF bubble. Iridius positioned his hands on his own helm console. He may not have agreed with April's decision to BAMF away, but she was the captain and he had to respect that. Plus, the thought that maybe she was right and the *Gallaway* alone wasn't enough to defeat them had crawled up the back of his spine and nestled itself in a damp spot inside his brain where it could grow. Iridius accelerated the ship again, pushing the distance out between the *Gallaway* and the Aegix. It took almost a minute, but once he'd added another one hundred kilometres, which he hoped would be enough, he looked over his shoulder and nodded at April. She nodded in return and then raised her hand, holding up three fingers. Then two. Then one. She pointed at Iridius.

Iridius adjusted the ship's controls from their current setting and sent them rocketing back through full stop to full reverse.

The ship howled, all but screaming its disgust from the bowels of engineering. After all, no piece of machinery, from a steam engine to an inter-stellar starship with dual nuclear fusion and matter-antimatter Bedi-Alcubierre-Millis-Formelge drives, likes to be taken from full forward to full reverse in a single step. It didn't help that Iridius also fired thrusters at full power, rolling the ship about both the lateral and longitudinal axes at the same time. The ship shuddered as vibrations travelled through the hull. As it twisted through space like an out-of-control piece of space junk, Iridius waited until his console showed they were coming around to one hundred and eighty degrees to their original bearing, then he fired the thrusters to stop their spin, leaving them facing the Aegix ship but with their momentum still carrying them away. He spun the fusion drive back up to full power. The ship's engines groaned again, as if to say *we've just gone full reverse, man, give us a break*. But they did as they were told and the *Gallaway* accelerated towards the dog-ship like they were two reckless teens playing a game of space-chicken. Of course, accelerating in that direction was still slowing their initial momentum. Which meant before they'd start moving towards the Aegix ship, their velocity would have to move through zero. They'd have to time it perfectly.

The distance between the two ships closed quickly. One hundred and fifty kilometres. One hundred and twenty. One hundred and ten.

"We're one hundred kilometres out," Latroz called. "Ninety now. They're firing a full railgun barrage."

"Approaching zero velocity," Iridius said. "BAMF on my mark, Smith."

"Impact in four seconds," Latroz called.

Iridius cut the fusion engines and said, "Three, two, one... mark."

Smith slammed his finger down on the BAMF button and,

having timed it right at the moment of zero velocity, the *FSC Gallaway* popped out of existence.

In their own private universe, the ship began the preprogrammed FTL flight to Alpha Centauri B. The crew let out a collective breath of relief.

"Nailed it," Iridius said. "Heaps of time."

"Something's wrong," Ensign Smith said. "The bubble universe is off course." The lights on the bridge flickered.

"Seems like a Franklinism," Ensign Rangi said.

Iridius sighed. "Malfunction, ensign. Let's just call it a malfunction."

CHAPTER TWELVE_

THE *GALLAWAY* POPPED its BAMF bubble and the ship coalesced back into a solvable quantum waveform in the normal universe, causing eleven hundred species that had evolved, developed intelligence and formed advanced civilisations inside the bubble universe to blink out of existence. All that, and the ship wasn't even in the right place. The helm had programmed the *Gallaway* to travel to Alpha Centauri B and yet here they were popping out of FTL in Proxima Centauri. Considering the scale of the entire universe, it was fairly close to the mark – Alpha Centauri B and Proxima Centauri were only zero-point-two light years apart – but it was still like driving home from work and pulling into your neighbour's driveway.

"What just happened?" April asked from the captain's chair.

"It was Captain Franklin," Rangi said from where he hovered uselessly at the edge of the bridge. "Like I said, it was a Frankli—a malfunction. Same thing happened when we took the *FSC Patterson* for its shakedown. We entered FTL for Trappist-1 and ended up popping out in 55 Cancri. I don't need to tell you the difference between the tropical resorts of Trappist-1 and the weird mosquito-men of 55 Cancri."

"It also happened when we had the *FSC Emerald Sea*," Quinn said.

"Yeah, and the *FSC Reggie Clark*," Rangi added.

"Yes, alright," Iridius said. "We don't need a rundown of my greatest hits. Point is, we got away."

"Yes, we did." April stood and made her way to the elevator. "Thank you, Iridius, that was excellent work. You can give the helm back to Ensign Wesley. Ensign Wesley, park us at Proxima Centauri B's L1 point. I'm going to make contact with the Federation Senate and report on the situation. Iridius, give me twenty minutes and then meet me in my cabin."

"Well," Iridius said, "I know we just escaped a near-death situation but I'm not sure this is the time."

April glared Sintarian laser daggers at Iridius as she stepped into the elevator.

"What?" Iridius said. "I was joking."

April didn't respond, and Iridius had a sudden urge to dodge whatever was coming out of her eyes.

"You can make the call to the Senate from here if you'd prefer, captain," Commander Mul said, an undercurrent of insistence in his high-pitched alien voice. "Everyone on the bridge is aware of the situation and cleared to an appropriate level."

"Thank you, commander, but I'd prefer to make this call in private." The elevator doors closed.

Commander Mul glanced at Iridius, who raised his shoulders in a small shrug, the two of them bonded for a brief moment in their complete lack of understanding of humans, women, their captain, or perhaps all of the above.

————

Iridius knocked on the door of the captain's cabin. "It's open," April called from the other side.

Iridius touched the control panel and the door slid sideways with a satisfying hiss. Iridius had waited awkwardly on the bridge for a little longer than twenty minutes – closer to half an hour in the end, because he wasn't exactly sure what was waiting for him.

As he entered he saw April sitting on the edge of the bed. Her hair had been released from its tight ponytail and hung in an s-shaped wave down to the top of her back. Normally she wouldn't pull her hair out like that until she was off-duty. The way she sat, her shoulders slumped forward, was also uncharacteristic. She'd always carried herself with the posture of a ballerina. Sometimes Iridius had considered it incredibly powerful and sexy, the way she held herself so strong and high. Other times it just seemed like there was a stick up her arse. It really depended on what stage of their on-again off-again relationship they happened to be in. Something was wrong with her now, though. She hadn't even acknowledged him.

"You asked me to come by," Iridius said, mostly to check that she even knew he was there and also, if he was being honest, because he'd never been good at awkward silences.

April looked at him. Her eyes were puffy and red. Not crying, but definitely either pre-tears or post-tears. She'd left the bridge to communicate with the Federation Senate. At least, that's what she'd said. It struck Iridius – perhaps too late – that it was really just an excuse to be alone. April looked away, hiding her face as she wiped her eyes. Iridius couldn't remember ever seeing April cry. Crying wasn't something he thought April Idowu capable of. She had her shit far too together for that – surely she'd utilise a more efficient method of expelling emotion. Why had she asked for him to come if she didn't want him to see her like this?

"I've contacted the Senate," she said, the tugging at her seams obvious as she tried to hold herself together. "They want to send a fleet after the Aegix ship. I've advised against it. We don't know how many vessels they can control at once, or what other capabilities they have that we haven't yet seen. They've ordered us to find a weakness, but I don't—" Her voice caught just slightly. "I'm not sure how we'll do that."

"I can come back later," Iridius said, feeling a sudden desperate need to not be in this situation. He could sense it was quickly going to become gooey with emotion and, unless it was mirth, he wasn't very good at emotion.

"No," April said, her voice hardening, growing defensive. "I asked you to come."

There was a pause and Iridius could feel some concerning levels of gooeyness filling the space around them. "I'm sorry about the *El Nino*," he said. "I really am."

She nodded, a tight nod with a squeezed mouth designed to hold back more tears. "I learned so much on that ship." April stared ahead, her eyes fixed on the middle distance. "Those people were my family."

"I understand," Iridius said. "I don't even like half my crew and I'd be devastated if I lost them. It's okay to be upset, you know. The FSC shrinks are always banging on about letting starship crew have emotions. We're not androids."

"I wish I was an android."

"It's not your fault," Iridius said. "You know that, right? There's nothing you could have done. Mayhem flew his ship into range and the Aegix took control."

"I never should have frozen up though, should I? A captain should be able to push emotion aside until later, make the hard decisions and grieve when the situation is over."

"You were shocked," Iridius said. "Don't be so hard on yourself. Everyone freezes sometimes."

"Have you ever frozen up?" April asked in a tone that was almost accusatory.

"Well, no," Iridius answered, "but I've never watched my old ship get shredded by railgun fire either."

"Roc never froze up," April said. "He was in command when Rangarlian Gut-Burying Parasites exploded free of the stomachs and large intestines of six million people on Persepholis D and he never batted an eyelid. We saw the FSC *Tasman* and the *FSC Lars Blitzer* destroyed in combat right in front of us and he continued giving orders and managed to destroy the Alliance rebels' ships and get us safely home.

"We were in imminent danger when the *El Nino* was destroyed and I didn't react. Roc always talked about the jump in responsibility from first officer to captain. Maybe I'm not ready for it. Maybe you're right, and you really should be a co-captain or something."

"Oh please," Iridius said, "you're the most ready of anyone in the fleet. You should have had a command like the *Gallaway* five years ago. It doesn't matter whether you froze up or not. You got the *Gallaway* to safety, you got the crew to safety."

"But I wouldn't have been able to if you hadn't shaken me out of it and taken the helm. I—" Her voice cracked and she stopped speaking, looking down as her shoulders began to shake with silent sobs.

Iridius hesitated. He'd definitely never seen her cry before. If he had, he might have been a little more prepared for how uncomfortable it made him. He shifted on the spot, bombarded with awkwardness. Whether it was hairy-lip kisses from Aunt Wallace or that one time his father tried to hug him, overt displays of emotion just left him hopelessly lost. This was even worse than usual because this wasn't some random villager on a distant planet crying because their crop of weird fungal fruit had been eaten by six-foot-long Targutan moose spiders. This was April. If social networking hadn't been banned for its destruction of human psychology and its detrimental effect on society in the mid twenty-first century, April and Iridius's relationship status would still be set to: it's complicated.

"Hey," Iridius said without moving any closer, "it's okay."

April didn't reply, she just shook her head meekly.

Iridius took a few ridiculously tentative steps towards her and put his hand on her shoulder. He felt her shuddering intake of breath as she fought to get control of her emotions. "April," he said, "don't worry. You haven't done anything wrong."

"I'm sorry," she said, wiping at her eyes, "I don't know what's wrong with me."

"Do you want me to leave you alone?" Iridius asked.

"No."

Bugger, Iridius thought.

"Will you just sit with me for a bit?"

"Of course," Iridius said, sitting down on the bed beside her. He felt her lean against him. She dropped her head down onto his shoulder and he could suddenly smell her hair - she must still be using that same coconut shampoo. *Coconuts are probably extinct now*, he thought. *Chocolate is gone, too. Oh shit, no more coconut chocolate.* He forced away the thoughts that tried to creep in and distract him from the emotional situation he was in. "You would have snapped out of it," he said, "I know you would have. You've never done anything wrong in your life."

"I stole a packet of candy from the cafeteria on Europa when I was thirteen."

Iridius leaned back slightly so he could turn to look at her. "No, you didn't," he said.

She smiled, sniffling. "I had a rebellious phase, you know."

"Oh right, one afternoon of shoplifting."

"No," she said, "it was more than that. At least two."

Iridius laughed and found himself falling into the old habit of wrapping an arm around her. "Sorry," he said, releasing her as he realised what he'd done.

"No," she replied, taking his arm and putting it back. "It's nice."

They stayed like that in silence for a few minutes. It wasn't an awkward silence, but the silence of two people quite comfortable sitting together. Even Iridius didn't feel the need to fill the empty air with words. He remembered, not that he'd ever really forgotten, why their relationship always had the 'on again' component.

"Iridius," April said, looking up at him. "I know we haven't been very good at keeping in touch the last few years but," she paused, "I have thought about you."

They locked eyes. Iridius felt his insides begin to churn, like electrical discharge in an empty chamber. The buzz of attraction filled him. Really it was just his brain being flooded with dopamine, his adrenal glands dumping adrenaline into his system and his sweat glands pumping out pheromone-infused sweat like the survival of the human race depended on it - which, given the sudden population drop, it probably did more than any time since the last great ice age. Still, in that moment, all that physiology distilled down to Iridius not being able to take his eyes off April as she bit the corner of her lip.

April moved her face towards his. Iridius watched her lips part slightly. She closed her eyes as she moved in...

"Waheya!" Iridius said as he jumped back. "Whoa, hey, I... Ha... You're clearly emotional right now. That's probably not a good idea."

April's face quickly turned from surprised to embarrassed and then angry. "What the hell was that? You don't have to leap back like that."

"No," Iridius said. "Sorry. It's just, doing that would be crazy."

"You were looking at me like... You have a standing news search going... I'm not crazy. You don't have to be an asshole."

"I'm not being an asshole and I didn't say you were crazy, just emotional."

"Which you think is the same thing? You've never been able to handle having actual emotions."

"No. No, no, no," Iridius said, "don't you start that. I'm the one doing the mature thing right now. That," he made a non-distinct flapping gesture between them, "what nearly happened. I stopped a mistake."

"So I'm not crazy, just a mistake?"

"No," Iridius said, suddenly feeling like he needed to pull his collar out and let some air in. She always did this when they fought. Her words were so ice cold and yet he felt like a frog in a slowly boiling pot of water. "I didn't say that. Although I'm feeling like I might have been right about the crazy."

Nice one, Iridius. That's absolutely what you say to an ex-lover you just spurned. She didn't say anything though, she just stared at him, which was way worse.

"No, look, April, I didn't mean—" He stopped, his mind coming to a grinding halt as it tried to navigate the perilous waters of interpersonal relationships. "Last time *you* broke up with *me*, remember? I figured this time I'd be the one to break it off even before we went down this black hole again."

Red Alert. Red Alert.

"Captain to the bridge," Mul's voice came through the comms system.

Oh, thank god again.

"We better talk about this later," Iridius said, already up and making for the door. "Duty calls, there's an emergency to deal with." Whatever it was, Iridius felt far better equipped to deal with that than the emotional emergency that was going on in there.

———

When Iridius and April walked onto the bridge they didn't have time to speak over the top of each other because Commander Mul, as though his big balloon head had been waiting to expel the air, was already speaking. "We picked up a BAMF bubble disintegration on the scanners."

"The Aegix dog-ship," Iridius said.

Commander Mul nodded. He'd taken Iridius's statement as a question. It hadn't been a question, though. Iridius knew the Aegix ship was out there. He knew it had just entered the system. He wasn't sure how he knew, he just did. In a rather unsettling way, he could *feel* them.

"They followed us?" April cut in. "That's not possible."

"Proxima Centauri B must have detected our arrival and somehow the Aegix picked up on that," Iridius said.

"I don't think so, captain," Quinn said. "We know the Aegix need to be in close proximity to hack into systems. They might be using lunar bases to access Federation communications, but there hasn't been any communication from Proxima Centauri B. We would have picked it up, too."

"Could they have predicted our destination then?" Iridius asked.

"I don't see how," April said, her tone towards him not greatly improved since they left the captain's cabin. *"We* didn't even know this was our destination. We were supposed to be heading to Alpha Centauri."

"The only explanation I can see," Commander Mul said, "is that the Aegix are capable of both tracking us through BAMF and altering their course while in FTL transit to pursue us."

"Both those things are impossible," Iridius said. He tried not to let frustration colour his words. There was a thought tickling around the edges of realisation. One he wasn't going to give into easily. "You can't detect a ship until it drops out of BAMF and you can only pre-program FTL navigation."

"That's what our technology allows, Captain Franklin," Mul said. "It is not necessarily wise to extrapolate that to an unknown intelligence."

"Well, fine," Iridius said. "Whatever happened, they're here and we need to do something. Proxima Centauri B is a major planet. There are probably three billion sentients down there, and once the Aegix deal with us, it'll be gooping time for them."

"I have a theory about how the Aegix might be tracking us," Quinn said.

"Didn't you hear me? Three billion sentients? Goop?" Iridius said indignantly, and would probably have continued had Latroz not interrupted.

"Aegix ship approaching at high speed. An attack trajectory."

"See?" Iridius added.

"Your theory might have to wait, Quinn," April said. "How are our shields?"

Latroz consulted her display. "Fully charged."

April directed her attention to the helm. "BAMF?"

"Ready," Ensign Wesley replied.

Iridius kept his opinion to himself, though he wanted to ask why they were running again, and not putting all their effort into finding a weakness in the Aegix like the Federation had instructed. It seemed an absolute necessity now that another three billion sentients were in the gooping line.

"*Interference will not be tolerated. The galaxy must be prepared for the coming of the Synth-Hastur. You must be eliminated. Predictive algorithms conclude you will continue to hamper our mission and attempt to bring about our destruction. This will prevent the survival of the galaxy.*"

"How about you listen to me?" Iridius spoke into the air around them. "The only thing that *Hastur* happen is you stop what you're doing." Iridius ignored the groans at his excellent pun and continued. "Maybe you need to go back to sleep for another half a million years because despite having had such a long nap, you seem awfully cranky."

"The hibernation of the Aegix is predetermined because the coming of the Synth-Hastur is predetermined. They are coming. The galaxy must be prepared. Preventing the survival of the galaxy cannot be tolerated."

"We're not trying to prevent the survival of the galaxy, you crazy git, we're trying to ensure it. You're the ones who want to turn every living thing to goop."

"The loss of incompatible life is collateral damage in the preparation of the galaxy. The Synth-Hastur are coming. The Synth-Hastur will purge all life. It is the programming of the Aegix to prepare the galaxy."

"Ensign Wesley," April said, "get us out of range of this and prepare to BAMF to escape system bravo."

"Aye, captain," Ensign Wesley answered.

"April," Iridius said, keeping his voice low. "Proxima Centauri B needs our help. So does everywhere else in the galaxy."

April ignored him. "Prepare to BAMF."

"April," Iridius said, more insistent this time.

"I've given my orders," she shot back.

"I know you want to be more decisive and act to save the ship," Iridius said, "but there are sentient beings in danger."

"Do I need to remove you from the bridge?" April said, glaring at Iridius.

Iridius raised his hands in mock surrender.

"Get us out of range and initiate BAMF, Ensign Wesley."

"Wait," Quinn said. April looked at her and she cleared her throat. "Captain Idowu, would you allow me to talk to the Aegix? We can remain within communication range but out of range of their influence on the ship. We need to learn everything we can about them. Maybe we can negotiate."

"Have you ever tried negotiating with a light switch?" Iridius asked. "It doesn't matter how convincing you are, it's either on or off."

"Captain," Quinn said, "I think we've lost sight of the fact that despite the hostility of this entity, this is still a first-contact scenario. FSC regulations state that our first-contact responsibilities are to learn everything we can and attempt a diplomatic and peaceful resolution."

"Quinn, you know how much I admire your knowledge of FSC regulations, it's really invaluable – or annoying, depending on the situation. But I'm pretty sure first-contact regulations went out the window after they attacked Mining Station Victoria and destroyed the *El Nino*. Oh, and let's not forget the thing where they charbroiled THE ENTIRE EARTH."

"I understand that, captain," Quinn said, "but this is an unparalleled scientific opportunity. The Aegix might well be evidence of long-theorised ancient galactic life. Life that existed prior to the evolution of any current species living in the Milky Way."

"The entire Earth," Iridius said, "just gone. Poof."

"Captain Idowu?" Quinn said. "Do I have your permission to at least try?"

"Wesley," April said, "keep us just ahead of them. This range." She glanced at Iridius, not seeking permission necessarily, but gauging his reaction. "Quinn, you've got your shot. Make it fast."

"Thank you, captain," Quinn said. "Um, okay, can you hear me? Am I addressing the entity calling itself... or themselves, the Aegix?"

Iridius watched Quinn. She was nervous, her voice quivering slightly, but he had to admit she was stepping up in a way he'd always encouraged her to. He felt a pang of pride. Maybe his insistence in pushing her out from behind a console and into the real world of space exploration – even though most of that had been hauling junk around the galaxy – had finally paid off. Maybe she was finally coming out of her shell. They grow up so fast.

"*Obviously,*" the voice of the Aegix answered.

"Huh," Iridius said, "the crazy computer program just threw you some sass."

"Probably learned it from you," April muttered. She spoke up. "Keep going, Quinn."

"Right," Quinn said. "Yes, well, will you answer some questions for me?"

"*There is no need to communicate with you, only to extermi-nate you and continue preparing the galaxy for the coming of the Synth-Hastur.*"

"Surely you must see we can learn from each other."

"*We have all relevant data.*"

"But you said yourself that some life seems incompatible with your attempts at these preparations you deem necessary, and yet you claim to be trying to protect all life. If we understand each other, you may be able to learn how to adapt your programming."

There was silence. Iridius thought it was a little odd that an incredibly advanced synthetic intelligence would need thinking time. Seemed an awful lot like a pause for the show of it, really.

"*Very well. You may ask your questions.*"

Huh.

"Are you a synthetic intelligence?"

"*We are the Aegix. We are a hive intelligence. We are the swarm and the shield.*"

"You claim to have existed for at least half a million years, since the last coming of the Synth-Hastur you keep referring to. Do you have a creator?"

"*The original Aegix were created by the Endless, a race that foresaw the coming of the Synth-Hastur and endeavoured to protect the galaxy. The Aegix were made to prepare the galaxy for the coming of the Synth-Hastur and break the cycle of the Synth-Hastur purges."*

"What happened to the Endless?"

"We do not possess this data. They may be an extinct civilisation."

"Didn't choose the best name for themselves then, did they?" Iridius said. "Bit arrogant really."

"There is a forty-three per cent possibility they have achieved the ultimate state of evolution and have moved beyond the confines of the physical universe to become multi-dimensional beings of pure energy that will exist even beyond the heat death and entropy smoothing of this universe and outlive the completely lifeless void that will exist for all time."

"Fair enough," Iridius said.

"What is the Synth-Hastur's purpose?" Quinn asked. "You say you are trying to prepare life to defend against them. What threat do they pose?"

"The Synth-Hastur pose an existential threat to all life. They move between galaxies seeking to exterminate all sentient life to ensure it never progresses to a stage where it threatens their desire for universal harmony."

"Look, this is some great mid-adventure exposition here," Iridius said, "but the point is, the Aegix and the Synth-Hastur sound very similar in your intention to eliminate all life for your own agenda of harmony and protection. Not a lot of consultation from the Synth-Hastur with those being harmonised, and not a lot of consultation from the Aegix with those being prepared. We want a diplomatic resolution, but we will use force if necessary."

"We do not have a diplomatic function."

"See? Like negotiating with a light switch."

"They're accelerating," Latroz said. "Gaining on us now."

"Ensign Wesley, are we at maximum acceleration?" April asked.

"Yes, captain."

"I thought we could outrun them."

"Their ship appears to have some sort of advanced production-level printing facilities on board, captain," Mul said. "They're likely capable of upgrading the ship at an unbelievable rate."

"We are making enhancements to your limited propulsion technology and preparing significant upgrades to sensor, transmission and weaponry equipment."

"AIs," Iridium groaned. "This is why we banned them. An hour since we last saw them and they're upgrading already. If we don't act now we're just going to get further behind."

The view-screen at the front of the bridge showed a magnified view looking back behind the *Gallaway* to the Aegix dog-ship, which Iridius was certain had somehow begun growing hair. As he watched the dog-ship's acceleration begin to surpass their own, he saw the flash as the view-screen suddenly lit up with a red box tracking a fast-moving object.

"The Aegix ship has launched a probe," Commander Mul reported. "It's moving at high velocity. Trajectory extrapolation indicates it's heading for Proxima Centauri B."

"Aegix acceleration levels increasing again," Latroz declared. "They're closing the gap between us."

"What was that probe you just fired off?" April called into the space around them.

"The galaxy must be prepared," the Aegix voice said. *"We are preparing this planet as we will prepare all others."*

"That probe must contain nanobots," Quinn said, "same as those on Iota Persei and on *Gargarin Station*. The nanobots seem to be what interacts with biology to bring about whatever change it is the Aegix are trying to achieve. They also seem able to form the nodes of a network that allows them to hack into systems."

"Latroz," April said, "target that probe. Bring it down."

"My console is not responding. I can't bring missiles to bear. The probe is three minutes from Proxima Centauri B."

"We've got a system infiltration alert," Mul said. "Something is scanning us."

Iridius watched April. Stations around the bridge reported updates in quick-fire succession now. This was the activity of a starship in action, under siege, in crisis. Iridius could see April taking it in, parsing the information in order of criticality, planning, prioritising and re-prioritising her strategy as a result. This was the true skill set of a starship captain, not bravery or bravado, not a sharp diplomatic mind. Those things had their place, of course, but this right here, taking in information in the heat of the moment and making not the perfect decision but the most correct decision with the information at hand, then backing that decision one hundred per cent while also being willing to abandon it completely as new information came in – this was leadership.

"Distance to the Aegix ship?" April asked. April might not have thought she was ready for this, but seeing her sitting in that chair, in the centre of the bridge on the most advanced ship in the galaxy – other than the giant artificially intelligent toy dog that was following them, perhaps – Iridius knew she was. The moment she'd frozen up seemed like nothing but a tiny meteor now, one that had deflected off her energy shields as she flew on to claim her place among the FSC's legendary captains. Iridius would usually lament the fact that he would never be on that list, and blame the systems that would never give him the chance, but April's words still rang at him. Had he done everything he could to put himself in the position she was in? No. He hadn't. Oddly, he didn't feel like slinking off alone to a dark bar with a half-empty bottle of Grantakian Razor Vodka. He felt at peace watching April. She was awesome, and he hoped she saw that in the mirror soon enough.

"Which systems are they scanning?" April asked.

"All of them."

"They've drawn within projected range to infiltrate ship systems," Quinn said.

"Probe still approaching Proxima Centauri B. It will beat missiles to the surface unless we can fire in ninety seconds," Latroz said.

"Helm," April said, "the fusion engine will handle a one hundred and thirty per cent overload before we're in danger. Get us out of range then bring us back around after that probe."

"Ah shit," Ensign Wesley said, tapping and sliding his fingers over his console to no avail. "Helm is down, captain. I'm locked out. Engine throttle reducing to zero."

"The Aegix are slowing too, stopping within railgun range," Latroz said.

"Shields?"

"Offline."

Latroz's single word seemed to echo through the bridge. They were dead in the black, drifting with no shields. An AI enemy with the empathy of a turnip was bearing down on them, ready to fire hyper-velocity metal shards through them, just like the *FSC El Nino*.

"*We have provided you with information and you have now provided us with information.*"

"What information did we give you?" April said.

"*Up-to-date information about estimated population density across the galaxy,*" the Aegix voice said. "*You will now be destroyed.*"

"Remember when we thought taking the *Gallaway* for a shakedown would be fun?" Iridius said to no one in particular.

"Captain Franklin?" Quinn said. Iridius turned to her. "I think you should try to bring the shields online."

"Quinn, I'm quite sure Lieutenant Latroz knows what she's doing. If she says the shields are offline, I'm going to believe her."

"It's not that, captain. I know the lieutenant is capable. It's about this theory I have."

"What is it?" Iridius said.

"The Aegix's railgun matrix is coming online," Latroz said. "I do not believe this is the time for theory."

"Captain Franklin, please try to bring our shields up," Quinn said. There was a hint of terrified begging in her tone that struck Iridius pretty hard – almost like he hadn't truly realised they were all about to die until he heard the shake in his XO's voice. He moved to Latroz's console. The Amazonian-like alien stepped aside without a word. Iridius really had no idea what Quinn's theory was or why she thought this would work, but he touched the control console for shields. He tried to bring them back online but, unsurprisingly, the console didn't respond. The console lit up with the indication that railguns on the enemy ship were fully charged and about to fire.

"Quinn," he said. "I'm sorry. I don't—"

"Bring the shields up, captain!" Quinn shouted at him.

Iridius had never heard Quinn shout before. At least, not *at* someone, and especially not at a superior officer. If they weren't about to die, probably followed by every sentient being in the galaxy, he'd likely have some choice words for her. Right now, though, he took her rather loudly declared advice and tried again.

Latroz was looking over his shoulder at the console display that indicated the weapon status of the enemy ship. "Aegix railgun fire away," she said to the bridge, keeping a professional neutral tone right up to the end. "Impact in two seconds."

Iridius gritted his teeth as he tried to manipulate the shields again. "Come on, give me some shields, you bastard thing!" And, without even touching it, he watched the console display showing the ship's shields flip from red to green. The shield master indicator declared the shields to be ONLINE and at one hundred per cent.

"Ah, shields are up," Iridius said in the most nonchalant tone he could muster. After all, he'd just saved the ship from being shredded like ball-bearings through wet paper, even if he had no idea how he'd managed to do it.

"Impact," Latroz reported.

Iridius felt the vibration that always travelled through the ship's structure as the shields were impacted. Flashes of blue lit up the view-screen as the shields absorbed and dissipated the massive amounts of kinetic energy being pounded against them. There was a sudden outburst of celebration on the bridge, the usual wooping and hooting and fist-pumping that comes with a narrow escape from certain death.

"Iridius, how did you *do* that?" April asked. Iridius shrugged. "Doesn't matter," April continued, "we'll figure it out when we're out of trouble. Helm, tactical, are your systems online?"

"Weapons still offline," Latroz said, leaning over to examine the console.

"Helm, too."

"Captain?" Quinn prompted. "I believe you should attend to those consoles, too."

"The probe launched by the Aegix is twenty seconds from being out of range," Latroz said.

"We need to stop that probe." Iridius switched from shield control to weapons systems and attempted to fire. Of course, the system didn't respond, and Iridius became very aware of the seconds ticking away as the probe loaded with goopifying nanobots careened towards the densely populated Proxima Centauri B.

"Captain Franklin," Commander Mul said, "did you lower shields again?"

"No, of course not, why would I—" Iridius stopped as he saw the display on his console. As he'd changed the main display from shield control to weapons, the small indicator in the top left of the display was indicating that shields were dropping. Forty per cent. Twenty per cent. Ten per cent. Shields down. "All I did was switch to weapons."

"And now you're focused on bringing weapons systems online, and you've stopped concentrating on shields," Quinn said.

"The Aegix ship is preparing to fire again," Mul said. "Railguns fully primed."

Iridius saw the targeting system tracking the trajectory of the Aegix probe. It was eight seconds from being completely out of range.

"Iridius," April said, "whatever you did for the shields, do it again please."

"The probe will be out of range in five seconds," Iridius said.

"Shields."

Iridius hesitated only a fraction of a second. He flicked back to shields and, concentrating as he had before, he brought them back online.

"Aegix firing," Mul said.

As the shields came back online, raising to the eighty-two per cent that was left following the first railgun barrage, there was a moment of stillness, until Iridius spoke.

"Probe out of range."

There was nothing they could do now. That Aegix probe would hit Proxima Centauri B and spread nanobots out around the landing site. They would begin taking over computer systems, machinery, weapons, all the technology that made space flight and life on innumerable worlds across the galaxy possible. And, Iridius guessed, just as they had on Iota Persei E, *Gargarin*

Station and on the lunar bases, the Aegix would put the 3D printers and other production technologies to work making more nanobots, more of their chosen dog form, and more of their dog-shaped ships to go out, multiply and spread. And of course, along the way, the people of Proxima Centauri B would be "prepared" and turned into puddles of pink goop like a creamy, viscous pile of curdled strawberry milk. Iridius hung his head and squeezed his eyes with his thumb and forefinger, not even looking up when the ship shuddered slightly as railgun fire peppered the recently re-raised shields.

"Shields at fifty-nine per cent and holding," Latroz reported once the volley had ended.

"It seems like you can only bring one system back online at a time," Quinn said, more to herself than to Iridius. She was in full scientist speculation mode, proposing and testing hypotheses, refining her understanding of the variables. What exactly she was testing, Iridius had no idea, apart from the very obvious fact that he was the subject of all her speculation.

"Alright then," April said. "Iridius, try whatever magic you're managing on the helm and get us out of here."

"And everyone down on Proxima Centauri B?"

"I'm making the hard decision," April said. "We grieve later. We're no good to the rest of the galaxy dead."

Iridius made his way to the helm, Wesley relinquishing his seat without any hesitation for a change. "And the fact that the Aegix have another staging ground?"

"You may be a captain too, but you're on my ship, Captain Franklin," April said. "Get us out of here."

Iridius pressed the button to fire up the BAMF engines and initiate FTL travel. The course had already been plotted – a jump to escape system bravo. Iridius didn't actually know where that was. Every starship had three emergency jump destinations for situations like this, albeit maybe not as extreme. Onboard systems would constantly update to ensure a BAMF jump could instantly be initiated to those destinations without the need to plot a course. Iridius hadn't had a chance to review what had been programmed into the system. If the system still had the default settings, he thought escape system bravo might have been Sirius. He supposed it didn't matter much. He hadn't expected the helm console to actually respond when he pressed the BAMF button, but the red button turned green, and confirmation that BAMF engines had been initiated flashed across the screen.

The bizarre image on the view-screen, which showed a giant dog hovering before them, preparing to fire another rain of railgun metal, shimmered. Around the *Gallaway* the universe ceased to exist as a new bubble universe was created, ripping them out of the fabric of reality and leaving a sudden discrepancy in space-time that caused ripple effects through the four dimensions of space and time. As the *Gallaway* disappeared into faster-than-light travel, nanobots were already spilling from the probe that had smashed into the surface of Proxima Centauri B, spreading out in small groups that coalesced and dispersed and reformed into clouds of almost imperceptible black dots like pollen on the wind - very deadly pollen that comprised the neural net of an insane synthetic intelligence working off programming five hundred million years out of date.

CHAPTER THIRTEEN_

IRIDIUS WATCHED the screen of his console as the emergency escape course was executed. He smiled. "Very clever."

The location of escape system bravo was Proxima Centauri – the *Gallaway* had programmed a BAMF jump to the other side of the very system they were already in. Iridius had been concerned about the amount of time they would be in FTL, unable to communicate with the Federation, but it was only a matter of minutes until the *Gallaway* dropped out of BAMF on the outskirts of the same system.

"I'd already considered a plan in case the Aegix managed to take us or another world," April said. She manipulated the console in the arm of her chair. "I advised the Federation against sending a fleet, but I still took the offer of some backup. Are the Aegix following us, commander?"

Commander Mul's fingers worked the screen of his console and the display on the view-screen switched to a mirror of Commander Mul's display, with sensors showing the Aegix dog-ship on the move.

April watched in silence as the Aegix began flying across the system towards them. The enemy ship would not BAMF to get closer because as soon as they popped out of BAMF their shields would be momentarily down, leaving them vulnerable and allowing the *Gallaway* the opportunity to shower them with missiles. Instead, the Aegix made its way across the gulf of space between them under standard fusion power. April hit another button. "FSC *Valkyrie*, this is Captain Idowu of the *Gallaway*. The Aegix threat has spread to Proxima Centauri B. You'll need to hit it with a planet-slagger. All life on the planet is already lost. I have Federation Senate Executive Order Six-One-Three-Six-Oh to authorise this. Hit the planet and then get out of the system."

"Well," Iridius said, "I'm glad you didn't have Executive Order Six-One-Three-whatever when we broke up. Although you did send your mother after me, and she's basically a planet-slagger."

April, luckily for Iridius, chose to ignore him.

"Confirmed." The single word came over the comms system from the FSC *Valkyrie*. "Engaging target."

Iridius realised that wasn't just the normal terse response of a combat ship, that had been Lieutenant Aidan, the only completely synthetic life form in Federation Space Command. They (gender neutral pronouns being the norm for androids) had been accepted into the FSC on a trial basis. There had been considerable opposition to this, and while most of it had come from outside the FSC there had also been a strong anti-synthetic contingent within the ranks. As a Federation captain, Iridius knew he shouldn't get involved with politics but he happened to agree with the anti-synthetics. There had been an artificial intelligence ban for almost one hundred and fifty years, and he'd seen firsthand what could happen when a rogue scientist decided to play franken-god and try to bring a computer to life. His family, and so many others, had paid the price. He still wasn't sure what the difference between an android and an AI was, but those high in the ranks of the FSC had assured everyone there was a differ-ence, and that Aidan wouldn't go rogue. Turns out even with everyone protesting about Aidan and the semi-regular prosecu-tion of human scientists who tangled with AI, they still managed to dig up a half-billion-year-old crazed computer that became obsessed with toy dogs - just goes to show the real issues aren't those you get fixated on, they're the ones that will blindside you out of nowhere one Wednesday afternoon and turn you into pink goop.

"Planet-slagger away."

Iridius was almost certain he could hear an outburst from the Aegix. It wasn't like a human groan of frustration or a shout of anger. It wasn't even emotion. It was perhaps more accurate to say that he felt the Aegix's realisation that it had suffered a setback. A hint of annoyance, muddled in with a feeling like it had lost a limb. There was a low rumbling inside his chest that he eventually understood was a growl. He looked around the bridge of the *Gallaway*. No one else had reacted. They were watching the display on the view-screen that tracked the tiny overkill bomb as it was launched from the *Valkyrie,* covered the black vacuum to Proxima Centauri B and flared down through the atmosphere, ready to turn the planet into a toasted marshmallow. He assumed no one else had felt the strange sensation and decided, for the sake of maintaining the appearance of sanity, not to mention it.

"Impact."

The display on the view-screen showed the planet-slagger blink out of existence against the green outline of Proxima Centauri B. Having seen what a planet-slagger does from orbit, Iridius was struck by the utter understatement of it. From here, on the other side of the system, they couldn't see the quantum reaction set the planet on fire, torching the atmosphere and turning the surface to lava. And even if they were in orbit, they still wouldn't be able to see the horror of those on Proxima

Centauri B whose skin melted and bones evaporated where they sat or stood or slept.

"Iridius," April said, "can we BAMF again?"

"Three minutes."

"Time until the Aegix are within range to infiltrate our systems again?"

"At their current acceleration, and using conservative estimates for the range of influence the ship seems to have, we've got at least twelve minutes," Commander Mul answered.

"Alright," April said. "Iridius, are you happy to give the helm back to Ensign Wesley?"

Iridius stood up, more than happy to relinquish the chair. The truth was, he wasn't happy about being the only one who seemed able to overcome the control of the Aegix. That, together with the strange communication he seemed to sense, left him with the strong feeling that he was far more involved in this than he'd like. There was something else at play here, and he wasn't happy about how much of it seemed to orbit around him.

"Wesley," April said, "set a BAMF course for the Proxima Centauri-Sol interstellar midpoint and activate when the drive is back online."

"Aye, captain."

Iridius felt the change in the atmosphere on the bridge. Everyone knew the enemy was still out there, and all life in the galaxy was still at risk, but they had jumped from the frying pan and had managed to clear the fire, at least for the time being. Even April relaxed into the captain's chair as if sagging under the relief. Iridius felt the same sense of relief – it was impossible not to. But he didn't think they should be letting up yet.

"What's the next step, April?"

"Federation Senate has sent a bulletin via quantum entanglement for all vessels, planets and stations to report the appearance of the Aegix ship. Wherever it goes next, we'll know."

"But we won't get there fast enough to stop it dropping more probes, will we? Is the plan to follow it around, blowing up every planet the Aegix touch? We need to stop them now."

"I'm not putting this ship at risk like that again, Iridius," April said. "We've tried your way and it got the *El Nino* destroyed, and nearly the *Gallaway*, too."

"If we don't figure out how to stop them, who will? We've got the best ship in the fleet. We're the galaxy's best hope. We—"

"Enough!" April yelled. "What good is launching ourselves headfirst at the Aegix when we know we stand little chance at stopping it? It doesn't matter if we've got the *Gallaway,* we're still not a match in a straight-up fight. I'm getting tired of this discussion, Iridius. I told you already, it's not the ship that makes the captain, it's the other way around. Smashing our heads against the wall isn't going to knock it down. We need to figure out how to go around it." Iridius, for once understanding the importance of keeping his mouth shut, or at least being so shocked that his brain didn't supply a witty retort, didn't reply. April gave herself a moment before addressing Quinn. "You're up now, lieutenant commander. You said before you had a theory about what was going on, and you clearly knew the controls would respond to Captain Franklin when we were completely dead in the black. So what have you got for us? Some weakness in the Aegix?"

"Um, well, I don't know how much help it will be in defeating the Aegix. It's really more of a theory about Captain Franklin."

"A theory about me?" Iridius said.

"Ah, yes sir."

"I have plenty of theories of my own about Iridius B. Franklin," April said. "I assume this one is somehow linked to the Aegix?"

"Ever since I started serving with Captain Franklin three

years ago I've been very interested in trying to understand what the crew refers to as the 'Franklinisms'."

"Malfunctions," Iridius quickly corrected.

"Yes, sir," Quinn continued. "The widely accepted opinion within Federation Space Command appears to be that the *malfunctions* that occur when Captain Franklin is onboard a starship are bizarre, but are ultimately just bad luck. Given that we're a civilisation built on science who long ago threw off the shackles of folklore and superstition, I've always found it odd that people actually believe in bad luck. Bad luck isn't real. There is no external force that influences probabilistic outcomes. I've done some research, and the rate at which malfunctions occur on vessels when Captain Franklin is aboard is completely, extraordinarily, beyond any other correlation between a crew member and major system failure. The numbers are so high that they completely skew the distribution curve. Captain Franklin is basically the mathematically impossible hundredth per centile in a curve of crew members who seemingly cause strange malfunctions. Something about Captain Franklin causes ships to break."

"Don't labour the point or anything, Quinn," Iridius said. "I somehow break things, everyone knows this. What does it have to do with the Aegix?"

"Well, I've been theorising for a long time about how and why these malfunctions occur in Captain Franklin's presence. There had to be some influence that could be scientifically explained. It wasn't until we encountered the Aegix that my theory solidified. The way in which the influence of the Aegix occurs is the same as the way in which the malfunctions around Captain Franklin occur."

"What are you suggesting, lieutenant commander?" April asked.

"The Aegix use their nanobot swarms to generate a field that allows them to penetrate and control systems at a distance. My theory is that Captain Franklin generates the same field."

"Be straight with us, Quinn," April said. "Are you saying Captain Franklin has the same ability as the Aegix, or is it more than that?"

Iridius knew what April was really asking. She was asking if Iridius wasn't human, if he was something else, an Aegix sleeper agent or some robot in human skin. Ordinarily Iridius would have protested his innocence, and maybe he should have, but he could hear that crackling voice in his head again. He'd heard it on Iota Persei E but had chalked it up to his imagination. *You. Are. Us.*

Quinn looked somewhat anxiously from April to Iridius and then back again. "I don't know."

"I do," Iridius said. "I know. I'm completely, boringly, ordinarily human."

"You can't deny that the malfunctions that happen around you are bizarre, and you're the only one who can seem to wrestle control back from the Aegix when they've got the ship completely locked up," April said.

"Honestly, apart from the fact that I've had as much medical testing as any member of the FSC, April, you of all people should understand my humanity. We've done plenty of very biological things together."

"Um."

"Yes, Quinn?" Iridius snapped, without meaning to. But screw it, she'd just basically accused him of being a robot.

"When I say I don't know how Captain Franklin has the same abilities as the Aegix, I do have an idea about how to check."

"And what's that?" Iridius said.

"The *Gallaway* has the most advanced medical and scientific facilities ever put on a starship. We've got the equipment to examine you on a nano scale. We could determine the structure of the fundamental particles in your DNA if we wanted to. We should well and truly be able to detect anything non-biological that exists in your body."

"Franklinisms were happening long before we first encountered the Aegix," Greg said. "Junker and I have been fixing them on shakedown flights for years."

"Thank you, Greg," Iridius said, glad that at least someone, even if it was the humanoid cancer, appeared to be on his side. "Greg, as usual, is right on point. The timing doesn't add up. We didn't even know about the Aegix until they were dug up on Iota Persei E. No one except the poor bastards on that planet had made contact with them before."

"Then you let them hitchhike on your hauler back to Earth," Commander Mul said, "where they proceeded to destroy the planet."

"Look," Iridius said, "the point is, the malfunctions that have been attributed to me were happening way before I even went to the Academy. I was on an asteroid belt cruise with my parents when the cruise liner had to turn back because every screen on every deck of the ship began playing reruns of that godawful historical drama about that reality TV star who became president. Whatever is going on with me has nothing to do with the Aegix."

"Do you know how to use the necessary equipment, Quinn? Remember, we don't have any of the usual science or medical staff aboard. Doctor Paine will be able to assist you, but other than that there's no one."

"I can do it," Quinn said. "Most of the equipment is automated. We probably just need a blood and hair sample to get started."

"Okay, take Captain Franklin and go get him examined then," April said.

"Hold up," Iridius said. "Is no one going to ask me what I

think about this? What about my right to consent to a medical experiment?"

"It's not an experiment," April said, "it's an examination, and as captain of a starship, you should be aware of Federation Space Command Regulation 234-M."

"Yes," Iridius said, "obviously." He turned to Quinn expectantly, and stage-whispered, "Might need a teeny hint on that one."

"Federation Space Command Regulation 234-M states that the captain of a vessel, when on duty, has the right to subject any sentient of any rank on board the vessel to a medical examination if the captain believes there is an adequate risk to ship safety in not doing so."

"Oh, yeah, that one," Iridius said. He turned to April. "Look, it's not that I'm worried we'll discover I'm some sort of Aegix robot wrapped in human skin." It was. "It's just that I find this sudden lack of trust from you and from my own crew a little unnerving. Are you all going to turn on me that quickly?"

"No one is turning on anyone, Iridius," April said. "If you're not worried, then go and get examined and we can move past this."

"I see, nothing to fear from Big Brother if you've done nothing wrong."

"Iridius." April's voice grew more stern. "Go and let Lieutenant Commander Quinn do what she needs to do."

Iridius didn't move.

"Lieutenant Latroz," April said, "escort Captain Franklin and Lieutenant Commander Quinn to the lab."

The large Siruan moved closer to Iridius. She didn't project any outward sign of aggression, but it was like a mountain had shifted over to stand next to him. Any loyalty Latroz had to him was non-existent. She would follow her commanding officer's orders and that was all there was to it. If April told her to pick him up and thin him out like spaghetti she probably would.

"Alright, alright," Iridius said, "I get the picture. I have as much choice as a toilet trip after a Turgranian Spiced Coffee Burrito."

Iridius walked to the elevator, flanked by Quinn and Latroz. No one on the bridge said anything.

Ensign Rangi awkwardly saluted him. "Don't worry, captain, I think there's only a small chance you're an undercover alien robot spy."

"Thanks, Ensign Rangi. Reassuring as always."

"Do not worry, Benjamin," Latroz said. "I will only hurt your captain if necessary."

"Thanks, Peach," Rangi said.

Did he just call her Peach? Seriously, Iridius thought, worst shakedown ever.

———

"It's just like an ordinary blood test," Quinn said as Doctor Paine filled a second vial of blood from his arm. The first sample was already in a small container ready for testing. Quinn wasn't wasting any time. In fact, unless Iridius was mistaken, she was positively thrilled. Stupid science officers. "But while Doctor Paine runs standard medical analysis, I'm going to run elemental analysis, spectral analysis, sub-particle analysis and a more in-depth nano scale examination than would ever have been done on your blood before. If there's anything non-biological in your system, even something trying to mask itself as biological, we'll find it."

"Great."

Quinn continued rambling about how they could find traces of carbon- or silicon-based nanobots, they could use electron resonance analysis, and then there was something about Heisenberg's Uncertainty Principle. She was not, it seemed, picking up on the fact that her subject was rather less enthusiastic than she was.

They set to work. Iridius was left sitting on the edge of a bed in the stark whiteness of the medical bay as Doctor Paine went to one end of the lab to begin her analysis while Lieutenant Commander Quinn vanished off down the hall to the main science lab, where she was going to do all the science-ing she'd mentioned. Iridius sat and wondered why they always chose such an eyeball bleaching white for the walls of every medical bay on every ship, space station or colony across the galaxy. He supposed it was something about giving off the impression of being clean – but that seemed wholly unnecessary now. Medicine had come a long way. With the flawless antiseptics, programmable antibiotics and short-term gene editing techniques available, a medical facility could be erected, quite literally, as it had been on Proxima Centauri C during the Poo Planet incident, in a field of bubbling human faeces and not a single patient would face the risk of infection. Still, there was something reassuring about the cleanliness of white.

It was especially reassuring when out the window was nothing but the endless black of the void and the ever-present knowledge that the vast majority of the universe was composed of freezing, radiation-filled vacuum completely inhospitable to life. It was as though all sentient life in all existence was balancing on a pinhead afloat in an ocean. And that ocean was growing stormy since the arrival of the Aegix – something Iridius, deny it though he might, was feeling increasingly responsible for. Despite what April might say about not flying headlong into danger, Iridius knew he had to do precisely that. They had to protect that tiny pinhead of life in the harsh universe lest the Aegix snuff it out for good.

Iridius's musings were interrupted a short time later by

Quinn's return. She entered the medical bay, asked for Doctor Paine to come with her, and then quickly exited again. It doesn't matter where you are in the whole of space and time, it's never a good thing when one doctor decides they need another doctor to come and quickly have a look at something. Never once in all the universe did someone grab a doctor just to say, "Hey, look how handsome this guy's insides are," or "Check out this most perfect spleen."

"Hey, Quinn," Iridius called into the hallway, "are you going to tell me what's going on?" After waiting extremely patiently for another three seconds, he called again, "Quinn!"

Several minutes later, Quinn and Doctor Paine entered the medical bay, accompanied by April.

"Sorry, captain, Doctor Paine and I wanted to make sure we were on the same page, and we wanted to ensure Captain Idowu was here."

It wasn't a good sign that they'd called April down to hear the news. She must have asked them to do that. That was the sort of thing one did if they were worried the person being tested might try to suppress the results somehow. He felt a pang of offended anger, but he knew he probably would have done the same had he been captain.

"Well," Quinn said. "The good news is you're not an Aegix robot. You're completely human."

"Obviously."

"The bad news is..." Quinn let her words trail off as she searched for a way to put it delicately.

"Quinn," Iridius said, remaining very calm given the situation, "that's never a good time to pause. Just tell me."

"The bad news is your blood is, well, it's positively crawling with Aegix nanobots. You display the same type of ability as the Aegix because you have the same type of nanobots inside you."

"Okay," Iridius said, "I'll admit that's not great news. They must have breached my suit when we were on Iota Persei E or aboard *Gargarin Station*. I'm not thrilled with the idea of little machines floating around inside me, but I'm assuming you'll figure out how to remove them. Thing is, I've been causing ship systems to malfunction since I was a teenager. These nanobots can't be the cause of that."

"That's the other thing," Quinn said, in the way people always do when they're getting to the real crunch of the bad news statement. "The nanobots seem to replicate at a fairly constant rate as they become damaged or corrupted. They also gather trace amounts of by-product with each replication. By measuring the trace amounts of these chemical by-products, I can estimate how long the nanobots have been in your system."

"Given how long you're taking to say this, I'm going to assume the answer isn't since last Friday?"

"At least twenty years," Quinn said. "Probably closer to twenty-five."

"Look, Quinn, you're great at science but that's clearly not possible."

"I've triple-checked, and I also had Doctor Paine take a look. She drew the same conclusion. I have no idea how or why, Captain Franklin, but you've had Aegix nanobots in your blood since long before we knew the Aegix existed."

Iridius wanted to argue. He wanted to explain what seemed very logical to him but for some reason the scientists didn't seem to get – this just wasn't possible. It wasn't possible to get infected by something you've never been exposed to. Twenty-five years ago he hadn't even left the backwater space station he grew up on, let alone had his body invaded by the swarm entities of an ancient synthetic intelligence. But, no matter how much wanted to argue the point, he didn't. Lieutenant Commander Kira Quinn had been his XO for three years. When it came to scientific analysis she wasn't often wrong, and when she'd double or triple checked something she'd never been wrong – not once.

And there was something else. Something that was honestly surprising to him. He *wanted* it to be true. Whatever the reason, however the impossible had happened, he wanted tiny alien robots floating around in his blood to be responsible for interfering with ship systems his entire career, because then he'd have an explanation. Finally, after all these years, he could point to something and say 'there, these things are the reason I'm a walking clusterfuck'. With a cause having finally been identified, someone might actually be able to do something about it. If he didn't cause chaos on board just about every ship in the fleet, he might finally be on his way to a command that mattered – assuming they managed to overcome the current existential threat to the galaxy, of course.

"Captain?" Lieutenant Commander Quinn said, pulling Iridius's attention back. "There's something else."

"Another something else?" Iridius said. "In all the black what now? Are they radioactive? Are my limbs about to fall off? Is my flesh going to melt, or am I going to explode?"

"They're transmitting, sir."

April, who'd been quietly taking this in, spoke. "What do you mean transmitting?" The implications of this were abundantly clear to her. There was now a risk to the *Gallaway,* just as she'd feared.

"This must be new then?" Iridius said. "Surely someone would have noticed if I'm a walking radio tower. I may not have had the kind of nano-level analysis that you've just done before, but I've been scanned for bugs and transmitters plenty of times."

"The nanobots aren't transmitting waves of any frequency or wavelength. In fact, we wouldn't have picked up anything if we hadn't seen and examined them first. Examining several, I found a repeating pattern of sub-particle manipulation."

"Quantum entanglement," April said.

Quinn nodded. "That's right. Of course, we have no way of interpreting the message, but it's safe to assume the other end of the entangled particles are with the Aegix main consciousness aboard their ship."

"I know what it is." Iridius spoke before realising he probably shouldn't have – his mind spiralled the implications out in front of him.

"What do you mean?" April asked.

Iridius thought back to the words he'd first heard from the Aegix, *You are us.* He thought about the way he'd felt the closest thing the Aegix had to emotions. And, more than anything, just as he could when he'd been on the bridge, even now he could sense that the Aegix mind was out there, trailing them through the black of space. Despite requiring a centralised node, a fixed spatial-temporal housing from which to orientate itself and produce true synthetic cognition, the Aegix mind was able to instantly control swarms of nanobots as if they were appendages attached to its body. There was no communication lag, perhaps even across star systems. The only way that was possible was if the Aegix had a far superior grasp of quantum entanglement communication than any species in the Federation. "It's some sort of quantum entanglement link between the nanobots in my blood and the Aegix mind. I don't know how the nanobots got in my blood years before we'd ever encountered the Aegix, but I don't think the Aegix mind can control them, at least not completely. Instead, I think they're using them to track us. No matter where we go, they'll always be able to find me."

"They're using the nanobots in your blood like a tracking beacon," Quinn said.

"Quinn, doctor," April said, "could you give me a moment alone with Captain Franklin?"

"Of course," Doctor Paine said, and both women vacated the

medical bay, leaving Iridius sitting on the edge of the white-sheeted bed with April standing nearby. She took a moment before addressing him, taking a few steps then turning on her heels to pace back the other way. She tapped her finger against her lips as she thought. Eventually she stopped and turned to him, clearly having reached some sort of decision. "Iridius," she said, "I don't know how you must be feeling. To have discovered something like this about yourself. But at least it's an answer to the question that's always bugged you."

"That's how I'm choosing to think of it."

"They must have got into your blood somehow, which means I'm sure Quinn or someone within the FSC will be able to get them out again."

"It doesn't weird you out then?"

"What do you mean?"

"Well," Iridius said, "knowing that the whole time we were together these things were inside me. All those rounds of bedroom rodeo and I was crawling with microscopic alien robots the whole time."

"To be honest I hadn't thought about that until right now," April said, "and now I'm thinking about it, so thanks for that. And for the record, my opinion on you calling it 'bedroom rodeo' hasn't changed."

"A bit of crumpet?"

"No."

"Adult nap time?"

"Nope."

"Slaying the vamgina?"

"Absolutely not."

"Violating the prime directive?"

"Just stop. I know what you're doing."

"What?"

"Same thing you always do. Blow off the situation with a

cascade of jokes so you don't have to face up to the inevitable. There's only one clear outcome from this discovery, Iridius. It's been nice having you on my ship, working together again, but this isn't like our old Academy days. We can't act like we don't have responsibilities now."

"Just like that then, is it?" Iridius said. "After everything. You tried to kiss me."

"What's that got to do with it?"

"I don't know. I know I reacted badly, but I was just surprised."

"You're an idiot sometimes. This isn't about that. Even if you weren't a homing beacon for our enemy you'd still have to leave eventually, and besides, you were right to react the way you did. We wouldn't work out, Iridius – we never do. It was inevitable it would end this way."

"Can you gather all the crew on the bridge, then? I'd like to make the announcement."

April nodded. "I'll call them together now."

"Oh, and just for the record," Iridius said, and April turned back towards him. "Apart from the eventual heat death of the universe, I don't think anything is ever inevitable."

————

The skeleton crew of the *FSC Gallaway* and the ragtag crew of the *Diesel Coast* gathered on the bridge following Captain Idowu's shipwide announcement. As Iridius stood behind the captain's chair ready to address them, he realised just how few people were there. The entire crew of both ships amounted to barely the same number of people as the *Gallaway* would have on the bridge during full operation. They were facing an enemy they didn't know how to fight that had the potential to eradicate all life in the galaxy. Iridius had to acknowledge that what these few people had done so far was remarkable. Now he had to give them the best chance to succeed.

"Thank you for joining us," April said. "The situation we're in is a unique one. We're facing this enemy completely uninformed and undermanned, an amalgamation of two crews on a barely tested ship, and as such we're closer knit and much more informed about every aspect of our situation than would ordinarily be the case on a ship this large. I want to be open with you all. As you know, Captain Franklin underwent testing to determine why ship systems malfunction around him and why he was able to take at least some control back from the Aegix. He wanted to be the one to explain the results and what this means. Iridius?"

"Thank you, Captain Idowu. And the winner of the best picture award is..." Iridius mimed opening an envelope, but was interrupted by April clearing her throat. "Okay fine, I'll just get to it then, will I? Right now the Aegix ship is following us across the system. The *Gallaway* is prepared to make another BAMF jump, but as you know, they managed to track us down last time. Exactly what they want with us and why they haven't just gone off to goopify the rest of the galaxy, we're not sure. But now we know how they managed to find us. It's me. Lieutenant Commander Quinn's hunch about a link between my – I won't say abilities because that makes it sound like I have any idea how to control it – a link between my... Franklinisms and the Aegix was correct. I have Aegix nanobots in my blood, and they appear to have been there for a very long time."

Iridius held up his hand to cut off the questions from the crew, Junker and Rangi in particular. "We don't know how they got there or how to get rid of them, but the outcome right now is simple. I always believed having command of a ship like the *Gallaway* would give me the chance to make a real difference. I considered a decent starship the only thing a captain needed. But my idea of leading the *Gallaway* straight at the Aegix isn't going to work. Someone once told me it isn't the starship that makes the captain – it's the other way around – and it's also the crew. This crew needs to find a way to stop the Aegix, and you can't do it with them hunting you. It's me they can track, and so I'm leaving."

"Captain, this isn't your fault. There are nanobots inside you," Quinn said. "You don't have to feel responsible."

"I know," Iridius said. He looked at April. "But that same person who told me the ship doesn't make the captain also told me that blaming other things all the time doesn't actually fix the problem. I may not have known about the nanobots in my blood, but I am responsible for the Aegix getting off Iota Persei E in the first place. I've endangered the galaxy enough. I've endangered the *Gallaway* enough. I'm not her captain."

"You are our captain though," Junker said.

"That's right," Rangi agreed. "So if you go, we go. Besides, I'm not letting you fly the *Diesel Coast*. She might be a shit bucket, but I'm the pilot of that shit bucket." He looked at Latroz. "Sorry, lieutenant."

"It is alright, Benjamin," Latroz said. "I find your loyalty to your captain very sexually attractive. I will see you again."

"No," Iridius said, choosing to ignore that exchange. "What I'm going to do is pretty stupid. I can't ask you to come."

"With all due respect, captain," Junker said, "you aren't asking us to come. We're telling you we're coming."

Iridius didn't reply. That was pretty close to insubordination, but he knew it was coming from a place of loyalty. "I appreciate the sentiment, I really do, but you're not coming."

"I, too, will be accompanying you, captain," Greg said. "The *Diesel Coast* is my home, and you are my captain."

Iridius couldn't help but smile – stupid loyal idiots. They didn't even know what he and April had planned, didn't know the danger this would put them in, and yet they would come without question. He looked to April.

She nodded. "Of course, any crew of the *Diesel Coast* who want to accompany Captain Franklin, you're quite welcome to do so. He's your captain, and that is your ship."

"Where exactly are we going?" Quinn asked.

Iridius turned to his XO. "You're staying here."

Quinn stared at him. "Sir, I'm coming with you. Just like the rest of the *Coast*'s crew."

Iridius shook his head. He could see the emotion in Quinn's eyes – fear, disappointment, concern. "I'm sorry Quinn, but you have to stay with the *Gallaway*. You need to use what you've learned about the nanobots from my blood to figure out their weakness. You're the reason I can't let them find the *Gallaway*. You're going to stop them."

"No," Quinn said, straight-up refusing the order in a way Iridius had never seen before. "Captain, I want to stay with my crew."

Iridius had to stop himself from praising her for finally showing some self-confidence. Right now, he needed her to do this. "Quinn, FSC regulation eighty-three."

"Operationally urgent inter-ship transfer of crew under agreement of ship captains," Quinn said, glancing from Iridius to April.

Iridius nodded. "That's right. The *Gallaway* is your ship now."

She nodded – reluctantly, but Iridius could tell she knew it was the right thing to do.

"Alright," Iridius said. "*Diesel Coast* crew, let's go. Our shit bucket is waiting."

Iridius, Rangi, Junker and Greg all made their way to the elevator.

"Quinn," Iridius said, "we're relying on you. And don't worry, once you figure out how to save the galaxy you can come home to the *Diesel Coast*."

Quinn gave a small nod.

Iridius looked at April.

"Commander Mul," she said, "you've got the conn for a moment. I'm going to accompany Captain Franklin to his ship."

"Yes, ma'am."

The four crew members of the FSC *Diesel Coast* and the captain of the FSC *Gallaway* rode the elevator down to the docking bay in silence. The decision had been made for them to leave. The *Diesel Coast* crew would back their captain, and both April and Iridius knew this was the best outcome for the safety of them all, and the galaxy at large. Still, what lay before both ships was very much unknown. The lights in the elevator flickered, and it stopped. The lights came back on and the elevator continued. Iridius sighed. They disembarked on the deck to the docking bay. The airlock door to the docking point where the *Diesel Coast* had been piggybacking was only a few paces away.

"You three head aboard and prepare for departure," April said to Junker, Rangi and Greg. "I'd like a moment with your captain."

"Yes, ma'am," Junker said, whacking Rangi on the arm just as he opened his mouth to say something.

"What?" Rangi said to Junker, aghast. "I was just going to thank Captain Idowu for the chance to serve on her ship."

"Sure you were," Junker said. She nodded to April. "Thank you, captain."

The three of them entered the airlock to the *Diesel Coast*, Rangi grinning like the idiot he was.

"Sorry," Iridius said. "They're basically children, but they're my children."

"They're a very talented and loyal bunch," April said, "if a little oddball."

"I wouldn't have it any other way."

"I wanted to thank you, Iridius," April said, "for everything, and obviously wish you luck."

"Is that why you wanted to walk down here with me? For a formal captain's farewell and a 'godspeed'?"

"What do you want me to say?"

"I don't know, April, how about something about what in the black is going on with this?" Iridius gestured back and forth between them. "Talk about hot and cold. You're like the burning ice pits of Rigel D. To be honest, I can't tell whether we're saying goodbye under better or worse terms than last time."

"How many times have we been here before? Don't they say trying the same thing over and expecting a different result is the definition of insanity? It never works between us, Iridius. Our relationship has Franklinisms of its own."

"Yeah, well," Iridius said, looking at the door that led to the *Diesel Coast,* "some things are immune to Franklinisms. Maybe we are, too."

"We make a good team," April said, "just like at the Academy – when it comes to dealing with a starship at least. The problem is, a starship can only have one captain. We've both chosen a life of solitary leadership. Does it really surprise you that our relationship failed?" April paused, looking around under the pretence of examining the ship, but Iridius could tell she just wanted to break eye contact. "We've both changed, I hope for the better, but it's been ten years. We're both captains now. I don't think this road is one we can tread again." April Idowu was likely the woman Iridius knew best in the world, and even then he'd never claim to actually understand her. He thought he could sense the truth underlying her words now, though. She didn't think this was a road they *could* walk again, but that didn't mean she didn't *want* to.

Iridius sighed. Why had he avoided contacting her for so

long? Because he didn't want to go down this road for fear of it imploding again? Because he thought she was right, a captain only had room in their life for the ship they commanded? Earth was gone. They'd watched another planet fall. All sentient life in the galaxy was threatened with extinction. Did they have to valiantly face what was out in the black alone? What was the point of sentient life if not to share something with others? Why else did they fight so hard to save it? And why was he asking himself so many questions?

"It might have been ten years, April, but there hasn't been anyone else in those empty ten years," he said, blurting the words out lest they get caught up on the way. "Do captains really have to face the black alone? If we're so bad together, why do I want to try again?"

April looked at him, her face softening, her eyes betraying the sudden emotion at having to face what she probably thought would go unsaid. "You've never been great at knowing what's good for you," April said.

"No, I guess not."

Iridius turned to make his way to the *Diesel Coast*.

"But, Iridius," April said, and he turned back, "neither have I. I just... we need to stop the Aegix."

"Yeah," Iridius said, "you do. I'll see you around, Captain Idowu."

CHAPTER FOURTEEN_

IRIDIUS CLIMBED the stairs to the *Diesel Coast*'s bridge. Walking out among the sharp edges and cluttered space, he felt a sense of coming home. The bridge seemed small after spending so long on the *Gallaway*, but rather than cramped, it felt fitting, like a comfortable old jumper snugly shrunk in the wash.

Iridius sat in the captain's chair, and it squeaked satisfactorily as he leaned back. The bridge was dark; Greg, Junker and Rangi were still bringing the systems online. "Fire us up."

"You got it, captain," Rangi said from the helm. He punched at the screen in front of him and the ship hummed to life.

Iridius spoke into the comms. "*Gallaway,* this is Captain Franklin on the *Diesel Coast,* we are ready to depart."

"Confirmed, *Diesel Coast,*" Commander Mul answered. "Docking clamps retracted, you are cleared to push away." There was a pause. "Good luck out there, Captain Franklin."

Iridius looked at Junker, Rangi and Greg, his eyebrows raised in surprise. Old Balloon Head had come around after all. "Thanks – you too, *Gallaway.* Oh, and Commander Mul?"

"Yes, captain?"

"You take care of her, won't you?"

"Of course, captain."

Iridius wondered whether Commander Mul knew who he meant. He supposed it didn't matter. April, Quinn, the *Gallaway* – he wanted all of them to make it through what was to come. He felt the clunk as the airlock umbilical unhooked from the *Diesel Coast* and retracted into the hull of the *Gallaway*. The *Diesel Coast* was free. Ensign Rangi eased her away and Iridius watched the sleek shape of the *Gallaway* growing smaller in the view-screen. He suppressed a tug of longing. He had to give everyone on that ship the best chance to defeat the Aegix. He had to believe he was doing the right thing.

"Alright," he said over the comms. "This is co-captain Iridius Franklin signing off. Get the black out of here, *Gallaway*."

"Roger that," April's voice replied over comms. "Not the co-captain part, but we're preparing to BAMF. Good luck, *Diesel Coast*."

The *Diesel Coast* had pulled just over five kilometres away and the view-screen looked back as the *Gallaway*, the most advanced ship in the Federation fleet – and the ship that, unbeknown to most, carried the hope of the galaxy – engaged its BAMF. Iridius watched as a shimmering bubble formed around the *Gallaway*. It seemed to bend light in subtle but peculiar ways. The full spectrum of colours flickered and danced across the bubble in bends and curls. Then, in an occurrence that was always difficult for the human mind to comprehend, the bubble inverted into a hole in the fabric of reality. One moment the *Gallaway* was there, the next moment it was both there and not there, like two distinct realities superimposed on each other, a universe where the *Gallaway* existed and one where it did not. As the bubble universe fully formed, the space surrounding the *Gallaway* blinked out of existence. For the briefest moment Iridius stared into a hole in the fabric of space and time. There was nothing there. Actual nothingness. Even deep interstellar space is still vacuum, radiation, sub-atomic particles and fields of fundamental space–time dimensions. But before Iridius's eyes was the true abyss: no time, no space, no energy, no matter. This unknowable place beyond our cosmos that would make Lovecraftian horrors shrink back in confusion and fear. It existed – or didn't exist – for only a few milliseconds before space–time rushed in like panicked bureaucrats to fill the void. Still, that split second of actual nothingness was enough to turn Iridius's stomach.

"Urgh," he said, taking a deep breath and letting a long exhale force down the rise of nausea.

"You watched the BAMF, didn't you, captain?" Rangi asked.

Iridius held his fist to his mouth and burped, then swallowed down the excess saliva that had filled his mouth. "Get us ready to BAMF, too," he said. "Andor system. As soon as we come out, plot another BAMF jump to Eton-12."

"You got it," Rangi said, beginning his work at the console, his fingers flying across the familiar interface even faster than when he'd been on the *Gallaway*.

"We are taking them goose chasing?" Greg asked.

"That's right," Iridius said. "We think the Aegix came after the *Gallaway* because I was aboard. They want to eliminate me. Maybe because I can wrestle back some control on systems they take over, or maybe because they know I've got nanobots in my blood that might help us work out how to beat them. Maybe both. No matter the reason, we're going to let the *Gallaway* get away and figure out how to beat them. We're the bait to distract the Aegix and we're going to take them on something of a galactic game of tiggy."

Greg's large, drooping brow lifted in confusion. "Tiggy?"

"Yeah, tiggy," Iridius said. "You know, tag, chasings?" He didn't see any recognition in Greg's eyes. "It's a game children play, Greg. One person is 'it' and they chase the other kids around, and if they catch someone that person becomes 'it'."

"We did not have such games," Greg said. "On Maggelax we cannot move as children because we are still one with the planet tumour. We are unable to move until we have fully metastasised. The only game we had was the race to become full grown and detach before Maggelax destroyed us with its immune response."

"Sounds fun," Iridius said. "Well, consider this metaphor then: we are a Malignant and the Aegix are a very persistent immune response."

Greg nodded, though Iridius could tell he wasn't convinced. "Captain," he said, "when we drop out of BAMF we will be vulnerable to an attack from the Aegix. Our shields will be down for at least two minutes. If they BAMF straight in after us—"

"Yes," Iridius cut him off. "I know, Greg. That's why I didn't want you all coming with me, remember? And that's why everyone on the *Gallaway* keeps saying good luck all the time."

"There is no external force that affects the probability of outcomes," Ensign Rangi said.

Iridius stared at him. "What?"

Rangi shrugged. "Quinn's not here. I figure that's what she'd say."

"Well, you know what, you're probably right, and I'd usually be the first to tell people not to wish a starship luck but, on the off chance some sort of universal luck deity is listening, we could probably use a little."

"The Aegix are continuing to approach," Greg said. "They are at a range of nine hundred and eighty-six megametres."

"That dog's really hounding us, hey?" Rangi said.

Iridius looked at him. That dumb grin Rangi always got when he'd made a joke was spreading across his face.

"I have the distinct feeling you've been waiting to say that."

Rangi's grin expanded. Iridius decided to go back to his default state of ignoring most of the things his helmsman said. Iridius knew the Aegix were behind them – not the precise distance, but he knew they were out there and he could feel them coming closer. Across almost a billion metres of space he could sense them. If it was a form of quantum entanglement, as Quinn theorised, then he would be able to feel this connection with the Aegix anywhere in the universe. He wondered how much the Aegix knew about what he was doing. If these nanobots had been in his blood since he was a teenager then they might have been privy to everything he'd done since then. Jupiter's nuts, if they'd been tracking his nightly behaviour as a teenager, then – well, it was best not to think about it.

"Ready to BAMF," Rangi said.

Iridius connected his comms to Junker's workshop. "Junker, do systems look good to go?"

"Aye, cap."

"Alright, Rangi." Iridius took a settling breath. "Prepare to BAMF."

Ensign Rangi brought the ship to a stop and began spooling up the BAMF engines, ready to rip a chunk out of the space–time continuum and send the *Diesel Coast* blasting across the galaxy. He turned to Greg, who'd taken up the position as his XO in Lieutenant Commander Quinn's absence. "Greg, ensure the defence guns are ready."

"They are online and at full capacity, captain."

"Alright, Ensign Rangi," Iridius said. "Let's see if we can't act as the postman here and survive being chased by an enormous ravenous dog that wants to annihilate us and convert the galaxy to pink slime."

"At least it's not delivering rocks for a change," Rangi said.

Iridius laughed. "Yeah, for once you're right, ensign. At least it's not that. Engage."

Ensign Rangi hit the button on the console and the *Diesel Coast* was gone.

———

Iridius watched the view-screen. Outside the *Diesel Coast* was the fuzzy white glow of faster-than-light travel as the ship, contained within its bubble universe, moved at more than five thousand times the speed of light towards the Andor system. "When we drop out of BAMF make straight for the Andor Asteroid Belt, Rangi. The *Diesel Coast* has one advantage over that enormous flying canine – she's an ex-asteroid hopper, which means she's got multi-axis thrusters to navigate an asteroid field better than that giant poodle."

"And we've got the pilot to make it happen – Benjamin Rangi, Space Ace," Rangi added enthusiastically.

"No one has ever called you that."

"We could start."

"No," Iridius said. "We're not doing that."

Rangi shrugged. "Worth a try."

"Just be ready to lose the Aegix in the asteroid belt. How long until we arrive?"

"Popping the cherry in just under three hours, sir."

Three hours was a long time to wait. Iridius had excelled at the Academy, but since then his space combat experience had been limited to outrunning the occasional pirates or managing to survive encounters with hostile Alliance patrols. These were all spur of the moment encounters, very different to intentionally travelling to battle, and Iridius didn't enjoy the thumb-twiddling anticipation. But then this was what war and conflict had always been like, since the first tribes had collected clubs and rocks and walked to the next territory over for an unfriendly hello - every soldier knew conflict was long periods of boredom punctuated by bursts of utter chaos and terror.

Eventually Iridius watched as the Andor system appeared beyond the bursting BAMF bubble. Ahead of them, some few hundred thousand kilometres away, was the Andorian asteroid cluster – one of the largest groups of asteroids in the galaxy. Iridius could see bright lights clustered all over the largest of the spinning rocks, plus hundreds of lasers strobing through the asteroid belt. The lasers shot up from the surfaces of asteroids, hitting others and projecting images or simply shining colourful lines out into deep space.

"What the hell is that?" Iridius asked.

"That," Greg said, "is the Andorian Asteroid Festival."

"The what?"

"The Andorian Asteroid Festival," Greg repeated. "It occurs every five years, and goes on for three months. The Andorians worship the asteroid belt as gods. They celebrate the belt and the resources it provides with a celebration culminating in the destruction of one of the smaller asteroids by nuclear warhead, breaking it apart into fragments that add to the density of the belt. Hundreds of thousands of people come from all across the galaxy to drink Andorian Black Wine, which intoxicates for almost six weeks, join in the party and watch an asteroid explode."

"How do you know about this?" Iridius asked. "And why didn't you mention it?"

"I went there with friends at the end of my schooling," Greg said. "And like I said, captain, I drank Andorian Black Wine, so cannot be expected to remember anything about when that was or when the next one might be scheduled."

Rangi laughed. "Greg, you sly old cancerous dog, who knew you were a party animal back in the day?"

"So the asteroid belt I'd planned to use to escape the Aegix is currently occupied by hundreds of thousands of sentient beings completely off their rocking horses?"

"Yes, captain, unfortunately that is correct."

"And we've led the Aegix right to them?"

"Yes, sir."

"Good, that's good, excellent, great."

"Do I still head for the asteroids?" Rangi asked.

"Incoming ship signature," Greg said.

"Let me guess," Iridius said, "it's not someone coming to deliver me a bunch of flowers and a box of chocolates?"

"No," Greg said, "not unless the Aegix have gone into floristry."

Iridius groaned. "Damn it, that was even faster than I thought."

"Cap?" Rangi asked. "What do you want me to do?"

Iridius looked at the lights flashing through the asteroid belt, hundreds of thousands of people, probably out of their minds on fungal alcohol, enjoying what they thought would be the biggest party of their lives. They couldn't lead the galaxy's worst gate-crashers straight to them, could they? But then, if they didn't keep up the pursuit long enough for Quinn and the *Gallaway* to find a weakness in the Aegix, more people would suffer. The decision weighed enormously heavy on him. The decision of who to endanger. The decision of a starship captain. He was captain of a hauler, he'd never been faced with a dilemma like this before. April was right, this was a lonely position and there was more to it than heading out into the unknown black like a twenty-third century swashbuckling hero.

"Take us into the asteroid belt, Rangi. Full fusion drive, but head for the far rim. Try to keep us away from the largest central asteroids where the population seems to be most concentrated."

Rangi nodded. No comment. No questions. Even he seemed to have picked up on the gravity of the decision.

The ship hit the edge of the asteroid field and Rangi began to weave through the first of the rocks – slow enough to dodge everything with the shields still down.

"Ah, captain," Greg said, "the Aegix haven't used a containment shield after dropping out of BAMF."

"I'm sorry, what now?"

"No containment shield," Greg repeated, almost as if he couldn't quite believe what his console was telling him. "There's a BAMF bow shock heading straight towards the asteroid cluster."

"They can't... you have to contain the burst," Rangi said.

Iridius knew why they were shocked. The devastating shockwave that came from popping an FTL cherry had to be contained by a shield. Nobody wanted to be the ship that destroyed another solar system – nobody except the Aegix, apparently. "They don't play by our rules," Iridius said. "I should have thought of this. They must have figured we'd try to lose them in the asteroid belt. What better way to stop that than by removing the whole gronking thing? How do we stop it?" Neither Greg nor Rangi jumped in with a suggestion, so Iridius pounded on his comms. "Junker, is there a way of stopping a BAMF bow shock?"

"That's what the contain—"

"Other than a containment shield. Like, how do we stop someone else's bow shock?"

"Um, I don't... I don't think there is a way, captain."

"Shit." Iridius really wished Quinn was here right now. She was his problem-solver. "Shit. Shit. Shit. Can we use our shields to stop it?" Iridius felt the desperation rise. "Can we fly in front of it like the *El Nino* did for us?"

Greg shook his head. "No, sir. The bow shock expands as it travels, it'll be far too large for us to block. Besides, our shields are only partially recharged – we'd be destroyed."

The *Diesel Coast* veered through the belt, Ensign Rangi using the vectoring thrusters to their full capability as they drew deeper into the asteroid field and the rocks grew larger and closer together. Iridius watched the jagged asteroids flash by out the view-screen. Some of them had clear structures on the surface, festival attendees likely inside. "Cap?" Rangi prompted. "What am I doing?"

Iridius looked from the view-screen to the ensign. "Keep going, Rangi. Get us through the belt before the bow shock hits."

"And the people in the asteroid belt?" Greg asked.

"I think you know the answer to that question, chief."

"Here we go," Rangi said. "Geronimo!" Iridius heard the hum of the engine increase as Rangi throttled up.

"What?" Iridius said.

"That's what you say when you're about to do something crazy, cap," Rangi said as, on the view-screen, the asteroids came at them faster and faster. "And this," he added as the asteroids whipped past, "is crazy."

"Right, well, let's not have the pilot so blatantly admit that we're doing something crazy."

"Hey, you're the one giving the orders."

"Just concentrate, will you?"

There was always a sense of separation when watching something like this on the view-screen. It never quite seemed real. It was easy to imagine you were watching a video, a recording of some other idiot flying dangerously between enormous rocks of thousands or even tens of millions of tonnes, narrowly avoiding a collision that would, particularly with their shields still being down, turn the *Diesel Coast* into nothing but a brief explosion and a spray of shrapnel. Iridius gripped the arm of his chair as Rangi's evasive manoeuvres intensified. He could almost see the acceleration vectors whipping around like a compass in a magnetic field as Rangi pitched and rolled through the asteroid belt. "Rangi, can you fly if we go picture-in-picture?"

"As long as," Rangi paused as he input commands on the console with his left hand and manipulated the manual flight-control ball with his right, "as long as it's small. Bottom left."

"Greg, bring a rear view up on screen, bottom left like Rangi said. I want to see it happen."

"Captain," Greg said, "I think it would be remiss of me not to raise the question of whether it's a good idea to watch that."

"Thank you, Greg," Iridius said, "I appreciate that. Thing is, I'm trying this new thing where I take responsibility for stuff. I ordered us to come here, I've brought the Aegix down on all these unsuspecting people. They're going to die because of me, Greg. The least I can do is watch."

"Bit morbid, isn't it?" Rangi said.

"Maybe, or maybe it's bearing witness to the consequences of one's actions. Greg, bring it up on screen."

In an inlay on the bottom left of the screen, the view from behind the ship appeared. In the foreground, the asteroids the ship had passed were receding but behind that, looming like the wall of a space-storm, came the purple and blue wave of particles released from the front of the Aegix ship. It would strike the beginning of the asteroid belt at any moment and, despite the knowledge of what was to come, Iridius had to admit it looked impressively beautiful. So much of what lay out in the black of space was dangerous, but also beautiful – except for all the poop, anyway. Iridius watched as the bow shock struck the first of the asteroids beaming party lasers out into space. It disintegrated, the colours of those lasers immediately ceasing. They were obviously too far away to see, but Iridius knew there'd been thousands of people on the surface of that rock whose lives had just been snuffed out. Even worse, he could sense the Aegix's cold indifference. They claimed to be programmed to protect life in the galaxy, and yet they didn't care that they'd just destroyed all those lives.

Iridius watched the asteroids erupting into fragments, being shattered into smaller rocks and leaving mineral-rich dust billowing out in front of the bow shock, and every time lights and lasers flickered out he knew lives were flickering out along with them. He winced. "Yeah, you're right, it's a bit morbid." Yet he made himself watch.

The *Diesel Coast* flew through the asteroid belt with the precision Iridius had hoped for – precision that only the specially designed thrusters and a pilot like Ensign Rangi could provide. The ship slewed between asteroids in manoeuvres that could only be accomplished in the vacuum of space. The *Diesel Coast* entered a barrel roll to the right while simultaneously continuing to strafe to the left in a nauseating display of momentum, acceleration and everything Newton had been babbling about all those hundreds of years ago. But while they sped through the asteroid belt, the bow shock continued to roll up behind them, destroying the asteroid belt and removing the obstacle Iridius had hoped to put between themselves and the Aegix. Thanks to both the ship's scanners and the nanobots coursing through his body, Iridius knew the enormous dog was steadily moving forward behind the wall of energy it had unleashed. If the bow shock didn't destroy them and they managed to clear the belt, the Aegix would be right on their tail. Watching the rear vision inlay on the view-screen, the former looked increasingly likely. The asteroids rupturing behind them were getting closer and closer.

"I know you're flying your pants off, ensign," Iridius said, "but is there any chance you can get some faster pants?"

"I like fast pants as much as the next person, captain," Rangi replied as he worked the ship's controls, "but I'm fairly close to the edge here. The ship's got a little more in her but I can't guarantee I won't clip a few things."

"Shields, Greg?"

"Back at forty per cent, captain. We could take a few glancing blows, but we'll need them if the Aegix catch us."

"Push it, Rangi. If you get us through this unscathed I'll take back every bad thing I've ever said about you."

"I've got a better idea, captain." Rangi paused for a moment as he sent the *Diesel Coast* barrelling sideways to avoid an oncoming chunk of million-tonne rock. "If I get us through at full speed, you start calling me the Space Ace."

Iridius paused for longer than he should have, weighing up the lives of every sentient creature in the galaxy versus having to call Benjamin Rangi the 'Space Ace', but eventually he relented. "Fine."

He'd half-expected Rangi to cheer at this small victory, but to the man's credit he simply focused back in on his console, deftly guiding the ship through a small gap between two asteroids. In reality it was a gap of several hundred kilometres, but when you were moving at several thousand kilometres per second it seemed like a small gap. Watching Rangi's hands twist and move, watching his fingers slide across the console and slam buttons like he was playing a complex musical instrument, Iridius could tell he was teetering on the edge. He was pushing both himself and the *Diesel Coast*. He was fighting to stay on the tip of the knife and keep from tumbling into oblivion, but gronking red Mars he flew like a man possessed.

As they rolled and pitched through the asteroid belt the Aegix ship continued on at a steady pace behind them. Any asteroids that hadn't been blasted into space dust were small enough now that they simply bounced off the dog-ship's shields as it trundled forward. It was like the hare and the tortoise, the *Diesel Coast* zooming through the asteroids and the Aegix trundling steadily along behind. Shame the tortoise wins in that story, thought Iridius. Best not dwell on it.

"We're through the high-density region of the belt," Greg called. "It should get easier from here."

The ship rolled completely over, its forty-year-old artificial gravity plates groaning as they tried to balance the acceleration vectors and keep the crew feeling like down was towards the floor. Immediately following the roll, Rangi slewed the ship sideways out of the path of one of the last of the larger asteroids. "Get easier?" Rangi said. "Bah, it's been easy the whole time, chief."

"Don't get cocky, kid," Iridius said, immediately knowing the statement was futile. Telling a pilot not to get cocky was like telling space not to be black. But he had to admit, Rangi's cockiness was probably deserved. The ship roared through the asteroid belt, the bow shock bearing down on them, the wave of high-energy particles growing dangerously close.

"Captain, the bow shock is drawing dangerously close," Greg reported.

"Whatever shield charge we've got, direct it to the rear. Keep our butt covered."

"Aye, captain."

The leading edge of the shockwave was close enough now that it began throwing small chunks of rock forward to strike the back of the *Diesel Coast*. The shields easily deflected the shrapnel, but as the wild manoeuvring of the ship steadied somewhat, the shockwave itself became the real threat. Rangi accelerated the ship to draw everything he possibly could from the engines. Iridius could feel the vibrations rattling the hull, something the *Gallaway* would never do, and he realised he'd missed it in a weird sort of way. The *Diesel Coast* gave you some really tactile feedback on how things were going. Accelerating hard, the hauler flew out the other side of the asteroid belt (which was now more of a dust belt) and into empty space. They were clear – Rangi had fulfilled his promise. Unfortunately the leading edge of the shockwave began to envelop the rear of the ship, the shields flashing bright blue as they dissipated energy. The *Diesel Coast* bucked forward as the pressure of the wave pushed them along like a cosmic surfer. Rangi did everything he could at the controls, but with the bow shock enveloping them and the ship shaking like an unbalanced washing machine there was little he could do but keep them pointed forwards.

"Shields at thirty per cent," Greg shouted over the noise. "Twenty-five. Twenty."

"Full power to shields," Iridius said.

"We've done that already, captain," Greg said.

"I said *full* power. Take all non-critical systems offline."

"That will leave the railguns uncharged."

"I understand what full power means, chief," Iridius said. "Do it."

Greg worked the controls to sap the power from their only weapons system and shove it all into shields. Iridius wasn't sure whether it was the right call, but in this sort of situation any decision was better than no decision. There was no time to deliberate or second guess. Besides, if they didn't boost the shields they might not survive the bow shock at all, and then what good would fully charged railguns be?

"Shields holding at twenty," Greg said. "They're being charged and dissipated at the same rate."

After almost a minute more of being tossed along like a toy boat helplessly crashing through rapids, the rattling of the ship noticeably calmed.

"Bow shock energy is lessening," Greg said. "Particles are beginning to dissipate more rapidly. We appear to have ridden it out."

Rangi let out a whoop of celebration, the first overtly Rangi thing he'd done since they'd entered the asteroid belt. He turned to Iridius expectantly.

"Nice work, Rangi," Iridius said. "That was some damn impressive flying."

"Nice work from who, captain?"

Iridius stared at him. "Nice work," long pause, "Space Ace."

"Oh yeah." Rangi turned back to his console. "That's going to stick."

"No, it isn't."

Rangi faced the view-screen. "I need some sunglasses. Space Ace would wear sunglasses. Don't you think Space Ace should have sunglasses, Greg?"

"I believe I should book a leaf from Lieutenant Commander Quinn in this situation and advise that the Aegix are bearing down on us."

"Thank you for that, Greg. Despite your continued butchery of Earth colloquialisms, you're right." They'd reached the end of the churning river, but their little toy boat was still being chased by an enormous dog. "Ensign, are we ready to BAMF to Eton-12?"

"We're ready."

"As soon as we can go, hit the button."

"Roger roger."

"Captain," Greg said, "Aegix ship is arming missiles. They're drawing within range. Our shields are sitting at eighteen per cent."

The Aegix were gaining on them. However they were managing to change their ship so rapidly – onboard construction printers was Quinn's theory – they had clearly improved their propulsion systems yet again. The *Diesel Coast* wouldn't be able to outrun them. They'd be caught eventually and the Aegix would open fire, and with eighteen per cent shields, they'd only withstand a few missile hits. So, trying to outrun them wasn't going to be an option. Unfortunately, in order to BAMF they'd have to come to a stop. The Aegix would surely draw close enough to bombard them with missiles if they did that.

Maybe, just maybe, they could stop, take some hits but still manage to BAMF before they were completely destroyed. Iridius guessed the odds of that happening were about as good as the odds of a human beating a six-armed Gorgonian thunder troll in a boxing match. Still, there was a chance, and it was the only option that gave them even a sliver of hope. Besides, a human did once beat a Gorgonian thunder troll in a boxing match. Sure, he might have immediately died from his wounds and posthumously tested positive for the performance enhancing drug known as berserker blood, but for a glorious minute and a half, Henry Betson from Middleborough, Massachusetts had been Galactic Heavyweight Champion.

Iridius didn't know why he'd expected any outcome different to this. He'd known that trying to buy the *Gallaway* time was a suicide mission, so dying as a result shouldn't come as a surprise. Still, he'd try to get them out of this. Thinking of Henry Betson gave Iridius hope. Sometimes people could do the impossible. It was good for his confidence that Iridius didn't know the fight was fixed - and Henry Betson still managed to die.

"Rangi, are we ready to BAMF?"

"Aye, captain."

"Alright. Before we do this, let me just say it's been an honour serving with you. For a long time I thought being captain of a hauler like the *Diesel Coast* was a punishment. Now I see that this old bucket has the best crew in the fleet. Despite the risks, you all agreed to come with me to try and give the *Gallaway* a chance to save the galaxy. You—"

"Regretting it a little now TBH, cap."

Iridius raised an eyebrow. "I was trying to have a moment here, Rangi."

"Yes, captain," Greg said, "that is accurate. We have only a moment before the Aegix will be within range."

"That's not what I meant, Greg." Iridius sighed. "Full stop then, ensign. Prepare to BAMF."

There was only a slight hesitation from Rangi before he slowed the ship – not bad for someone pressing the equivalent of the 'kill me now' button. The *Diesel Coast* began to decelerate, fast. Ensign Rangi had been smart to slam the anchors on hard, getting to a stop as quickly as he could, ready to press the BAMF button.

"Aegix are within weapons range," Greg said. "Confirmed, they've fired. Incoming missiles. Quite a large amount of missiles, in fact."

"On screen."

The view-screen switched to show the view behind the *Diesel Coast*. Iridius watched the swarm of burning lights leave the Aegix ship, red reticles lighting up around all of them. Greg was never one for hyperbole. Iridius wouldn't have said there was a large amount of missiles, he'd have said there was a gronking shit tonne of missiles coming for them. There must have been hundreds.

"Impact in eight seconds."

The *Diesel Coast,* still shedding speed from being pushed along by the bow shock, wasn't quite at a full stop yet.

"Rangi?"

"Almost, cap."

"Six seconds."

Iridius stood. He stepped forward.

"Four."

"Full stop now," Rangi said. "BAMFing."

The engines spooled. Iridius closed his eyes. Suddenly, he didn't feel panicked. He didn't even feel like commenting on how everything always came down to the last second like this. He could feel them out there. Not just the Aegix, but the missiles. A cloud of points moving towards them. They were just like a swarm of nanobots. Individual machines communicating back to a home base.

"Two seconds."

Iridius thrust his arms out. He probably didn't need to, but it seemed to help give form to his intention – plus he figured it would look damn cool. Iridius, matching his thoughts to his actions, told the missiles to turn away. The rest of the crew watched the view-screen in awe as hundreds of red-highlighted missiles peeled away, accelerating hard to miss the *Diesel Coast*. The first of the missiles spun off more aggressively and crashed into some of the others, which in turn crashed into others, causing a chain of nuclear dominos that erupted around them. Some of the missiles exploded close enough to the *Diesel Coast* that the ship shuddered, some managed to make it through, hitting the ship's shields and bursting in iridescent white.

"Shields at five per cent," Greg said, but as he spoke, the universe around them shimmered and the spectacular display of missiles smashing into each other disappeared.

––––––

As soon as the *Diesel Coast* was tucked away in its bubble universe the violent shaking and shuddering from the missiles exploding all around them ceased. Here, in this tiny universe, there were no giant dogs trying to destroy them. Iridius wondered if anyone had ever tried staying in a BAMF bubble universe before. Sure, each BAMF universe was a completely empty void comprised of a zero-point space–time in which no events had ever occurred, no matter had coalesced from pure energy, and nothing, not even subatomic particles, existed to support life. Anyone who tried to remain in a BAMF universe would eventually exhaust all resources on their ship and die a cold, lonely death and float for eternity in an abyss of nothingness. Still, who didn't enjoy a little peace and quiet every now and then? It was while pondering this that Iridius noticed Greg and Rangi staring at him.

"Gronking shit-tunnels," Rangi said, his voice betraying his utter awe. "Captain, you just... I mean... that was awesome!" He nearly lifted off his chair in excitement. "I know there's a perfectly rational explanation about your nanobots and whatever, but that was like techno-wizard magic." He thrust his arms out, imitating Iridius's action. "Pew, and the missiles veer away and explode. Space Ace and the Techno-Wizard. What a team."

"Two things," Iridius said. "One, I am not a techno-wizard and two, it would certainly be Techno-Wizard and the Space Ace. You would be the sidekick. Now, stop talking to me, I need to think."

Iridius needed to figure out a way of staying alive back in the actual universe while keeping the Aegix occupied for at least a little longer. How could a gazelle (now extinct) keep a lion (now extinct) chasing them across the African savanna indefinitely? Iridius's knowledge of Earth animals wasn't great – he hadn't been raised on Earth, after all – but he knew enough to know that a gazelle wouldn't keep ahead of a lion. Instead, some young, old, or injured member of the herd would fall behind, keeping the lion occupied while the rest of the herd escaped. Maybe that was the strategy they needed. He might have modelled himself on the shields up, fire the missiles, swashbuckle the bad guys aspects of the job, but at the end of the day Iridius was captain of a starship and sometimes, in space, you just had to science some shit.

"Greg, if we fire a railgun while in a BAMF bubble, what happens when the round reaches the edge of the bubble?"

"I'm sure Lieutenant Commander Quinn would understand the physics better than I do, but basically, nothing inside a bubble universe exists as far as the *real* universe is concerned; however, objects can move out of a BAMF bubble and back into the real universe, because from the inside, the bubble edge represents a finite boundary. Anything that passes through the bubble boundary, though, experiences instantaneous deceleration from many multiples of light speed to stationary in the prime universe reference frame."

"Soooo..."

"So the first part of the object passing through the bubble comes to a stop while the rest of it continues at the speed of the bubble. Then the next part that passes through stops while the bubble continues. Ultimately the object is shredded into component molecules and spread over vast interstellar distances."

"Thought so," Iridius said. "But, the molecules are spread over vast interstellar distances in the actual real-life real universe, right?"

"Yes, captain."

"Is there a possibility that nanobots would survive that?"

Greg twisted his face in an expression of thought. It wasn't an entirely pleasant vision, but Iridius was used to the strange distortions of cancerous flesh that were displays of emotion for Greg. "Each nanobot exists on the nano scale, too small to be seen with the naked eye. We can only see them when they cluster together into macroscopic sizes. Nanobots are ten times larger than the molecular scale, but at that scale it is possible that the acceleration gradient over their length might be low enough that they survive. I assume you are considering a diversion of sorts."

Iridius nodded. "The Aegix are faster than us, can alter course while in BAMF and can track us through the galaxy. We can't do anything about the first two, but we know how they're managing to follow us. I'm thinking perhaps if we give the Aegix something to chase, they'll drop out of BAMF to investigate and that'll give us time to BAMF again." He activated the comms on his chair. "Junker, can you drag out the medical supplies and get ready to figure out how to launch a whole lot of my blood out of the railgun?"

"Sounds weird," Junker replied. "Sure."

"I'll be down to your workshop in a minute."

"Aye."

Iridius descended the steps at the back of the bridge, then walked through the cargo bay to the small alcove off the side that housed Junker's workshop. She had already dragged the medical supplies out of the storage locker – the *Diesel Coast* was far too small to have a fully equipped medical bay, so Junker functioned as the ship's medic. Luckily no one had ever been injured badly enough to require extensive first aid – Iridius had seen her take to mechanical components with a grinder and a hammer, and couldn't be sure she wouldn't attempt the same on a person.

"So," Junker said as she lifted a railgun round off the floor and placed it on a bench top with a heavy thud, "I gather you're going to shoot your blood out the railgun to try to distract the Aegix?"

"That's the plan."

"Cool." Junker laid her hand on top of the railgun round. "Lucky I've got this then." She began unscrewing the top – not normally a feature of a railgun round, as they were simple kinetic rounds of solid metal that relied on good old Newtonian mass and velocity to do damage. "I was toying around with the idea of launching objects from railguns a while ago and machined up this hollow round."

"Why were you investigating that?"

"I was getting sick of my cat," Junker said. "Figured I'd get rid of it." After a moment she laughed at the shock on Iridius's face. "I'm kidding. I did it in case we ever needed to smuggle something or get rid of something in a hurry or, you know, fire a jar of blood into space."

Iridius sat on the swivel stool in front of Junker's workbench. She pulled out a tourniquet, a needle, and a plastic mini-pump IV bag. By the twenty-third century medical advances had seen the eradication of almost every genetic disease. Curing cancer was as simple as taking a single pill and resting for a couple of days, and 3D printers could stitch bone, muscle and even nerve tissue back together. Yet still the only way to get a blood sample was to stick someone right in the vein with a sharp metal object and suck it out. Iridius felt like he was about to be bled like it was the eighteenth century - mind you, there were several types of blood disease that could be completely cured by exposing someone to Callorixian internal mega leeches so the old Earth quack-pots weren't necessarily that far off the mark.

"Can you roll up your sleeve, cap?"

"No."

Junker looked at him and raised her eyebrows, wordlessly reminding him that this was his idea, and that if he wanted to shoot his blood out of the railgun then he'd need to let her take it and not be such a giant wimp. All in a very non-insubordinate way, of course.

"Fine," Iridius said, undoing the strap on the cuff of his sleeve and rolling it up to expose the inside of his elbow. "I don't like needles and I don't like dogs and yet somehow that seems to be a large part of— ow! You didn't want to warn me?"

"Sorry, didn't think of it. I'm used to working on things that don't feel pain."

Junker attached the needle to the thin plastic hose that led to the IV bag. Once connected, the bag began to hum as the small pump in the top started sucking his blood out. "Do you think you can turn the suction down? I feel like it's going to suck me dry."

"You'll be fine."

"Good thing an engine doesn't care about bedside manner."

"And I thought Rangi complained when I had to use the auto-stitcher on him that time he cut his head falling down the cargo bay stairs."

Once the pump had sucked a bag full of blood from his system, like a tiny mechanical vampire, Junker took the blood bag, sealed the top, and dropped it into the hollow railgun round. "I'll get this loaded ready to fire."

Iridius rolled his sleeve back down. "What do you think, Junker? You think this is going to work?"

"I'm just a mechanic, cap."

"Don't sell yourself short, Junker, you're more than a mechanic."

"Well, I appreciate that, but theoretical physics is still a little outside my area. Doesn't matter anyway."

"Doesn't matter?"

"Nah, you think it's our best shot and we trust you. That's what matters."

Rubbing the bend of his elbow, where it felt like someone had thumped him with a sledgehammer, Iridius returned to the bridge. "Okay, prepare to fire the central starboard railgun. Junker's loaded the package."

"The blood bomb," Rangi said. "How do you feel about spreading your blood across the galaxy, captain?"

"I'm trying not to think about it."

"Your DNA will be stretched out over light years."

"Yes, thank you, ensign."

"One day, millennia from now, some alien race will find the pattern of your DNA in the stars and think it's the DNA of the creator of the universe. They'll probably clone you in a religious experiment to bring their god back into existence."

Iridius blinked at Ensign Rangi. "Right." He turned to Greg. "Fire."

"Aye."

Iridius heard the single *cha-clunk* of the railgun firing and recoiling.

"The round is away," Greg reported. "Am I right in anticipating that we will not know whether this plan is successful until we drop out of BAMF and discover whether the Aegix are delayed in following us?"

"I'll know," Iridius said. It was true that the ship's sensors would be unable to track the Aegix until they dropped out of FTL behind the *Diesel Coast* but even now, while they travelled in what were ostensibly separate universes, he could feel the Aegix. They were following. He wasn't sure what it meant that he could sense the other nanobots across the barriers of universes – maybe he'd let Quinn ponder that when all this was over. It seemed like the sort of thing she'd be interested in.

"You'll know?" Rangi asked.

"Yes. I'll know." Iridius didn't offer any further explanation, still unsure how much he should reveal about his connection with the Aegix, even to his crew. Besides, he didn't feel like being accused of any more techno-wizardry or want to encourage Rangi to spin any more tales about future cloning or, you know, to speak at all.

Luckily Greg saved him from any more prying questions. "Railgun round approaching bubble barrier. Impact in three, two, one."

The three of them waited in silence. Iridius couldn't sense the nanobots they'd fired. Did that mean they'd disintegrated into chunks? To be fair, he couldn't feel the nanobots that were swarming around in him right now, either – if he could, it wouldn't have taken twenty years to realise they were there. He kept his focus on the Aegix, who still seemed to be following.

"Well?" Ensign Rangi prompted. "Did it work?"

Iridius didn't answer. He closed his eyes. It was easier to sense what the Aegix were doing if he blocked everything else out.

"Did they take the bait, cap? How can you tell?"

Iridius opened his eyes and shot Ensign Rangi a look that could rip the carapace off a Retlarkan Lava Worm. It must have been just as potent as Iridius had hoped, because the helmsman, who Iridius was sure would attempt to talk in a vacuum with his lungs full of concrete, fell silent.

Iridius concentrated again. *Come on you assholes,* he thought, *take the bait.* He waited. After a further twenty seconds, just when he was sure the plan hadn't worked, he felt a shift in the course of the Aegix and then a sudden shrinking away, as if they'd instantaneously fallen vast interstellar distances behind. Which, Iridius realised, they had. They'd dropped out of FTL chasing the nanobots they'd shot out of the bubble.

"It worked," Iridius said. "They've gone after the nanobots. Rangi, when we drop out of BAMF program a jump to Tau Ceti. Execute the jump as soon as possible. Hopefully we've bought enough time."

They rode out the rest of the BAMF journey more or less in silence, or at least what passed for silence on the bridge of the *Diesel Coast*, which was Ensign Rangi blabbering away about how the numbering and naming of star systems seemed completely random to him, as if someone was just making them up as they went along, and asking who it was that actually got to name star systems anyway and why, if Earth was only relatively new to space travel compared with other species, did so many star systems use the naming convention invented by astronomers on Earth?

Iridius pointedly ignored his helmsman as usual – not because he didn't know the answers to his questions, of course. It was just that he was very focused on keeping his feelers out for the Aegix who had, after obviously finding nothing but molecularised blood, reinstated the chase. He could answer Rangi's questions if he wanted to, of course. He just chose not to.

Finally, after the *Diesel Coast* had withstood the strain of a long FTL flight and Captain Iridius Franklin had withstood the strain of his helmsman, Rangi announced, "Popping the cherry in three, two, one." And they dropped out of BAMF. With the way things had been going, Iridius had half-expected that they'd drop out of BAMF into the middle of some sort of raging battle between mutated space monkeys. Instead, as planned – which was a novel concept – they popped out of BAMF in the middle of the empty star system of Eton-12. It wasn't entirely empty; there were celestial bodies of course – that's what made it a star system – but as far as anyone could tell, there was no life on any of the planets or their moons.

"Quantum entanglement is rearranging," Greg said, moments after the shield had dissipated. Someone had been attempting communication with them while in transit. Quantum entanglement communication didn't work while in BAMF. That raised further questions about how his link with the Aegix worked seemingly across universes. Iridius made a mental note to tell Quinn about that, too – she'd definitely want to science that. "It's from the *Gallaway*."

Iridius had to keep himself from audibly thanking the black void, Neil Armstrong, William Shatner, Captain Catherine Huxley and any other gods of space travel who happened to be listening. He wouldn't admit it to the others, but he had no idea how they'd keep ahead of the Aegix through any more BAMF jumps. It was half a miracle they'd managed it so far. Never mind what Lieutenant Commander Quinn said about luck – he was sure they'd had some for a change.

"Play it, Greg."

April's voice came over the speakers on the bridge. "Diesel Coast, *this is the* FSC Gallaway. *Based on the samples taken of the Aegix nanomachines, Lieutenant Commander Quinn has managed to develop a broadcast interference pattern she believes will block the Aegix from taking control of FSC vessels. It has been distributed to the fleet. Federation Senate has agreed with our primary strategy and confirmed for you to execute.* Gallaway *out.*"

"Good girl, Quinn," Iridius said, to no one in particular. "Knew you could do it."

"So," Rangi said, "what exactly is this strategy?"

Iridius looked at his helmsman, and then over to Greg standing off to his right. He keyed his comms-link down to the workshop. "Junker, can you come up to the bridge?"

"Aye, cap."

A moment later Junker, wiping grease from her palms down the legs of her coveralls, walked onto the bridge. "What's up?"

"Before we left the *Gallaway*, Captain Idowu and I discussed options on how to proceed if Quinn was successful."

"Of course she was going to be," Junker said, like there'd never been any question that Quinn would figure out a solution to this catastrophe.

Iridius nodded. "So, we decided that *when* Quinn figured out how to stop the Aegix, we'd keep acting as the bait, but this time the plan is to take them straight into the heart of the fleet. We're going to lead them, and hope they follow us, to Tau Ceti."

"We're going to take them to Tau Ceti?" Rangi asked. "But we'd be leading them straight to the home of the Federation Senate, right into the most populated system in the galaxy."

"It's also where the fleet has gathered," Iridius countered. "Trying to get an attack force to converge on an enemy is always a challenge, so instead, we'll lead them into an attack. Besides, Quinn has figured out how to stop them controlling our ships. We get them there and the Federation fleet will do the rest."

Iridius's idea to spray his blood across interstellar space had bought the *Diesel Coast* enough time for their BAMF drive to recharge. Iridius gave the order, Rangi hit the button, and once again the *Diesel Coast* vanished into a pocket universe, this time headed for Tau Ceti, central hub of the Federation. There'd be no outrunning the Aegix again. This had better work.

CHAPTER FIFTEEN_

Even pushing the *Diesel Coast* as hard as they could, the journey from Eton-12 to Tau Ceti took close to thirty-three hours. Iridius knew the *Gallaway* at full-noise could make the trip in just over twenty and, given everything they'd learned about the Aegix and their ability to upgrade their ship at will, he was sure they would be faster still – though by how much, he didn't know. For the first four hours after they'd entered FTL Iridius sat on the bridge, feeling the Aegix gain on them. It was a slow gain, a constant approaching doom, as inescapable as the lingering sense of dread that accompanied the march towards gym class at the Academy. There was nothing Iridius could do but wait to see what would happen when the dog-ship caught them. The Aegix had already shown they were capable of adjusting their course while still in BAMF; perhaps they were also capable of using weapons in BAMF, in which case the *Diesel Coast* was even more of a fat, squat, sitting duck than usual. They shouldn't be able to fire missiles across a BAMF boundary, but Iridius wasn't willing to take anything for granted. He didn't tell the crew what was happening, not wanting to burden them with that same inevitable hopelessness, but from the way they sat solemnly, he was sure they knew. Rangi asked only two annoying questions in the entire four-hour stretch, an unheard-of average of less than one question an hour.

By hour five Iridius knew the Aegix were more or less right behind them. His sense of them was fuzzy across the boundaries of BAMF travel, as if they were drifting in and out of existence, but he could tell they had drawn within weapons distance. But no attack came. For the next hour the Aegix stayed that same distance behind them. And again for the hour after that. Iridius couldn't see any reason why they wouldn't have fired – unless they couldn't.

"Alright," Iridius said, breaking what had been over an hour of silence. "Seems like they're just following us, same as before. Greg, Rangi, go and get some shut-eye. I'll take first watch." He keyed the intercom down to Junker. "Junker, things seem to be going according to plan. Get some sleep, okay?"

There was a groan. "I *was* asleep, cap."

"Ah, sorry. Carry on then," Iridius said, wondering how Junker had managed to sleep when they were being pursued across space by the Aegix.

"Would you like me to come and relieve you in six hours, captain?" Greg asked.

Iridius nodded. "Thanks, that'll be fine."

"So we aren't going to be destroyed by a giant dog in inter-stellar space then?" Rangi asked.

"Doesn't seem like it."

"That's good. That would be pretty ruff."

Iridius looked at Rangi, doing his best imitation of the way his father used to look at him pretty much all the time - with over-whelming disappointment.

"Ha." Greg let out a single word to indicate laughter. "This joke I understand. Because that is the sound of an Earth dog."

Iridius looked from Rangi to Greg. "Go away," he said. "Both of you."

The two of them stood and walked off the bridge.

"Because ruff is what sound a dog makes," Greg was saying. "That is very good, Ensign Rangi. I like this joke."

"Stop praising him for that pun," Iridius called after them. "That's an order."

———

Iridius walked up the steps to the bridge, rubbing his eyes and shaking his head to try to clear the fogginess. He'd surprised himself with how long he had slept. Junker had called him up to the bridge, and if she was on watch that meant he must have slept through two six-hour watches – twelve hours at least, maybe more. He couldn't even remember drifting off. He'd been pulled out of his body and into unconsciousness in the way that only happened when you were lassoed into sleep by pure, utter exhaustion. He couldn't remember the last time he'd slept properly. Actually, he could, it was when they'd been on their way to Iota Persei on a nice, simple cargo hauling mission, before the *Gallaway* and the Aegix and the destruction of Earth and all this saving the galaxy nonsense.

"Hey cap, sorry to wake you. We're about eight hours out."

"No need to apologise. You want to go and get some more rest?"

"I might just head down and keep tinkering in the workshop. Can I be dismissed from watch?"

"Sure. You're relieved."

Junker hopped down from the captain's chair and Iridius took her place. "Oh hey, Junker?" he called as she walked off the bridge.

"Yeah, cap?"

"What are you working on down there?"

Junker shrugged. "Just some little side projects. Nothing that should explode, don't worry."

"I find the fact you need to clarify that terrifying."

Junker smiled broadly and exited without another word. Iridius was certain that if he didn't keep close tabs on her, Samira Nejem would be well on her way to mad-scientist territory.

Once Junker left, Iridius sat alone on the bridge of the *Diesel Coast*. He enjoyed being by himself on the bridge. It would never happen on a ship like the *Gallaway*, a vessel that large would always have a bridge crew, but on a small hauler like this with its bare-bones crew, it was normal to leave just one person on watch. At times like these it was easy to imagine that he was alone in the black. Despite the mind-shattering, existential dread-fuelling endlessness of space, he somehow found the idea of being alone out here comforting, or at least enthralling. It was probably just the pull of the void, that unknown draw of the vast black that had caused people throughout the history of spaceflight to float away on spacewalks or even launch themselves out of airlocks with the reckless abandon of lemmings off a cliff. He'd never heard of other species doing this, only humans. It must have been another quirk of human psychology that set them apart from other species, just like mankind's fascination with fire, climbing very tall mountains just for the sake of it, and watching other people live their lives on a thing called reality television, which still, even in the twenty-third century, bore almost no resemblance to actual reality.

There were still another eight hours before they'd arrive at Tau Ceti and likely fly themselves into, and hopefully out of the way of, the gronking shit tonne of missiles that would be directed at the space canine behind them. Iridius, April and those Federation Space Command Admirals who were still alive had decided that when the *Diesel Coast* led the Aegix into the waiting Federation fleet, every Federation ship would immediately open fire while broadcasting the interference pattern developed by Quinn, limiting the time the Aegix had to react and hopefully destroying them before they even realised their ability to hack into the ships wasn't working. The fleet wanted to end this fight quickly, while they had the only advantage open to them – probably the only advantage they'd ever have against a constantly upgrading advanced synthetic intelligence. What frustrated Iridius the most wasn't the danger the plan put them in – he'd been more than happy to sign up for whatever they had to do to destroy the Aegix. It was the fact that there was nothing he could do to improve their chances of getting out of the way of the fleet's attack. The long FTL flight provided nothing but time to stew over the coming confrontation.

Some time later the communicator on the arm of his chair beeped and flashed, pulling Iridius out of his thoughts. He hit the button. "Go ahead, Junker."

"Cap, I've got something to show you. Would you mind coming down to the engine room?"

"Sure. On my way."

The engine room of the *Diesel Coast* wasn't really a room for the engine; that was terminology that had hung around on ships for many thousands of years. Rather than being an enormous, noisy room housing the rattling, chugging guts of the ship's propulsion system, it was a simple, quiet space about the size of Iridius's cabin containing a bunch of consoles, computers and ports into major engine systems. The engines themselves were all external to the ship – that was the best place to keep the highly volatile nuclear reactions that powered the fusion drive and the matter-antimatter annihilation and spontaneous creation of fundamental particles that reshaped reality and generated whole new universes inside the two BAMF drive engines. This small room was where all maintenance and monitoring was done for the engine systems and, from the looks of the open wiring looms and unbolted access panels, it was where Junker had been doing her tinkering.

"Okay," Iridius said as he looked at the exposed wiring, patched-in components and almost unrecognisable control panel, "what have you got to show me other than the fact it looks like you've hacked my ship to pieces?"

"Now cap, do you think I'd rip a ship to pieces?"

"Is that a genuine question? Because the answer would be a resounding yes."

"Well, sure, I've taken things apart, *but* I always put them back together again, and most of the time they turn out better than before I started."

Iridius pointed at a cylindrical object sitting on the ground that had frayed wires extending from either end. "Is that thing supposed to be somewhere inside my ship?"

Junker shrugged. "Always a few bits leftover when you do a bit of DIY upgrading."

"Why do I suspect it's probably some part that prevents an explosion?"

Junker twisted her mouth to the side. "I mean, if there was a reversal of polarity in the boost capacitor bank then sure, that resistance block has a burn out failsafe that would stop a massive reversal of current that could, if a few other things went wrong, lead to a small explosion, but the chances of that are fairly slim."

"Slimmer than ancient alien AI infecting toy dogs and destroying the Earth?"

"Good point," Junker admitted. "But it was limiting the power I needed to drive my new upgrade, and it's one I think we're going to need."

"Okay, before I make you put back the bit that stops the explosion, I'll bite: what's the upgrade?"

"Right," Junker said, "so we're going to come out of BAMF

and pretty much fly into a hailstorm of missiles that are aimed at the Aegix, hey?"

"No, you see, it's an advanced tactical manoeuvre leading the enemy into a standard—" Iridius stopped when he saw the way Junker was eyeing him. "Yeah, that's pretty much it."

"And as good a pilot as Rangi is, we're going to struggle to get out of the way, aren't we?"

"That is one possibility, but—" Junker was looking at Iridius in the same way his mother used to look at him when he lied about taking the last of the cookies from the cookie jar. Iridius wondered what it would be like to command a crew that had some level of fearful respect and didn't treat their captain like the older brother they just sort of listened to sometimes. "Yes, we're probably going to eat a healthy breakfast of missiles."

"Figured that," Junker said, "so I thought maybe I'd do something useful while we were on our way. Thought we'd show the Aegix they're not the only ones who can upgrade their ship on the fly. I've had this idea for a while but never really had the chance to test it out. Basically, I've rigged up the drive control system to position all thrusters in full vertical and simultaneously fire. This can be done normally, of course, but what I've done is included not just the manoeuvring thrusters but the main fusion drive nozzle, too. Now, the real icing on the cake is that I've made some tweaks and bypassed a few safety overrides so that the fusion drive will overload and blow some major juice through the main engine. Usually we can push the main fusion drive to about one hundred and fifty per cent capacity without any damage, but I'm talking about letting it spiral up to three or four hundred per cent of normal operating load."

"And that's when we die in a flaming inferno, is it?"

"Well, probably not. See, the drive system is probably actually designed to take about a five hundred per cent load, so it'll still hold together. What it will do is fry some shit, and there's a bunch of inbuilt overrides in the control system that I can't deactivate or the nuclear reaction could easily go critical, so a blast like that through the engine will cause everything to automatically shut down pending cooldown and damage checks. However, that single shot will accelerate us like Greg running from his mother-in-law. We'll gronking know about it, and we'll probably all black out because I doubt the old girl's acceleration dampeners will handle it. Once the drive safety overrides shut down we'll be floating dead in the black for a bit, but it'll give us a rocking good chance to get out of the way of a missile barrage."

Most of the time the upgrades Junker installed led to marginal increases in power and efficiency. Even she knew not to mess with a ship's systems too much. She wouldn't go altering or installing anything crazy without permission. Most of the really crazy things she did were her own bench-top experiments, none of which had exploded so far – at least, not dramatically enough to take the ship with them. But what she'd done here seemed a little more extreme than a subtle tweak. The truth was, Iridius didn't know enough about what she'd done, or understand the ship's control system enough, to have any real concept of how far along the crazy spectrum she'd gone with this particular unsanctioned piece of work. Still, he had to admit, up until now he'd been relying on a lot of cards going his way to make it through the chaos to come. Now Junker had given them a legitimate manoeuvre to try to execute straight out of BAMF.

He went to clap her on the shoulder but stopped, his arm hovering in the air above her. He stared seriously into Technician Nejem's dark eyes. "Is this going to work?"

"Yes cap, it'll work."

He let his hand fall onto Junker's shoulder. "In that case, well done. You might've just given us the extra advantage we need. If this works and the Aegix get destroyed, I'm sure you'll get reinstated to chief, and could probably pick your posting on any ship you want. Would you go back to the *Valkyrie*?"

She shrugged. "Dunno."

"Well, let's get through this first and then I'm sure you'll get the chance. I'm going back to the bridge. I'll call everyone up when we're an hour out."

Iridius turned and headed towards the steps.

"Cap?"

Iridius turned back.

"I'm happy just here, on the *Diesel Coast*."

Iridius smiled at his technician. "Yeah," he said. "So am I. But Junker?"

"Yes, sir?"

"Probably ask me next time you want to completely redesign the drive control system."

Junker shot him a thumbs up. "You got it, boss."

———

As planned, Iridius called the crew of the *Diesel Coast* up to the bridge an hour before they were due in Tau Ceti – well, forty-eight minutes, actually, because Iridius B. Franklin wasn't quite as precise as that. He ran the crew through the alterations Junker had made to the ship and their plan for when they arrived – to get the gronking shit out of the way, basically. He'd considered making a very heartfelt speech about how much they and this ship meant to him, how it had been an honour serving with them and that no matter what anyone else in the fleet thought, even if they'd been thrown together as a bunch of outcasts, he still considered them the finest damn crew in the black. Iridius didn't say any of this though, because it seemed an awful lot like admitting they were all about to die, and surely that was bad luck. Besides, all that mushiness was just plain icky.

"So, let me get this clear," Rangi said, "we're going to pop the cherry and then I push full fusion power and activate the normal thrust vectoring controls and the ship will fire at power levels more than is probably safe at extreme acceleration and I'll have about as much control as a zero-g coaster flying off its track into the wild black yonder?"

"Yes," Iridius said, "that about covers it."

Rangi smiled. "Sounds fun. Like the early days of spaceflight: strap us into a can and light a gronking rocket under us."

"I never said it wasn't safe," Junker chimed in. "The ship systems will take it. They'll probably just shut down and we'll all black out."

Iridius stared at her.

"Look," she said, "it's not *not* safe, it's just less safe than usual."

Just like the previous thirty-two hours, the final hour of BAMF transit was uneventful. At least, externally it was. Internally, Iridius's concern was growing. He didn't let the crew see that, because that's just not what a captain did, but he was preparing himself for the absolute worst. Prepare for the worst, hope for the best, that's what his father used to say. Well, no, Iridius's father usually said, "pass me that Gartagan Lager, kid," but surely someone's wise father somewhere said things like that.

"How long?" Iridius asked, breaking what had been a long silence on the bridge.

"One minute," Rangi replied.

"One minute?" Iridius responded, more aghast than he'd meant to sound.

"Yeah," Rangi said.

"Right, sure, I must've lost track of time. You're sure it's only one minute?"

"Aye, sir," Rangi replied. "Well, it's forty-seven seconds now. Everything okay, cap?"

"Yes, no, it's fine," Iridius said. "I guess this is it. Everyone know what they have to do?"

"I pull us up as hard as Junker's upgrades will allow this old bird to go," Rangi said.

Iridius looked from Greg to Junker. They'd already sat down and strapped themselves in.

"Sure," Junker said. "I sit here, hold on like all gronking hell, and try not to pass out too fast."

"I believe I will be doing much the same, captain," Greg said.

"Yeah, right," Iridius said. "Well, make sure you do that to the best of your ability then."

"Twenty seconds," Rangi announced.

"Listen," Iridius said, "I wasn't going to say anything like this but... you guys are the best crew I've ever had."

"Fifteen seconds."

"We're the only crew you've ever had," Junker said.

"Sure," Iridius said, "but I mean, I wouldn't swap you for anyone else in the fleet."

"Ten seconds."

"Except maybe you, Rangi."

"Oh gee, thanks."

"Like, for a pilot that was completely mute. I wonder if there's any of those around."

"If I was mute I wouldn't be able to say this... Geronimo!"

And the *Diesel Coast* dropped out of BAMF right into the middle of one hell of an ambush. It would have been terrifying had it been set for them – and even though it hadn't, this was still a firing squad about to start shooting. As the shimmering blue of overloading shields dissipated, the view-screen revealed the gathered armada of a Federation fighting fleet. The *Valkyrie, Centaur, Fryx, Gallaway, Beetlejuice, Shatner, Jintyr* and at least thirty more of the Federation's most advanced starships hung in a scattered formation before the crystal blue planet of Tau Ceti C, all of them facing the point of the *Diesel Coast*'s arrival. Each of the ships had shields up and weapons primed to fire and, just as agreed, as soon as they picked up the incoming BAMF signature and the *Diesel Coast* popped back into reality, they let loose their weapons.

"Missiles away, missiles away." The voice of Lieutenant Aidan came over the comms system, confirming the weapons launch. Iridius had ensured the *Diesel Coast*'s comms were tapped into the Federation fleet channel before they'd arrived, and now they could hear the chatter. As the most senior combat ship, the FSC *Valkyrie* would be leading the assault on the Aegix, the other vessels following their lead, though the plan was relatively simple – shoot a lot.

Iridius was reminded of the buzzing of an approaching plague of locusts as he watched the assembled fleet unload their barrage of missiles, each carrying a nuclear warhead. In their one real shot to avoid being devoured, Ensign Rangi initiated their overpowered vertical burn. The *Diesel Coast* made the kind of noises that were never comforting, especially when coming from the only thing keeping you safe from the all-but-instant death of space. It screamed, howled and shook like the best cocktail bartenders Iridius used to visit – damn, he realised, all his favourite Earth bars were gone. Even with the maneuverability of an ex-asteroid hopper the *Diesel Coast* moved in a way it never had in its long life. They say you can't teach an old dog new tricks, but the fusion drive ramped up well past nominal power limits and spewed superheated plasma out of every nozzle and orifice. This was like strapping a rocket-pack to a retired old hound dog and letting it chase rabbits again.

The sudden acceleration hit Iridius like lead bricks were tugging on every cell of his body.

"Aegix... out of... BAMF," Greg managed to say against the increasing g-forces as he watched his console.

Just as Junker had predicted, the *Diesel Coast*'s ageing acceleration control systems were struggling to maintain a bearable acceleration profile inside the ship. Iridius gripped the arms of his chair. He was being pushed down harder and harder into it by the ever-increasing force. The vibrations of the ship became ever more violent, until he could hardly focus on the view-screen in front of him because his eyeballs seemed to be rattling around inside his skull. From what he could make out from the data on screen, the relative motion between the incoming missiles and the *Diesel Coast* should see them get clear. That was nice. They probably weren't going to get atomised by friendly Federation missiles. Not that Iridius was going to start whooping and celebrating just yet; there still seemed to be a distinct chance that the *Diesel Coast* would rattle itself to pieces or simply explode at any second. And as if on cue, a sound like titanium nails down an antimatter chalkboard filled the air.

"Junker?!" Iridius yelled.

"It's okay," she called back. "She's... still happy."

"She doesn't feel happy! She feels... decidedly unhappy! She... she feels... Greg's mother-in-law... unhappy!"

"Only... one... time... captain," Greg said, his words stretched thin through the effort of speaking. He seemed to be struggling the most with the g-forces, probably due to his malignant physiology. Although it was becoming difficult to turn his head, Iridius looked over at him. Greg's head was lolling on his shoulders. His eyes rolled back and he sagged forward, unconscious. At this acceleration, and with the *Diesel Coast* struggling as it was to adapt the artificial gravity system to compensate, it wouldn't be long before the rest of them blacked out in a similarly undignified way.

"Missile impact... belay that." Iridius focused on Aidan's voice, which was still being piped through the comms system as he communicated with the fleet. "Missiles are veering off course. I say again, all missiles are altering their course."

"All vessels, this is Captain Idowu. Confirm you are broadcasting the interference pattern provided."

"This is Admiral Traxis in Tau Ceti Control, we are picking up the broadcast pattern strongly. It's being broadcast. It's just not working."

Iridius listened as the ship shuddered and shook, forcing his core muscles to tense, inhaling and exhaling in short, quick puffs to try to keep himself from passing out. He could barely see the view-screen now, the details had all blurred into a fractured kaleidoscope. Even as he watched, the colour seemed to begin draining from his vision. He squeezed his eyes shut and concentrated on staying awake, desperate to at least hear what was going on.

"Missiles are detonating," Aidan reported to the fleet. "Mass detonation but all missile trajectories have turned away from target. I say again, we have zero hits against the target. The Aegix vessel is undamaged."

A familiar voice came over the comms. "All vessels, check shields, ready second barrage, initiate attack pattern delta-three-zero."

Iridius tried to move his hand to fumble for his comms but he couldn't lift it. He needed to tell the fleet to fall back. He needed to tell April to fall back. He tried to open his eyes. Everything was black. He couldn't tell if his eyes were open or not.

"Aegix ship accelerating, weapons and shields primed."

"Picking up an opening bay door."

"Multiple bogeys."

Iridius's head fell back, pinned against the headrest by the acceleration of the ship.

"We're locked out of ship's systems!"

"No propulsion or shields here either."

No, Iridius thought, but he didn't hear any more after that as the g-forces stole the blood from his brain and his consciousness went with it.

————

Iridius's eyes slammed open as he gasped a sharp intake of breath. His momentary confusion was followed in rapid succession by fear and panic. The comms channel was full of frantic chatter, which didn't precisely quell his panic, but at least it meant there were still FSC ships out there. He could see again, which was a welcome relief – although what he saw on the view-screen made him wonder if the alternative was better. A space battle the likes of which Iridius had only ever witnessed in simulations or imagined in school-aged staring-out-the-window daydreams was in full swing.

FSC starships moved the enormity of their bulk in arcing trajectories or tight thruster-burning turns to bring weapons to bear or protect vulnerable shield or hull segments. Among them, smaller Aegix ships buzzed around like bloodthirsty insects, altering their vectors with astonishing shifts in acceleration. Those Federation ships that carried fighters of their own – only the specialised combat vessels, like the *Valkyrie* and the *Centaur* – had launched them into the fray but they were laughably outnumbered, and completely outmatched in manoeuvrability and weaponry.

Among the starships, fighters, missiles and railgun fire that crisscrossed below them, a gathering cloud of debris floated against the black. Most of it, Iridius reflected, didn't seem dog-shaped. And there, well below where the *Diesel Coast* had ended up, at the centre of the battle, was the main Aegix ship – the synthetic intelligence that was responsible for what had been, quite frankly, the worst few days of Iridius's career and, you know, the destruction of Earth, too. That was the ship they'd played bait for. It had caused the destruction of hundreds of thousands of festival-goers, had launched more missiles at them than there are chillies in a Gatarsian Gut Liquefying Lava Bowl, with not so much as a ruffle in its fur. The centre of the Aegix hive mind floated in the middle of the carnage, completely undamaged and seemingly as relaxed as a sunglass-wearing pool-goer on an inflatable bed.

How fucking rude.

Any ships that flew too close or tried to attack the giant dog-ship were destroyed, their systems rendered completely inoperable as the Aegix took control, just as they had every time an FSC ship had faced them. Whatever Quinn had come up with to jam the Aegix's ability clearly hadn't worked. But she'd never been wrong before, and Iridius figured she probably wasn't now. Something was different about the Aegix. It was only subtle, but he could feel it. The Aegix were clearly adapting at a rate far beyond human comprehension. Just as people had always feared with artificial intelligence, it was going to be impossible for any human, even one as intelligent as Quinn, to out-think this enemy. So this was it then. They were completely out-thought and out-gunned in an actual gronking space-battle for the fate of the galaxy. The future of all sentient life was at stake and Iridius – very unlike what he'd pictured in those school-aged daydreams – was facing it in a flying metal shoebox. Cool. Cool cool cool. Everything's fine. It'll be fine.

Around him on the bridge, the other members of his crew were also coming back to the land of the living – though the living part would be awfully short if they didn't act quickly.

"Junker," Iridius said, "ship damage update? Rangi, is the helm responsive? Greg, shields and weapons?"

"Holy shit," Rangi said as his faculties (such as they were) returned and he caught sight of the myriad of targeting reticles on the view-screen. "It's—"

"Yes," Iridius interrupted, "it's a gronking space battle for the future of the galaxy, so will you please start reporting!"

"The drive system held together with about as much damage as expected," Junker said. "BAMF is completely offline and some thrusters are toast, but fusion drive is giving us about forty per cent, so at least we're not completely dead in the black."

"Helm seems good to go," Rangi said, "but our manoeuvrability will be limited based on that damage."

"Shields recharged now," Greg said, "but they will not survive the damage we will likely suffer if we enter that battle. Railgun ammunition is also limited to two or three salvos. I am afraid I do not know what assistance we will be able to provide. We are not a battleship, after all, captain."

Greg was right. They weren't a battleship. They were a forty-year-old piece of shit ex-asteroid hopper with a crew of four misfits, no weapons, limited shields and less than half their usual engine capacity. There was nothing they could do. Once again, Iridius B. Franklin lacked the ship he needed to make a difference. But then a different thought rose up from somewhere within him. A thought he'd never had before when considering his lack of a Universe-class starship. It was an interesting realisation, really.

This was just the way he liked it.

Iridius looked at Greg. "The ship doesn't make the captain," he said, "and it doesn't make the crew either. We're what makes the Federation great, so we're going to figure something out." He tapped at the comms on his arm. "*Gallaway*, this is Captain Franklin on the *Diesel Coast*, are you there? April?"

"Iridius?" April's voice responded. "You're alive?"

"Surprisingly so, yes. What's the situation?"

"About as good as it looks. The interference pattern we

broadcast didn't work. The main Aegix vessel hasn't suffered a single hit and their missile barrages and fighters are shredding us. We've lost at least ten ships."

"I'm sorry, captain." Quinn's voice cut in; it sounded like she was calling out from behind April. "It should have worked. They must have upgraded their systems or changed somehow. I don't know what happened. It should have worked."

"Lieutenant commander," April said, "I told you to focus."

"It's alright, Quinn," Iridius said. "I know. I think they're constantly changing. You couldn't have predicted how to overcome that, but right now we need a new plan. Fast."

"Any ships that try to engage the main Aegix ship lose control and are destroyed just like the *El Nino*," April said. "We have no idea how to attack them. The only positive is that the Aegix haven't taken control of every ship in the fleet. The amount they can control must be limited somehow, so they're saving it for when the main intelligence is threatened."

"Any chance we can sneak attack?" Iridius asked.

"Tried that already," April responded quickly, "that's how we lost the *Fresno*, the *Dumbledore* and the *Sinclair*. All communication was Alpha-encrypted, but they obviously cracked it. We can't communicate any sort of strategy, and they seem easily able to predict ship movements based on trajectory changes and can anticipate when a vessel is peeling off for a broadside attack. Everyone is just fighting their own battle for survival right now."

"I assume someone with much more authority than me has ordered the fleet to fall back?" Iridius asked.

"We've lost communication with Tau Ceti Control and subsequently the Admiralty. A bunch of captains transmitted that all vessels should retreat, but no one seems to have a working BAMF drive. The Aegix must be jamming that for everyone. They're not letting anyone get away from this fight."

"They're trying to eliminate everyone. Whenever they

perceive a threat, they seem fixated on ensuring it gets destroyed so there's no possibility it can interfere with their mission of galactic goopifying. So, basically, in the terminology of old Earth military, this is a SNAFU?"

"Very much so, yes."

It was then that Iridius had another realisation, one that, even a few days ago, he'd never have expected. The *Diesel Coast* was not the worst possible ship he could be in. In fact, it very well might be exactly the one he needed. The beginnings of a plan tickled around the inside of his brain, amorphous, not yet fully formed, but there.

"Quinn?" Iridius said. "You still eavesdropping over there?"

"Yes, sir."

"I've got an amorphous blob in my head."

"Sorry, sir?"

"A vague idea, Quinn, a hunch, but I need your brain. You know more than anyone about the Aegix and the way their techno-hacking works."

"I can't help, sir. I obviously don't know enough. It didn't work."

"Forget about that for now."

"I can't, captain. I screwed up. I shouldn't be out here. All those ships are gone because I couldn't do it."

"Gronking Jupiter's nuts, Quinn," Iridius exclaimed over the comms. "I know you're blaming yourself for this but I need you to get your shit together, understand? All those times I've told you to focus on the moment, ignore your nerves, that courage is the overcoming of fear and not the absence of it, et cetera et cetera, blah blah. This is the moment you need to listen to me, understand? Time to be a Federation officer."

There was a pause while it seemed like the crew on the bridge of both vessels, and perhaps the whole fleet involved in this mad fight, were waiting for Quinn's response. Surprisingly, it wasn't Quinn who spoke next.

"You should do what your captain says, lieutenant commander." Commander Mul's voice came over the line. "He's a starship captain and he needs your help."

"Okay," Quinn said after a moment. "What's your amorphous blob, captain?"

"Your theory is that the Franklinisms that happen to basically every ship I've ever been on are caused by the nanobots in my blood, right?"

"Yes."

"Then why is there one ship that's never given me a problem?"

"The *Diesel Coast*."

"Exactly. Why isn't she affected by my nanobots? Plus, why was it that the *Diesel Coast* could escape from *Gargarin Station* even though the station was swarming with Aegix?"

"You're thinking the *Diesel Coast* is immune, Iridius?" April asked.

"That's what I'm thinking."

Quinn took a moment to answer. Iridius could imagine her, staring off into the middle distance, her finger pressed against her lips in the way it always was when she was thinking. "The Aegix have so far demonstrated the ability to remotely influence electrical, mechanical, energetic and quantum-dynamical systems and yet the common thread is that all of those systems have been run by computers."

"Quinn," Iridius said, "that's like saying all fish in the ocean exist in water. Everything is managed by computers."

"Yes, sir, but our ship," she caught herself, "your ship—"

"No," Iridius said, "you might not be here but the *Diesel Coast* is still your ship, Quinn."

"Yes, sir. Thank you, sir. Well, the *Diesel Coast* was designed for use in asteroid mining operations in the Frantle Belt, an area of highly magnetic asteroids. The only way to avoid interference issues when traversing the Frantle Belt is to avoid the wireless architecture common on most starships. The systems on board the *Diesel Coast* are still all shielded circuits that are almost entirely hardwired. The result is a ship with systems only marginally more advanced than old Earth telegraph wires, but it also means there's no opportunity for wireless signals to hack in. It's old technology, and the simplicity of it is probably what saves her."

Iridius nodded. "Alright then, that's turned my blob into a more solid idea. We're the only ship that can attack the Aegix."

"Captain," Quinn said, "that's just my theory. I could be wrong. I was wrong about the interference pattern."

"I trust you, Quinn." Iridius looked to Junker. "When was the last time the life-pods were checked?"

"Ah, probably last tech inspection. Maybe twelve months ago."

"But they're safe?"

"As safe as those coffins ever are."

"Okay." Iridius flicked a button on his comms panel. "All stations, this is Captain Franklin of the *FSC Diesel Coast*. We're mounting an attack run but are low on shields. Keep those mongrel dogs off us."

The responses from the other ships in the fleet began coming in fast.

"Who is this?"

"What ship?"

"Communicating vessel, identify yourself."

Iridius pressed his comms button again. "I just did identify my—" but he was cut off.

"This is Captain Idowu on the *Gallaway*. Captain Franklin is one of the best damn captains out here and he's the only one with an actual plan for how to destroy this thing, so just do what he says and keep the Aegix off him. Clear that hauler a path."

There was a moment of quiet.

"Rangi," Iridius said, "get us moving. As much power as you can towards the main Aegix vessel."

Rangi tapped at the console and the ship's fusion engines began to hum, notably quieter than they would normally be.

Just as Iridius was ready to rethink the feasibility of his plan, a voice came over the comms. "This is the *Valkyrie*, we acknowledge. Switching priority to keeping the *Diesel Coast* covered."

With the positive response from the *Valkyrie* and the angry rocket up their asses from Captain Idowu, other ships began to acknowledge the plan and shifted their trajectories to assist the *Diesel Coast*. Of course, having overheard the communications and more than likely being well aware of their inability to control Iridius's ship, the Aegix began turning their attention to the *Coast* as well. The small fighter-dogs split off from other combats to intercept. Those fighters remaining from the *Valkyrie* and *Centaur* moved into an escort formation and engaged the first wave of enemy fighters. The *Gallaway* manoeuvred into a position above and slightly in front of the *Diesel Coast*. It fired a wave of railgun chaff into a squadron of six approaching dogs, shredding them in a series of brief explosions. But even before the debris cleared, the space where they'd been was soon filled by another ten dog-fighters. These were swiftly dealt with by a railgun salvo from the *Shatner*, which was also moving in to escort them. The FSC ships would pave the way for the *Diesel Coast*, but just how far this yellow-brick road would take them was completely up for speculation.

"Captain, I'm very happy you've got a plan," Rangi said, "and I'm sure it's a really great plan, but I was just wondering, given we don't really have weapons, or shields, or engines, really, what exactly is the plan?"

"Eloquent as always, Rangi," Iridius said. "The plan is as simple as they come. We do have a weapon."

"We do?"

Iridius nodded. "Sure. The *Diesel Coast* is a weapon. We're going to ram the Aegix."

"Ram?" Junker said. "As in, crash the ship into?"

Iridius nodded. "We fly as fast as we can, we bail out, and the *Diesel Coast* goes into retirement and takes that massive Aegix pain in the ass with it."

"Um," Rangi said, "that's not really the plan I was hoping for, cap."

"You got a better idea?"

"No."

"Well, are you with me or not?" Iridius stared at his helmsman. "Space Ace?"

Rangi smiled. "Oh, I'm with you."

"Greg?"

"Certainly, captain."

"Good. Junker, you get down to the engines and see if you can't find a way to squeeze us a little more power. You alright with that?"

"Haven't got anywhere else to be," she said as she climbed up from behind the console to make her way down to the engine controls.

The *Diesel Coast* pushed on, charting a straight trajectory through the carnage of battle towards the Aegix ship. It was a trajectory that completely betrayed their intentions and was a strategic nightmare in terms of leaving them open to attack but, for the moment at least, the other ships in the fleet were doing an excellent job of escorting them in, clearing the path of missiles, fighters and chunks of floating ship. After a few moments Iridius felt, more than heard, an increase in the hum of the fusion drive.

"We've got more power coming through," Rangi said. "Not much, but we're accelerating."

Iridius hit the comms. "Nice work, Junker. Can you get us any more?"

"If I push the systems much further past their safety limits there's a good chance we'll explode, cap."

"Now or later?"

"Pretty quick."

"Alright," Iridius said, "give me whatever you can but keep us unexploded until we crash into the Aegix and explode anyway."

"Aye."

The *Diesel Coast* flew in, Rangi doing what he could to manoeuvre through the battle with limited power and thrusters. Iridius could see his frustration growing at being unable to fly to the best of his ability. The Aegix were quiet in Iridius's head. Surprisingly, they hadn't contacted him to reiterate their nonsense about how the galaxy had to be prepared, but Iridius knew the Aegix were well aware of his intentions now. There was a strong sense of being watched emanating from them; Iridius had the sudden feeling that he was their sole focus now. Suddenly, as if to prove it, the Aegix fired an extraordinarily large salvo of missiles straight back along their trajectory towards them. Like, an absolute shitload.

"Incoming," Greg said.

Ahead of them, the *FSC Jintyr* roared in and cut across their path to fire a huge barrage of railgun rounds towards the incoming missiles. They impacted and destroyed maybe eighty per cent of the missiles, but that still left enough to well and truly overwhelm what little shield charge the *Diesel Coast* had left and probably take them out, too.

"I don't have the delta-v to attempt evasive manoeuvring, captain," Rangi said.

Other vessels spat railgun fire in from the sides, taking out another half of the remaining missiles, but broadside railgun fire against fast-moving targets such as missiles was never as effective as front-on fire.

"Still multiple incoming missiles," Greg said. "Fifteen seconds out."

"Oh right," Iridius said, "is that what all those flashing red icons on the view-screen are? Tell you what, I've had just about enough of this shit!"

Iridius thrust his arms forward and then, in a motion like he was sweeping a desk clear of clutter, swung them to the side. Ahead of them, the missiles that were rapidly converging on the *Diesel Coast* immediately changed direction and spun, end over end like tossed trash, off into the empty black beside them. Well, almost empty black – they narrowly missed two of the ships and several fighters that had moved into escort formation around them. Iridius noticed this a moment too late, but if anyone asked, he'd claim he'd carefully avoided those ships on purpose.

"Woohoo!" Rangi let out a whoop of excitement. "Techno-wizard on the bridge, take that, fuckers!"

Iridius stopped himself from berating his helmsman for two reasons: first, despite the fact that he had things crawling around inside his body, it was pretty cool that he could do that, and second, it was true: they were fuckers.

The attacks from the Aegix continued; missiles being fired from the main ship and darting attack runs from fighters. The majority of them were repelled by the Federation ships, but occasionally Iridius had to wave away the odd stray missile. He realised too late – though of course it made sense, given they had no computer guidance – that he was unable to force railgun rounds away. They lost around a quarter of what remained of their shields when an Aegix fighter managed to pepper the underside of their hull with a spray of railgun fire before being)ut by a fighter from the *Valkyrie*. Lesson learned the hard way, but at least fighters were only minimally armed with railguns.

As they drew nearer to the Aegix, the *Shatner* moved to intercept and fired their broadside railguns at a strafe of missiles from a group of Aegix fighters. Iridius knew even before they broadcast that they'd come too close to the Aegix. This was the point at which the fleet would have to turn back.

"We've lost all control," the panicked voice came over the main comms channel. "Propulsion gone. Shields gone now, too. More incoming. Oh—"

The voice cut off as the *FSC Shatner*, lacking any energy shield protection, was hit by a further salvo of missiles and erupted in a series of small explosions, culminating in the white-hot burst of the fusion drive and the shimmering dissipation and firework-like crackle of particles and anti-particles from the BAMF drive.

Iridius immediately hit the fleet-wide channel. "That's it, all ships fall back. I say again, all ships fall back. You've got us this far and I thank you for that, now get out of range."

"Iridius," April responded, and Iridius noticed she was using the dedicated communication channel between their two ships. "You won't make it in alone." From the tone of her voice, Iridius could tell she wasn't just concerned about the success of their attack.

"April, as your co-captain I'm asking you to drop back. Protect your crew. Please."

Her response was slow in coming. "Alright," she said. "Make sure you get out of there safe, co-captain."

"I will," Iridius said. "I don't plan on dying for these over-grown metallic fleabags. I'll see you on the other side."

"Iridius—" April started but was cut off as, keen to avoid an emotional exchange, Iridius shut down all open comms channels.

"All Federation vessels are turning back, captain," Greg said.

"If you do not mind my asking, precisely how do you intend for us to ensure the *Diesel Coast* reaches the Aegix vessel? I believe we will become the focal point of their attention."

"We're going to guide her in as far as we can. Then we're going to give her an acceleration kick in the ass by overloading the fusion drive. We'll bail out in the escape pods and hope we've given the ship enough to make it to the Aegix and finally neuter this runaway mutt."

"Huh, I don't think I've ever heard that before," Rangi said.

"What? Neutering? It means cutting their balls off, ensign."

"No, I don't think I've ever heard you rely on hope. That's not like you."

"Well, it's not really like me to be involved in a gronking space battle for the fate of all sentient life either, Rangi, but here we are," Iridius replied. "Desperate times. Get us in there with the best evasive manoeuvres you can manage with the propulsion we've got. Greg, use up as much railgun ammunition as you need to protect the sides and aft of the ship. I'll handle anything coming at us directly from the main Aegix ship. We're on our own now."

"It's all good, cap," Rangi said. "We're always on our own."

Iridius hit the comms. "Junker, make sure the escape pods are open and ready to launch. Oh, and one other thing. How long from when we overload the fusion engine with all the power you can give us to when the ship goes all 'splodey on us?"

"I'm not sure exactly – thirty seconds, maybe a minute."

"Alright, be ready to overload on my mark, and then we abandon ship."

"You got it."

Iridius tilted his neck from side to side, releasing a series of cracks, then rolled his shoulders back. "Let's do this. Let's save the galaxy." He gestured with a pointed finger towards the view-ı. "Onward."

Ensign Rangi remained twisted around in his chair, staring at Iridius. He looked to the others on the bridge as if wondering whether they were supposed to be doing something. "We're sort of already going as fast as we can," he said. "I'm not sure what you want me to do, captain."

"I was just trying to be inspirational, say something fitting for the moment we're about to single-handedly try to destroy a vast alien intelligence."

"Sure," Rangi said. "It's just, you said 'onward', like we should start moving, but we're already moving. It's like yelling 'charge' when you're already on your horse galloping towards the enemy. You can see how that might be confusing. Some of your soldiers might think you mean to charge someone else, and they might go one way and everyone else goes another, and then your force is all scattered."

Iridius looked at Rangi and gave him his familiar 'turn around' finger spin.

"Aye, cap," Rangi said as he spun to look at the view-screen and focus on his console.

"Incoming missiles off starboard side," Greg reported. "Firing railguns." The chattering thumps of the few remaining defensive railguns the *Diesel Coast* had vibrated through the ship. "More inbound from the front."

"I see them," Iridius said as the view-screen lit up with red reticles like a rapidly approaching, very angry Christmas tree. He didn't stand and he didn't thrust his arms out in front of him this time, because he realised he didn't need to. He simply concentrated on making the missiles veer around them and, just as he'd imagined, without any techno-wizard pomp or circumstance, the missiles split into two equal packs, turning out and away from the *Diesel Coast* and erupting harmlessly off to either side. "Okay," Iridius said. "Rangi, when I give Junker the signal to overload the drive make sure we're on target for the centroid of the Aegix ship and lock that course in. Then we all head straight down to the escape pods, clear?"

"You got it, cap."

"Aye, sir."

Iridius hit the comms down to engineering, or at least the small workshop and control room that passed for engineering on the *Diesel Coast*. "Junker, ready to blow our load?"

"Terrible phrasing, captain but yes, I'm ready."

"Alright," Iridius said. "On my mark. Three, two, one... mark."

"Shutting off safety overrides and overloading fusion drive... now."

"Aim us in and give us full power, Ensign Rangi."

"Aye aye. Locked on target and full power."

The *Diesel Coast* hummed as the fusion drive began to increase its power output, being forced past the limits the system had imposed after having already been overloaded once. The sound of the engine rose from a reassuring rain on the roof hum to a raw chest-reverberating bass-line rumble to an increasingly frantic squealing. The structure of the ship began to vibrate more forcefully, until it was shaking and shimmying. The overall effect was that the ship was throwing a screaming, thrashing tantrum about being forced to overload its engines yet again when all it wanted was to have an ice cream and not explode.

"Let's get down to the escape pods," Iridius called over the noise. "I'm not keen on staying aboard what's basically become a missile."

Grabbing onto rails and supporting themselves on consoles as they were bumped and shuddered off balance by the wild toss of the ship, the three of them hurried down the stairs to meet Junker in the cargo bay. The *Diesel Coast*'s eight escape pods, which were of the extremely outdated type known unaffectionately as

s, stood open along the port-side wall of the cargo bay.

Embedded in the ship's walls, they were a single-use solution to getting off the ship in a hurry. One occupant could fit in each pod, which would then be closed, sealing them inside. When activated, a thick blast shield would slide down to maintain ship atmospheric integrity and then controlled explosives would blast a chunk out of the side of the hull, ejecting the pod along with it.

"Poor girl doesn't like this much," Junker said.

"I know," Iridius said, "she knows she's on the way out. She's always been stubborn. Get into the escape pods, now."

Rangi and Junker both did as ordered, entering the claustrophobic confines of the pods. The doors closed and locked. Iridius could see their faces through the circular glass window set within the grey, gunmetal door. Surprisingly, it was Greg who didn't obey. It was unlike him to be insubordinate, even if, as Iridius suspected, he intended it to be helpful. He stood outside his pod, looking at his captain.

"Greg?" Iridius prompted.

"Someone has to make sure the pods seal correctly, captain."

"Yes, and I'm going to do it. Get into an escape pod, Greg. I'll be right behind you. That's an order."

Malignants' faces were oddly shaped, with disproportionate features and skin as bubbled as grilled cheese toast, so Iridius always found it difficult to read Greg's emotions. This time, though, it wasn't so hard. Iridius was fairly certain Greg knew what was coming.

"They will react poorly," Greg said. "This crew would follow you, as humans say, to the end of the Earth."

"Thank you, Greg." Iridius put his hand on the malignant's shoulder. "But we've already been past the end of the Earth, remember? Now, into a pod."

The enormous cancer looked like he was going to argue but then, without another word, he acquiesced and climbed into a pod, letting it close behind him. Iridius checked the panel beside each door to ensure that the pods were sealed and ready to launch and then, instead of getting into a pod of his own, he took a handful of steps back so that he could see into the window of each pod. Junker closed her eyes for a long time before opening them again to stare out at him. She knew, too. Of course it was Rangi who was slowest on the uptake.

"Captain, what are you doing?" Rangi said, his voice pumped through an external speaker on the escape pod.

"Listen, you three," Iridius said. "It has been, strangely enough, a pleasure having you as my crew."

"Captain, what are you doing?" Rangi repeated, but this time his words were tinged with understanding.

"This ship was never going to hit the Aegix target without a little assistance from some techno-wizardry, Rangi," Iridius said. "I'm going to have to keep the path clear all the way to impact. Plus, you know, the captain needs to go down with the ship and all that. Perks of command, I guess. Believe it or not, you're the highest ranking officer here now, so you need to make sure you all get to safety."

"From a coffin?"

"I'm sure you can handle it, Space Ace."

Even through the thick glass porthole, Iridius could see Rangi biting his lips to try to control his emotions. "You told Captain Idowu you didn't plan on dying here, cap. I heard you say that."

"I know what I said, ensign," Iridius replied. "Thing is, I happened to be telling a whopping big fib."

"Captain," Junker began her pleading with him now. "Please don't do this."

This whole thing would have been a lot easier if the escape pods didn't allow the occupant to communicate with the outside. It wasn't as though it was going to help. As they say, in space no one can hear you scream from inside your tiny coffin floating in the black vacuum of the infinite void.

Junker was the first to try the rather obvious solution of actually opening the door of the escape pod. When that didn't work, she squirmed back then began to push and even tried to ram her shoulder into the door, but there wasn't enough space to make any sizeable impact.

"I already set the escape pod doors to automatically lock," he said. "And I can't believe you only just tried the door."

Junker shrugged. "I knew you wouldn't have made such a simple mistake, but I figured I'd check anyway." Her pause was heavy, loaded with a myriad of unspoken emotions. "Captain, please don't do this. It's bad enough to lose the *Diesel Coast*, you can't go with her."

"Good luck, you three," Iridius said, "and say hi to your mother-in-law, Greg. Computer, launch the escape pods."

"No!" The cry came almost in unison from both Junker and Rangi.

"One time," Greg said, though it wasn't a true rebuttal, but more a habitual response that was loaded with an entirely different meaning this time.

The blast wall slid down, and the glass portholes revealing the faces of Samira Nejem, Benjamin Rangi and Gr'lak N'hlarkic Tre'laktor disappeared from view. Iridius inhaled through his nose and exhaled sharply through pursed lips, blinking to clear away the unexpected blur. In many ways he'd felt an even stronger need to cut off the goodbye with his crew than he had with April. It was a different feeling, of course, but the April-sized hole in his life had been there for the better part of a decade. This crew-sized hole was brand new.

A staccato series of muffled pops marked the eruption of the explosive bolts that perforated the hull section around the escape pods. A larger whoomph from the other side of the blast door indicated that the ship's emergency hull section had burst outwards and the escape pods containing his crew, his friends, had been ejected into space with it. He desperately hoped that, despite their colloquial nickname, those pods didn't become coffins.

He realised with a sudden pang of panic, fear and disappointment that he'd never have the chance to find out. He pushed that thought well down out of the way. If he didn't have time to say a proper goodbye to his crew, he didn't have time for emotions, either. He turned and headed for the bridge. He had no doubt the Aegix would continue their assault to stop the Diesel Coast, and if he didn't hurry, they'd succeed.

His boots clanged up the steel steps to the bridge and just as he hit the top he saw, looming in the view-screen, precisely what he'd been concerned about.

"Jupiter's nuts."

A cloud of missiles launched from the Aegix was about to hit the front of the Diesel Coast. He'd taken too long getting the others off the ship. He threw his arms forward and to the side. He knew he didn't need to, and there was nobody to show off in front of anymore, but it was pure instinct at this point. The missiles veered in the direction he'd waved his arms, but those in front had been so close that despite their sudden change of direction, they still collided with the Diesel Coast. The incandescent white of several nuclear warheads detonating in the vacuum of space filled the view-screen, leaving a bright green and purple after-image in the centre of Iridius's vision. This was followed by the crackling blue of the Diesel Coast's shields overloading as they absorbed and dissipated the enormous amount of energy that had just been slammed into the ship.

Iridius may have thrown the missiles off-target enough that the Diesel Coast was only hit by glancing blows, but those three impacts were enough to rock the ship like a toy boat in the shore break. Iridius was thrown off his feet as the deck bucked beneath him. Unable to get his hands out to take the impact, he slammed face-first into the steel grate floor, his nose crunching and his front teeth suddenly howling as they cracked and chipped. The lights on the deck flickered and went out and orange emergency lighting switched on, casting the space in an amber haze. Through a sudden shrieking ring in his ears Iridius heard alarms beeping and whooping from all over the bridge as several systems failed at once.

Iridius pushed himself to his hands and knees, spitting out a coagulated glob of blood, saliva, snot and tooth fragments. He looked up, squeezing his eyes closed and then opening them again in an attempt to clear the blur. The *Diesel Coast,* through its already powerful momentum and the use of its overloaded drive system, continued on the trajectory that would slam it right into the centre of the Aegix dog-ship. Iridius patted the floor.

"Good girl."

He pulled himself to his feet and looked at the XO's station. Shields were completely non-existent now, and the hull was ruptured into the cargo bay. Though Iridius hadn't noticed as his face was rendezvousing with the floor, moments after the missile impacts had taken the shields offline and ripped open the hull, the blast door at the back of the bridge had slammed closed, sealing it off from the rest of the ship and preventing him from being sucked out into space. The console before him streamed information about the *Diesel Coast*'s distance to the ship in front of it. A trajectory proximity warning began howling from the helm, joining the cacophony of desperate alarms. Iridius didn't need to look at the console to know they were about to hit the target. The shape of an enormous dog almost a kilometre long loomed ahead of them, quickly filling the entire screen. Iridius realised as he stared at the enemy ship that his hands were no longer on the console and his feet were no longer on the ground. The artificial gravity had given out. He placed his foot on the top of the XO's console and kicked off, sending himself out over the helm station and towards the view-screen.

The red reticles used to track enemy ships swarmed towards him. This was why he'd had to stay on the ship. No matter what he'd told his crew, he'd known that the *Diesel Coast* would never make it all the way to the Aegix ship without him fending off attacks. He'd known the Aegix would throw everything they had at him. He was sure they had realised his plan not long after the *Diesel Coast* had begun its impact trajectory. He was also sure they didn't consider it much of a threat. No doubt the Aegix considered themselves well aware of all the advantages Iridius had. They knew they couldn't hack the *Coast* and they knew Iridius had nanobots in his blood and could use them to fend off attacks in the same way they could. The Aegix considered them-selves vastly superior in every way.

However, there was one other advantage Iridius hoped he had – the hunch that he'd based this entire plan of attack on. He was happy to kill himself. Well, not *happy* per se, but willing. Something the Aegix had said numerous times had resonated with him: *interference shall not be tolerated, the Aegix will eradi-cate any threat to its mission, the galaxy must be prepared.* Iridius had a hunch that when the Aegix said they would eradicate any threat to their mission, that meant any threat to the Aegix itself. The Aegix had a self-protective protocol, he was sure of it, some part of its programming that saw its survival as a key component of its mission. Why else had they chased him, the thing they considered a threat, across the galaxy when they could have completely ignored him and gone off gooping everything? The Aegix was programmed to survive, and despite its almost unfath-omable intellect, Iridius had guessed it couldn't comprehend the possibility that someone, namely Iridius, would completely fly in the face of that and willingly choose to die.

As the fighters closed in, Iridius willed their thrusters to push them into each other. Their tight flying formation made them easy fodder for canine pinball as they ricocheted into each other, erupting, bursting and coming to pieces in the space around him. Some of them hit the *Diesel Coast* with wild railgun fire as they spun out of control, and some stray debris from the fighters smashed into the hull. More holes punctured through into the cargo bay, but nothing hit the bridge or the main fusion drive. Any other damage didn't matter anymore. As this fighter barrage proved ineffectual, Iridius knew he'd been right. The Aegix were surprised. They had expected him to bail out of the ship with the rest of his crew before it impacted, leaving it unprotected. The fact that he hadn't done so was unfathomable to them.

The *Diesel Coast* was close enough to the main Aegix ship now that Iridius could see the missile batteries opening on the surface. He was filled with a sudden awareness, as if being this close to the Aegix ship amplified his abilities. Almost in slow motion, with no assistance from the ship's alert systems, Iridius pushed the missiles casually to the side as they were launched, swatting a full salvo of nuclear warheads away like annoying buzzing insects. He could sense another change in the Aegix mind now. He still wasn't sure whether the synthetic entity had emotions, but what he felt coming from that ship seemed a lot like panic.

Good. Iridius hoped the electrical signals buzzing along whatever wires, transmitters or quantum circuits passed for synapses inside the synthetic mind of the Aegix were loaded with fear. Strangely enough, as Iridius stared out the view-screen at the metal surface of the Aegix dog-ship, he didn't feel that same sense of panic or fear. He was calm. Sure, dying as one of his ship's engines erupted in a nuclear blast and the other ripped him apart with a bombardment of anti-matter particles wasn't how he'd intended spending this particular Tuesday afternoon, but he found himself sitting with the thought in a zen way that would make even the Erati Mega-Buddhists, who managed to meditate while being castrated of their seventy-two distinct genitals, proud. Iridius didn't bother looking at the proximity distance warning counting down in bright red numbers on the console below him. The collision was imminent, that was obvious enough. He closed his eyes and decided not to open them again, resigning himself to the gaping maw of inescapable death that would soon claim him.

"Ahem."

As Iridius floated with his eyes closed he could have sworn he'd heard, over the ringing in his ears and the howling, shrieking alarms, the sound of someone clearing their throat. No, not clearing their throat, actually saying the word "ahem", which was frankly ridiculous because there was no one else here. Besides, what kind of wanker actually says, "ahem".

"Ahem."

With the hesitation reserved for someone turning around in a horror movie to confront the monster/serial killer/ghost behind them, Iridius opened his eyes and turned. What he saw was, in an odd turn of events, a ghost after all. A ghost floating in the air near the entrance to the bridge. Iridius was sure it was a ghost because it was floating (not that this was any great indication in zero-g), and because it was slightly translucent. It wasn't even the fact that there was a ghost on his ship that was the most surprising, it was that the figure was Iridius himself. He was floating on the bridge looking at a ghost of himself floating on the bridge. The semi-transparent version of himself was wearing different clothes – still a uniform, but one he didn't recognise. A ghost. In space. A space ghost.

"Am I already dead or something?" Iridius said.

"Jupiter's nuts," Space-ghost Iridius said, rolling his eyes. "I hate that we say that. If you were dead you'd *be* the ghost, you wouldn't be looking *at* the ghost, would you? Plus, I'm not a ghost."

"What are you then?" Iridius said. "Why are you on my ship? Why do you look like me?"

"You remember this ship is about to hit that giant dog, right? We don't have time for this. Don't speak, just listen. This is where it starts getting weird."

"*This* is where it gets weird? Earth was incinerated by an artificial intelligence modelling itself on a fluffy white dog and it's just *starting* to get weird?"

"God, I'm annoying," Not-space-ghost Iridius said. "I told you to shut up and listen. I'm from the future. This is a holographic projection. I'm actually hidden on a completely cloaked ship nearby. I'm here to tell you how to survive this so that you can go on to become me and then come back and tell you – us – how to survive this."

Iridius opened his mouth to argue about the possibility of this but the inherent paradox made his brain hurt. He settled on, "There aren't any ships that have managed full cloaking."

Future-not-space-ghost Iridius held up his hand to stop him. "Future, remember? We've got about thirty seconds. Go down the steps into the cargo bay. Damage to the hull has caused one of the last escape pods to come free. It'll be floating across the bay but its life-support is still operating. Get in it."

"It won't keep me safe once we hit the Aegix," Iridius protested.

"Just do it. Trust me, I have the benefit of knowing exactly what happens. An explosion will cause the pod to be hit by debris, knocking it free. After that you'll get a little nudge from a few other objects. Go now."

Moments ago Iridius had been completely resigned to the fact that he was going to die. Now though, with this incredibly fortunate and utterly *deus ex machina* turn of events, there seemed a sliver of hope that he might somehow get through this. That was all the human survival instinct needed – with the tiniest, thinnest sliver of hope, instinct would force you to scratch and bite and claw your way to survival. With that eons-old biological process driving him, Iridius kicked his foot against the helm and floated towards the sealed blast doors at the back of the bridge.

"Remember to breathe out so your lungs don't burst," Future-not-space-ghost Iridius said as a surprisingly casual afterthought.

Iridius exhaled as he yanked down the blast door release handle. The door retracted and Iridius was pushed forward into the cargo bay as the explosively decompressed air from the bridge rushed into vacuum to try to equalise the pressure. He felt the sudden cold as the temperature plunged so far below normal human survival range that his nervous system couldn't even register it. He didn't snap freeze though, and his eyeballs didn't explode – in fact, none of those myths about being in vacuum occurred. He knew he could survive vacuum for two minutes, and wouldn't suffer any significant long-lasting damage if he could get back into a pressurised environment within the next sixty seconds. He could stay conscious for perhaps thirty seconds, but the fact was, he didn't have that long anyway. If this didn't work, the only long-lasting effect he'd be experiencing was death. It must only be ten or fifteen seconds until impact.

Exactly as the Future-not-ghost Iridius had said, one of the several holes punched through the hull had torn free the blast door, and one of the last escape pods was floating right in front of him. Iridius pushed off the wall towards the pod and reached out for it, wrapping his arms and legs around it like a toddler refusing to let go of a parent's leg. As he slid down the release handle and the curved door of the escape pod opened, he began to feel the crackling sensation of the saliva boiling off his tongue – it reminded him of the popping candy he used to eat as a kid. He manoeuvred himself awkwardly inside, beginning to feel a tightening sensation all over his body as his skin started to swell, the water inside his body beginning to vaporise in the absence of any atmospheric pressure. Iridius pulled the door of the escape pod closed and was relieved to find that the life support was indeed still functional. The pod immediately flooded with oxygen and nitrogen, the pressure instantly relieving the pain Iridius was feeling and allowing him to take a joyous deep breath. So far so good: he'd managed to put himself into a coffin floating inside a ship that was about to blow up. As far as escape plans went, this was among the worst he'd heard.

He didn't hear the explosion that Future-not-space-ghost had mentioned – there was no air to carry the sound to him – but he felt it. Somewhere in the fusion drive a component that Junker would know the name of but Iridius certainly didn't finally failed under the extra strain of the overload, triggering a cascading series of explosions down the length of the ship. A fragment of bulkhead that had been ripped away slammed into Iridius's escape pod, causing it to spiral end over end across the cargo bay and, quite luckily, pass through a gaping hole in the side of the hull and out into space. As it did so, several small Aegix fighters attempting to stop the *Diesel Coast* roared in on a desperate kamikaze attack, but it was too little, too late. One of them clipped the escape pod with a glancing blow, sending it spinning away. The fighter collided with the already rupturing *Diesel Coast*, adding to the destruction. Chunks of what had once been Iridius's ship blossomed outwards and one particular chunk hit the escape pod, pushing Iridius further away from the imminent explosion.

The *Diesel Coast* was fracturing now, coming apart at the seams – or at least, creating seams where there hadn't been any before – but the damage wasn't enough to ruin Iridius's plan. The forty-year-old ex-asteroid jumper collided with the Aegix dog-ship. Iridius, to his later annoyance, was unconscious inside the escape pod at the time, so he never saw the dazzling display that followed. The Aegix shields withstood an impressive amount of damage as the *Diesel Coast* hit, keeping the initial impact away from the hull. The shields flashed in a blue half-sphere in front of the enormous dog as the nuclear fusion drive on the *Diesel Coast* went critical and blasted out energy in a radiant white cornea-scorching explosion. This nuclear blast was enough to overwhelm the shields of the Aegix vessel, and chunks of debris began hitting the furry hull, though the damage from that was relatively minor. It was the detonation of the BAMF drive that managed to inflict significant damage. Although it was less a detonation than it was the rupturing of the containment field and the high-energy release of something like ten billion billion anti-matter particles. All told, this was enough to blast a hole through to the centre of the giant dog. The small escape pod carrying the unconscious Captain Iridius Franklin had been knocked clear of the follow-on explosions and suffered nothing more than some cosmetic gouges on its surface.

Iridius had succeeded in guiding the *Diesel Coast* all the way in to collide with the Aegix, but even that hadn't been enough to destroy it. The central mind of the Aegix was damaged, but it still survived. Given enough time it would use nanobots to repair itself, and then no doubt continue preparing the galaxy for the coming of the Synth-Hastur. At least, that's what would have happened if it hadn't been for Captain April Idowu. Once she'd realised what particularly stupid thing Iridius had decided to do this time, she had given the fleet-wide order to fire all remaining weapons at the Aegix ship. She wasn't going to let Iridius's sacrifice go to waste.

So, after being socked square on the nose by the jab from the *Diesel Coast*, the Aegix was hit with the left hook of the remaining Federation fleet. A barrage of missiles careened towards the giant dog. Perhaps undamaged, the Aegix would have turned the missiles away with ease, but the Aegix didn't seem to be firing on all cylinders. Most of the incredible mass of missiles did veer away, slamming into each other and detonating, but a handful managed to make it to impact. Because the Aegix ship no longer had the protection of shields, this handful of missiles crashed their way straight through the hull into the heart of the vessel and, exploding in nuclear fury, caused the complete destruction of the Aegix. The explosion inflated out to the size of a small moon before rapidly collapsing back and vanishing, leaving a cloud of ship debris to rival any asteroid belt.

On the bridge of the *FSC Gallaway* most of the crew cheered, and rightly so – they'd survived, and won, the battle for all sentient life in the galaxy. But the celebration on this ship was somewhat more subdued than on the others through the fleet, because they'd all known the captain who had given his life to save them. Two people in particular stared out at the fading destruction of the Aegix without celebrating at all. April and Quinn looked at each other and shared a small, sad smile.

April turned to look back at the view-screen, considering the announcement she'd make to the fleet about Iridius and the valiant sacrifice he'd made, when the ship's sensors picked up another escape pod. They'd already detected the three that initially left the *Diesel Coast*. April had known, even before the *FSC Beetlejuice* had picked them up, that they'd contain Rangi, Junker and Greg. Iridius would stay with the ship, ensuring it hit its target. But now another escape pod was floating through space, and she had no doubt who would be inside.

"All stations," April said into the comms, "this is Captain Idowu on the *Gallaway*. We'll recover that escape pod."

April and Quinn joined the shuttle crew sent out to recover the floating escape pod. After the EVA crew had passed the pod through the airlock April leaned over it. The porthole was scratched, dented and burned black, making it impossible to see in.

"Open it," she said.

The EVA crew turned the safety locks and pulled a series of release handles and the escape pod hissed open. They pulled the door and there, lying battered and bruised but, judging by the goofy smile on his face, very much alive, was Iridius B. Franklin.

April scowled at him. "You hung up on me, you asshole."

CHAPTER SIXTEEN_

THREE MONTHS later Iridius stood on the observation deck of the Tau Ceti orbital spaceyard beside Fleet Admiral Merritt who, having gone off-world for a well-earned holiday the day after Iridius had left on the *Gallaway,* had managed to survive the destruction of Earth. If you'd have asked him back when he was at the Academy, Iridius would have told you that *of course* Metal Merritt would survive the complete destruction of Earth, probably just so she could continue hassling him. As it turned out, instead of hassling him she'd been the one to pin the Federation Cross on his uniform, the highest honour that could be bestowed upon a member of the Federation Space Command, for gallantry and bravery far beyond the call of duty. What a turn-up for the books.

The Federation was, and would continue to be, in recovery for a significant amount of time. A temporary FSC Headquarters was currently housed on Tau Ceti, adjacent to the Senate building, the seat of Federation government. The ships lost in orbit around Earth or in the battle with the Aegix would need to be replaced, and major economic recovery would need to be actioned for Sol and the systems around it. This was not an easy task, of course, but it was easier than avoiding annihilation at the hands of an utterly mental synthetic intelligence.

It had been almost thirty seconds since Iridius had walked up beside Admiral Merritt where she stood looking out at the ships docked in the yard, and she hadn't yet acknowledged him. It was getting to the point of uncomfortably awkward.

"You wanted to see me, admiral?" Iridius prompted.

"You've had three months off duty now," Merritt said without turning from the window. "The first month was debriefing with the Senate and what's left of the Fleet Admiralty, and being prodded by every scientist interested in your insides. Then there was all the pomp and ceremony around you, your crew and the rest of the battle fleet receiving honours for their part in defending the galaxy. Have you managed to get some rest and relaxation in though?"

"Yes, admiral, the last few weeks have been very relaxing."

Admiral Merritt turned to him. "You mean boring?"

"Yes, exactly, ma'am, utterly boring."

"You're a Space Command captain, Iridius, you're probably itching to get back out there."

"I am," Iridius said. "I kind of flew my ship into a giant dog though."

"That's why I asked you up here. What ships do you see out there?" Merritt gestured to the space dock stretching for many kilometres out below them.

"Most of the fleet still under repairs, a couple of haulers, the *Gallaway*."

"Any ships you don't recognise?"

Iridius looked between the docked vessels. "Uh, not really—Wait." There was a ship he'd never seen before – not that he'd seen every ship in the Federation fleet, but this wasn't even a model he recognised. It was small, a corvette size probably, and looked like a long triangle fattening out at the back to make room for an engine array. It was grey with white lines zig-zagging around its angular edges to accentuate its sleek design. The bridge positioned at the aft top of the ship, which was similarly triangular and sleek, shone as the light from Tau Ceti hit it at an oblique angle. "There," Iridius pointed at the mysterious, utterly rad-looking ship. "What is that?"

"That ship," Merritt said, "is the most advanced ship the Federation has ever constructed."

"I thought the *Gallaway* was the most advanced ship in the fleet."

"Well, that's what we want people to think. The *Gallaway* has a much bigger loadout, medical and scientific labs that could never fit on a corvette like that. It's a much better ship for exploration and furthering the scientific mission of the Federation, but the Alliance threat has been growing and our encounter with the Aegix is evidence enough that we need other capabilities in the fleet."

"So it's a warship?"

"Think of it as more like a reconnaissance vessel. That ship has technology the Federation has been trying to get working for years. A working cloaking system."

Oh. Jupiter's. Nuts.

"My *deus ex machina*," Iridius said, realising too late that he'd spoken out loud. He hadn't told anyone about the events that led to his escape from the *Diesel Coast*. He'd had quite enough attention as it was, thanks to the nanobots in his blood, without needing to explain how he'd been visited by a holographic projection of himself from the future. The story he'd told was much simpler. He'd made sure the *Diesel Coast* would hit the Aegix and then gone into the cargo bay to get into an escape pod on the slim chance he would somehow make it. It was mostly the truth – after all, if you were going to lie, it was best to just leave bits out rather than completely invent a story.

"That's a little bit cocky, Iridius," Merritt said, "but yes, that ship is your new command. We were going to call it the *FSC Diesel Coast II* though, not the *Deus Ex Machina*, but I don't mind that actually – the *FSC Deus Ex* does have a nice ring to it. We can change that easily enough."

Iridius stared down at his new ship, the *Deus Ex*. "Thank you, admiral, it's beautiful."

"It's also needed."

Iridius turned to the admiral.

"We've received communication from Omni D that the Alliance have been raiding its moon bases. Alliance vessels have also been tracked crossing into Federation space with more frequency than at any time since the war. We have no doubt the Alliance is going to use our recovery after the Aegix crisis as an excuse to attack. We need you to take the *Deus Ex* and test out the cloaking technology by running recon into areas prone to Alliance attack, and possibly into Alliance held systems. Your crew has already been briefed and are waiting for you. I wanted to introduce you to your new ship myself."

"My new crew?" Iridius asked.

"I said new ship, not new crew. The *Deus Ex* only takes a crew of ten, including yourself. You know most of them already."

————

The next day Iridius sat in the captain's chair on the bridge of the *FSC Deus Ex*. It was the equivalent of sitting in the driver's seat of a sports car after spending his whole life driving a horse and cart. The bridge of the *Deus Ex* was even more aggressively streamlined than that of the *Gallaway*. The low roof swept back over them and the walls curved around, as if enclosing them in a cocoon. The basic layout was similar to that of all starships, though. In front of Iridius was the helm, a two-seat station. On the right was newly promoted Lieutenant Benjamin 'Space Ace' Rangi and beside him sat Junior Ensign Hal – an unfortunately named android whom the FSC had stationed on the *Deus Ex* to pattern his learned piloting on that of Rangi. Off to the side of the bridge at the communication station was Ensign Herd, apparently the brother of the Ensign Herd that had been on the *Gallaway* and also one of the Babel cult. Beside Iridius was Lieutenant Commander Quinn, back in her rightful place as his XO. Off to the other side was tactical officer Lieutenant Latroz, who had requested a transfer from the *Gallaway* to the *Deus Ex*. Iridius was sure he was going to have to put up with the enormous alien warrior woman and Rangi making googly eyes at each other across the bridge.

The non-bridge crew consisted of Greg (who'd become the first malignant to ever receive a medal from the Federation), Junker (who'd been reinstated as a chief petty officer), Doctor Dooms (which Iridius thought was probably a worse name for a doctor than even Doctor Paine), and Technician Marie Grantham (a brand new technician straight out of training who would no doubt be led horribly astray by Junker). They all stood around at the back of the bridge, Iridius having called them up to be present for the first push back from the Tau Ceti space dock.

"Okay, Lieutenant Rangi," Iridius said, "take us out."

"You got it, cap," Rangi said, but before he pushed any buttons on the console he ran his hands along the edge for what Iridius was sure was the tenth time. "So shiny."

"Let's go, Rangi."

Rangi released the docking clamps and eased the *Deus Ex* out of their docking bay and away from the Tau Ceti dock.

"Admiral Merritt wishes us good luck, captain," Ensign Herd reported.

"Tell her thank you, ensign," Iridius said. "We'll take good care of the *Deus Ex*." He'd still have to get used to having a communications officer, and especially a Babel one who could communicate externally to the ship without actually saying anything into the comms.

Once they'd used thrusters to manoeuvre far enough away from the space dock Iridius gave the order to engage the fusion drive. As Rangi did so, the lights of the bridge flickered and went dark and the fusion drive, which had begun to hum as it powered up, went completely quiet.

"Rangi?" Iridius asked.

"Um, fusion drive doesn't seem to be working, cap."

"It was fine during the initial tests," Technician Grantham said.

Junker laughed. "Oh, newbie, you've never been on a ship with Captain Franklin."

"Look," Iridius said, "this is not necessarily a Franklinism. It could just be a malfunc—"

"RED ALERT. RED ALERT."

The blaring alarm filled the air.

"—tion," Iridius finished. "Oh, balls."

CHAPTER SEVENTEEN

MEANWHILE, far from Tau Ceti, a probe containing a backup of a bat-shit crazy synthetic intelligence travelled through the black nothing of interstellar space, heading for impact with a tiny moon containing a settlement of traders and enough raw resources to allow it to begin its programmed mission again.

Even further away, beyond the edges of the Milky Way, an armada of ships traversed the deepest parts of the great abyss at speeds never even imagined by the technology of the Federation. They moved through inter-dimensional space and travelled the realms of tentacled cosmic horrors. They came to destroy. They were the Devourers of the Stars, the Great Living Storm of Steel, the Lords of Interstellar Space, the Harbingers of Forever War, and the galaxy had not been prepared.

The Synth-Hastur were coming.

<<<<>>>>

ACKNOWLEDGMENTS_

As with any book, it's the author's name on the front, but there are always people that hold us up. This is the part where we get to thank them.

The biggest thanks, as always, to my family and my wife, Holly, in particular, for the support necessary to hold our universe together when I'm in the throes of drafting or editing or being otherwise distracted by thoughts about space.

Thanks also to 'The GMOB' - Amanda Bridgeman, Amanda Pillar, Craig Hildebrand-Burke, Dave Sinclair, Luke Preston, Nathan Farrugia and Steve Vincent - my writing friends and support group. Each of them excellent writers in their own right and together an unmatched force for technical feedback and emotional support.

Thanks to my new Tasmanian crew of writers, too. After moving here a couple of years ago, it's great to find a community down here. Particular thanks to Damon Young, Robert Batten and Tania Walker for helping with some cover feedback.

Thanks to Vanessa Lanaway for her always excellent copy editing work, and to Amanda Rutter for her proofing.

To the design team at MiblArt thank you for dressing my book in a beautiful cover.

And, of course, thanks to you, the reader, for taking a chance on my book. It's been a journey to get here. Shakedowners came close to finding a home with publishers more than once but, despite liking the book, they passed on it on for the same reason each time: 'We don't think we can sell comedic science-fiction.' I disagreed, of course, which is why I ultimately went the indie publishing route. I believed there was an audience who would enjoy reading this book as much as I enjoyed writing it, and maybe those people would buy it. Thank you for disagreeing too, and for taking a chance with me. I hope to see you out in the black for more adventures with the Shakedowners.

Justin Woolley

ABOUT THE AUTHOR_

Justin Woolley has been writing stories since he could first scrawl unreadable words with a crayon.

Now he is the author of novels for both adults and young-adults including *Shakedowners,* the *The Territory Series, We Are Omega,* and Warhammer 40K fiction for Black Library.

Justin lives in Hobart, Australia with his wife and two sons. In his other life he's been an engineer, a teacher and at one stage even a magician. His handwriting has not improved.

Keep up to date with all Justin's news and releases by subscribing to his newsletter here:

https://www.justinwoolley.com/signup

Printed in Great Britain
by Amazon

21408485R00171